Enjoy !!

Rochelle Bradley

The Double D Ranch

A Fortuna, Texas Novel

Rochelle Bradley

DEDICATION

To all grandmothers, especially Elaine, Ganelle, Undine, and Vera.

ACKNOWLEDGMENTS

I'd like to thank my family, especially my awesome husband and wonderful mom. I appreciate your ever-present support and encouraging me to follow my dreams.

Thank you Hadley and Nik for inadvertently helping to name The Double D Ranch. Who knew a car ride conversation about bra sizes would be interrupted by a question from the nine-year-old boy in the backseat: "What's a double D?" Thank God for the suburban cattle farm we happened to drive past that became this mom's scapegoat.

To my NaNoWriMo writing friends, Sarah, Chris, Beth, Darla and Lillian, who were there when I gave birth to the Double D, thank you for the shared laughs, brainstorming sessions, and helping me find my voice. I apologize for testing my punny names on you.

My gal-pals from My Favorite Muffin Mondays, Kathryn, Cathy, Dawn and Stacy, you are the best! Thank you for being available to answer all my questions, no matter my caffeinated state.

CHAPTER 1

Josiah

WHAT SOUNDED LIKE AUTOMATIC GUNFIRE had Josiah Barnes running out of the barn and into the warm Texas afternoon. He gasped for air while his heart galloped. Cupping his eyes to shield them from the sun, he squinted at the Double D ranch house. On the front porch, he spied Jessie Davidson watching a car leave the property. Chewing her bottom lip, she leaned against the railing with a hand raised in farewell.

With his hands on his knees, he bent and sucked in a deep breath. Instead of fresh air, he inhaled dust from the plume of grit the vehicle had kicked up. He coughed then closed his eyes as relief flooded him. Jessie hadn't been in harm's way.

Josiah had a promise to keep to Jessie's grandmother. On Undine Davidson's death bed, the ailing woman instructed, "The Double D is Jessie's now. She'll need you, Josiah dear. You'll always watch over her, won't you?"

He'd replied, "Yes, Ma'am, I swear." It had been an easy promise to make because he loved Jessie and suspected the old woman had already known.

For the three years after Jessie inherited the ranch, he'd worked alongside her and his admiration grew daily. She'd handled last spring's flash flood, which had decimated the longhorn herd, better than expected. The tender way she cared for the orphaned calves was one thing he loved about her. He witnessed the rancher's spirit catch fire in her soul.

1

He intended to keep that promise even if it meant keeping his distance from Jessie. She'd made it clear love wasn't a high priority with her disdain for romance and men. He scrubbed his face. Could he safeguard his heart? One side of his lips bowed. It was too late, she'd already stolen it.

He strained to see the vehicle that held Jessie's attention. The wind shifted the dust cloud, and he caught a glimpse of the gold 1970 Cadillac Deville as it fishtailed out of the driveway sending a spray of gravel into the air.

"Son of a bitch," Josiah muttered with a laugh. The car could be considered new compared to the owner, Undine's best friend. *That old woman can be as ornery as a horny bull.* Hopefully, her unscheduled visit hadn't brought bad news. "Other than the yard." He frowned and studied the parallel tracks the Deville left. The muddy ruts arched precariously close to the side of the barn. A renegade dirt clod still clung to the weathered wood.

He shook his head and glanced back at Jessie. She'd sat on a porch swing sucking her bottom lip. The enduring quirk informed him she stewed about something.

Determined to find a solution to whatever problem Jessie faced, Josiah took long strides to the porch. An orange blur ran in front of him then darted between his legs. He nearly tripped over the three-legged barn cat.

"Are you trying to lose another paw, Tippy?" Josiah scolded then reached down to pet her. The petite tabby rubbed against his hand, purring. He smiled and glanced up to find Jessie watching. A sweet smile touched the corners of her lips and she patted the swing next to her.

It was an invitation he couldn't refuse.

Josiah leaned back, stretched his legs out and crossed them. He closed his eyes and sighed. He could picture them sitting on the swing in the evenings, him with a beer and Jessie with a sweet tea, while twins played in the yard.

Tippy jumped onto his lap, landing on his junk. "Oh." He snapped forward and lifted the small cat from his thighs.

"You okay?" Jessie asked, first glancing at the cat then his face. She transferred the small kitty to her lap and placed a hand on his arm.

The temperature rose and his pants felt too tight. He rubbed his damp palms on his jeans-clad thighs. Her grandmother's face flashed in his mind, reminding him of his promise. He cleared his throat. "I'm fine."

"It's a good thing Tippy is tiny."

"Yeah." *But I'm not.* Josiah scratched the back of his head. He needed a diversion from his swollen package. His mind raced to find something, anything to talk about. "What did Ms. Hardmann want?"

"Have you heard about the town prankster?" A toothy grin blossomed. He eyed her plump bottom lip and was tempted to taste her.

The reason for the visit hadn't been bad news after all. *Ms. Desire Hardmann had wanted to gossip about Fortuna shenanigans.* He relaxed against the swing's back and nodded. "The guy is hilarious. He's hit more than one store sign, switching or removing letters."

Jessie's auburn hair shifted on the breeze, dancing in the sunlight like a flame. Josiah's heart sped up at the sight.

"Sounds pretty harmless. What did they say? Desire knew he'd struck again but didn't have all the details."

Jessie leaned closer, her full lips parted in an expectant smile. He'd kissed those lips once, and he ached to relive the day. He swallowed and pulled his gaze away from her mouth to her emerald eyes sparkling with mischief.

Not trusting his hands, he stood.

"Well, one of the guys drove past the community center and the scrap-booking class turned into a 'crap' booking class. The C went missing on the McDonald's help wanted sign." He grinned, stuck his fingers in his front pockets and rolled back on his booted heels.

"Just the letter C? How odd." She cocked a brow.

"The sign used to say 'now hiring closers', but now it states they're hiring 'losers'." He laughed, and she chuckled, shaking her head. He caught a whiff of her strawberry shampoo.

The laughter caught in his throat as he spied the white truck turning into the driveway. "You okay with this?" Josiah asked, nodding at the truck. A grimacing B.J. Johnson sat behind the wheel.

She shrugged. "Yeah, believe it or not, he's invited. He's picking up donations for the senior center."

Josiah raised an eyebrow. Beside him and her dad, Jessie tended to be gun shy when it came to being alone with men. "I'll be here if you need me."

"I know and I appreciate it." She gave him her reassuring smile.

Josiah reluctantly sauntered to the barn as the truck pulled to a stop near the front walk. He watched Jessie's face brighten as a dark-haired man exited the vehicle. The earlier relief he felt evaporated and turned to dread.

Johnson got out of the truck and, with a confident swagger, approached Jessie. From the doorway, Josiah heard them talking in amicable tones. She nodded then led the visitor to the front door. With one last glance outside, Johnson followed her into the house.

Josiah balled his fists and turned to pace the long barn aisle. Jessie's father, Brad Davidson, had volunteered a time or two with Johnson at the senior center. He could maim Brad for suggesting Johnson work with her, especially after the warning the older man gave him. According to Brad, Johnson suffered through a messy divorce and didn't care for women right now. Johnson might be good for Jessie, helping to draw her out of past hurt, or he could be trouble. If Josiah would've been a gambling man, he'd bet on trouble. He didn't want to throw the bitter divorcé in with the woman he worked hard to protect but it was out of his hands. For now.

He stopped in front of an empty stall and kicked the door. It did little to calm the building angst.

Jessie

"You ready?" Jessie hesitated, embarrassed about the collection Grandma left. She led B.J. up the hardwood stairs to the second floor. The scent of his musky cologne preceded him.

B.J. smirked. "Born that way."

"I doubt it." Her hand gripped the metal doorknob. When she'd inherited the Double D Ranch from her grandparents, the cache in the upstairs bedroom came as a complete shock. She took a deep breath and closed her eyes, steeling herself for his reaction. The area behind the door once housed Grandma's sewing room but now…

The mess was as awe-inspiring as it was overwhelming, which had been why she enlisted the help of the reluctantly altruistic B.J.

"Well?" he grunted, crossing his arms as he waited. A hard worker, the thirty-two-year-old man had caught her eye a year ago with a smile that lit his face. The smile disappeared, however, when his wife left him for another man. Now the handsome man scowled as a hobby.

Her hesitant fingers tightened around the smooth knob, slowly her wrist shifted, and the latch popped. The door opened a crack. "You ready?" she repeated, taking another deep breath.

He shifted his feet with impatience. "Already said I was."

Words could do little to describe the mess or the enormity of it. It wasn't the worst thing she'd ever encountered but Jessie found it embarrassing, nonetheless.

She could've had a cleaning party with her best friends, Kelly and Mona, but they'd heckle her to hell and back with what they'd find, plus the whole town would find out in no time. She didn't want her grandma's neurotic obsession, the Davidson version of the skeleton in the closet, to become known.

Then there was Josiah. He'd keep the secret. But being confined with the cowboy made it hard for Jessie to breathe. Her father trusted B.J. and laboring beside a stranger would be easier than dealing with the funny feelings bumping elbows with Josiah caused.

No, B.J. was her only option.

She swallowed then pushed the door open. The hinges creaked, filling the silence.

B.J. blinked twice. "What the hell?"

Books -thousands and thousands of paperback books, all romance novels- were stacked in neat rows from floor to ceiling. The bedroom was full save for a three by three space on the floor. It was a dark closet with book wallpaper. To say her grandmother had loved to read was an understatement.

B.J. pushed on the stacks a few times but nothing moved, it was solid. He whistled low.

The confounded man stood with hands on hips staring at the twelve-foot ceiling line. "How am I going to reach the top?"

"I planned ahead, knowing you weren't ten feet high." Jessie retrieved a four-foot step stool from behind the door. She unfolded it and he climbed up. In the hallway, a stack of plastic storage totes waited to be filled. She retrieved one and placed it next to the base of the ladder.

"This is going to take a while," he mumbled.

What a genius. "Ya, think?" She took the six books he handed her and lined them in the plastic tub. They worked in silence as they filled the tote. She tried to keep focused on the books he passed and not the potency of the cologne.

Several of the books had worn spines and dog-eared pages. Memories of Grandma flitted to mind. When Jessie was in elementary school she'd climbed into her grandma's warm lap and asked, "Why do you read them?"

Grandma's eyes had crinkled as she smiled. "Love, child. They are filled with love. Everyone wants to live happily ever after. Someday, Jessie, you'll find it too." She'd tweaked Jessie's nose then tickled her.

"Hey, Jessie," B.J. spoke, startling her. He glanced down from the ladder. "You're gonna need more tubs. What the hell kind of books are these, anyway?" He stared at the cover of a scantily clad woman leaning against a bare chested man in leather pants. "*Werewolves in Heat?*"

"Grandma had a thing for romance novels." Jessie shrugged, feeling her

5

face heat.

"Honey, it was more than a thing. She hoarded the damn books."

B.J. was right. One stack near the wall held one hundred and forty books. Some stacks had thinner books, equaling more. B.J. handed her one called *Hot Hawaiian Sunrise*. She regarded the happy couple on the cover. Young, good-looking and, no doubt, rich.

Jessie was grateful for the longhorn cattle ranch her grandparents left her, even if it hid her grandmother's secret. Her grandparents each died within a year and her breath hitched thinking about them. Josiah had worked for her grandpa Don but stayed on as foreman when she inherited.

As if on cue, Josiah's sun-kissed face peeked around the corner. The dusty tip of his boot and a stray piece of hay sent her mind reeling to the night he'd found her crying in the hayloft. The memory of his lips on her neck sent a shiver down her spine.

He pointed to B.J. who reached for more books, and mouthed, "You okay?"

Her heart tripped when she gazed into his curious eyes framed with a brow etched with concern. She gave a thumbs up then waved him off, slightly annoyed yet comforted he was checking on her.

Jessie rubbed her temples. Her head began to throb due to the pungent scent of B.J.'s cologne.

"If my calculations are right, there aren't thousands plus thousands, but thousands times thousands," Jessie said in a soft voice. The number of books blew her mind. All four bedrooms were good-sized, but the paperback hoard was housed in a room twenty feet long by thirteen feet deep. The ceiling sloped, so the outer wall was eight feet high while the inner was twelve. Jessie sighed, grateful both upstairs bedrooms weren't filled to capacity, and thankful Grandma's collection consisted of pressed and bound paper and not taxidermic animals.

"Over a hundred thousand?" B.J. whistled. "Damn, that's a lot of smutty books."

They filled one plastic bin to the brim then started on another. "You're going to need a lot more of these storage totes if your estimate is anywhere near accurate." He took another handful and passed them off with a grimace as if romance might give him cancer.

She took the books, curious to what had motivated the authors to write. Romance: the one thing neither she nor B.J. wanted. She sat the books aside then inspected the stacks. The room overflowed with sex, love and romantic intentions. It was a virtual nightmare of false hope and unrealistic expectations.

Her grandmother had been a hopeless romantic and had dreams for Jessie. She sighed and tried to ignore the guilt corroding her heart. No, she was better off removing romance from her life. Including the books, even if she felt she'd be disappointing her grandma.

Due to bad relationships with men, who showed more interest in her double-D bra size than her personality, and an incident with a drunk family friend, she'd decided to forgo romance, love and men.

Yet she stood working beside one man and trying not to think about another. Especially when Josiah made her treacherous body feel funny tingles in places she thought she'd turned off.

According to her father, B.J. thought women were of the devil, thanks to his adulterous ex-wife. Jessie and B.J. weren't threats to each other, so they formed a sketchy friendship based on mutual wariness and distrust of the opposite sex. She figured being considered Satan's spawn was better than trying to fend off a horny man she wanted nothing to do with.

CHAPTER 2

Jessie

FULL OF BOOKS, THE PLASTIC totes were heavy and hard to manage. Jessie and B.J. carried them to the unused dining room table. Amazed at how much an amassed amount of paper weighed, she rubbed her sore arms. Jessie took deep breaths, grateful to be in the large open room.

B.J.'s nose crinkled as he inspected the box. "I can't believe your grandmother read all these. Are you sure she did?"

There was one way to prove her grandmother had read all the books. Jessie fished one out of the plastic bin and opened it. U.L.D. had been scribbled on the inside of the cover. Handing the book to B.J. with the cover open, she pointed to the mark made in pencil.

"Uld? What's that?"

"Not uld, silly. U.L.D. Undine Love Davidson. Grandma marked each book she read with her initials."

"Her middle name was 'Love'?"

Jessie watched as he pulled out several other novels and flipped them open. He found each branded with U.L.D. Sometimes in pen, pencil or marker, sometimes the initials were printed or written in scrolling letters.

Jessie smiled. "Undine Love: sounds like undying love."

B.J. grunted, one eyebrow raised. "The church ladies will appreciate these sexy books."

The church would hold its bazaar in a few weeks and they always accepted donations.

"You are not taking these to the church, are you?"

"I might. It'll liven things up a bit."

She smacked him on the arm with a novel. "You will not! Take them to the senior center instead. That way Pastor Peacock won't pitch a fit."

"Are these books like blood to sharks? Are the old ladies going to run over each other with walkers or beat each other with canes as they swarm the free book shelf in a frenzy? What is it with these stories anyway?" He held one trying to ascertain the magnetic qualities.

She brought her hands to her hips. "Old ladies won't beat each other to get a book."

"They might for a cheap thrill." His lips curled into a smirk.

He had a point. Jessie's thoughts wandered to the contents of the books and she absently thought, "How many relationships have been affected by romance novels?"

"Affected for better or worse?" His face held more questions, but he waited.

"Worse mostly, I think." She held a book and waved it around, her annoyance flaring. "These things are full of false hopes. If a woman gets them planted in her head, she's going to be sorely disappointed in real life. The poor guy who lives with her will never satisfy her because the bar is set too high."

"Falling in love is a false hope? I've never heard a woman say that before." He returned the displaced books to the plastic tub.

Falling in love? That wasn't what she'd said. She hadn't been considering love, more along the lines of the bedroom. But whatever. "Have you ever read one?"

His eyes widened as he stepped back from the books. "What? Me? Hell no!"

She narrowed her eyes as she grinned. "I dare you to read one. No, more than one so you learn the pattern. At least three."

He shook his head. "Now why would I want to read these trashy things?"

She shrugged. "Because they're trashy? You got something against sex?"

He harrumphed. "Not sex. Just women."

"That's a problem. I guess that's why God gave you hands." B.J.'s face turned bright red. He crossed his arms. Stifling a laugh and to save him from embarrassment, she started on a tangent. "There are fundamental flaws in all romance novels."

"Besides being fiction?" he smirked.

"Yes, besides being fiction." She succeeded in not rolling her eyes. "One: the man always satisfies the woman one to three times before joining the fun. That never happens in real life."

"Satisfy?" He tilted his head inspecting her.

"The big O."

His brows lifted. "Ah. Up to three times?"

"With his tongue." She crossed her arms. "What man has a magic mouth?"

"Well, I've been known to…" He licked his full lips as if she lit his hunger.

Following his tongue with her gaze, her whole body heated. "Stuff it, Johnson. Giving her multiple orgasms before getting your jollies? Once maybe but two or three? Completely unrealistic. If a woman bases the actions of her man on these books, he'll always be lacking."

"I see your point. You've only said one. Anything else?"

"So much more." She chuckled to find him intrigued. She began ticking them off on her fingers. "Two: stellar sex negates all previous difficulties in life. Three: after a random short period of stellar sex, with multiple orgasms each time and the weight of the world forgotten, they can now get married. Usually, it's within three months. What American wedding can be planned in three months? All the venues are booked a year in advance. Four: now that the magic mouth recipient and spouse are happily hitched, within three months of meeting each other, they can start having babies. There's no getting to know each other or seeing if their lusty relationship will last, only more stellar sex."

"If you have such a problem with these stories, why do you read them?"

Jessie turned, jogged to her bedroom and picked up a book on the bedside table. She touched the cover, a wave of nostalgia hitting her. She'd practically given up on it but her grandmother had whispered in her ear for years. Hope: the true reason she continued to read. A deep seeded hope one day she'd have her own happily ever after but she couldn't admit it to B.J.

Midnight Love was a typical romance. Guy meets girl, they deny interest then wham, bam, thank you ma'am, they were in the sack.

She returned to the dining room and handed the book to B.J. who flipped it open to see the telltale initials. "So?"

She pointed to the cover featuring the ripped body of a mountain of manly muscle. The cover model resembled her foreman, Josiah. No wonder last night's dreams about the cowboy had been so spicy.

The image of the perfect man with light brown hair, green eyes, long lashes, chiseled jaw, perfect straight teeth, and tight jeans with a substantial bulge on long legs. His strong, flexing arm reached for a brunette with hooded eyes in a form-fitting dress. His fingers caressed her cheek and she seemed to purr.

Fiction remained safer than reality because it was fake. She could end a relationship by closing the pages.

She shrugged. "Because I like to use my imagination."

"Him?" The incredulous man stared.

She drew in a deep breath and couldn't believe she was having a conversation about passion with a stranger. It was less far-fetched than longing for Prince Charming.

She snatched the book from him and opened the chapter she'd enjoyed the previous evening. She cleared her throat. "*Armando cupped her breast and thumbed the hard nipple making Nevaeh arch her back. He nibbled her neck making his way down her wanting body. He lingered over the pink buds making her moan his name. 'Armando, I want you in me now.' Her voice deep and lusty, begged. 'Not yet, my sweet,' his lips whispered against her inner thigh. He spread her legs wide and glanced longingly at her. 'You're so beautiful.'*" Jessie snapped the book shut. "What is he? A freaking gynecologist?"

B.J. took the book and opened it to where her thumb held the page. "That's all in there?" He peered at her with a predatory smile. "Wow. This is like porn."

"Yep. And you wanted to take them to church."

"Hmm." His gaze dropped to the page and followed the words.

She snatched it out of his hand again with a grin. "Three books. Can you handle it?"

"Are they all like this?"

"Pretty much. You can't have this one, but you can pick any of these," she offered, swinging her arm over the totes of books.

B.J. pulled out books and read the back covers. He set them aside. He glanced at her with a smirk and dug deeper into the plastic tote.

Josiah

As the spring light waned, Josiah knocked on the front door then pushed it open, not waiting for a response. "It's me." Jessie stood within view on the edge of the entry. He nodded at B.J. as he sized up the visitor standing with an open book in hand.

Josiah chose the front entry instead of the rear for a reason. He'd observed movement in the dining room window. The animated conversation had him worried about Jessie getting hurt again. He waited a while, hoping the conversation would end, but his nerves got the better of him and impatience won out.

Johnson's sickly sweet cologne permeated the air, but he appeared to be behaving himself, which was a good thing. Josiah wouldn't hesitate to throw the other man out of the house and off the property if he felt Jessie was being threatened in any way. He could handle himself in a fight if need be, but he hoped it wouldn't come to that. He wasn't too intimidating with a dirty "Hammered" bar t-shirt and a hat ring halo. He ran fingers through his hair and wiped his boots on the doormat before going further into the home.

"Why didn't you come in the back?" Jessie noted his front door entry as unusual. Normal was the rear kitchen entry, the laminate floor and shorter route to the bathroom with the shower. He always showered before hitting the road. Her green eyes blinked and a beautiful smile appeared on her lips.

"I didn't want to interrupt dinner." His stomach churned and his cheeks warmed as he glanced from Jessie to her guest.

"Thanks, Josiah, but B.J. isn't staying. He's got some reading to do." Her voice was light and teasing. She seemed at ease, and B.J. moved toward the door. Josiah relaxed some.

"Yeah, well, on that note I'll take my homework and skedaddle." There were six books in Johnson's arms.

"Why don't we hold off on donating these until you've had a chance to validate those four flaws? You might need to do more research." Jessie walked the guest out.

Josiah stood with her at the window of the dining room and watched the truck disappear. With Jessie now safe, Josiah could conclude his workday and go home but whenever he left Jessie, he was like Tippy the three-legged cat. He wasn't whole.

Jessie

The fresh showered version of Josiah Barnes entered the Double D kitchen and sat across from Jessie. No longer a dirty cowboy but a squeaky-clean kid. She could smell the spicy scent of shampoo on his damp hair. He wore a t-shirt and jeans, no boots but athletic shoes. He had a college degree and worked the ranch as her foreman but sometimes, like now, she was reminded of the sixteen-year-old boy who'd almost died.

It had been a horrible night. She shivered recalling the memory of Josiah's compact car getting the jaws of life to pull the unconscious high-schooler out.

Had eight years passed since the accident? She shook her head and sighed.

Josiah would rather dance than step on a cat's toes or crash his car instead of hit a stray dog. When he swerved into oncoming traffic, to miss hurting an animal, there'd been consequences but a man who cared about animals was special.

What a way to meet a friend.

That thoughtful high school kid sat across from her, now a handsome man. He smiled, his head slightly tilted as if contemplating her thoughts. "Remembering?"

She studied the kitchen. The walls were pale yellow, a remnant of her grandma's touch she liked. The updated cabinets were white. A treasure trove of memories resided here. She learned to cook in this kitchen at Undine's side but those memories weren't the ones that flooded her mind.

The teenage Josiah's eyes showing complete horror and regret, yanking the wheel of her F150, and the angelic, comatose face of a cute boy, all flashed in her mind. Jessie could have killed him, all because of a dog. She rubbed her arm, and closed her eyes.

He leaned forward and stretched a hand across the table, his long fingers touched hers and her breath hitched. The tears welled at the tender touch, she inhaled deeply trying to stymie the guilt. Neither his family nor hers placed blame on her. In fact, to this day Josiah took the blame but tried to make light of the incident by joking about their failed attempts to take each other's lives.

She quoted from their ongoing debate. "You wouldn't have killed me."

Josiah smirked and leaned forward. "Well, I'm glad I didn't." Jessie was about to say something but he quieted her with, "It's nice you're thinking of me."

Could he be flirting? She hoped not, but after all the talk about orgasms and sex her mind wallowed in the gutter. Her face heated. She didn't want to view Josiah as sexy but she wasn't blind.

Jessie swallowed and changed the subject. "Are you going to Hammered tonight?" Hammered wasn't the only local watering hole for the younger crowd but they sold the best grub around.

"I was, but not anymore."

"Did your hot date cancel?" She had witnessed several girls flirting with him, especially the bartender's daughter. Josiah was fun-loving, well-mannered and charming too. He would make the right woman a fine husband someday.

He laughed, scratching the scruff on his chin. "No date. I was going for dinner. Tonight's the Fortuna Fish Special but I've got to miss it. Mom is having pot roast." Family dinner trumped dinner alone. He glanced at the clock on the wall then rose.

"I'm not sure which sounds better." Jessie had joined the Barnes family often and knew from firsthand experience his mother, Prairie Barnes, was an excellent cook.

"You want to come?" He paused at the door and glanced over his shoulder.

It didn't surprise her when he invited her to his parent's home. An invitation she occasionally took him up on because eating alone all the time sucked. Mrs. Barnes didn't mind when she joined them for dinner. With five children, the three boys being sixteen and older, there was always plenty of food.

"No thanks," she said.

With a stiff nod, he opened the door and walked out. From the window, she watched as he started his small pickup truck. He met her gaze and winked, earning a grin. He pulled into the darkness. She wrapped her arms around her chest. The taillights faded as emptiness settled.

With a sigh, she retrieved *Midnight Love* from the dining room table then settled into a leather chair in the living room to read. Armando wed Nevaeh within three months and they had a baby within the year. She sighed and tossed the novel into the plastic tub full of books then turned out the light.

CHAPTER 3

Josiah

JOSIAH LEANED AGAINST THE WALL and glanced into a catchall filled with old tools and debris.

"Ready to clean out this old stall?" Jessie asked with a grin.

"Can't think of a better way to spend the morning." Actually, he could and it involved less clothing.

Jessie might be petite but was more than capable of handling anything in the stall. She was strong and, now that she set her mind on the task, determined. She would get it done with or without his help. Jessie wanted, not needed, his help and it had him giddy.

Tippy ran in the barn door, jumped on a wheelbarrow and licked her back. Her ears shifted, and she crept back to the entry. That was when Josiah heard a vehicle pulling up the drive. Johnson again. He stepped out of his truck and nodded at Josiah.

"Hey Jess, your romance novel convert has returned," he called over his shoulder.

Jessie straightened and wiped dusty hands on denim-clad thighs. "It's only been three days. Could he have read all six books?" she murmured aloud, walking to greet the guest.

Josiah, wary of the other man, followed them into the dining room. He offered to help Johnson put the heavy totes in the truck bed. The sooner Johnson left the easier he could breathe. Figuratively and literally, because, once again, Johnson smelled as if he'd taken a cologne bath. Once they'd loaded the tubs, Johnson drove off.

She watched the truck kick up dust as it pulled onto the main road. "That's odd. He didn't say much about the books other than he read them."

"He's probably reading the juicy parts," he suggested. Johnson didn't seem like much of a reader. His gut told him the man wasn't as philanthropic as he let on. Josiah was as curious as Jessie when it came to Johnson's interest in the risqué books. "Where's he taking them?"

She regarded him with wide eyes. "Oh, God, I hope he doesn't take them to church." She bit her bottom lip.

Josiah's lips lifted in a lopsided grin. "That sounded like a prayer to me."

She giggled, a sound that was music to his ears and lightened the load his heart had been carrying since the other man's arrival.

Jessie

As Jessie and Mona Little entered the bar, Hammered, Lisa Ford blindly brushed past them. Hurrying toward the ladies' room, the distraught woman tried to cover her tear streaked face.

"Hey, what's up with Lisa?" Mona pulled Jessie to the side and pointed.

Jessie shook her head. "I don't know. Maybe she and Parker had another fight." This wouldn't be the first time it happened in public. Parker barked at his wife until she became cowed and quiet. Jessie's heart always went out to the older woman.

Kelly Greene sat with her parents. She waved and joined Jessie and Mona. The women found a high-top table near the pool tables. Kelly's gaze circled the room then she spoke loud enough to carry over the din. "You missed it."

"What? Do tell." Mona leaned forward with a grin.

"It was horrible. I wanted to smack that man." Her green eyes narrowed in on Parker Ford as he leaned over the pool table with cue in hand. His cue ball-like head reflected the light. "Lisa worried about finances and he fought with her at their booth. She tried to keep it quiet but you know Parker." She shrugged.

"Like a locomotive horn." Mona patted Kelly's folded hands.

Kelly tended to be a fixer. She helped people and animals out of sticky situations. It worked well for her second grade students but not so much for adults who didn't care for the intrusion. Usually, Kelly's endeavors focused on family and close friends. Jessie studied her childhood friend. Had Kelly placed herself in a dangerous position?

Kelly stared at her hands. "Ms. Hardmann confronted him."

Mona slammed both palms on the tabletop. "Oh. My. God."

Jessie snickered and searched the room for the spunky old woman. If anyone could put the cantankerous man in his place, it was her grandma's best friend, Desire Hardmann. She found her sitting with one of her younger employees. The petite woman in her eighties appeared the epitome of a grandmother sporting a sweet smile, rosy cheeks and a pink sweatshirt with a goose on it. All she needed was fluffy, white hair but she opted for an unnaturally dark, short Spock-like do. Desire caught Jessie's gaze and winked.

"She could've got herself killed," murmured Kelly. "She walked right up to Parker, poked him in the chest, and lit into him. I thought my ears would bleed." Her eyes glazed, one corner of her lips lifted in a grin and her voice continued in whispered awe, "I've never heard half the things she said before. I don't think he'll be able to sit for a week because she ripped him a new one."

Jessie glared at Parker as he taunted his pool partner. "Serves him right. Stupid man." Her voice came out a feral growl and sounded bitter even to her own ears. She sat back and glanced around the dimly lit room. On a stool at the end of the hardwood bar Josiah nursed a beer. *Why hadn't he stepped in when Lisa and Desire dealt with Parker?* From personal experience, Jessie knew the cowboy wouldn't sit idle when a woman was abused. "Why didn't he do something?"

Kelly and Mona glanced in the direction Jessie stared. "He was going to. Josiah stood up and started over to them. He looked madder than a hornet but Desire beat him to Parker. When Desire took a breath, and before Parker could open his mouth, Sawyer stepped in." Kelly's gaze shifted to Sawyer Hickey, Fortuna's resident playboy.

"What?" Mona and Jessie chimed at the same time.

"Yeah. He bet Parker couldn't beat him in pool." Kelly shrugged both shoulders. "It diffused the situation."

Sawyer glanced at their table and gave them a two-finger salute sending Kelly and Mona into a fit of giggles. Kelly and Mona were both single and, unlike Jessie, actively seeking a man to fill the role of significant other.

But Sawyer Hickey?

Sure, the man had a ripped body and a dark swath of hair but he flirted with anything that had a vagina. Those were Kelly's words, not hers. She couldn't believe the way her friend stared at the man now. Jessie could appreciate the way his jeans hugged his tight butt, but he was a few years younger and immature; besides, who'd want the last name Hickey? She could hear it now, "there's a pair of Hickeys on the Double D." Sawyer's kids would be little Hickeys. Jessie stifled a giggle as she thought of a voicemail message for the Hickey residence: If you need a Hickey leave a message and we'll make sure you get one.

Jessie searched for Josiah again. He sat in the same place nursing a beer and talking with Hammered's owner and resident bartender, Holden Dix. Holden worked his magic behind the long hardwood bar straight out of an old time western with a plethora of carved wood and glass shelves holding whiskey bottles like trophies. He welcomed another customer at the bar and passed the guy a frothy mug and two paperbacks.

Huh?

The man, in his forties, took the items with a laugh and a nod. Jessie reassessed the room. There were four men with their noses in books. B.J. leaned over an open paperback in a corner booth, his empty plate pushed to the center of the table.

Jessie slipped away from her friends. She took deep breaths to soothe her nervous stomach as she wove through the tables. Jessie slid in the booth across from B.J. She watched his dark eyes roam back and forth on the page. His, and the other men's, interest in the romance novels intrigued and baffled her. She remained quiet for a full five minutes before he glanced up startled.

"You must be at the good part," Jessie teased.

He held *Midnight Love*, the romantic escapade about Armando and Nevaeh. "Armando is using his magic mouth. Again." His cheeks grew pink.

"Are you taking notes?" She tried to hide the giggle that escaped by covering her mouth with her hands. It didn't work.

A slow smirk grew on his full lips, and the red went all the way to the tips of his ears. "I could have written the book."

She grinned with evil intent. "Braggart. There's one way to prove that claim." She paused at his shocked expression, sucked in a quick breath then blurted, "I won't hold you to it though." Jessie's heart hammered in her chest and she bit her bottom lip.

Why did those words fly out of her mouth? It had sounded like another dare. By B.J.'s narrowed eyes and predatory smile, it was a dare he'd wanted to take her up on.

She couldn't meet his gaze so she surveyed the men with romance novels. *What did B.J. say to start the trend?*

His face masked, Josiah assessed the situation in the corner booth. He would sweep in if she needed him. She smiled and lifted her hand, it seemed to relax him.

After B.J. left, Jessie perched on the barstool next to Josiah. Saturday was their night to eat together. She usually paid. He called it a job perk, but it was the only one.

A romance novel sat open on the bar top with a warm beer next to it. A sidelong glance at the man beside her revealed he wasn't reading anymore. "Good book?"

"Eh, I've read better." He stuck a napkin in between the pages to mark the spot then set it aside. "You hungry?"

"I wouldn't be sitting here if I wasn't." She turned in her seat and signaled Holden.

Holden pointed to the pile of menus but she shook her head, having memorized it years ago. He took their order and handed off the ticket to his daughter, Piccadilly, who winked at Josiah. She went by Pixie, Pixie Dix.

Fortuna, Texas deputy Benjamin Moore entered the restaurant and sat a couple of seats away. He nodded in greeting then scanned the room. His gaze settled on Mona and lit up. Jessie leaned closer to Josiah and elbowed him. "Is Ben sweet on Mona?"

"Yep. Has been for a while now."

"How did I miss this?" Ben wasn't Mona's type. He was shorter than the other men Mona usually dated and more reserved, with short cropped brown hair and dark brown eyes. The man had upper body strength as the tight t-shirt tried desperately to hide.

Josiah tilted his head, his blue eyes held her gaze. "I'm not surprised you hadn't noticed. You're not into love."

Jessie's jaw dropped. She couldn't argue. He was right. But just because she wasn't interested in a relationship didn't mean she should be blind to those around her.

Holden's wife went through the swinging door into the kitchen, her arms laden with dishes, barely missing Pixie as she came out. She placed plates of hot food in front of them. The young woman leaned against the bar beaming at Josiah. "Need anything else?" Her eyebrows wiggled.

He flashed a brilliant smile in return. "Nada, Darlin'."

Pixie blushed and left before a frowning Jessie could ask for blue cheese dressing to go with her wings.

Josiah seemed more interested in his food than the barkeeper's daughter. Jessie didn't want to examine why she felt so relieved. Between bites they talked about the ranch, their day and romance books. During this time, two other men came and went with paperbacks. Had Holden Dix become a romance novel pusher?

CHAPTER 4

Jessie

SITTING WEEDING A FLOWERBED, JESSIE spied a truck coming up the driveway. B.J. parked and exited the pickup ready for his fix of paperback love. He smiled, a slow, sexy grin making butterflies in Jessie's stomach take flight. She bit her lip and glanced toward the barn. Jessie drew in a deep breath. She wasn't alone, and it empowered her to put on a smile and greet her guest.

Glancing down at her grimy hands and clothes, she found her arms the same color as her red tank top. Strands of her long auburn hair had escaped the ponytail, and she used her shoulder to wipe it away from where it stuck to her damp face.

"You're getting sun." B.J. shielded his eyes as he glanced at her.

Hot, even for a spring day, it was pushing one hundred degrees. She stood and stretched, arching her back to free it from the moist, clinging tank. "I'm hot."

"I'll say." B.J.'s gaze roamed her body, lingering on the exposed cleavage.

The compliment brought heat to her cheeks that had nothing to do with the sun. "Shut up."

"I like your grandmother. She was an eclectic woman. You mind if I-?" he asked pointing to the house.

"No, go right ahead." Jessie took the pile of weeds and stuffed them into the yard wagon. She wiped her forehead with the back of a hand trying not to streak dirt across it.

B.J. walked toward the front door with an empty bin he had plucked from the truck bed. She tried to keep her eyes, along with her mind, off his form-fitting khakis.

Grandma would have liked B.J. or, at least, his concerted effort to educate the male population. Jessie had done some sleuthing and found he'd dropped her grandma's books to several Fortuna civic offices and businesses, including the small hardware store Nailed, and he'd even delivered to a few places in Nockerville, the town next door.

On Jessie's weekly Saturday night rendezvous with Josiah, she checked Holden's novel supply. Grandma's books were accumulating initials. B.J.J., H.O.D. and J.E.B. were in *Naughty and Nice*. B.J., Holden and Josiah had read it.

B.J.'s biceps flexed under a white polo shirt, as he brought the novels out, put them in the truck-bed and secured them. The taxiing of the plastic tote had caused the embroidered company logo to tip and shirt collar to pull open sideways exposing dark chest hair. He righted his shirt under her watchful scrutiny. Finger combing his head of silky black hair gave him a roguish appearance. Today he wasn't manager of the Longfellow Property Management Company. No, today he was pimping romance to anyone in need. He leaned his fit body against the side of the white truck.

"I know you've taken books to Prime Cuts Barbers, and to the police station and fire station. My father talked to the mayor the other day. Guess what I heard? You make frequent stops there too." She paused wanting confirmation but he only grinned. "You've been a busy boy, B.J."

"That's not the half of it."

He didn't elaborate, and it drove her crazy. "Amanda Layer said her husband, Willie, tried to act out something from one of those books and it nearly killed her."

He quirked an eyebrow. "She didn't like it?"

"No. She loved it. She could have died of pleasure. Willie works at the feed store. Where else have you taken those books?" Her hands rested on her hips but she couldn't help but smile.

He pushed off the side of the vehicle and leaned so his lips were an inch from her ear, as if he wanted to tell her a secret. "I've taken them to the Silver Oaks Retirement Community and Twin Hills, the country club in Nockerville. I feed the need at the feed and seed store. People are reading about being hammered at Nailed and getting nailed at Hammered. I've left some at Prime Cuts Barbers but also the Tease Me Salon. That's right, women are interested in what the men are learning. They want to experiment. Let me correct that, they want to be experimented on."

His breath on her neck sent a shiver to every female part. All the reply she could muster was a simple, "Hmm."

"I've given enough books to Stitts' Travel Center for the truckers to be entertained for a few weeks. Holden Dix has been going through them and has handed them out to his fishing buddies. That reminds me, Garren Teed wanted some for his law office. They're circulating. Your grandma would be pleased. They're making people happy." His finger skimmed her cheek causing her to sigh.

Jessie's heart shifted into high gear at his nearness. She'd better watch out, or he'd claim more outlandish things and want to prove them. And, heaven help her, she'd be tempted to let him. She clenched her eyes shut, she did not need to want a man.

The front door slammed, Jessie's eyes popped open to find Josiah, his lips pressed in a firm line, striding down the path holding an ice-cold lemonade. His focus never left her. Relief washed over her like a cool breeze.

B.J. backed away with a scowl.

"Jess, you're a mess." Josiah spoke softly. He rubbed his finger across her forehead then offered her the lemonade. She sighed at his gentle touch.

She guzzled the drink, emptying half in a single breath. "Thanks. That hit the spot."

Josiah didn't retreat but remained standing there. "I need to speak to your friend a minute." An awkward moment passed. "Alone," he intoned.

"All right." Jessie drew the words out, glancing from one man to the other, "I'll see you, B.J."

Once inside, she ducked into the dining room and peered out the window. In boots, hat and tight jeans, Josiah was about the same height as B.J. but when he leaned in on the other man, he seemed a giant. Both wore poker faces, but B.J. kept shaking his head with hands held in surrender, as if Josiah was accusing him. Her past and the assault were a sore spot, and not common knowledge.

Jessie

Jessie stomped away from the window to the mantel. She picked up a framed photo of Donald and Undine Davidson. She closed her eyes and sighed. A few years ago, after her grandparents died and ownership of the ranch passed to her, she fell into depression.

The pressure of running a working ranch, even now three years in, could be stressful but then she'd felt clueless, stricken with loneliness and grief. Her father had tried to help, but he threw himself into the operations of his ranch, dealing with his own grief.

During this time of adjustment, Rusty Kuntz returned to Fortuna with a smile and a zest for life that had appealed to her. Rusty, her father's childhood friend, was the uncle she'd never had. They hung out a couple times and the attention he showed had taken the edge off her grief.

Uncle Rusty had visited every year while growing up but this latest visit hadn't been so fun. A shiver shook her body, and she swiped a stray tear away, angry he could still make her cry. She hated the man.

She returned the picture and took a deep stuttering breath wishing her grandmother was still there to hold her.

She balled her dirty hands and traipsed to the kitchen. Turning on the water, Jessie pumped soap onto her palms. She lathered and scrubbed, wishing she could get rid of Rusty's lingering residue on her life like the dirt down the drain.

Rusty couldn't get to her. He remained in jail but the memory still haunted her. The day had gone from bad to worse. Breaking her grandmother's favorite mug and getting a flat tire, added to the disappointment of having no date for the Cattlemen's Ball. Rusty had lent a kind ear, poured her a drink, and they watched a comedy. They drank too much. Then he turned on a movie she'd never seen before and soon there was too much flesh showing. Porn.

She gripped the side of the sink basin and gulped air. Some uncle he turned out to be.

It got worse. Thank God for Josiah. Storming into Rusty's mother's trailer, the cowboy found Rusty's overweight body smothering hers as he ripped at her clothes. She had wanted to gag; his breath stank and she couldn't breathe. Her head swam, and she sobbed. She'd let herself fall into that vulnerable position with a man. It wouldn't happen again.

Josiah

When Josiah returned from his talk with Johnson he found Jessie sitting at the small round kitchenette. She appeared to be asleep with her elbows resting on the table and chin in her hands, but her eyes fluttered open and regarded him. She leaned forward, inhaling the steam swirling from her tea cup.

He frowned as he scanned her. "What's wrong?" His fingers curled

24

around the top rung of the ladder-back chair.

"Nothing." She smiled at him, at least; he thought she did. Her lips had moved but her eyes remained emotionless.

He tried relaxing his shoulders and taking a deep breath. He pulled out the chair and lowered himself onto the seat.

She dunked a tea bag into the hot water. "What did you say to him?"

He leaned back and crossed his arms. "A warning."

"A warning about what? How not to get a paper cut when reading a book?" The venom in her tone surprised him. She took a sip of tea then said softly, "I appreciate your concern but it's not necessary. B.J.'s not going to hurt me."

"Like you trusted Rusty not to hurt you?" He regretted the words the second they left his mouth, but, dammit, he didn't want to see her upset again.

Jessie sucked in a deep breath, and her green eyes glittered with tears before she stared into the mug as if trying to get control. "It's not like that at all. B.J.'s been hurt before, he understands."

"Having a bad breakup is different from being accosted and nearly raped," he stated. He hated to say it, to throw the past in her face, but she needed to be cautious.

"I won't let it happen, okay? I don't plan on getting close. As you so poignantly pointed out, I'm not 'into love.' Anyway, my relationships aren't your business. So don't worry about me."

"I can't help but worry, Jess." It hurt to care. This was getting too close to admitting the truth. He wiped sweaty palms on dirty jeans.

"You aren't my brother or my bodyguard." She took a big breath, her voice rose in pitch. "God knows, you're not my man. I don't pay you to be a guard dog, so back off."

Being protective came with loving her. It instinctively came out when other men came around. She was returning to the old Jessie, and he'd be damned if he let some loser come in and set her back again. He slapped a hand on the table. "Somebody's got to do it."

Jessie's red face glared. "You think I can't make my own choices?"

"Look how it'd turned out last time." He crossed his arms again. His heart raced, and it had nothing to do with the low cut of her tank top.

Jessie growled deep in her throat and slammed her palms on the table. "B.J. is not going to assault me."

"Maybe not physically. His wife left him. He's bitter and angry at the world. I don't want to see that anger turned on you."

"Let it go. It's not your concern. He's not going to hurt me," she repeated in a feral growl.

"But what if he does? What if I'm not there for you?" He hated voicing his biggest fear: failing her as a man. It would kill him. "What's it going to do to you, Jess?"

"Nothing. Because nothing is going to happen." She stood, breathing through clenched teeth. "I'm not going to shut down. I won't need to be institutionalized. You'll still have an employer."

Josiah jumped up scraping the chair across the floor. "You think I'm worried about job security?" He held her gaze, trying to slow his hammering heart. He clenched and unclenched his fists. "You don't know me very well." He stormed out of the house, slamming the door, hopped in his truck and drove off as fast as small town gossip, with the image of tear-filled eyes seared into his mind.

Josiah

Josiah drove to the Big Deal ranch and saddled a horse. He rode the bay hard out into the rolling hills heading for the highlands. On the crest of the hill overlooking a small dry riverbed, he could see for miles. Twilight fell as he faced the Double D where, soon, Jessie would turn on the outside lights.

His heart ached for the stubborn woman.

He'd been waiting a long time for her to come around. It was time to face facts. After knowing her for eight years, she still had no interest in him and probably never would. Don and Undine had seen the love in his eyes and counseled him to be patient. They seemed to understand he and Jessie belonged together. Jessie, on the other hand, thought of him as a brother.

Yet together they had become a team, the yin and yang of the Double D. There had been peace and harmony until he'd upset the balance. Hell, if he was the boss, he'd fire himself too. She had every right. He'd acted the jealous fool with Johnson and the relationship was none of his business.

He ran a hand through his wavy brown hair. He'd been such an idiot. Being patient was one thing but wasting time was another.

He should have had the guts to ask her to the Cattlemen's Ball. Three chances that day, and each time he chickened out. Maybe if he'd asked her out, and she'd agreed to be his date, he could've kissed her in the hayloft instead of fighting Kuntz.

"Come on, Sundance, let's go home." He sighed and turned the horse towards the Big Deal. The bay eagerly headed back to the barn.

His stomach knotted in protest. Time to talk to Jessie's father.

CHAPTER 5

Jessie

THE SUN WASN'T UP BUT Jessie had been awake for hours. She hadn't slept well. Already dressed, with coffee brewing, she heard a vehicle pull into the driveway. Opening the back door, she frowned at the man standing there. "Dad?"

"You don't sound happy to see me." The tall man grinned and grabbed her in a bear hug. He rubbed his bushy mustache against her neck, tickling her in the same manner as he had since her childhood.

"What's wrong? Why are you here?" *Josiah*. Horrid thoughts sifted into her mind.

"Josiah swapped with me. He thought you might need time apart. You've got me and Curly Moe." He pointed to the barn. Curly, her dad's foreman and his best friend, entered the building.

"It takes two of you to replace Josiah?" She elbowed her dad gently in the gut.

"What happened? Did you two have a lovers' spat?" He sat at the kitchen table where she placed a boot-shaped mug of black coffee in front of him.

"Something like that," she mumbled. "Oh, Daddy, I was horrible. I was moody and upset and I snapped at him."

"He must've given it right back." Her father put his hand on her shoulder and squeezed.

"He held his own." Biting her lip, she nodded. "Why?"

"The poor guy has been eaten alive with guilt. He's afraid you'll fire him."

28

"I should. He's bossing my dad around now." She poked him in the chest and gave him a lopsided grin.

"No, child, this was my idea," Brad admitted. He sipped the dark brew and waited.

Jessie sighed. "Josiah warned B.J. off."

Her father rubbed his chin. "Yes, B.J. told me."

The event happened yesterday, late afternoon. "Why did B.J. call you?" she asked through clenched teeth.

"B.J. and I are in the same book club." He grinned sheepishly and shrugged as if it was no big deal.

Imagining her father and other men sitting in a circle analyzing the plot and characterization of a book had her laughing until she snorted. She wiped her eyes.

"We don't read the same book. There are six of us and we read different ones. The next week we switch so within a month and a half we will read all six. The novels have common themes. Usually we discuss what women would find attractive about the book, besides the guy on the cover."

Jessie's jaw dropped. Her father wasn't much of a reader unless it was tool or equipment catalogs. "So do you have a woman in the group to help you locate those attractive properties?"

"Um, no."

"It's a crap shoot then. You guess which parts the women like?" Her eyebrows lifted.

"Um, yes." He scratched his chin again. "Well, it sounded good originally. You wouldn't want to-?"

"No." She laughed again. They could find another guinea pig. When the giggles stopped, she took a big breath. "What did Josiah tell B.J.?"

"B.J. didn't say, but he mentioned Josiah had words with him and it concerned you. He asked me about Josiah. He wanted you safe, and I assured him Josiah was that."

"Good. I guess I need to go find Josiah." She bit her lip again. "

Brad leaned and folded his hands on the tabletop. "No. Let him stew a bit. Here's what you're going to do." He suggested she wait until lunch then go find him. Josiah had traded work on the Double D to sweat out a full day's work at the Big Deal. Her father's idea sounded wise but before she confronted one man, she needed to face the other.

Her dad stood but paused at the door. His gaze turned serious. "Daughter, you can't have two cocks in the hen house."

29

Jessie

She felt out of place in this business setting and second-guessed her visit because of its personal nature. The nutty smell of the hazelnut latte hung in the air and comforted her. She hoped B.J. would accept it as an apology. After all, it was her cowboy, Josiah, who had accosted him on her ranch and a five-dollar drink was a small price to pay.

Jessie found her courage stuffed somewhere under the seat, pulled it out and drew a deep breath. Taking the final sip of her latte, she savored the double caffeine dose from the coffee and cocoa. Her procrastination now over, she set the empty cup aside with a sigh. She picked up his drink then left the safety of the truck, venturing into the unknown.

Painted soft blue, the lobby walls featured several satellite photos of Longfellow's managed properties. The plump receptionist smiled at her as she shifted the phone from one ear to the other. She pointed to a seat and returned to typing. After a few minutes, she greeted Jessie then informed Mr. Johnson about his visitor.

B.J., the office manager, greeted her with a handshake. She followed him to a square office with fluorescent lights but no windows. His cologne permeated the air. She sunk into a small leather chair bouncing her knee. He sat behind his desk. After shutting the laptop, he focused on her.

"This is a pleasant surprise." He accepted the latte then leaned back and took a sip. His eyes closed a moment as a small sigh escaped. "Thanks. Is there something I can do for you?" He gazed at her like one of those models on the cover of a romance novel would stare at a woman: with bedroom eyes.

The latte left a dab of foam on his top lip. She watched as his tongue darted out and licked it clean. She blinked, straining for the reason of her visit, but she couldn't recall. *Oh, yeah. The truth.* She tried to swallow but her mouth went dry. "Well, I talked to my father this morning." *That was smooth.* "I didn't know you started a book club." *Not much better.*

A mischievous glint sparkled in his dark eyes as his lips formed a slow smile. "Yeah, well, what do you want to know?"

"I recommend adding a lady to the group. That way you have an expert in all things… girly." She shrugged, surveying the room.

"*All* things?" he asked with eyebrows raised.

Jessie's gaze snapped to his. She felt like a rabbit cornered by a fox, a foxy fox. Her face grew hot, and she cleared her throat. "All things literary, that is. I suggest Ophelia Cox, the Fortuna librarian."

There on the credenza behind his desk, sat eight or so romance novels. Had he added his initials to the inside covers? Her fingers itched to check. Did the four unrealistic points hold any merit? Could he be schooling men in the art of magic mouths? She swallowed.

"Did you drive all the way to town to find out about my reading habits?" He studied her like a lion watching a wounded gazelle.

Again, her mind sprang to viewing B.J. as a dominant animal. *No, that isn't it. He's a predator and I'm the prey.* She didn't want to be eaten alive unless it had to do with a magic mouth. The room temperature seemed to rise twenty degrees. She shifted in her seat, a bead of sweat trickling between her breasts.

"I came to find out what Josiah said to you yesterday," she admitted.

At the mention of the other man's name, his face changed to that familiar chiseled scowl. It was smooth, unyielding and as sexy as one of those steamy novel cover models. His hardness drew her. She wanted to touch him and it scared her. She didn't trust men and B.J. did not trust women but she couldn't deny the attraction. Why was he acting angry? She didn't belong to Josiah. Neither did she belong to B.J.

"He warned me," he stated.

"That's what Josiah said. What, specifically, did he warn you about?" She needed the details.

"Why don't you ask him?" He crossed his arms and lifted an eyebrow in challenge.

"I will but I came to you first." That settled the ruffled feathers a little. "I was hoping you'd tell me so I wouldn't have to talk to him again."

His dark gaze assessed her. "He said you've been through some bad stuff in relationships and I should be careful with you. It felt like an open-ended threat."

"Why would he do that?" she muttered. "You and I aren't dating."

"It might seem that way to him. All our interactions revolve around romance... novels." He grinned wolfishly then added, "And he's in love with you."

Jessie shook her head. *No way, not Josiah.* He hadn't ever been anything but friendly. No sideways glances or silly nicknames. No flowers or dates. B.J. had to be wrong. Josiah was more of a younger brother, a hot, muscular brother, but a brother none-the-less. They were friends and the only benefit to the relationship was an occasional dinner. He protected her and therefore the Double D. That was what friends, and employees, did.

But it didn't equal love, did it?

"He *is* in love with you. He's jealous because he thinks we're becoming an item." The property manager seemed satisfied with her reaction. The man exuded confidence and wore a cocky grin.

God, his ego is getting on my nerves.

Crap, that wasn't going to work. Jessie stood, fumbling with her purse. Her relationship with B.J. wasn't evolving , she wouldn't let it. She needed to nip whatever preconceived notions B.J. had in the bud, right now. "Your cock's not in my hen house!"

Jessie fled the building, as fast as she could, with B.J.'s laughter ringing in her ears.

CHAPTER 6

Josiah

THE MORNING STARTED EARLY FOR Josiah, in fact, he'd never left the Big Deal. He stayed in the bunkhouse with Curly Moe and Gimme Malone. His talk with Brad lasted longer than he'd planned but they hashed out some items. They'd swapped ranches, and work, for the day. Brad had assigned Josiah to ride with the cowboys, to move the herd from one grazing zone to another. As the sun rose, he mounted Sundance and followed Arlon Topp and two others.

The April day grew warm and the smell of earth, vegetation and animals assailed his senses. He loved riding and had often suggested Jessie get horses. The animals were work, but they were worth it.

Cole Dart rode beside Josiah and nodded in greeting. The cowboy kept his blue eyes open and mouth shut. Over the last few years he'd changed, but cancer could do that to a man. Before being diagnosed and treated, Cole had been a loud-mouth rabble rouser but now he'd become a devoted family man. If Cole suspected Josiah wasn't in his right mind he said nothing. They rode next to each other for a while and the silent company comforted Josiah's ailing heart.

By and by, they conversed about the books they'd read. "Have you read *The Visitation* yet?" Cole asked him with a smile.

"No. Never heard of it."

"It's a good one." Cole blushed under Josiah's shocked stare and explained, "It's different but has a happy ending."

Cole had a thing for romance novels. Maybe he knew a thing or two about romancing shy women? Josiah steered the conversation towards women, trying to be vague.

"Is this a love worth fighting for?" Cole asked him, prompting Josiah to retreat within himself and list the ways he loved Jessie. Like the way she soothed orphaned calves when she bottle fed them. Hell yes, it was worth fighting for.

The men spent the morning driving the herd to fresh pastureland. They pressed forward, corralling the rebels and motivating slowpokes. In a barren canyon the cowboys' job became easier thanks to natural boundaries. During this part of the trek the rhythm of hooves trampling stone put Josiah into a memory trance.

Josiah thought Jessie was a strong woman, or at least she had been until the Kuntz incident. Although she'd been grieved when her grandparents passed and perplexed about running the ranch she hadn't been emotionally compromised to the point of losing herself. Sad red rimmed eyes, yes. But rolled into the fetal position didn't happen until after Kuntz left his mark.

He clenched his jaw, let out a long breath and imagined beating the living tar out of Kuntz all over again.

Josiah had been poised to knock on Kuntz's door when he heard Jessie shouting his name. Peering in the sidelight, he observed empty bottles of whiskey on the table, beer cans on the floor, the flickering of the TV and Jessie's feet thrashing. He'd thrown open the unlocked door and stormed inside.

As pissed as a beat piñata, Jessie swore a torrent even as tears streaked her face. Stunned to silence, she recognized Josiah. He would never forget the smile of relief that exploded on her face.

Fortunately, the intoxicated Kuntz was a stupid man and had become incapacitated. Once upon a time, Kuntz might have been in the army but his physique went AWOL a long time ago. If he hadn't been so big and heavy she'd have overpowered him, but in that state, he had her pinned. He tried to grope what he thought were breasts and mumbled something about double Ds but, in actuality, he squeezed a dirty sock.

Josiah had kicked the old jerk in the side. Kuntz rolled off Jessie and onto his back. His naked body hadn't been aroused at all. Josiah had dropped to her side, fearing the worst. Curled up and snuffling, she clutched her torn shirt closed. He took off his shirt and covered her then called the sheriff.

Jessie hadn't been raped or beaten. And that turned out to be a good thing for everyone. Especially Kuntz, because Josiah could have killed him.

He never knew rage until that night. His entire body had trembled with pent up fury. His heart turned black and his vision red-hot. If not for focusing on Jessie and her needs, Kuntz might have met another fate.

When Kuntz had lunged at him, the drunk tripped on his own underwear but still took a swing. Kuntz took two fists to the face, the second breaking his nose, before succumbing into a blubbering mess on the floor.

A quick glance at the TV revealed circus clowns getting it on. He'd pushed the power button to end the torture. He shook his head trying to get rid of the scariest image seared onto his optic nerve. Jessie had teetered on the verge of mental breakdown. She'd ended up hating clowns.

She didn't trust men except her father and him. The privilege of holding her trust warmed his soul. He'd protected her that time but what if he couldn't next time? He recognized something feral in Johnson's eyes. Hell, maybe he'd been jealous of the competition. Josiah had a promise to keep, and he'd do all he could to honor it by keeping Jessie safe.

No matter what relationship he dreamed about, right now he was an employee and friend; at least, he hoped he was still both. He sighed and nudged Sundance in the side.

Jessie

The prairie grass grew tall, but Cowboy, the ATV, had no problems traversing the backcountry trail. Jessie felt the sun's heat but a cowboy hat shaded her eyes. The weathered trail held the telltale signs of recent passage: cow chips. Behind her, latched to the back with a bungee, sat a small cooler full of grub. She stopped near a grove of trees and slipped the cooler's strap over her shoulder then followed the trail on foot. Thanks to her dad, she knew where the ranch hands were headed. She brought food for all four cowboys, Arlon, Gimme, Cole, and Josiah.

Arlon, a man in his sixties, was a lifelong horseman whom her father trusted. He gambled too much and lived alone in a trailer. Tanned, tall and skinny, his nickname should have been slim. Gimme, the baby of the ranch at twenty-one, was wiry and topped out at 5'8". He wasn't afraid of work but tended to talk too much. The other man, Cole, was about her age. He might have been bald but she couldn't be sure because he never took off his hat. His shoulders were wide and the way he slumped forward all the time reminded her of a gorilla.

The cattle lowed as she approached. Arlon rode up beside her on a roan horse. She sat the cooler down then touched the horse's velvety snout.

"Hey, boss lady, what brings you up here?"

"My father thought y'all might be hungry," she said with a smile.

"He sent you to check on Josiah. I promise, we ain't done him in. He's been a great help. He's funnier and smells better than Curly."

Jessie giggled. Arlon was a funny, dependable man, and she liked him. He offered to carry the cooler, so she handed him the strap. He hoisted the cooler to his lap and pointed. She walked to where he indicated: a flat area semi-devoid of debris. Arlon lowered the cooler to the ground and rode off to find the other cowboys.

Josiah appeared first, hesitating then he strode toward her. She sat on a blanket and removed sandwiches, potato salad and chips. She knelt arranging everything for the men, but this was for Josiah. If he hadn't shucked Double D responsibility, she never would've come.

B.J.'s words echoed in her mind: *he's in love with you.* She tried to push those powerful words out of her thoughts Her hands flew to her hair pulled back in a navy bandanna. She inspected her denim shorts and t-shirt. Did he consider her pretty? Her face heated. Glancing up at her wayward employee, she smiled.

"Hey." His reciprocating smile lit his face like the sun lights the earth. Her heart hammered faster as his gaze traveled over her.

"Hey." She patted the ground next to her. She inspected him but he didn't seem any different, although maybe quieter than normal. She handed him a ham salad sandwich. "Listen, Dad sent me here with a scheme to lecture you but I don't intend to. So if he asks, pretend I read you the riot act, okay? The real reason I came is to apologize. I shouldn't have snapped at you. You did what you thought was right."

"Your love life is none of my business," he admitted. "You had every right to be angry."

Jessie crossed her legs and scooped some sides onto his plate. "That's true, but I trust you, Josiah." She took a deep breath and asked a hard question. "Was B.J. acting weird? Did you hear something in town?"

"No, but I wanted to make sure of his intentions. I don't want to see you hurting, Jess." He accepted the plate and stared at it.

"I appreciate you not spilling the details to him." Her voice became a soft whisper.

"That's yours to reveal, if and when the time comes." Josiah touched her cheek.

The gentle caress reminded her of B.J.'s words regarding the younger ranch hand. "He thinks you're in love with me."

Josiah stiffened. His gaze roamed Jessie's face as color crept to his cheeks. "How about you?"

She swallowed and, needing to turn away from the intense stare, pulled out the other plates. The awkwardness grew. She sighed dramatically. "I s'pose I could do a whole heck of a lot worse than your sorry keister." She flashed a teasing grin and watched him relax.

He took a few bites of food. "Johnson's paranoid since Carlotta left him."

"I'm not dating him. I'm not dating you. B.J. shouldn't be acting paranoid. It's none of his business who I date."

"Ah, but it's his business if he's contemplating asking you out." Josiah sighed. "Jess, I've seen the way he ogled you while you worked in the garden. Johnson studied the landscape of your body not the yard. At Hammered, he watches you as if you're the main course. He's biding his time."

"He's been burned. He's-"

"Safe?" he asked in a soft voice. "He's read all those romance novels. He's lonely and horny. It's a dangerous combination."

A snort sounded. "Lonely and Horny? Aren't those nicknames for the Nocker twins?" Gimme asked Arlon as they sat on the blanket. Cole moseyed over to join them.

Arlon winked as he piled potato salad onto a plate. "What are you kids planning?"

"We're going to run away and elope." Josiah announced grabbing the chip bag away from Cole.

"How to you feel about that, Miss Jessie? You'd be stuck with that burr under your saddle," Arlon teased.

Her mind raced. Grandma Undine had eloped with Grandpa. They'd skipped the formalities and saved money. She'd left her past in Austin and came to Fortuna. This Jessie knew from the room full of novels. The whittling away of the hoard left a corner of a piece of furniture exposed. A table of some sort and under the table was a box full of Undine's diaries.

The men laughed, bringing her back to the conversation. Poor Josiah's face shined bright red. "She's plumb numb with fright," teased Gimme.

"Actually, Josiah's okay," she admitted with a small shrug. He'd be a great husband and dad, and probably was cute naked, but she wasn't going to say that out loud. "It's the planning of the elopement. A sudden vacation is almost as hard to plan as a wedding. Plus, we have to consider the children." She gave Josiah a conspiring wink.

A chorus of "What children? You don't have any children," rang out.

"I have a whole herd of them." She grinned and gathered the desolated food containers. Cole handed her the dirty paper plates. At least the cowboys had stopped teasing Josiah as they returned to work.

Josiah lingered, folding the blanket. "Thanks for the diversion."

"I found my grandmother's diaries and she and Grandpa eloped. I got sidetracked. Sorry if it got you in trouble," she said.

"It was nothing I couldn't handle."

"Hey, Arlon," Gimme called from the saddle. "I think we need to let Josiah and Miss Jessie have some alone time so they can do something about being lonely and horny." He chuckled and slapped his knee.

This time anger, not embarrassment, turned Josiah's face bright red. His lips pressed into a thin line while his hands balled into fists. His tight biceps threatened to stretch his t-shirt to the point of ripping, like the Hulk. This had to do with her honor not his reputation. Gimme would get it unless she calmed Josiah.

She covered the pocket of his shirt with her hand. The strong steady rhythm of his racing heart coupled with his warm hard chest had her second guessing her touch. He stared at her small hand with an open mouth.

With a glare, she focused on the offender. "My father didn't send me up here to roll around in the bush with a cowboy."

"Shut up, Gimme, before you get yerself fired." Arlon growled as he saddled up. "No harm meant."

"It's fine," Jessie said with a wave. "Besides, I rode a cowboy here and I don't have an itch to ride another."

CHAPTER 7

Jessie

"YOU SHOULD HAVE SEEN THE room before." Jessie spread her hands and stood in a vacant space where novels had once been stacked. "This crater used to contain the books now circulating around town."

"Dang." Josiah's first trip into the hoard left his voice a hoarse whisper. Mesmerized by the inventory, Josiah's childlike expression fascinated Jessie and she couldn't help but watch as he soaked it all in.

So far B.J. had removed a couple thousand books but the outside wall remained hidden even though the skylight now let light into the room. The previous day, under a pile of Harlequin Blaze novels, B.J. had discovered a hard wooden corner, surprising them both. After she shifted a few hundred books, the culprit showed itself. Jessie suspected there weren't as many books as she originally calculated.

A wood desk, narrow but heavy, seemed familiar. She enlisted Josiah to help pull it free. She didn't need the physical strength, but she didn't want to be alone. They slid it out into the open space and he wiped dust off with a bandanna. It was old, heavier than it should have been, and honey colored wood. Pecan? They glanced at each other over the desk and grinned. She moved to the other side, noticing the three side drawers had wood pulls. It wasn't a pretty table, but it was an antique. He knelt, inspecting the underside, while Jessie ogled his backside.

Josiah stood, and she watched as his hands slid across the wood surface causing her heart to speed up. Was she jealous of a desk? "Here it is." His long fingers found a latch. He pulled and the wooden top lifted to the side and a sewing machine rose into place. It was modern but housed in an old fashion casing, not unlike her spunky grandmother.

"I remember this. She bought it right before Grandpa died. It replaced an older model." She caressed the machine as memories and questions assaulted her. "How did the table become buried by books?" A quiet settled and she pulled open the drawers and shifted through the contents.

Josiah

Josiah contemplated the wall of books with his arms crossed. "She lived long enough to fill the room. It wasn't always like this," he stated.

"When was the last time you were in here?" Her small hand clutched his arm and warmth stretched through his body.

"Your grandpa and I brought the desk upstairs about a year before his death, but the room was empty except for a chair. The closet was full of patterns and fabric. Your grandma had high hopes for making this a sewing room." His hand closed over hers and squeezed. He took a deep breath, reluctant to move. "Mrs. Davidson was an avid reader, and the house was always filled with books. Every day I'd ask her where she was. The places changed daily. Tahiti, New York, the outback, Yukon Territory, Greece, Dayton. But there's no way she had this many stashed in the house."

"I agree. And there isn't a basement," Jessie said.

"But the Double D has barns." He shifted to face her.

Her fingers tightened on his bicep but she stared into space as if to pull an answer from thin air. "That has to be it, but how and why did she do it?"

"Maybe you'll figure it out as you read her diaries," Josiah suggested. "Desire might have helped her. She was here nearly every day after Don died." Two old ladies trying to wrangle stacks of romance books would have stuck out like a sore thumb and he never saw a thing. They could have been covert, moving them when he was out on the range, which was most days, or in the evenings after he'd gone home.

"Maybe." She glanced at him and her face turned pink as she withdrew her hand. Already the place where her hand had been cooled, and he missed her touch. She pushed the drawers shut and sighed.

Hiding a modern machine in an antique then surrounding it with risqué, paperback novels was weird. It wasn't romantic. It was neurotic.

Jessie

Days later, memories of Grandma Undine kept returning to Jessie. After her mom, Trish, died, Undine stepped in as Jessie's female role model. They baked cookies and made hot chocolate in the winter after school. Grandma taught her the basics when it came to cooking.

Undine had created Jessie's Halloween costumes and the high school theater group always asked for her help. Jessie smiled, proud they still used her grandmother's creations for plays. Undine sewed ruffled dresses for her granddaughter but Jessie had been a tomboy at heart. She'd loved to ride and climb trees and didn't care for the lovely dresses. She hoped she never hurt Grandma. Her grandma loved to sew, but Jessie hadn't had the patience for it. Still Undine had given her lessons here and there. Jessie wanted to put those lessons to the test.

Jessie plugged in the machine. She needed to find some fabric, even a scrap, to see if it still worked. There was nothing she needed to make, but she felt nostalgic.

Surrounded by stacks of paperbacks, Jessie used an old pair of underwear to test the machine. The needle worked on the slippery nylon like a hot knife in butter. Crazy thoughts entered her mind and a wicked smirk formed.

Jessie

In Hammered, along the wall with the jukebox, a new shelf filled with paperback novels stood waiting to be inspected. Jessie inspected the spines then pulled out a few novels finding five or more sets of initials in each. One had fifteen, so out of curiosity she opened to the prologue.

"I heard that's an interesting one," Josiah said from behind her.

"Why?" The cover depicted a bare-chested man with a pair of angel's wings bending over a sleeping woman. With body parts sticking out of the blankets, she appeared nude.

Jessie and Josiah walked to their spot at the end of the bar, sat and ordered.

"The guy isn't an angel but her neighbor. He's in love with her but she's not interested in love. She's career-driven. So he comes to her at night. He whispers in her ear and pretends he's a dream. She becomes smitten."

Josiah shrugged.

"That's creepy. Stalking, breaking and entering," Jessie pointed out.

"They were good friends. She gave him a key to her apartment. She trusted him. He thought of it as therapy. He would lie next to her and talk, but nothing else. Soon she longed to have someone special in her life."

"Would it work?" she asked, shooting a quick glance at him.

"What?"

"Reconditioning someone in their sleep?"

"Oh. I don't know." He blinked twice and a slow grin grew on his lips. "Maybe. It'd be subconscious."

"That'd be convenient. Many phobias could be cured."

Mona sat on the other side of Jessie, listening and waiting for a chance to critique. "All you need is a naked angel man to come and whisper in your sleeping ear that life is a bowl of cherries and all men aren't creepy old coots like Rusty Kuntz. The naked guy could rub your arm and murmur you'll soon find love. The perfect someone is out there. You just have to open your eyes. Convenient."

"I suppose a naked man with good intentions could be okay." Jessie forced a short laugh then bit her lip.

If Mona knew about Jessie's assault it must be common knowledge. She scanned the room, watching the other patrons, but nobody stared at her. Nothing out of the ordinary except Josiah who lifted one eyebrow in question.

Mona jumped off the bar stool and motioned to Josiah. "Hurry up and eat. Sawyer is waiting for a game."

Sawyer challenged Josiah to a game of eight ball. They each took a cue stick off the holder. "What should we play for?" Sawyer asked as he loaded the plastic triangle with numbered balls. Usually, the loser bought the winner a beer or an appetizer.

"How 'bout kisses?" Mona suggested with too much enthusiasm. Jessie's face grew hot, and she sent a prayer of thanks for the dim lights of the tavern.

Sawyer's predatory smile meant he agreed. Josiah hit solids into the pockets. He had talent but Sawyer was better. As the game drew to a close, Jessie slipped away to the restroom. She'd let Mona give the winner's kiss. Game two Sawyer chugged his third beer and Mona praised his every move. Sawyer's bragging, while in good fun, was more the focus than the actual game. He probably figured he'd get another kiss no matter what.

"Josiah, you need to win or Mona will be hard to handle." Jessie pointed to her giggling friend.

After he sunk a ball, Sawyer lifted Mona and spun her around. His next one missed. Josiah's turn.

"I agree. They're a bit obnoxious." Josiah inspected the table looking for the best opportunity. Thinking he found it, he stood poised.

"Wait." Jessie moved next to him and slid her finger along the cue.

"Hey, that's his staff. You're not supposed to touch his staff or balls." Sawyer doubled over laughing.

Jessie rolled her eyes. *Men.* She could be obnoxious too. She slipped under Josiah's arm, slipping between him and the cue. With one of his arms on either side of her, she faced the table and curled her fingers around the wooden cue next to his hands. She caressed the smooth hard wood pretending it was the best male body part... ever. She pursed her lips and moaned a little.

Together, she and Josiah leaned as he eyed the ball. His hard and warm body pressed against her back. She tried to ignore her body's response to his. "What are you doing?" His low voice and warm breath kicked up her heart rate.

"Shutting Sawyer up. It worked. You can thank me later. Now you better let me go so you can win this," Jessie said.

"Their faces were priceless." He rubbed his nose in her hair making her shiver. "I won't let you go. You're my good luck charm."

She laughed and turned to face him but sobered because they were nose to nose and pressed together. Her breath caught and body heated. "Josiah, you better win this game. Especially after I made a fool of myself." She hugged him, then slipped out and stood next to Mona at the end of the table. Mona had quieted and eyed her with curiosity.

Josiah won and the crowd in Hammered grew loud. Sawyer heckled Jessie and Josiah and congratulated them. She slung an arm around his waist and hugged him. "I knew you could do it."

"It didn't shut Sawyer up." Josiah grinned from ear to ear. "I don't think anything could."

"I know. We'll never hear the end of it, either." Jessie knew Mona planned to tease her till the cattle came home.

"Jess, I-" The smile slipped from his face.

"It's just a kiss." She faced him with head tipped and eyed his lips. Her heart tried to jackhammer out of her chest. "Go ahead and claim your winnings before Sawyer believes you've forfeited your right and tries to stake a claim."

He pulled her to him in a tight hug and kissed the top of her head. "Are you sure?" he whispered. She understood why he hesitated. This time making sure *he* wasn't the one to hurt her. But she wanted this more than she thought possible. Jessie stood on tiptoes and claimed his lips. His eyes widened, then closed, as he tilted his head. Their arms tightened around each other as the roar elevated.

CHAPTER 8

Jessie

HOLY HELL. JOSIAH BARNES IS *an awesome kisser.*

But that very public kiss had been a mistake. Not that it had happened, but it'd happened in a place assuring everyone in town would find out. The gossip bothered her. Folks' erroneous assumptions would ruin any prospect of Josiah ever having a real girlfriend.

B.J.'s scowl returned but even though she'd become the spawn of the devil again, it hadn't kept him away from the weekly book run. Undine's addiction had rubbed off on at least one member of the opposite sex.

The phone rang, bringing her out of her daydreaming.

"So…I heard about the kiss. When's the big day? I'd like to be a grandpa before I grow another gray hair." Jessie stared at the phone and shook her head.

"Sorry, Daddy, you'll be waiting awhile. Josiah and I aren't an item." *Although, everybody thinks we are.* She blew out an irritated breath.

After the awkward phone conversation, she wanted to flee the confines of the ranch. A change of scenery was needed, but she didn't want to visit Fortuna. Everywhere she'd go curious people asked her questions or stared. Like Desire, who wanted romantic details. Desire wanted to help plan the wedding.

She pulled open the truck door and threw her purse on the seat.

"Hey, Jess, where are you going?" Josiah walked out of the barn with a paper in his hand.

"Nockerville." She glanced away from him, not wanting to admit she was running from the rumors.

"Great. I need a few items Nailed doesn't have. Do you mind if I tag along? I'll drive."

"That's fine." She handed him the keys then retreated to the passenger side of the truck. As the truck bumped down the driveway, she feared he'd mention the kiss.

He switched on the truck's radio to fill the awkward silence. She chewed on her bottom lip and stuffed her hands under her thighs to keep from drumming her fingers. The more she tried to relax and enjoy the scenery, the more it backfired. Even with her head turned away from him, she heard each noise he made, from the cute sneeze to the mutter at a rude driver. He cleared his throat, and she chanced a glance at him.

She gulped, her heart fluttered and breath hitched. She examined Josiah as if she'd never seen him. *God, the man is gorgeous.* His light eyes gazed at the road and both hands gripped the wheel. She studied the slope of his nose, his long lashes and the day's growth of a beard. But her gaze narrowed in on his lips. Her body warmed at the memory of his lips on hers. She sucked in her bottom lip and bit it, trying to dispel the sensation.

His arm shifted when he turned the wheel, giving her traitorous eyes something new to study. The white t-shirt allowed an unencumbered view of his corded biceps as they flexed under tanned skin.

Jessie breathed a sigh of relief when she pushed open the door. With a wave, they went in opposite directions. The square shaped town had an old courthouse in the center and most of the shops circled it. She walked the town, happy to be anonymous. She found a sewing shop, talked to the owner and came away with samples and a bag of supplies. Jessie stowed them in the truck and went off in search of Josiah. She located him in a coffee shop reading *The Visitation,* the nighttime angel book. She'd recently finished it and passed it off to him.

The story was open to a page with a few romantic lines underlined. Willie Layer reenacted scenes from the book that had resulted in jail time. Josiah tapped the page near the highlighted quote and wore a faraway look as he pondered something and it probably wasn't anything to do with the health of pregnant cattle.

"That's not bad," Josiah said.

"The latte or the book?" Jessie slipped into the seat across from him. She knew how it ended- girl falls for dream guy. She liked the clever book.

"*The Visitation.*" Josiah grinned as he shifted towards her. "I believe dream therapy could work."

"Dream therapy? If it worked, everyone would be healed because everyone would get it. The world would be a happy, healthier place." She watched him over the rim of her cup as she sipped.

"It could work with someone you love." He stuck a napkin between the pages and closed the book.

"The heroine wasn't in love with the hero. They were friends. He's a horny stalker."

"He's crazy in love with a *stubborn* woman." Josiah quirked an eyebrow.

A nervous giggle escaped because she was being stubborn. "He's a peeping tom."

Leaning back and crossing his arms, he sighed. "I'm going to try it on you."

Surprised by the funny sensations those words caused, she slapped the palms of her hands on the table. "You are not sneaking into my bedroom naked!" Her loud words attracted the attention of the table next to her, making two older women laugh.

"Honey, he doesn't have to sneak. Just give the man an invitation." The older lady waggled her eyebrows, and both women giggled again.

Jessie's cheeks heated. She snapped her gaping mouth shut. She tried to resist the temptation to glance at Josiah but, once again, her treacherous eyes honed in on the man's lips. Josiah extended his long, denim-clad legs and crossed them. He wore a smug smile and tipped his hat at the women earning more giggles.

"It's not that, ladies, he has to wear this." She handed them the book with the half-naked man wearing feathery, white angel wings. She smiled, picturing bare-chested Josiah with wings. *Not a bad look.*

"Oh my." They eyed the cover then Josiah. It was his turn to change colors. "Good luck." One woman pointed out the window to a temporary Halloween store in a vacant pet shop across the street. *Oh my*, was right. Jessie winked at the squirming man, earning a sheepish grin.

Jessie

Thursday after five B.J. stopped by the Double D to get his weekly fix. He used curt replies bordering on rude. It irked Jessie that he let the gossip get to him. He scowled as he slammed the gate of his truck.

"You got a minute?" Jessie said, not making it a request. She pointed to the shaded porch.

"A minute."

She led him to the porch swing, and they sat for a moment. Jessie gathered her thoughts. B.J.'s heavy musk hung in the heat. She blamed the hot evening air, and not nerves, for the sweat trickling down her back.

"You haven't been around." A sad tone tinged her voice.

"Have you missed me?" B.J. asked sarcastically.

"Yes." She glanced at her sandals. Not B.J. per se but people in general. His mouth fell open then shut, twice, before she drew in a deep breath and stumbled on.

"I've been staying away from town and people for two weeks. It's a self-inflicted boycott. I've been lonely. Cabin fever is getting to me but I'd rather be alone than the subject of all the rumors."

"The rumors are still there." The familiar scowl hardened his features as he focused on the noise coming from the barn. Josiah worked on something with a power tool.

"Josiah and I are not an item." Jessie and Josiah's relationship was more complicated than friends and business associates but lovers they were not.

"I heard you were going to elope," B.J. stated. His piercing gaze bored into hers.

Jessie giggled then rolled her eyes. "First the people elope *then* you hear about it. Not the other way around."

B.J.'s jaw dropped and his brows rose. He rubbed his chin and glanced away as his cheeks grew pink.

They sat on the swing in silence a few moments, enjoying the breeze. She twisted on the wood seat and inspected the man beside her. Framed with long, black lashes, his dark eyes watched a butterfly flit from flower to flower. He caught her gaze and a seductive smile formed. *Seductive?* The bottom was slightly fuller than the top.

"Josiah and I aren't dating. We aren't lovers. I gave him a kiss for winning the game."

When B.J. left, he wore a smile. She hoped it wasn't the facts but her sincerity that won him.

Josiah emerged from the barn covered in sawdust. He pulled on the front of his blue t-shirt and shook it, sending grit into the air. Jessie swallowed, biting her lip as he ran fingers through his wavy hair. He spied the alien vehicle leaving and glanced at the porch. Jessie motioned for him and he sauntered toward her.

"B.J. heard we're planning to elope." She tried to remain emotionless as she scanned Josiah's endless blue eyes.

"Someone's been running his big mouth again." Josiah's hands balled against his side but otherwise he seemed relaxed. His gaze flicked to his truck then to Jessie.

"You'd let me know if we were going to elope, wouldn't you?" she teased.

"We can't take the children," he fired back.

She laughed. "What are you going to do?"

"I'm going to go visit Gimme and have a little talk." The fingers on one hand stretched and re-curled showing the language of the talk.

"After the talk add a 'ditto' from me." She smiled sweetly, and he nodded.

Josiah smiled, but it looked evil. He drove away, fishtailing out of the drive. She'd seen him enraged once before and Rusty hadn't fared well. A thought to warn her father came and went. They were big boys.

CHAPTER 9

Josiah

DUST ENGULFED THE TRUCK AS it came to an abrupt stop next to the Big Deal ranch's bunkhouse. Josiah put it in park and scanned the lot. There were several vehicles but one he recognized was Cole's beater. The truck was barely held together with duct tape and baling wire. None of the other cars shouted they belonged to the man he searched for. The barn-like building matched the other brown outbuildings on the ranch. He shoved the door open and strode to the main living area with heavy boots.

Arlon pushed a broom at the rear of the room but Josiah, spying the overflowing trash, remained near the entry with a wrinkled nose. The front room was a combination kitchenette and living space containing a secondhand sofa and wood table and chairs. Cards lay scattered over the table's surface as if someone lost a game. A range, fridge and microwave were sandwiched together on one wall.

"What can I do for you?" Arlon asked as he completed his pile. He bent his thin body over and retrieved the dustpan.

"Is Gimme around?" Josiah ventured further into the room and the smell got worse. "It stinks in here."

The old man shrugged. "I had chili last night."

Josiah laughed and followed Arlon into the bunkroom where, thank God, he breathed clean air. The room, with metal-framed beds, reminded Josiah of church camp dorms. The white beadboard walls made the room homey but the tiles on the floor were noisy. Most of the eight beds were tidy, like the one he'd stayed in, but two remained unmade. A few of the men lived at the ranch. The foreman, Curly, and Gimme were both residents.

Arlon swept the terracotta floor. He picked a pair of running shoes and threw them on an unmade bed then continued. "You lookin' fer Gimme?" Arlon asked coming closer.

"Yes, sir."

"Why?" Arlon stopped and leaned against the broom. He scratched his whiskered chin.

"I've got a matter I need to discuss with him." Josiah tried to keep his voice neutral but he couldn't help the level of anger coursing through his veins. It wasn't the old man's business, but he'd tell him if need be. He trusted Arlon to keep quiet.

"Well, son, you got a problem." He shifted the handle to the other hand. His gaunt face seemed pensive as he tilted his head. "Gimme is out with Curly and Cole near Settler's Ridge. He'll be gone all night." The old man's leathered face frowned, and he shook his head pushing the broom again.

Josiah swore and jabbed his hands in his front pockets then kicked the metal frame of the closest bed.

"What the hell are you doing to my furniture?" demanded Brad as he stormed into the room from the back door. His mustache twitched, revealing a reserved smile.

Josiah's mouth fell open but nothing came out. He hadn't damaged any property. "I need to talk to Gimme," he growled.

"You can do that, son," Brad said with a raised eyebrow. The man reminded Josiah of Sam Elliot. He wore a denim button-up shirt and jeans, dark boots and hat and a red bandanna.

"Not unless I ride an hour to get to him." Josiah rammed fingers through his hair. An hour.

"Malone isn't out on the range tonight," Brad said.

Gimme happened to be a Malone. The Malone family had been in Fortuna from the inception and most were decent folk. Gimme's great-grandfather once owned a small ranch, but he'd sold off the land before the depression and went into banking. Now the family split vocations, either running the banks in Fortuna and Nockerville or working local ranches.

"He's not? But Arlon said…" Josiah stared quizzically at Arlon.

Brad slid a sidelong glance at Arlon. The two seemed to communicate something telepathically. "What's this about? Why the urgency?"

Josiah shook his head. "I've got something I need to say to Gimme. The sooner the better."

"I didn't want the boy sent on a wild goose chase but he needs to cool off," Arlon cautioned.

"Is this about Jessie?" The father pinched his brows together.

"He's been running his mouth again." Josiah huffed out a breath. "It's time he shut it."

Brad shifted his weight and strode toward the back door. "Come on, son. He's this way. The fool talked back to Curly one too many times and now he's cleaning out the stalls with extra special care." Josiah followed close behind matching the Big Deal's owner stride for stride.

Josiah

Once inside the barn, Josiah drew in a deep breath. Brad headed for the small office he kept there. He stopped and sniffed the air. Over the scent of horse, leather, sawdust and straw, he smelled smoke. Above the last stall, a thin thread of white smoke twisted into existence then disappeared like a ghost. A grunt accompanied the next puff and a shovel full of muck landed in a wheelbarrow next to the open stall door.

"Dammit, Gimme," Brad yelled, "How many times do I have to tell you *no smoking in the barn.*"

"Shit," Gimme squeaked. Josiah grinned at the other man's reaction.

Josiah glanced down the aisle to the lit area with the wheelbarrow. Two horses poked their heads out, curious about the newcomers and one welcomed him with a nicker.

Brad flipped the office lights and called him in. Josiah's gaze traveled around the room, over the desk and two chairs then settled on the gray filing cabinet in the corner. A dusty rodeo trophy, with a couple medals roped around it, stood sentinel over a few framed family pictures. He walked closer to inspect them. Behind him Brad opened and closed a squeaky desk drawer. One photo contained Brad and his wife with gap-toothed Jessie around the age of seven. Josiah had always admired this picture of the young family. Another frame contained the group of hands taken at the Fourth of July picnic a few years ago. He and Gimme were both pictured. Arlon's arms were slung over the shoulders of Cole and Josiah. The photographer caught Gimme with his mouth open as if he'd tried to pronounce "provolone" instead of "cheese".

That was the thing about Gimme Malone, he didn't understand when to shut his mouth. While his sister and cousins worked in the finance industry, he didn't. The man tended to be uncouth and Josiah couldn't see him handling customers discreetly. He'd blab how much someone did or didn't have in their account. The man held nothing sacred but in the three years he'd worked on the Big Deal he hadn't been fired.

"I like that one," Brad said as he picked up the frame holding his family. "Those were happy times."

"Jessie looks like Trish," Josiah said, "but she has Undine's coloring." Someday he hoped to have a family too, but the thought losing Jessie chilled his soul. The car accident took Trish too young. Josiah placed his hand on Brad's shoulder and gave a small squeeze.

With a sigh, Brad turned and walked behind the desk and placed the photo next to another frame there. "I have something I need to show you." He sat in the chair and opened an ivory colored file. A white envelope slid out into his big hand. He held it for Josiah.

Still standing Josiah took the envelope and flipped it to read the address. The words "correction center" leaped out at him. He raised his gaze to Brad's and held it as the color drained from his face.

"Go on," Brad prompted.

Josiah pulled out the paper and unfolded it. He scanned the, chicken scratch for handwriting, letter. "Oh, hell," he muttered. He stuffed the envelope and threw it on the desktop then clutched the back of the small wooden chair. "She doesn't need this. Jess is doing well. She's finally acting like the girl she was before Don died. I don't want to see her hurting again." He scrubbed his face with a hand and drew a deep breath.

"There's nothing we can do to stop it. Rusty Kuntz will be getting out of jail soon," Brad hissed. He leaned forward placing his elbows on the desk and steepled his fingers. "He's paid his time."

Josiah's gaze narrowed. "I don't care," he growled sounding feral. "I don't want him near Jessie."

"I don't either," Brad glanced at the younger man. "I doubt he'll ever return to Fortuna. There's nothing for him here anymore." His head swiveled to a paneled wall that held framed photographs. Many of these were rodeo and contest winners, even a preteen Jessie held a medal in one. It had to be bittersweet for Brad to stare at the wall full of proud moments because several held the smiling face of Kuntz.

"We can't help that Rusty is getting out." Brad's tone was soft and understanding.

Josiah stared at the chair because he needed something to focus on. He clutched the back with a death grip while emotions threatened to take over. He noted the oak seat was split and narrow, barely wide enough for a butt, and the thin spindle legs were missing a support. It was a wonder it held the weight of an adult man.

"He has a hearing first then he'll be released. I'll keep you posted on the date." Brad shuffled some papers with a sigh.

Josiah accepted the dismissal with a nod then thanked the man.

Josiah

Leaving the office, he followed whistling to find Gimme using the shovel digging to get the corner clean. Josiah spied a romance novel under the man's cigarettes and tilted his head to read the spine. *The Cowboy's First Love.* The man hadn't seen Josiah standing there, which was a good thing because a rolling wave of anger hit him. He clamped his mouth shut in order to stop the obscenities threatening to erupt.

Gimme dropped the load of dirtied sawdust on his boot and swore. "God, don't sneak up on me," he said grabbing his heart.

Josiah smirked at the drama-king and scanned the filthy man. *How could anyone in town take him seriously?* Yet they did and someone had believed the rumors. That's why he stood in a barn breathing dust and staring at Fortuna's paramount male gossip-monger. Josiah opened his mouth to confront him but Gimme threw a shovel full in the wheelbarrow nearly hitting him.

"Hey, when are you going to elope?" he asked with raised eyebrows. The crass question left Josiah speechless. Gimme pulled out a navy handkerchief and dabbed his damp forehead. "It's not surprising with the way you moon over her and all, but it kinda shocked me *she* liked you that much."

"Shocked?" he gasped. "Why?"

Gimme sneered at him. "You're you and she's, well, she's her."

Josiah snorted.

"Why would the owner of a large ranch want a scrawny hired hand? She's a mature woman and you're a runt, like me." He leaned against the wood wall and crossed his arms.

Gimme's statements struck too close to home, making Josiah frown. If the twenty-one-year old Gimme referred to their age he could be right. Sometimes Jessie called him "kid." At twenty-four, well, pushing twenty-five, there was less than a three year gap between them. She might balk at the age difference sometimes but she didn't most of the time. He recalled one night in particular and grinned like a contented cat. "How could you ever know what a woman wants?"

A glowering Gimme pushed off the wall but stopped, leaning into Josiah's space. He placed fists on his hips. "I know how to treat women right. I'm something of a ladies man."

This was no Casanova cowboy. Josiah tried to hide a chuckle. "Right," he drawled.

"Besides, I have sisters, three of them. When you're surrounded by girls, you pick up a thing or two." He admitted this reluctantly, but not embarrassed, like revealing a trade secret. Josiah had two sisters of his own, one older and one younger, and knew there was some truth to the statement; but, one does not romance one's sisters. He figured Gimme's knowledge of how to treat women came more from the information he gleaned from romance novels than the real thing.

"Your old lady is a beauty. I bet she is *fine* when she's hot and bothered."

"All right. That's enough," Josiah bellowed, the rage coming anew. He straightened and leaned in. "You need to shut your mouth."

"You don't want to talk about your fiancée?"

"I don't want *you* to talk about her."

"Nothin' wrong with speculating." Gimme smirked.

"I'm warning you, Gimme," Josiah growled in a low voice.

"Or you'll what? Run to Jessie's daddy?" he laughed. "Go on, little cowboy, run to daddy. He can be your bodyguard. Now you can get into his wallet 'cause daddy's little girl is into you. You're lucky to bed that little lady. She's already a spitfire, but I bet when she sucks your-".

Josiah didn't let him finish, he pulled back his arm then released it to fly into Gimme's stunned face. The man cursed as he stumbled backward into the stall. He lunged at Josiah but missed when Josiah darted to the right. The men swung fists and danced around each other. Josiah hit Gimme in the face again. Blood trickled out of his nose. Gimme hit Josiah's stomach, knocking the air out of him. They shoved and wrestled, throwing each other against the wall. Finally, Josiah got Gimme stuck in a headlock. Josiah grinned grateful for the hours he wrestled with his two younger brothers.

"You will not talk about her," Josiah snarled.

Gimme elbowed him in the gut trying to get away but Josiah tightened his hold.

"Everything all right here?" Brad asked. He glanced at the men with quiet indifference. Gimme stopped wriggling like a worm on a hook.

"We're coming to an understanding," Josiah said with calm assurance.

"Is that so, Malone?" Brad zeroed in on the man held captive.

"Yes, sir," Gimme agreed in a defeated tone.

Josiah felt the fight leave Gimme as the man relaxed in his arms. He silently applauded Brad's well timed intrusion. He dropped his arms and let the foolish man go. Gimme scrambled to the other side of the aisle and grimaced. Already the man's eyes were swelling. With a confident smirk, Josiah knew victory belonged to him.

CHAPTER 10

Jessie

WHEN JOSIAH RETURNED FROM THE Big Deal, Jessie sat at the kitchen table opening the mail, which included a whopping vet bill. He greeted her with a nod but wore a scowl similar to B.J.'s and it aged him. The man walked as if his boots weighed a ton. He passed her without a word.

She watched him disappear into the hallway, appreciating the way his jeans hugged his butt. The pipes groaned as the shower turned on. She leaned over the table, placing an elbow on the surface with her chin in her hand. She closed her eyes imagining he'd shampoo his hair first. The suds would run down his back and chest. Her eyelids snapped open, and she sat straight against the chair's back. Pulled the bill into view, and with a long sigh, she reread the details.

Josiah plopped across from her giving her a scare. She took deep breaths to still her heart while studying him. She wasn't used to his light brown hair, now dark and damp, combed to the side. He smelled divine. She sucked in a quick breath and thrust a bag of chips in his direction. His blue eyes roamed over her then the table. He plucked a few chips from the open bag. "Mmm," he moaned with a smile. She hadn't realized how much she'd missed his smile until the shower revived it.

"Your mother called. She wanted to warn you to get dinner out. You're brothers are sick. We're talking projectile." Normally, she'd offer for him to eat and stay at the ranch. He'd slept on the sofa many times but not with the rumors. She would not add fuel to the fire.

"I can go to Hammered. The Fortuna fish special is tonight. Care to join

57

me?" he asked in a hopeful tone.

"No, thanks." Going out in public with him wasn't an option but staying home with him was a better one. *God, where did that thought come from?* She shook her head, admonishing the rebellious thoughts. Her brain must be sick of finances if it diverted to men, especially Josiah.

The bills were mounting. Running a ranch was expensive, hard work. Josiah pulled the paper towards himself then whistled. With his business management degree, he could help or, at least, give her some suggestions to cutting the debt. All she needed to do is ask, but the man did more than enough for her, and the business, already. She used accounting software to tally everything plus an accountant helped at tax time. She was making it, but barely. After the flood wiped out half the herd, business improved but not fast enough.

She needed to augment the Double D somehow. Her grandmother's sewing machine and diaries might help, but how? She sighed and pulled another bill out of an envelope.

"How's Gimme?" Jessie asked without glancing from the power bill.

She peered up and found a confident man with a satisfied grin. "He'll think twice before he shoots his mouth off again."

She smiled like a fool and fist-bumped him. She hoped Gimme had learned his lesson.

With a deep breath, she set the bills aside and went to switch wet clothes to the dryer. He followed. Some of Josiah's ranch duds were in the dryer. She pulled out the clean jeans and folded them into a basket belonging to him.

"Here, let me help," he said, snagging something before she could touch it. With a sheepish grin, he set the red plaid boxers in the basket.

If he's embarrassed by those, wait until he sees what's tucked inside the t-shirt he grabbed.

He held up the shirt and something fell at his feet. After placing the folded tee in the basket, he reached for the wayward garment. He picked up the turquoise string bikini undies. "I, uh… Oh."

She giggled when his thumb and finger pinched the fabric and held it as far away from his body as possible. The red reached the tips of his ears. "Those aren't your style," she teased breaking the spell.

"But they match my eyes," he said, batting his lashes.

Together, they laughed and worked as a team until they finished the chore.

Jessie

Jessie sat on the sofa staring out the large window at the land she called home. Her knee bumped up and down. She'd hate to lose the ranch.

Josiah entered the room and lowered himself onto the overstuffed leather armchair. His wavy brown hair had dried messy and rivaled a romance cover model. Tanned and muscular, he was clothed in tight jeans and boots. The body under those clothes could vie for model of the year. She didn't mind admiring his body when it distracted her from the account balance at the bank.

"Jess, you ever think about that night?" He stared at his hands.

"You wouldn't have killed me." The argument popped from her mouth.

"Not the crash," he said with a nervous chuckle.

"What night?" She studied his face.

"The hayloft…"

"*That* night." Her mind raced to the night he recalled. A better night than the accident. An evening celebrating life, not circling death. At twenty-two, she'd been eager for another school year to begin but leaving home always saddened her. Dad planned to drive her to the University of Texas. Her grandparents held a farewell dinner in her honor. After the meal, she'd slipped out and hid in the barn to gain composure. The younger cowboy found her weeping in the hayloft.

"Ever wonder what if?" Josiah swallowed as his gaze caressed her face.

What if they had made love? Jessie's heart hammered remembering their bodies intertwined in the hay. They'd shared an intense passion. Yes, the man's lips could be the inspiration for any main character in the novels upstairs.

"A long distance relationship would have been hard," she reminded.

"A relationship?" Josiah leaned back in the chair. He studied her with wide eyes.

Their friendship would have blossomed into more if cultivated. A relationship would have altered their lives. He'd have followed her to Austin. His schooling could have been derailed. It was a good thing he'd found the strength to stop.

Jessie knew if she'd tasted his love, she would have wanted more. The way Josiah had touched her, as if she were the most precious thing in the universe, yet with fire enough to scorch, she had little doubt she'd become addicted. He'd made a nest out of their shirts and lain her on it. Her bra wasn't anything fancy, cream with ecru lace and, as luck had it, she wore matching undies but Josiah never found out.

He'd kissed her breathless. His calloused hands caressed the soft skin of her abdomen. Her hands slid over his back and chest. The adoration that shown in the blue jewels of his eyes, startled her. She thought Josiah to be the most handsome man she'd ever gazed upon. Her hand had slid to his waist where she attempted to unbutton his jeans. She succeeded but his hand caught hers and stopped the forward progress. He kissed her again, long and hard then whispered, "I'm sorry, Jess. We aren't ready for this yet." Walking away shirtless, the man left her there alone. She'd felt stunned, then pissed. He'd rejected her. *What horny, college-aged man would walk away from sex?* He hadn't wanted her and her heart ached.

She came to admire his restraint. Yes, occasionally, she thought about that night. She considered it to be one of the few romantic encounters where she felt respected.

"Do you?" she countered, not willing to admit anything to him.

His lids slid halfway closed, and he grinned as if he knew a secret. He stood to leave and opened the front door. "Evenin', Jess." He pulled the door closed but stopped and leaned back inside. He waited until he held her gaze. "I'm coming tonight."

She remained frozen for a full minute then jumped up and watched him through the window. Her heart hammered in her chest. Long after Josiah left, she stood chewing her lip.

She knew of the visitation fad going around town. Men visited ladies at night, becoming the men of their dreams, but she hadn't expected Josiah to fall prey to this trend. *Stupid romance novels.* She had no clue what strange ideas he intended to whisper in her ear but she didn't intend to find out.

She put a hand over her thumping heart, and smiled.

Jessie

The phone rang in Jessie's pocket, and she awoke, bolting upright, and fell off the chair onto scratchy hay. *Hay?* She blinked, willing her eyes to focus in the dark.

Tied to the security system, the phone app alerted her the front door had opened. Grabbing the blinking device, she checked the time. *2:13 a.m.* She yawned.

Who the heck visits at 2:13 in the morning? Visits? She groaned, "The Visitation."

She sucked in a deep breath and jumped up with heart hammering. A jolt of adrenaline worked as well as a double espresso.

A thin beam of light split the darkness of the night, illuminating the edge of the loft door. After she'd brought her supplies to the barn hayloft, she cracked the rolling door open, hoping for a breeze to help nullify the stifling heat. From her perch, she spotted a small truck parked in the driveway. Her mouth went dry, and she groped for the handle of the door to keep from losing her balance. She squinted trying to see who's truck it belonged to. Both B.J. and Josiah had similar makes and colors but she couldn't tell in the dark. *Wouldn't that be something if the two of them came face to face in my bedroom... naked?* She chuckled.

Leaving the door open, she resumed her seat and fished her tablet out of a bag. She tapped it to wake the device. Her fingers messed up the password three times before she could login. The barn's Wi-Fi worked, but the program lagged as it loaded.

No lights in the house yet. She sighed.

Back in the day, she'd brought a few boys to the hayloft to kiss. Josiah's trip turned out to be a one-time deal. She shivered, remembering his lips pressing hers. She'd been able to get away with it at her grandparents' home because they had fewer ranch hands roaming the property. Her dad would've skinned alive any boy caught locking lips with her. What would her father do if he knew a man had entered her home with the goal of replicating a scene from a novel and whispering romantic intentions into her innocent, sleeping mind? She giggled.

The tablet linked to the laptop computer which sat on the dresser. The small camera pointed to the foot of her bed and the doorway. She leaned forward and examined the hallway where a night light helped to illuminate the floor outside the room. It seemed normal.

She toggled to another camera showing a black-and-white picture. The small, square, black unit, a baby monitor used for a sick calf that past spring, had been angled toward the king bed. She'd rigged a faux body under the quilt. For the ruse, she'd rolled towels for the legs and used decorative pillows for the rest.

A figure walked past the night light breaking the constant light and catching her eye. So far, the man-shaped shadow remained a complete mystery. He didn't appear to be naked.

She released a breath she didn't realize she'd been holding.

He paused in the doorway. She tried to zoom in, but the picture blurred. Did he sense the hoax? When he stepped away from the door, she jumped almost dropping the tablet. The bed shook as if a body sat on it but the pillows blocked her view.

Hair appeared next to the dummy's shoulder, then a face. She recognized her visitor. *Josiah. I can't believe it.* Her heart beat so fast she thought it might explode.

His lips moved but she couldn't hear. She pressed on the volume control but it was already maxed. Either he spoke so low the small camera couldn't detect it or the camera malfunctioned. Dammit, she wanted to listen.

He reached to touch her face but pulled back startled. With a grimace, he pushed the pillows off the bed and sat up.

Holy anaconda! He wore nothing but his birthday suit.

Josiah stomped out of the bedroom and she jumped up and, hiding in the darkness, peered outside, scrutinizing her house.

He stormed outside, slamming the door. The nude man paced back and forth on the drive. His lips moved but, again, she could hear nothing. Frustrated, she leaned out of the second story hayloft trying to glean his words.

Even from far away, his build suggested what her heart already knew, but she took the binoculars and focused. Josiah—upset and naked. Good lord. *If the man would only hold still.* Her heart ran a marathon while her brain stalled watching the hunky body.

The one-sided argument he'd been having ended when he yelled her name. She jumped behind the door to hide and closed her eyes. Her heart beat a rapid tune she hoped he couldn't hear. Jessie stole a couple of deep breaths before peeking again.

He stopped pacing and, with one hand on the hood, he leaned against the truck. With his backside towards her, his arm moved as if he scratched his upper thigh. A lot. And fast. What could he be doing?

She refocused the binoculars for a closer inspection. Oh, God, he wasn't. Oh, God, he was. He satisfied his manly need while moaning her name.

She pushed away from the door astounded yet strangely flattered. This could be the craziest night of her life. She'd never read about a hero yanking-off, at night, on a driveway. Her driveway.

This wasn't a work of fiction. She swallowed, trying to moisten her suddenly dry mouth. *He moaned my name.* A smile crept to her lips as a hot sensation spread through her body.

Josiah froze, except his head swiveled around as if noticing her missing vehicle. She'd hidden the truck behind the barn. He opened the door to his truck and pulled on his clothes and boots. He called someone, shut the door, and headed to the barn.

She squeaked and grabbed her items, moving them against the hay bales. The bales formed a wall and protected her from being seen. She checked her phone to see if he called her.

He pulled open the door and strode in, his heavy footfalls echoed in the barn.

"She isn't home. Are you sure she's not at Johnson's place? You're sure. Okay. Fine. What am I supposed to do now?" He paused, listening. "Thanks, I'll camp out in the loft. Yeah, you too. Sorry for waking you."

Her stomach turned to lead. Jessie couldn't escape. She sucked in her lip and hid behind the bale wall praying he wouldn't peer over. She held her breath and kept still.

Muttering, he climbed into the loft and settled on the other side of the bales hidden from her view. She ignored the urge to spy and waited. When she heard heavy breathing, she peeked around to see Josiah leaned against the bales, his arms crossed and legs crossed at the ankle. His head tipped back and features relaxed. A small smile tugged at his lips, parting them slightly. She stared at his lips, curious if he'd planned on using them on her in the bedroom. A shiver ran down her spine.

He resembled the much younger comatose Josiah. A lump rose in her throat. The man's face feuded with her heart to tempt fate. Would fairy tale endings, like Snow White or Sleeping Beauty, work if the man needed kissed? She licked her lips wanting to find out. *He'd wake up, then what?*

Drumming her fingers against her thigh, she watched his chest rise and fall. A wicked smile formed. She could perform her own version of the visitation. "Josiah," she whispered. "Josiah," she purred in a louder voice. "I liked you moaning my name."

Jessie froze with wide eyes when he swallowed and shifted his arms. The movement yanked his t-shirt exposing tanned belly flesh. Her mouth fell open as she fought the desire to reach out and touch it.

Jessie hugged herself with a frown. She couldn't get the hots for Josiah. She clasped the pillowcase full of her electronics and climbed the ladder.

Sleep would be fickle. Jessie's mind couldn't digest what had happened yet but her heart ached to run her hands over Josiah's body.

CHAPTER 11

Josiah

JOSIAH TRIED TO SNEAK INTO the kitchen, but Jessie sat at the table cleaning a pistol. He paused, wondering wryly if a day's growth of whiskers, hay sticking out of his hair and lack of sleep improved his looks any. She paused too, and her gaze met his. He swallowed and hurried to the shower.

Josiah exited clean, in fresh clothes, and felt less a fool.

He poured a mug of coffee. Years ago, before working on the ranch, he'd hated the stuff. Oh, how things had changed. He sat and ran his fingers through his damp hair, watching her.

"Did you have a good night?" Jessie's hand rubbed the long hard metal.

He didn't want his actions to push her into Johnson's arms. His stomach ached with worry. "Did you?" He sipped the hot java as she rubbed the barrel. He cleared his throat which had gone dry despite the liquid.

"It was entertaining." She smiled like the Cheshire cat. "Did you know I sleep with a hand gun?"

"Not last night," he mumbled.

"Josiah, about last night." She sought his gaze. "Please don't do it again. You could've been killed."

A smile teased at his lips as their old argument filtered through his mind. He leaned forward. Heat flared in his chest and continued to his face.

"If I woke startled to find a strange man in my bedroom, I'd shoot first and ask questions later. Don't do it again."

"How'd you-?" Josiah asked inspecting his hands.

"I have my ways."

Someone knocked on the kitchen door. Josiah glanced at the visitor and clenched his jaw. An odd sensation settled in his stomach similar to when Gimme had punched him there.

"Come on in," Jessie said. She glanced up from cleaning the gun.

Johnson entered with a smile and a gust of his cologne. It was unusual to see him without a scowl. He even greeted Josiah with an agreeable nod then inspected Jessie from head to toe. "You ready to go to town, Jessie?"

"Sorry, I'm moving slow today. I didn't sleep a full night." Jessie put the gun in the case and shut it. She stood and emptied her cup in the sink. "Josiah, just a reminder- keep your gun holstered and don't shoot it on the driveway."

"Yes ma'am. Did you like the caliber?" Josiah grinned. His face had to be scarlet to match the heat radiating off it.

Jessie giggled but tried to hide it. "Let's talk about guns later. Sometime today, I need items brought in from the old loft. There's only a few and you'll know them when you see them." Josiah nodded with a somber smile.

Jessie added, "I'll be home after I find out where Grandma's books are special delivered." She blushed when Johnson winked at her. He held the back door open, and they exited. Johnson opened and shut the truck's door for the lady. Josiah gritted his teeth, believing a wolf had led a lamb away.

As the truck turned around, Jessie glanced at him and the laughter on her face died. Josiah couldn't perceive how he looked—like a dejected boy. He needed to buck up and sucked in a deep breath, pasting a smile on his lips. Was it his imagination or was she staring at his lips? Testing his theory, he stuck out his tongue.

Her eyes widened. A blush accompanied the smile on her face. God, he loved when she smiled. Her gaze flicked upwards then the red on her face intensified before she drove out of sight. He stepped outside and inspected the side of the barn.

"Well, hell," Josiah muttered, scratching the back of his head. The usually closed, four-foot wide loft door remained open the width of a body. He chuckled. *She'd watched the whole thing from the hayloft.*

Jessie

Jessie mentioned she'd discuss Josiah's visitation with him. When her outing with B.J. was canceled because of an emergency at his work, she returned home but couldn't face Josiah. It was the logical way to avoid the strange tingles thinking of his lips, clinging jeans or naked backside caused.

She hid in Undine's sewing room under the guise of research. Jessie discovered patterns in the closet and tried different threads and hems with samples of cloth. She googled fabrics- natural verses synthetic fibers, durability and texture. Even surrounded by thousands of paperback novels, the textile rabbit trails kept her mind away from romance and men.

After she and Josiah had unearthed the sewing machine, she'd wondered what other furniture or items of value lay hidden under and behind the stacks of books. When her back ached, she stretched then shifted a few piles here and there until she'd found the closet. In the closet she discovered a treasure.

For a week, she kept to the sewing machine, cranking out idea after idea. Grandma Undine's sewing lessons resurfaced. She sat on the ground thumbing through a packet of old patterns and tried to decide which to create next. Nostalgia threatened to overwhelm as tears welled.

A knock startled her. She hesitated then walked to the door. Josiah stood on the other side. She stared at the locked door handle debating whether to pretend she wasn't there.

Josiah's muffled voice requested, "Open up."

She twisted the handle and opened the door a crack. His cheeks were sun-kissed, as if he just returned from the range. He wore a hat ring halo. He cocked his head as he scanned what he could see. One side of his lips lifted in a grin. Her voice left her. Why'd she open the darn door?

Josiah's boot wedged the door open further, and he thrust a plate with a turkey sandwich at her. "We need to talk."

"No." Jessie grabbed the plate then slammed the door. A turkey and cheese sandwich exactly how she liked it, with a dab of mayo. Her stomach rumbled in anticipation. She took a huge bite, closing her eyes at the divine taste.

"Listen, I don't know what you're doing in there but you need to get out."

"No," she repeated around a mouthful of food.

"Yes."

"No," she said louder.

"Do I need to get my gun?"

She gasped and started coughing. Her eyes watered and she patted her chest.

"Jessie, you okay?"

"Yes," she croaked. Her frantic attempt to purge Josiah's gun show from her mind hadn't worked. Would he shoot the door or use it as a battering ram? "What do you want, Josiah?" she asked in a tormented whisper.

"Kelly and Mona want to see you. Please come to Hammered," Josiah begged. "You can sit and talk with your friends and completely ignore me. I don't care, but you need to get out."

Jessie

Jessie sat in the corner booth at Hammered with Kelly and Mona. Clutched in her hand, she held a backpack filled with her creations. Josiah and Ben Moore sat at the bar, glancing time and again at the women. Jessie peered at the men then leaned forward. Catching her friends' attention, she lowered her voice, "You've got to promise me. Not a word to anyone."

Kelly and Mona shared a nod.

"I promise," Kelly added, folding her hands in her lap.

Mona said, "Cross my heart," while making the childlike gesture of an X over her chest.

Jessie placed the bag on the table. Opening the bag her friends reached in, touched and examined the clothing items.

Mona ran her fingers over the jade green silky item with black lace. "God, Jessie this gown is gorgeous. I love it."

"This is boutique quality. What do they cost?" Kelly held an ivory piece.

"That one is seventy. I sold one like it for the same price." It was an online auction site but still it was money in the bank. Jessie mailed the package earlier in the week.

"You should talk to Desire about running a small business." Being a second grade teacher, Kelly knew how to fund-raise, but not start a business.

"That's a great idea," Mona added with a grin. "She's hopped through all the hoops and walked where you're walking now. Her salon has flourished as long as I can remember. She should be able to make suggestions and tell you about taxes and other expenditures. If you need a loan, Stephanie Malone will be happy to talk to you." Mona had worked at the Fortuna Savings and Loan since high school. Seeing Mona's face at the drive thru teller window was something the residents of Fortuna could bank on.

"Thanks." With a shy smile, Jessie nodded, happy for the positive feedback, but she needed to see if handmade lingerie could be a big seller. Her heart and mind raced.

"Pick one and take it home," Jessie said.

"You're joking, right?" Mona said as she glanced at the green gown she'd just returned to the bag.

"No, I'm not. I need your help. I'd like you to wear the gowns and test how they hold up in the laundry. Can you do that for me?" Jessie held her breath while biting her lip.

Kelly and Mona shared another glance. Again they nodded in unison.

"I'd love to, Jessie. Thank you for thinking of me," Kelly said. She slid the silky cream colored gown to her lap. Tears welled in Kelly's eyes.

"Any special care instructions?" Mona asked.

"Don't give them any special care. Wash with like colors and put them in the dryer." Jessie stole another glance at the bar. Josiah lifted a long neck to his lips. Heat coursed through her body as he swallowed. After he placed the bottle on the bar, he wiped his palm on his thigh. Her breath hitched when his nude body flashed in her mind. She squeezed her eyes shut. The image didn't dissolve but played out once more.

"Jessie?" Kelly questioned.

"Why are you smiling?" Mona asked. Kelly elbowed Mona and tilted her head in Josiah's direction.

Jessie's cheeks heated, but she ignored her friend's suspicions. Instead, she passed it on to her foundling business. "There has to be a niche for quality, custom-made intimate apparel." If she found it, she could augment the Double D's income and save the ranch.

CHAPTER 12

Jessie

TEASE ME & MORE SALON was a legend in Fortuna, Texas, as was Desire Hardmann, the woman who owned it. People traveled miles to get worked over by the experienced cosmetologists. Clients filled every chair, including Barbara Seville's, Jessie's lifelong stylist. As long as Jessie could recall, Barb kept her workstation spotless.

Jessie caught Barb's eye and waved. The plump stylist winked without missing a beat in her conversation with client Polly Ann.

"He's devoted to his children. That says a lot about his character, not like my last three husbands." Polly Ann Amorous, a woman from Nockerville, told Norma Stitts, who sat in the chair next to her.

Jessie recognized the regular clientele. She enjoyed learning town happenings while flipping pages of a hair styling magazine.

"This will be her sixth husband if Polly Ann gets her way—and she always gets her way." Norma giggled making Polly Ann blush.

"Is he cute?" Barb asked, as she pulled the cape from Polly Ann's shoulders.

"He's distinguished." Polly Ann shrugged. She picked up her large pink Michael Kors handbag while Barb swept the cuttings on the floor.

From the chair on the other side of Polly Ann came, "That means—ugly but rich." Shandra Lear giggled at her declaration. With her brows dipped in consternation, Derry Yare worked on Shandra's hair. Like a mad scientist with a chemistry set, Derry worked hard to cover the gray.

"Who cares about his looks, is he good in bed?" Derry asked as she tried her best to wedge between the chair and the wall. She swiveled the chair so Shandra faced the other shop clients.

Polly Ann turned two shades deeper than the fuchsia cape that had been tugged from her neck. She opened her mouth to speak but Shandra cut her off, "With the help of a little blue pill."

The women tittered and Polly Ann shrugged again with a timid grin. "I'd give him a nine." She hesitated then continued, "with the pill." She giggled like a schoolgirl with her first crush.

Jessie covered her mouth to stifle a snort of laughter.

"My Hugh doesn't need that little pill. All his assets work just fine." Norma smiled. Her short white hair, soft and fluffy, resembled a lamb.

In her forties, and the youngest of the stylists, Joy Ryder made anyone who took a seat in her chair magically appear younger than seventy-five. A favorite of those who frequented the senior center, Joy loved working with the young at heart. Norma swore by Joy and tipped well.

"Hugh's favorite romance novel has a heroine with dark hair. One of these days, Sugar, I will let you color my hair like yours," Norma threatened. Norma and her husband, Hugh, owned Stitts' Truck Stop, which had the best coffee in Fortuna.

"We can be twins then," Joy teased as her black-bobbed hair swayed when she nodded.

Tease Me & More had wide windows lining Main Street and neighbors waved as they passed. Cars parked at an angle out front. In a silver sedan, Hugh Stitts flipped pages in a paperback.

Bunny Hopkins sat with a damp mop getting snipped by Heddie Hayer. The slender stylist cut as if she created a masterpiece. A long ponytail sat on the workstation counter freshly cut from Bunny's head. "How many times is it now?" Heddie asked her.

"This will make seven for me but between all the girls we're close to thirty." Bunny smiled proudly. Jessie admired Bunny and her five daughters because they donated their hair to organizations making wigs for kids with cancer.

"I wish I could donate but my hair has been treated so many times I'm afraid it's too brittle. Yours is lovely and as soft as angora." Heddie had vibrant orange, should have been red, hair heaped in a loose bun at her crown.

The receptionist Gloria Sass sat snapping gum and flipping pages in a tabloid. She hadn't acknowledged when Jessie entered the salon. The dark-haired beauty was close to Jessie's age and a high school dropout, but

Desire knew how hard it could be for an uneducated woman to make it in the world so she gave the girl an opportunity. While Jessie applauded Desire's heart, she thought the crappy receptionist sat on her sass too much.

Littered with crumbs, drink rings and used cotton balls with varying shades of nail polish, the laminated reception desk resembled a work of contemporary art—not one worth spit. The Tease Me Salon & More happened to be a well-loved small town hole-in-the-wall but, with Gloria here, it might now be considered a glorious mess. Jessie thumbed through a styling magazine but glanced up to find Gloria giving her the evil eye. She refrained from sticking out her tongue.

Jessie could credit Grandma Undine for her auburn hair. Barb loved styling the long, thick mass. She cautioned Jessie never to color it or she'd never get back to the original. It was more brown than red unless in the sun then it was fiery. Her dad said it matched her spirit. Rusty hosed down her zest for life. Recently she'd felt normal—mostly around Josiah or B.J. Trying to ignore the tingles the men caused, she shifted in her seat and plucked a new magazine.

The distraction didn't work because she remembered the first time she saw B.J. walking across the parking lot—the happy-go-lucky man radiated joy. The happiness had been magnetic, attracting Jessie. His movement had been carefree. He loved life before Carlotta, along with her lover, had dropped the baby bomb.

When she recalled the way Josiah moaned her name in the driveway, heat simmered in her core. She had a kinky fascination with it. Grinning, she turned the page.

"Jessie?" Desire purred reaching for her. She stood and took Desire's wrinkled hands. The petite woman wore her chestnut hair in a Vulcan-like pixie cut.

With the owner out of the office, Gloria was off her sass and tidying the desk.

"Ms. Hardmann, I'm happy to see you." According to Undine Love's diaries, she and Desire danced at the same place: The Cork & Screw. It didn't sound reputable. Yet Jessie would describe her grandma and Desire as confident, smart and courageous. It was hard to picture the elderly woman as a lithe dancer but she remained full of life.

"Child, you are looking more like your grandmother every day." Desire's gaze dipped to the young woman's chest. Yes, Jessie wore a size DD. She found it both ironic and apropos.

"Barb is ready for you, dear," Desire announced.

"I need to talk with you later." Jessie squeezed Desire, wishing to discuss the journals and business ideas right then. Jessie agreed with Mona and Kelly, it would be helpful to review details concerning an intimate apparel business with a woman. She loved her dad, but he was a guy, and to him skivvies came one way: white, tight and cotton. She'd done enough loads of laundry through the years to know that fact hadn't changed.

Barb shampooed, cut then shaped her auburn hair, leaving the length but giving it style.

Jessie paid Barb then, ignoring Gloria's glare, she entered the hallway leading to Desire's office. She wanted Desire's insight regarding small business but hoped Desire didn't offer to plan her and Josiah's wedding.

Jessie

Jessie knocked on the open door. Desire's eyes remained closed; she appeared to be asleep. Jessie turned to leave but then Desire's lids flickered open and she pulled out small earbuds.

"Sorry, dear, I was listening to Madam Butterfly." Desire motioned for Jessie to sit. "What can I do for you?"

Jessie blinked. "I found my grandmother's diaries."

"Oh, that's lovely. I'm glad you'll know Undine in a whole new way."

"You have no idea." Jessie blew out a long breath and plopped into the mauve fabric side chair. "They were from Austin."

"Oh. Oh my."

Understatement of the year. The Cork and Screw wasn't the most respectable place in the city yet it had been where strong confident women worked in their twenties. Themed like a Wild West saloon, the women created old fashion period costumes in bright colors. Undine went into detail about the frills. The Cork and Screw women, a whole parcel of them, had watched out for each other, like family. How they'd survived a fire and drunken brawls amazed Jessie, especially with a manager called Jim Dimwitty. Undine Love had been a favorite of the stage and that saved her from personal performances. She'd loved to dance. The dances' skill level along with their reasons to dance varied. For some it was the only job they could find while others chose to strip. According to the diaries, both Desire and Undine's natural talent and grace drew in business.

Betty Rohder, her grandmother's understudy, so to speak, had been a busty blonde and a favorite of those fellows who liked big bosoms. The nights Betty danced enabled her grandmother to have a night off and visit other places. On one such night, she'd ended up at a park with a sidewalk artist and band. Watching the families interact had created a longing in Undine's heart. Across the way, a man watched her. He hadn't been one of the regulars who frequented the club.

Jessie had skimmed the diaries enough to know her grandparents had met and married within a month. Just like those blasted novels!

When a small-yellowed envelope dropped from between the pages, Jessie discovered Betty Rohder had taken over at The Cork and Screw with a new number Undine had planned for such an occasion.

"It wasn't the same after Undine left." Desire closed her eyes an sighed. "Betty brought in crowds so I decided it was time for me to retire." She opened her them and winked. "I couldn't settle on one man like your grandma even if he was hung like a horse." She hugged her abdomen and cackled.

Jessie sucked in a breath choosing to believe Desire wasn't referring to her grandfather.

"I suppose you have questions." Desire leaned forward and peered at Jessie.

"Grandma was amazing." Jessie's eyes filled and her breath hitched. "So was Grandpa." He could've regretted his wife for being ogled by others but he'd accepted and loved her for who she was.

"Your grandpa knew a good time. Bet he had the ride of his life." She croaked out another witch-like shriek.

Jessie shook off Desire's sexual innuendo. "I have an idea for a new intimate apparel business. I'd like to get your opinion."

"Intimate apparel?" Desire tipped her head then a toothy grin erupted. "This sounds right up my alley."

Jessie nodded and fished in her purse for a notepad and pen. She settled into questioning Desire about the materials used at the dance hall to make the clothing. Coarse or fine fabrics? Lacey or smooth? How many layers? Jessie stayed longer than she'd planned but it was worth it because she itched to create.

CHAPTER 13

Jessie

FORTUNA RESIDENTS STREAMED INTO SUNDAY service. The picturesque white clapboard church could grace the cover of any Christmas card. Jessie studied the felt banners, with children's barely legible handwriting, naming God. She chuckled finding a favorite: Big Guy Upstairs. Glancing around the room, she speculated why such a large crowd gathered. Maybe the townsfolk of Fortuna felt guilty for reading all those naughty novels. How many men in the congregation were on B.J.'s delivery route?

She and Dad sat in their usual pew, midway on the left.

B.J. swaggered in and scanned the sanctuary. When he found her, he smiled and stepped forward. She tried to find the thermostat because the room's temperature spiked.

Kelly's brother, Forrest, stepped forward in greeting, intercepting B.J. The men became engaged in conversation and Forrest slipped a thin novel out of his suit jacket. B.J. scrutinized the cover then, with a nod, the book disappeared into his pocket.

Jessie blew out a breath when the organ played signaling the start of the service. A door creaked open, and the choir entered the sanctuary.

In the front sat a handful of elderly ladies, one being Ms. Hardmann. She chatted with those around her. Prudence Spender and Rose Bush pointed and compared books. Jessie elbowed her father, and he laughed.

"I can't believe they brought anything other than their bibles," Jessie whispered.

"Are they picking new stories for their boyfriends to act out?" Brad waggled his eyebrows. Somehow, he'd heard about the latest man arrested for reenacting a hero. He opened the bulletin and chuckled. Jessie glanced where he pointed on the paper. "Even Pastor is all about love."

Jessie bit her tongue to keep from laughing but the evidence was there in black and white: The Book of Love. It referred to 1 Corinthians in the New Testament.

Lily White and Daisy Fields clutched their suitcase-like purses while discussing the upcoming bazaar. The event's flyer passed from one to the other. The bold letters—USED BOOKS 50c—in bright red were sure to get all of Fortuna's romance junkies to come.

Josiah plopped next to Jessie, startling her. After a quick side hug, he shook hands with her dad. She wished he'd opted to sit with his family but she hated to admit she liked the way the polo shirt clung to his strong, sexy body and revealed every muscle. She closed her eyes and took a deep breath. With the mantra of "look at the choir, look at the choir" in her head, she opened her eyes and her gaze dipped straight to his long legs. His silver belt buckle read "Don't mess with Texas" but she yearned to mess with it. Darn Josiah, for sitting beside her.

Jessie glanced over her shoulder and the Barnes family hurried up the main aisle and filtered into the pew behind them. She waved at the oldest Barnes child, Maggie, who was home from Dallas, visiting the family.

Jessie elbowed Josiah. "Who's that?"

"Maggie's boyfriend, Guy. He's an engineer." Josiah moved his jaw as if he sucked on marbles. She got the impression he wasn't thrilled with his sister's choice.

Jessie turned her head to survey the out-of-towner. The man inspected everything as he listened to Maggie's father, Bridger, explain something. Guy caught her gaze and nodded.

Jessie spun around. "He's cute. Does he have a brother?"

Grimacing, Josiah opened his mouth but his mother, Prairie, hushed his three younger siblings, so he snapped it shut again.

During the prayer Jessie peeked at Josiah. The clothes were different but his handsome face remained the same. She focused on the tanned skin of his face, noting the freckles. His eyelashes curled over his cheeks. *It's not fair men get all the best lashes.* She sent a prayer, a suggestion, to God regarding eyelashes.

Jessie had always gotten along with the Barnes family but how would his mother react if she knew Jessie had watched her naked son shooting his gun? Her cheeks warmed. She shouldn't think of her employee moaning her name but she couldn't concentrate on the minister's words.

She glanced at Ms. Hardmann. The old lady would laugh at Jessie's predicament. She winked at Jessie as if she had ESP. Jessie smirked and returned the wink.

Josiah

Pastor Drew Peacock's sermon pertained to love, God's love for the masses and how to show it to one another. Josiah had one kind of love on his mind—the romantic kind.

Pastor suggested they welcome their neighbors with love and ask a few questions to become acquainted with each other on another level. One question worked so well it might have backfired. "Tell me about a unique or quirky habit of yours?" The noise level in the sanctuary grew as most of the congregation talked about romance novels.

Josiah glanced at Jessie, seeing her raise her eyebrows. Pointing a gun at him, made from her index finger and thumb, she grinned. He swallowed, fighting the urge to raise his hands in surrender. She brought her finger to her lips blowing imaginary smoke away from the gun and his body went hot. He swallowed and couldn't pull his gaze away from her lips. If only her moist lips could give him special attention.

Her face turned red and her eyes widened. He chuckled and wiggled his eyebrows. She quickly turned away from him and greeted his father in the next row.

Josiah turned to the same pew and came eye to eye with his grinning eighteen-year-old brother, Matt. They grabbed hands in greeting and shook.

"Do you have any new annoying habits since yesterday?" Matt asked him.

Josiah countered, "Staring at your ugly mug."

Matt rolled his eyes and snorted because he and Josiah were practically twins. Matt gripped Josiah's hand tight to the point of pain. Josiah squeezed back, keeping a smile pasted in place. "How about you? Any new annoying habits?"

Matt challenged him with raised eyebrows and a grin. "I'm going to keep fantasizing about your boss." The young man's gaze dropped to Jessie's backside.

Josiah's smile faltered and his grip tightened. Matt didn't have a chance with Jessie but it irked Josiah that his little brother thought he might. The brother's childish battle of the death grip caught their mother's attention and she scowled.

Jessie and Brad welcomed his sister's boyfriend. Josiah released his brother's hand and stepped to Jessie's side as Maggie said, "Meet my boyfriend, Guy. He's from Houston."

Jessie smiled at the man and Josiah felt relieved when she didn't blush. However, his twelve-year-old sister stared with goo-goo eyes. Tori leaned closer to Guy, squeezing his other brother, Gabe, in the process. Tori, tall for her age, was the same height as Gabe.

"Hey," Gabe whined, "Get back." He elbowed his sister.

Guy turned to the siblings. "Are you two twins?"

Tori giggled and turned three shades redder. Her eyelashes fluttered as if they might take flight.

Gabe crossed his arms and, with a grimace, huffed, "No way. I'm almost seventeen and she's twelve."

While it irritated Gabe, it also bothered their mother because she had twins but one of them had died. His mother paled and sank to the pew with an unreadable mask on her face.

Josiah turned away from his family, pushing memories of Moriah back into the recesses of his mind. The pain leaked out though, causing his heart to ache. He failed protecting someone he loved once—he'd never let it happen again. He chanced a glance at Johnson and found him eying Jessie like a piece of juicy meat. Johnson focused on Josiah. A small sneer tugged on Johnson's lips and Josiah wanted to wipe it off with his fist. He inhaled and shook the violent thoughts away.

When they sat again, Jessie nudged him in the ribs and showed him the bulletin. She wrote: "You know Ms. Hardmann?"

Of course he knew her grandmother's best friend. She'd been visiting Undine daily after Don died but they'd conversed little beyond pleasantries. "I love her Caddy. Why does she look like Spock?"

Jessie snickered and rested her small hand on his arm. "Ever talk to her?"

"Not really."

"She's a dirty old lady," she whispered.

"She never smells bad," Josiah countered.

"Not that kind of dirty."

Josiah's jaw dropped. His mother tapped him on the shoulder and pointed to the Pastor. Chastised, he focused his attention forward.

He gave a sidelong glance at Brad and Jessie, the father holding his little girl's hand. He would try his damnedest to keep Brad's little girl worry free. There must be a way to put his education to work.

He shifted in his seat as he stole a peek of Jessie. The little dress hugged her in all the right places. She moved and her shoulder touched his then stayed there. He angled his head, seeing if Johnson watched. Johnson's face turned a shade of deep red as Josiah stretched his arm out and rested it on the pew back behind Jessie. He didn't drop his hand over her shoulder but bided his time. The air conditioning kicked on, blowing on them, giving Jessie goosebumps. Josiah lowered his hand, rubbing her upper arm. She pressed closer to him. Though she pretended to be intent on the sermon, at her soft sigh he grinned like a fool. His insides ignited. It was a pleasant burn, a yearning desire. Sweat trickled down his back.

If only he lived on the Double D property. That morning his father scolded him about his career choice. "You're a cowboy. You didn't go to college to become a cowboy." His dad had turned to Guy as they ate breakfast together. "He has a degree in applied business. He could be CEO of any company if he put his mind to it. A few more classes and he would've had his masters." Josiah stared at his eggs to avoid the disappointment on his father's face he always wore during these discussions.

"Leave him be, Daddy," Maggie said, coming to his rescue. "He's doing what he loves."

Josiah had winked at his older sister and straightened his spine. "I am running a business, Dad. A cattle ranch is a legitimate business. The equity is livestock. I know it's hard to think of animals as equity but it's lucrative." *Most of the time.*

Josiah's father had shaken his head. His parents were both professionals. Doctor Bridger Barnes was the premiere pediatrician of Fortuna while Prairie Barnes taught at the elementary school. Poor Maggie disappointed them too. Her career as a professional student had caused many debates.

Undine had rehired Josiah when he returned home from college; he'd meant it to be a temporary thing. Undine, clever lady, had dropped the bomb, "I'm giving Jessie the ranch." She'd gaged his reaction, probably noticing his heart stopped then started again in a racing frenzy. Then the clincher, "She'll need you, Josiah dear."

Josiah moved back in with his parents and stayed. *Free rent—you can't beat that with a stick.*

The Big Deal's bunkhouse could be another option to be closer to Jessie. Brad wouldn't mind having Josiah on the property. In fact, Brad already told him he was welcome to a bed.

Space was plentiful at the Double D, but people would gossip. People already did. He could tell it bothered Jessie and he didn't what to add to the rumor mill but, ah hell, he didn't mind being branded a couple. If he could convince Jessie, he'd be a happy man. Plus Kuntz was due to get out of prison soon. To protect her, Josiah needed to be close.

Still, the thought of living near her was tempting.

If he moved to the ranch, what was to keep him from sneaking into her bedroom again? *Nothing.* Maybe she'd be willing to polish his gun. He shifted the bulletin over his crotch. One side of his lips lifted in a smirk.

CHAPTER 14

Jessie

THE CHURCH SERVICE ENDED AND most filed out shaking hands with Pastor Peacock. Ignoring the stares, Jessie grabbed Josiah's hand and pulled him behind her. She'd already warned him. In the hallway, she found Desire putting her jacket on.

"Ms. Hardmann, I'd like to introduce my friend Josiah." Jessie released his hand but placed her hand on his arm.

Desire's eyes lit up then her gaze lowered to his belt buckle. "Are you still caring for the Double D, young man?" she asked.

"Yes Ma'am. Every day."

"That's nice. It'd make Undine and Don happy." Desire's gaze shifted toward Jessie.

"So what do you think of him?" Jessie leaned forward and giggled.

Rubbing her hands together, the older woman asked, "You want an *ass*essment?"

"Yes, Ma'am." Jessie covered her mouth to keep a belly laugh from escaping.

Josiah grinned with an endearing smile as Desire's gaze roamed his body. This wasn't a quickie.

JESSIE ELBOWED HIM. "SPIN AROUND."

Josiah shook his hips as he spun. She envisioned him preforming that little shimmy naked on the driveway. Her blood simmered, and she mimicked Desire using a hand to fan her face.

The hallway remained empty except for a few people talking near the

80

entry. Brad and a few other men visited with Pastor Peacock. Waiting, her father kept glancing back.

Desire raised an eyebrow in a Spock-like manner. "Do you want the church version or the other?"

Josiah and Jessie shared a glance as a family filed past. "Church," they chimed together.

"Very well." The old woman placed a hand on Jessie's shoulder. "The church version is: Honey, if I were you I'd get on my knees and play." She cackled the Halloween laugh. "You know it goes both ways, don't you?" Desire poked Josiah in the stomach.

"He does." Jessie mumbled and pulled him out of Desire's reach.

"That's good to hear, dear. I'm going to go help the organist. He's visually impaired." With a sweet smile, Desire walked toward the sanctuary. She paused and leaned back into the hallway. "One Eyed Willie has a nice organ."

Josiah and Jessie hustled out the side door and into the afternoon sun and burst out laughing. Red faced, they laughed until tears streamed. "I told you," Jessie squeaked.

Josiah

Josiah walked Jessie to the truck. He leaned against the metal frame and crossed his arms while she scanned for her father.

Josiah smiled. *The tables have turned.* Now Jessie had to wait for Brad, who talked to Ophelia Cox. Brad blushed, handing Ophelia a book, then received one in return. The older man fished in his pocket and pulled out his phone. After pushing a few buttons he handed the device to the grinning librarian. She took the phone and tapped on the surface.

"What's he doing?" Jessie asked putting a hand up to shade her eyes.

"Your dad just got the lady's number." Josiah made a mental note to congratulate Brad later.

A soft squeak escaped Jessie and her eyes widened. "That's new. Dad hasn't dated in years." Her gaze narrowed with new interest as she watched the couple interact.

The after-church crowd had thinned. Far up the sidewalk the church's side entrance opened and an elderly gentleman in a gray three-piece suit held the door for Desire. He held her elbow as they moved toward the handicapped parking space. Josiah nudged Jessie to get her attention then pointed. Her worry dissipated when she witnessed Willie and Desire walking close together. Desire whispered in his ear and grinned.

The elderly couple stopped in front of a tan sedan waiting for Willie. Desire turned to hug him. He stooped to kiss her cheek. It was sweet to see the older folks showing affection.

Jessie clutched Josiah's arm, surprising him. Her eyelashes became dewy, and she wore an angelic smile that tugged on his heart. He stepped towards her and put his arm around her shoulders and didn't pull away. In fact, she slung her arm around his waist and flashed a smile just for him. The heat of her body pressed against him made his blood race. He tried to take deep even breaths, but inhaled the fruity scent of her shampoo. He swallowed and refocused on the older couple. His mouth dropped open.

Jessie's fingers tightened into his skin when Desire's hands, once on Willie's back, dropped lower and she double goosed him. Jessie's body vibrated as she chuckled.

But Desire hadn't finished. Her hand slid between their bodies and she fingered Willie's pant zipper.

Josiah glanced at Jessie. "Not only does Willie play the organ, Desire likes to play too."

Jessie threw a hand over her mouth to cover a snort of laughter. "You're terrible." She giggled with teary eyes.

One of Willie's hands circled around Desire's back, holding her close but the other snaked up her chest, stopping to cop a feel of her fun bags.

Josiah gasped. "Willie's as bad as Desire."

"Tell me when it's over," Jessie said turning into his chest and closing her eyes. His arms encircled her. His heart hammered, and he hoped she couldn't tell where most of his blood rushed. *Get a grip, Barnes.* His heart clenched as the tender moment ended too soon when a car door slammed, and the vehicle drove away.

"All right, it's safe. They've gone," he murmured next to her ear and she shivered.

Jessie opened her eyes and gasped. Her gaze shot over his shoulder. In his peripheral vision, Johnson stood scowling with his arms crossed.

Jessie pushed against his chest and tried to step away. He wouldn't let her go, not yet. Let the other man brood. "I like her," he said. Jessie stopped moving and inspected him. "Desire is an unusual woman." A lopsided grin formed and her lips mirrored his.

"I can't believe what they did." She shook her head.

Church would never be the same again. "It's going to be hard to keep a straight face every time I hear the organ."

Jessie giggled and hit him. She snorted then laughed harder. She hid her face in his chest again. Josiah chuckled and held her close, amazed how easy he could purge Johnson from her thoughts. He swiveled his head to find the other man frowning. With the girl of his dreams in his arms, he couldn't help the smug smile that formed.

CHAPTER 15

Josiah

"WELCOME TO THE DOUBLE D," Josiah said with a bow as he opened the door. Kelly and Mona giggled and pushed past him to Jessie, giving her hugs.

He went to the kitchen and sliced lemons for lemonade, humming while he worked. The giggling continued, raising and lowering like a song. Jessie let out a belly-laugh. He smiled at the sound of her happiness. He added the slices and sugar to a pitcher then added water and the lemon juice. Almost done, he stirred then stuck it in the fridge for later.

Josiah followed the voices finding Jessie, Mona and Kelly sitting at the dining table with shears snipping pale blue and ivory fabrics. "Hey, I'm heading to town. Besides pizza, do you need anything?" Jessie waved him off with a smile. The dining room burst into giggles after he'd left. He bent to check his fly, but it was zipped. He shrugged.

Josiah hadn't a clue what the women were doing, but he liked that Jessie wasn't holed up in the bedroom with that blooming sewing machine running. He worried the isolation would get to her.

When Josiah announced the grub was on the kitchen table, he heard the excited voices of hungry women. Josiah had been the mule to get the food, but he waited until the ladies filled their plates before taking a slice.

They ate and laughed at the goings-on in life including the latest town prankster's letter swap. Josiah witnessed the spectacle while in town.

"Apparently, he has a cache of letters," Kelly said.

"With every hit he gains more," Mona pointed out before taking another bite. Her eyes rolled back as she hummed. "Good pizza."

"The employee said the sign advertised a weekly pizza sale," Josiah said. The women gazed at him, he continued. "Originally, it read 'Large triple meat pizza $9.99—worth every penny'. The kid said the prankster's handiwork had brought in record sales." Josiah rubbed his chin and laughed.

"Josiah," Jessie begged.

He lifted his gaze to hers. The way she'd said his name went straight between his legs. He turned away and picked up his lemonade. After chugging the cold drink he faced the women again, all still eager to hear the shenanigans. "The new message read 'triple meat—worth every penis'."

The giggling at the table rose like a crescendo. Josiah ignored the many mentions of penises and continued to eat standing next to the counter.

The discussion turned to the Cattlemen's Ball. Ben had worked up the nerve to ask Mona. Kelly and Jessie shared a look.

"Ben shocked me," Mona said with a shy smile. "I'd hoped to ask Sawyer, but he didn't return my calls."

"Ben's cute," Jessie mused.

"I think so too," Josiah chimed in with a grin. He opened the pizza box and stole another slice.

"Are you going to go, Jessie?" Kelly asked.

Jessie glanced at Josiah like he'd have an answer. The others glanced between them. With his mouth full, his face heated under the women's stares. The hopefulness on Jessie's face made his heart lurch. He swallowed the temptation to ask her on the spot.

Dancing meant she'd be touching men, him mostly,—Josiah hoped, but getting up close and personal with other dance partners as well. Sawyer might try to grab her butt. Ms. Hardmann would enjoy it but not Jessie.

Jessie shrugged. "Did anyone ask you yet?" she countered, deferring to Kelly.

"Actually, I've had two men ask me," Kelly admitted. Her cheeks turned pink.

Mona voiced Josiah's unspoken question, "Who?"

"Details, Kelly, details," Jessie said.

"I'm not going to tell you. Not yet. I haven't decided." Kelly's lips formed a firm line, and she crossed her arms.

"Ah, come on. We're your best friends," Jessie pleaded.

"I bet it's the student's father. The cute one who took her out for coffee." Mona laughed when Kelly rolled her eyes. They pressed harder, getting Kelly flustered and near the breaking point, but a knock on the kitchen door saved her.

Josiah opened the door for the honored guest. "Well, if it isn't my heart's Desire." He offered a hand. The old woman took it, her cheeks pink at the attention.

Josiah poured Desire a glass of fresh lemonade then refilled his. The conversation steered toward the dance again.

When filled with friends, the kitchen was cozy and homey. Home. Josiah hoped Jessie would find a way to keep the ranch. He gazed out the small window over the sink. The sunset painted the rolling Texas prairie in golden hues. With a sigh he turned to study Jessie. She tucked a stray strand of hair behind her ear. Her eyes crinkled in mirth and lips tipped at something Desire had said. He could kiss the old woman for helping Jessie forget her problems.

"I thought about asking Willie but his depth perception is off and my innocent feet would be victims. Mind you, that's the only innocent part of me." Desire laughed. "I'll consider slow dancing with him but find somebody younger to swing me around the dance floor." Desire wiggled her penciled brows at Josiah and he nearly dropped his lemonade.

Jessie

Jessie led the girls to the dining room with coffee and chocolate chip cookies. They munched while Jessie told Desire her plans. "I've picked up a few bolts of fabric to try out. Do you like it?"

Desire took an interest in the swatches of material. Her knotty fingers caressed the textiles. "This is nice. There's strength in the fibers but it's flexible too. It will give and take with the human body."

"Here are a few of the patterns I've found," Jessie said as she passed them to Desire.

The older woman whistled then wiped a tear from her eye. "Ah, the memories…"

The women shuffled the pieces of paper depicting patterns, each finding a favorite.

"Wow. This is exquisite. Undine had great taste," Kelly mused. "The gown is a classic."

"And sexy." Mona snatched the rendering and traced a line with her finger.

"Undine was a classy lady," Desire said. "I wish she was here to see you,

Jessie, dear. She'd be so proud her buttons would pop." She patted Jessie's hand then gave it a gentle squeeze.

At Desire's feet sat a large black carpet bag. She opened it and shuffled the contents. She took care to extricate a wide file then flopped it on the table in front of Jessie.

Jessie's hesitant fingers opened the metal latch. As she withdrew the first piece of delicate onionskin paper, her heart wedged in her throat. The charcoal sketch of a woman in slinky clothes stared back at her. "Holy crap," she muttered. Jessie's breath caught realizing the woman bore a face so like hers it had to be her grandmother.

"Let me see," Kelly said as she pulled the paper to where she, with Mona over her shoulder, could inspect it. The young women studied the drawing, their faces a mask of rapt awe.

"Hey, Jess, I'm going to get the mail." Josiah stood in the doorway to the kitchen. She startled then waved him off with a nod.

Jessie reached into the file again and pulled out another drawing. She swallowed and her face heated. "Check this out." Another charcoal sketch, this time a woman stood in a teddy with stockings and high heels. The woman's haunted eyes gave Jessie a sense of loneliness.

"Good God!" Kelly's jaw dropped and her gaze volleyed from the paper to Jessie's face.

"Jessie, it's you. Wait until Josiah sees this." Mona laughed.

"It's Undine Love before she'd met Don. Jim Dimwitty drew this. I have one too." Desire found a matching picture of another woman—her younger self. She wore a fuzzy baby doll robe and panties with stockings and heels. She pouted with one finger on her lip, like Betty Boop.

Josiah leaned over the table, his hands held a thick pile of envelopes. "Who are they?" His brows raised as he scanned the lines of the drawings. Jessie's heart leapt when his gaze roamed her lips then dropped to her chest. With every raise and fall of her quick breaths, his complexion became ruddier.

"Nobody you want to hug after church," Jessie whispered, escorting him out of the room. He caught her meaning and winked into the room of women.

Josiah

"Hey, can I talk to you for a sec?" Josiah pulled out two pieces of mail. They had a red notice stamped on them. He wasn't happy about this revelation. "Do you want to tell me what's going on?"

"It's not working," Jessie whispered. "We're barely squeaking by. I'm doing this," she thumbed toward the dining room, "to supplement the income."

He placed his hands on her slender shoulders and squeezed. "Jess, look at me. How bad is it? Are you afraid you will lose the Double D? Are you planning on downsizing and selling off the land?" It couldn't be that bad yet.

She bit her lip when it trembled. He wanted to protect and comfort her. He needed to be her rock of security so he took her into his arms. She closed her eyes as he pulled her against him. Her soft curves molded against his chest. He rubbed small circles on her lower back until she relaxed. And for a few seconds everything felt right.

Josiah rested his chin on her head. He kept his breath regular but worry nagged at him. If she sold the ranch, she'd have to leave. He'd have to leave too, then he wouldn't see her every day. He needed to see her as surely as he needed air to breathe. Squeezing his eyes closed, he nosed her hair and inhaled. The familiar strawberry scent helped calm him. He couldn't lose Jessie. They couldn't lose the ranch. His eyes popped open with new resolve.

"Let me help you, Jessie. I can double check the office work." Josiah stroked her long hair. She nodded, staying in the comfort of his arms. He didn't want her to leave the embrace, but he had to start. "Come on, show me where it is."

She pulled away and led him to the office. The room was a dark cave. She stumbled inside, running her hands over the wall for the switch. The sage green office had a large L-shaped desk laden with printer, books, checkbook and laptop within easy reach.

The brown leather desk chair had once fit Don Davidson's body, but it swallowed Jessie's when she sat to power up the laptop and click open the accounting software. She gave Josiah access to the receipts and the bills. It was more than his job in jeopardy.

"Thanks," Jessie said. Her lips turned upwards in a weak smile then she sucked in her bottom lip.

"Hey, don't worry. Not yet. We'll figure it out." Before he could stop himself, he reached out and traced a finger from her cheek to her chin. Jessie's eyes widened, and she stepped back. Dammit, he hadn't wanted to frighten her.

Josiah sat in the chair, pulling it to the desk. He gazed at her. The ranch numbers weren't a complete mystery to him, thanks to her grandfather, but it'd been a long time. He drew in a deep breath and clicked on a file. He scanned the document. He frowned at the tallies. This vet treatment pricing seemed outrageous. He opened the desk drawer and searched for a pen. He started a list: find other vet bills and verify pricing with Brad—top priority.

Jessie

Jessie paused at the office door. No man had ever sat in her grandpa's chair but him, yet, with Josiah it felt right, like Grandpa would approve. He was a good man; he'd saved her from Rusty and he'd helped run the ranch after her grandparents died, so if anyone could help the Double D, it was Josiah. She felt grateful he was hers. Jessie sucked in a startled breath at the thought. She shook her head trying to banish the idea from her head before it took root in her heart.

Josiah's face seemed ethereal in the dim wash of the computer light. He glanced up and held her gaze. Jessie forgot to breathe. Her face still tingled from his gentle caress. When he retreated to the screen, she breathed again.

Women's laughter pulled Jessie away from the melancholy of the office to the living room where Kelly and Desire had moved to the long brown leather sofa. Mona rested on the burgundy recliner's seat edge. They'd scattered papers across the cocktail table.

Jessie perched on the sofa arm with a soft sigh. She inspected Kelly and Mona's eager faces as they discussed various outfits and styles.

"Is your man giving you trouble?" Desire asked in a soft voice. Concern pinched her brow.

Jessie shook her head and gave a brave smile. "Who, Josiah? No, he's great. He is checking the computer for me. He's staying way past what I'm paying him."

"There are other forms of payment," Desire suggested with an evil grin. Kelly and Mona giggled.

"So here's what we think you should make." Kelly pulled Desire's picture forward and then a clothing pattern. "It's like the robe she's wearing, see?"

"What materials do you have, dear?" Desire's gaze never left the drawings.

"I don't have anything gauzy." Jessie took a mental inventory of the yards of fabric samples and bolts while tapping her chin. "I might have material that'd work for the slip." She shrugged. Should she diversify? The gowns had hits on several auction sites and many inquiries concerning cost and production time. She'd timed how long it took to make one from start to finish but if she could enlist help, it would take less. So far, it paid for itself, but with every order, the business expanded. She needed to keep costs low and buy in bulk, but she couldn't do that until she had regular clientele.

Jessie chewed her bottom lip. What would happen to the ranch if she shirked her daily duties to sit at the sewing machine all day? She knew the answer. Josiah would pick up the slack.

"Come on. Follow me." She led them to the office, knocked then opened the door. "Sorry to bother you but I need to get into the closet."

The room boasted a large walk-in closet, one long rack lined the wall. She stored office supplies, like reams of paper and ink refills in it, but now her completed creations hung there. Churning, her stomach turned into a ball of nerves.

The women huddled around the dark entrance as Jessie opened it. "The new material is in the back. I have a few bolts. Check it out." She swallowed then clicked on the light. She monitored the doorway, so the light didn't bother Josiah.

Josiah glanced up and winked. She didn't have time to react before his gaze dropped following the words on the screen again.

"Oh, Jessie, this is beautiful," Desire's voice rang out. Jessie stepped into the crowded closet as Desire held a pale blue piece with ecru colored lace. "Is this one of yours?"

Jessie glanced over her shoulder to check on Josiah. "Yes. I made it a week ago." It was a trial piece, she'd made to fit her body, not a client's.

"Your grandmother would be proud. It's a work of art, honey. This neckline is absolutely stunning. I wish I had talent like you. My talents lie elsewhere." Desire snickered.

"Ms. Hardmann, look at this." Kelly slid the plastic bag off the fabric in the back corner. It was a remnant of a contemporary tone on tone white, but it shimmered. "I love these swirls."

"This is it," Desire declared. "It's bridal white. You need to create the robe set in this."

"But-"

"Not see through? I know. You can do it, Jessie, you're like your grandma, you've got call girl in your blood."

Never in her wildest dreams would Jessie have ever thought "grandma" and "call girl" uttered in the same sentence not only, make sense, but compliment and inspire her. Jessie smiled and wanted to hug the older woman.

Desire continued in a soft voice, "Every woman has a little call girl inside her, it's just finding and teasing her out into the world that's the hard part. Some women embrace it, some deny it and some, Jessie, pretend it's not there."

Resting her hands on her hips, Jessie accepted the challenge. "I can do it."

"While it's true, every woman has a call girl inside, it's also true-" Glancing toward Josiah, Desire cleared her throat and continued, "Every man wants to be inside a call girl."

Giggling, Mona picked up the bolt of fabric. She covered it again then hauled it out of the closet. Kelly and Desire followed Mona out of the room, everyone leaving except Jessie.

She turned off the closet light then paused at the hallway door, watching Josiah type something on the computer. A grin grew. How would Mr. Barnes react if Jessie's inner call girl appeared? Her whole body hummed in agreement, he'd like it. She fled the room before she did something stupid.

The girls pinned the vintage pattern on the white fabric. Their enthusiasm was contagious and Jessie shook off lingering doubt and smiled. Her friends believed in her.

"More coffee? It's decaf." Jessie skipped into the kitchen to fill the requests. She brought mugs for everyone then returned and got a cold beer for Josiah. He deserved a treat and while Desire's suggestion tempted her, Jessie tried to keep her mind out of the bedroom as she set the beer on the desk.

CHAPTER 16

Josiah

WHEN JESSIE SAT A COLD beer bottle next to him, Josiah's hand shot out and caught her before she tried to leave. "Thanks, Jess." He rubbed his thumb in circles on the back of her hand.

"Any luck?" Jessie asked with hopeful eyes. When he didn't answer right away, she sighed, making his heart hitch. He hated when she fretted.

"Jess, I'm still growing familiar with the way you do things. There's a few tricks we can glean from other ranchers. Have you asked your father?" He tried to sound optimistic, but the numbers weren't good.

"Yeah, in the beginning, but he was more interested in telling me how to breed longhorns than filing paperwork," she replied with a frown.

"I'm not through yet. Go and have fun with your friends, especially Desire. That lady's a hoot." Josiah smiled, wishing he could pull Jessie onto his lap and ravage her lips. He'd kiss her senseless if it made her forget her problems. Hell, he wanted to kiss her again, period.

"I know. I wish Grandma was here."

"Wouldn't that be something to see them together?" Josiah chuckled. "You're lucky to have Desire. She lives life without shame and full of zest. We all could learn from her."

Jessie tilted her head and stared at him with an odd expression. Her gaze zeroed in on his lips. Her free hand covered his, skimming her thumb across his skin, causing goosebumps. His heart raced at the surprise caress and words stalled in his throat.

She stared at their hands and frowned then pulled away with a jerk, breaking the connection. A blush spread across her cheeks. Her lips parted a breath then stole away without a word.

For a solid ten minutes, he fantasized about Jessie's hands gliding over him the night they'd stolen away together in the hayloft. With a sigh, he sank back in the desk chair and drank half his beer, letting the coolness of the liquid quench the heat of desire.

Jessie

After her friends had left the ranch, Jessie tidied the kitchen then worked on sorting the piles of fabric they'd cut. She placed them in gallon baggies and toted them to the office closet. Through the clear baggies, Jessie knew Josiah could see the white material, and knew he was smart enough to realize if it concerned Desire it might be risqué. His gaze followed her as she hurried from the room, yet he hadn't asked any questions.

She vacuumed the living and dining rooms. It was after eleven, but the little bits of white thread bothered her. When she'd finished the chore, she checked on Josiah and found him still staring at the computer screen. She glanced at the wall clock—midnight.

He yawned and stretched. Jessie swallowed as she watched the t-shirt tighten around his arms and chest. She needed him to leave or he'd probably stay. "Aren't you tired? Don't you want to go home and sleep? You've been at this long enough."

"I'm not going home. Not until I'm done." Josiah yawned again then shook his head.

Jessie narrowed her eyes and studied him as he scrubbed his hand over his face. After a full day's work then hours hunched at a computer, he was beat. She suspected there was a reason for his hesitation.

Ah ha! The Barnes' had a guest staying with them. Maggie's boyfriend Guy Manning. "Is Guy staying at your house?"

"He's staying in my room." Josiah scratched the scruff on his chin and slumped over the desk.

"You have to bunk with another man?" Jessie teased noting his furrowed brow. "It's better than sleeping with one of your brothers."

"I can sleep on the downstairs sofa, but I can't go to bed at a decent time because my family stays up late watching movies. I wake and leave before dawn." He tried to stifle another yawn, but it didn't work, and she caught it.

Jessie's heart went out to him. *Poor guy.* "That's ridiculous. You can't get decent sleep in the middle of all that chaos. You can sleep here." She shrugged then tried to swallow the panic she felt bubbling inside. *This is Josiah not some random man.* "It's still a sofa but you won't have seven other people to contend with."

"Nope, just one." He cocked a brow and grinned.

"Take it or leave it," Jessie said with hands on her hips.

"I'll take it." He shut the programs and cleaned the space while Jessie foraged in the hallway linen closet. Josiah had stayed for a few middle of the night, crack of dawn work-related incidents.

The flash flood last spring was one such crisis. Mother Nature washed a passel of baby Longhorns away and drown the adults. The Big Deal and the Double D had both suffered losses. Most of the calves had died. Through round the clock working they'd managed to save a few. The recovery took days—weeks. Josiah and others had stayed coming and going at all hours.

But this was different, they'd be alone. A shiver ran down her spine.

She set the sofa with a sheet, taking care to tuck it in, laid a quilt over it, then placed two pillows on the arm. Retreating to the chair, she watched as he settled on the sofa and pulled off his boots. Her body relaxed on the soft leather as she closed her eyes.

"Jess," Josiah's voice stirred her.

Her heavy lids opened. A side table lamp cast a pale glow. "Hm?"

"I have an idea how to earn a few extra bucks." His hands rested on the edge of the seat as he leaned forward. His brow furrowed as he stared out the window into the darkness.

She snapped forward. "What is it?" The excitement in her voice made her cringe.

"I'm not going to say yet. It's something I've been considering for awhile." Josiah's fingers drummed the seat, and she waited. He took a deep breath and said, "You can save money if you don't pay me anymore."

"Of course, I do," Jessie growled. It didn't surprise her one bit he'd sacrifice his wages for the Double D. He loved it as much as she did. Letting him go wasn't the answer either. It wouldn't be home if Josiah wasn't here. She covered her face with her hands and whispered, "Thank you for offering, though. Oh, Josiah, what are we going to do if we lose this place?"

He scooted to the edge of the seat and he took her trembling hand. "We won't, Jess. Do you hear me? This is our home, we'll make it work." He squeezed her hand, and she tried to smile, but her mind flooded with the "*what ifs*".

Josiah

Against everything in him, Josiah tore away from Jessie and went to get ready for bed. It was either that or he'd pull her into his arms and kiss her. The memory of her placating smile and tear-filled eyes hung heavy in his heart. He took a deep breath and gripped the edge of the porcelain sink. He was a coward. She needed him and he'd bailed because he feared losing control

"Get a grip," he growled to the image in the mirror.

He pulled off his shirt, wadded it into a ball, and threw it at the hamper. It went in. "Score." Next went his socks, followed by his jeans. One sock lay bunched against the bottom of the wicker hamper mocking him—*if you aren't going to score with your girl, at least you did with your stupid game.*

In the laundry room, he found a clean shirt and pair of jeans for the next day. He padded over the cool tile through the kitchen. Stopping to turn on the outside lights, he checked to make sure the door was locked before he picked up the romance novel he'd been reading. Three chapters remained in the steamy, action-packed tale.

The hallway light silhouetted the furniture enough to maneuver through the dark living room. He set the book and clothes on the coffee table then stretched out on the sofa. With the pillows situated, he pulled the quilt to his chest and sighed. Maybe he'd put off the exciting conclusion until the next morning.

Josiah closed heavy lids and listened. He strained to hear her, envisioning her slipping into a spaghetti-strapped nightshirt. He placed his hands behind his head and smiled. The water turned on then off. The light flipped off, and all became quiet. They hadn't said good night, and he wanted to find her.

A slight shuffle, a light step in the hall. He wasn't one to let fear grab him, but Tippy, must have sneaked into the house. *Might as well call the fuzzball to sleep with me.* Josiah peered over the top of the sofa.

"It's me," Jessie whispered. "Sorry, I need to check the front door."

She must be paranoid after his nocturnal visit. This time, she locked him in. He smiled and watched her profile. Whatever she wore, the top hugged her double Ds. Oh yeah, the view from this sofa was much, much better than his parents'.

She placed a palm on the door's cool glass. How many times she'd entered through that door? He sat up and squinted. Something on her face reflected the dim outside light. She tilted her head, and he sucked in a breath realizing tears streaked her face. A fierce longing washed over him. Josiah wanted to run to her, pull her into his arms and make her forget. He stood, forgetting his tent pole, and shifted his weight. He didn't want to frighten her. "Jess?"

Turning her head away, she sniffed and wiped her face.

"Come here," Josiah called softly. Jessie surprised him when she didn't hesitate. He wrapped his arms around her and kissed her forehead. Neither said anything. He lowered them to the sofa where she cried and hiccupped. Josiah tucked her against his side, they fit together. He smoothed her long hair and rubbed her arm as she snuggled closer to him. That's how she fell asleep. Jessie's breaths deepened and her body relaxed. He tried to ignore her warmth pressed against him.

Her hand dropped to his lap, and Josiah sucked in a sharp breath then blew it out. The heat from her fingers made him rock hard. Geez, even a sleeping Jessie could turn him on. How in the hell could he sleep like this? He grinned, he would take this torture over his parents' sofa any day.

Hours later, he awoke hot and uncertain of his surroundings. His eyes adjusted as he recognized the living room and Jessie's body spooning him. The sweet smell of her strawberry shampoo made him sigh. The clock on the wall ticked, and her breathing remained even.

Needing to move his arm from its cramped position, he shifted trying not to wake Jessie. He froze as she stretched out her legs. He used her stirring to move onto his back then stilled as she sat up. Damn, her sleep-tousled hair was gorgeous. He wished he'd been the one to make it messy

She yawned. It was too early to rise.

Josiah sensed her debating—return to her room or stay with him. A cold, empty bed must not have been appealing because she turned over and used his bare chest as a pillow and slid her arm around his waist. He'd almost fallen asleep when she did the unthinkable, making his heart jump start. One leg moved between his, rubbing his gun. He held his breath hoping Jessie wouldn't feel his heart trying to jackhammer out of his chest.

The best night of his life but sleep wouldn't come easy. "Take it or leave it" she'd said. He'd take it any day, all day and all night too. Josiah kissed Jessie's forehead, and she sighed. He realized he could perform the visitation right then, and he whispered, "I love you, Jess."

CHAPTER 17

Josiah

A LOUD KNOCK WOKE JOSIAH. Jessie bolted upright. She kicked the quilt and slid off the sofa with a thunk. He rubbed the sleep out of his eyes and a bed-headed Jessie did the same. He grinned at her. "Mornin'."

She smiled back. "Morning."

The heavy-handed pounding continued. "Coming," she grumbled loudly. He watched her bottom as she moved to the door.

Jessie halfway opened the wood door. Outside the day was damp and gray. A cloud of cologne permeated the air. The man at the entry cast a long shadow, his face chiseled with concern. *Johnson.*

"Did I wake you?" Johnson asked Jessie. Josiah sat up and frowned as Johnson's gaze roamed the braless tank top and plaid pajama bottoms hanging low on her hips exposing her flat belly. Jessie fidgeted and crossed her arms, as uncomfortable with Johnson's lecherous gaze as Josiah was.

Josiah scanned Johnson. He wore jeans today, not khakis, but still an embroidered work shirt. Sunglasses topped his head even though the day was overcast.

"Yeah, but that's okay." Jessie said. "What can I do for you?"

At this offer, Johnson smiled wolfishly. "Well." He seemed to give it serious thought, which pissed off Josiah. "What if you and I-"

"Who is it?" Josiah called, knowing damn well who loomed at the door. From his angle, Josiah had a fine view of Jessie's profile and backside. He could also see the fire blazing in Johnson's dark eyes, and Josiah smirked.

Johnson forced the door the rest of the way open, slamming it against the wall and making Jessie bounce back a few steps. He glowered at Josiah relaxing shirtless on the sofa. The quilt covering Josiah's lower half made him appear naked. Johnson resembled a snake ready to strike with his jaw jutted out and fists balled. No way in hell this piss and vinegar man deserved Jessie.

Johnson turned to Jessie and uttered in a low trembling voice as he jabbed her with his finger, "You said you weren't involved with him." She rubbed the spot and glared. Josiah clenched his teeth, ready to bloody the angry man if he touched Jessie again.

Josiah's eyes narrowed. Maybe he could get rid of B.J. without saying a thing. He stood, and the quilt fell away revealing something men deal with when they woke—morning wood. Josiah shifted his boxers. He caught the other man's gaze and a slow sneer formed on Josiah's lips.

Jessie gaped at his crotch, pink creeping to her cheeks. She swallowed and a hint of a grin tugged at her lips. He shifted his hips side to side making his manhood bob. Josiah made a gun shaped with his finger and thumb, and she tore her gaze away from between his legs to follow his hand to his mouth. He blew imaginary smoke mimicking her gesture from church. She gasped and clapped her hands over her mouth. He waggled his eyebrows. Her brows rose as she continued to watch.

Josiah couldn't be sure how his peacock show affected Jessie, but he knew how their guest felt. Johnson's nostrils flared on his red face and his crazed eyes widened. Johnson spun around and leaned into Jessie's personal space. She crossed her arms again. "You lied to me. I knew I shouldn't have believed he was only an employee." He spewed a litany of accusations, curses, and declarations like "women are in league with the devil." As he ranted, his face turned a deep shade of fuchsia.

Josiah's coloring probably matched Johnson's, but he kept his anger in check because Jessie's expression was one of pity mixed with annoyance, not fear. She chanced a glance at Josiah and he rolled his eyes, earning a giggle. This sent the thirty-two-year-old Johnson on another tangent. "Another lying woman. Big surprise. I hate liars-"

Jessie sucked in a deep breath and interrupted, "Are you done?" Her hands gripping her hips, uncovered the tiny tank-top straining to hide her taut breasts. "Well, you are now."

Johnson's mouth snapped shut, and his gaze dropped to her chest where it hovered until she started in on him. "Who pissed in your coffee this morning? You storm into my house and yell at Josiah and me for what reason? This is my home, and I'll do as I please. I don't answer to you. You aren't my dad or my boyfriend. You've never even asked me out. I don't know what you are to me. Heck, are you even my friend?

"And for your information, after Josiah and I tried to kill each other eight years ago, we've been close. He'll be a part of my life because we're friends, and I trust him. He's not going anywhere, and if you have an issue with him I suggest you leave." Again she crossed her arms, her voice low and firm as she tapped her foot.

Josiah couldn't hide his smile if he tried. Jessie told Johnson to take a hike if he couldn't respect their relationship. His heart raced, and he longed to mosey over and kiss her until her toes curled. That would send Johnson running.

Johnson shook his head and placed a hand on her arm. "I thought we might have a chance-"

"A chance at what?" Jessie asked, shaking off his touch. Josiah wanted to high-five her.

"A chance to be together—to be happy." Johnson's voice brittle, he inspected his shoes.

"How can we be happy? You think I'm a liar. I'm not okay with that."

"Why do you think I'm here? I was going to ask you out, but that was before I knew the truth," Johnson growled, lifting his gaze to hers.

Josiah adjusted his manhood and picked up his jeans. Johnson closed his eyes and took several deep breaths while Josiah and Jessie exchanged a look.

"What truth?" Jessie cocked her head glaring at Johnson. One recent truth brought to light—Jessie's grandmother had been a stripper. Another was that Undine Love and Don Davidson had fulfilled every one of those four points in the novels Jessie spouted as untrue. Her grandparents' love had erased the past mistakes, forged the future, had a baby, and they'd lived happily ever after.

"The truth that you slept with him." Johnson pointed an accusing finger at Josiah.

Josiah wouldn't confirm or deny anything. He'd let Jessie do that. Josiah scratched his chin with his knuckles and sported a cocky grin. Yeah, he'd held Jessie all night long. It had been a dream come true.

Josiah slid his jeans over muscled legs, careful to tuck in his package, making a show of it for the other man. Her cheeks blossomed pink while Johnson's reached an unnatural shade of red-violet. Josiah didn't bother buttoning the jeans but left the fly open. They hung on his hips exposing the edge of his boxers.

"I did." Jessie admitted, shocking Josiah but making his heart gallop.

Johnson balled his fists like a three-year-old about to throw a fit. Josiah took a few steps toward Jessie.

Jessie started laughing. Her braless tank didn't stop the girls from jiggling a mesmerizing dance. Josiah frowned because Johnson had zeroed in on Jessie's rack again. Josiah cleared his throat earning a glare.

Jessie frowned at her guest. "You're talking sex, aren't you? See that man over there, B.J.? He's hot and sexy. He's got the body and face like the cover models on those erotic novels and you think I could snare him." Jessie shook her head making her hair flare. "Wow. If you think he'd choose me, that's a compliment. Thanks."

Josiah's heart sung. His face hurt from the huge, wicked smile he wore. He enjoyed seeing Johnson's seething gaze scour him from toes to crown.

Jessie stepped towards Johnson and poked him in the chest. He retreated a step.

"Let me tell you something else, Mr. Johnson. If I had Olympic sex with Josiah, I wouldn't wake up wearing my pajamas."

"Nope," Josiah agreed with a grin. That was a fact.

Jessie poked Johnson again sending him another step backward. "The sofa? I don't think I'd ride my cowboy all night long on the sofa."

"More like under the dining room table." The Desire-like suggestion flew out of Josiah's mouth before he could stop it. The chairs remained pushed back from the previous night and a couple could fit under the table. His face heated as she gaped at him with raised brows. He stood like a halfway-naked, cowboy Peter Pan.

"I was thinking a bed, but whatever floats your boat."

She didn't deny Josiah or kinky dining room sex. But if she wanted the king size bed, hell yes, he'd take it. His heart hammered. He shifted his manhood again. *Down boy, she didn't mean right now.*

Scowling, Johnson accused, "You're in love with him, aren't you?"

Jessie prodded Johnson again and this time, he stepped backward over the threshold. "B.J. Johnson, all I'm going to say to you is—it's none of your dang business!" She slammed the door in his shocked face. Jessie took a deep breath then opened it again. Johnson hadn't moved and stood wide-eyed, rooted to the spot.

"Furthermore, I will bring the books to Holden Dix at Hammered, so you won't have to travel to the liar's house of hell." She slammed it again.

"I can't believe I'm going to do this," Jessie mumbled, throwing a glance over her shoulder, "Hey Josiah, watch his face." She took another deep breath and yanked the door again.

Josiah stepped up behind her to witness Johnson's expression.

"And Josiah Barnes is moving in with me."

Johnson's face went from shock to determination as he took a step toward Jessie. She slammed the door quick then leaned her forehead against it. Josiah waited for a pounding fist. Jessie blew out a deep breath when she heard an engine turn over, and the white truck pull away.

Johnson's scent dissipated and Josiah breathed easier. A weight had been lifted. He reached out and caressed Jessie's shoulder.

"Did that just happen?" She whispered. "It's like a breakup. How is that possible?" Her hand clamped on his.

Josiah kept his tone neutral. "You like him, don't you?"

"Once I thought I did. He used to radiate joy, but the happiness is gone." Jessie sucked in her bottom lip and peered at him through her lashes.

Josiah squeezed her shoulder. "Let's make some coffee."

Jessie turned, slinging an arm around his waist and he threw an arm around her shoulders. With her free hand, she trailed fingers across his chest. "You've been reading too many romance stories. You know, not every girl wants a hairless man."

"Really?" Josiah scratched the stubble on his chest.

She shrugged as her cheeks turned pink. "Yes, really."

He'd shaved the hair off his chest after discussing a hairless hero with Sawyer. Somehow they'd dared each other to manscape although Josiah was sure Sawyer took it to the extreme. Now the hair was growing back, and he wasn't smooth anymore. The stubble felt prickly. It gave him goosebumps when she touched him.

"Did you do this for a girl?" Jessie's fingers continued to graze his chest, making his gaze shift to the floor of the dining room. "Let it grow, Josiah. It's part of you and you're perfect. If the girl doesn't like you for who you are, then she's not the one. Move on." Words of advice from the girl not "into love."

Jessie thought he was perfect. Josiah grinned absorbing the words.

CHAPTER 18

Jessie

THE ANGER-LACED INNUENDO JESSIE had spouted at B.J. should have mortified her, but Lord Almighty, he deserved all of it.

Josiah's striptease in reverse got Jessie's blood pumping. She smiled at the tall, half-naked cowboy with bed head and bedroom eyes. Holy heck, that man was fine. She couldn't turn away from the tanned skin of his muscled arms, shoulders, and chest as he reached into the cabinet. He filled the coffee pot with water while she scooped the grounds into the filter. She couldn't stop staring and the cocky smile he wore spoke volumes.

Thinking of something other than the front of his unbuttoned jeans might help to normalize the situation. Jessie needed to take care of her man—house-guest—dang-nab-it. She let out a long breath. "What would you like for breakfast?"

"Hotcakes." One of Josiah's eyebrows raised while his persistent smug smile remained.

She tried not to laugh as she fished out the ingredients. He added then stirred and blended the mixture. *This feels right. Normal.* They'd always worked well together and now was no different. She warmed the griddle, and he took a seat at the table.

She sighed, and flipped a pancake.

His brow pinched as he studied her. "What's up, Jess?"

"It was nice not waking up alone."

Josiah picked up his mug of steaming coffee and held it near his lips. "I could do without Johnson stopping by. He's not much of a morning person."

She giggled until she snorted. Jessie sat a plate full of hot food at each of their places. While they ate, he scanned her.

"Those plaid pajama pants are familiar." Jessie froze with her fork in front of her mouth. He tilted his head before adding, "They're mine."

"That would have got B.J.'s panties in a bunch," she snickered. "You left them here, and they're comfy."

"They look better on you. Besides, my gun needs a bigger holster." The cocky smile reappeared even though his face turned red.

The phone rang and Jessie let out a breath she'd been holding. The rotary dial phone still hung on the wall giving her the excuse to leave the table. She grabbed the handset and leaned against the counter. "What's up, Dad?"

Jessie glanced up to find Josiah staring at her pair of double Ds not so well covered by the tank top. Her blood simmered beneath the surface. She grabbed a dishtowel and threw it at him, hitting his face. She covered the receiver. "Stop being so male."

"Hey, you said I was perfect." Josiah flashed a wicked grin.

"Your body, not your mind." Jessie's face heated. She focused again on the conversation. "Really? Yeah, we can get out there. I'll ride Cowboy. Oh, um, Josiah? He's here eating pancakes. We'll be out the door in ten minutes. Love you, Daddy."

Jessie cleared the plates. "There's a fence down."

"That's not anything new. We can handle it. But I'm getting a vibe it's something more." Josiah frowned. From his seat, he reached out and touched her arm.

"Dad says it's vandalism. He found the wires cut, and the post rammed. Curly's doing a count trying to assess how many cattle are missing." Jessie bit her lip.

"Gone? Someone took our Longhorns?" Josiah jumped up and spun around.

Jessie watched as his gaze volleyed between the dirty dishes, the doorway, and her lips. She stared at his lips, remembering the way he'd moaned her name. Her heart rate skyrocketed, and a heat wave rolled through her body.

Josiah took two steps toward her, pressing her against the counter. He bent touching his lips to hers, almost reverently, as he stroked her face. He tasted like syrup, coffee and passion, a combination that had her hungry for more. She groaned, a needy guttural sound, opening, wanting more.

He stepped backward with a grimace. She frowned, confused by the ache his absence caused.

"Oh God, Jess, did I do something wrong?" Josiah shuffled his feet as if he couldn't decide to stay or go.

Jessie crossed her arms hiding her pert nipples.

"I'm fine, Josiah," she whispered in a husky voice Jessie wouldn't have recognized as hers. He jumped back with wide eyes as Jessie stretched an arm towards him and he fled the room mumbling, "Gotta go save the herd."

Jessie might have been mad if he hadn't wanted to help the animals. She let him go.

Josiah

If they wanted to mend a wire fence, they'd need tools. Josiah searched the old barn for the post hole digger, wire crimper, and other items they might need. He attached the trailer to the ATV and loaded it, then waited for Jessie.

His stomach felt unsettled. He hoped he hadn't scared Jessie and could kick himself in the keister for giving in to the temptation of her lips. The sensation of their moist warmth had yet to fade.

Tippy jumped onto the trailer and blinked golden eyes at him. He reached a hand out and she rubbed against it and purred.

"At least I can tell when you like my touch," he mumbled. *Too bad women can't purr.* The tabby answered with a trill and a mew. He reached to pick her up and scratched under her chin. "You're a pretty girl."

"Thanks," Jessie said with a grin. She reached to pet the squinty-eyed kitty.

Josiah shelved the urge to tickle Jessie under the chin and set the cat down. "Ready?" he asked giving her a sideways glance. She'd changed into tight jeans, his favorite pair with a small hole at the top of the rear pocket, and a loose t-shirt. He swallowed. That shirt belonged to him. Jessie wearing his clothes felt right, as if it marked her as his.

She nodded and helped to tie down the load. Josiah motored out of the barn and waited until she closed the door, barely missing Tippy as the cat zoomed outside. Jessie handed him his hat, then climbed on the ATV behind him. With the extra weight of the trailer, they had to travel slower. They followed a trail up a slight grade through pastureland then turned and followed a creek bed for twenty minutes.

Jessie grabbed Josiah around the waist over a rough patch of stones. He grinned, purposely taking the bumps. She didn't loosen her grip once the trail smoothed out. He liked her slender arms gripping his sides.

"You good?" Josiah asked after peering over his shoulder. She chewed her bottom lip.

Jessie gave a reassuring squeeze and met his gaze. "Just worried about the animals. I hope they're not hurt." Her warm breath against his ear made his blood pump faster, so did her words. He worried about the animals too. There'd be hell to pay if someone hurt them. He gave a stiff nod, and when Cowboy accelerated Jessie squeaked.

Josiah skirted the herd so as not to startle them. He waved to a pair of Big Deal cowboys as they circled the Longhorns.

In the distance, two horses grazed and Brad moved debris. Brad stood beside the mess of mangled wire fencing, and the splintered wood post.

"Daddy, who would have done this?" Jessie asked dismounting the ATV.

"I don't know. There's light color paint on the post." Sweat beaded Brad's forehead, and he wiped it away with a navy bandanna.

"Have you called Ben Moore? He can get it analyzed." Jessie stood staring at the mess of tumbleweed-like wire balls.

"I put in a call, but it's a big county," Brad answered. "I took pictures with my phone before I touched anything but the fence needs repaired and I can't stand here all night waving my hands."

"Hey, Jessie, take a look." Josiah crouched over the splintered pole. He pointed to the discolored wood. She knelt beside him. *When Desire said get on your knees and play this isn't what she had in mind.* "Know any angry men with a vehicle that color?"

She gasped. Her doe-eyed gaze searched his. "It's the same color as B.J.'s truck. He wouldn't have, would he?"

"You rejected him." Josiah stood and offered her a hand. He frowned and paced toward the trailer. He stopped and stared at the tools, not needing anything but a moment to think. When Josiah glanced up, Brad's gaze bored into his.

It was hard to stomach vandalism. No matter how mad he was at a person, he'd never risk their livelihood or destroy their property, but would Johnson?

Josiah's mind flew to money and the meager amount of funds to refill supplies. His heart hurt watching Jessie contemplate the same thing as her gaze darted around the ruined wire fencing, chewing her lip and clenching her fists.

He sucked in a deep breath. Standing around worrying wasn't going to get the job done. "Don't worry, we can recycle most of this wire," he said with a reassuring nod. Josiah slipped on work gloves and grabbed the post hole digger. He worked getting the old post's stump out. Soon his back and forehead were damp.

"What happened, son?" Brad kept his voice low. He dug the spade into the opposite side.

Josiah cast a cautious glance at Jessie before answering. "Johnson stopped by the Double D today and made some heavy accusations." He let Brad digest the information while he watched Jessie examine tire tracks and a few hoof prints. She followed them to the pavement. She shaded her eyes and scanned the road. The road didn't have a cattle guard so the escaped animals could be anywhere.

Josiah continued to dig around the base of the old post. He knelt beside Brad, and they wiggled it until it pulled free. Thank God for leather gloves, or their hands would've been hamburger. Together they hoisted the new post into the hole and set it. Brad held it in upright while Josiah filled in around the base.

Jessie removed any debris she found from the roadside. She kept glancing over her shoulder as if she thought someone watched them. Nobody drove the road unless they had to. It was a rural roundabout way to Nockerville with homesteads and ranches but no businesses.

"Daddy, can I take Duke and see if I can locate the lost children?"

Both men glanced at Jessie. The children reference made Josiah chuckle. Josiah's breath caught as some of Jessie's auburn hair escaped her ponytail, floating on the wind.

"Take Lucy, I brought her for you." Brad helped Jessie up like she was a little girl.

Jessie

Lucy, the tan buckskin mare with a black mane and tail was guided away from the other horse. Jessie clucked her tongue, and Lucy picked up the pace. They headed northeast.

Jessie's mind and emotions swirled. A malicious crime on her property against her animals was bad enough to give her an ulcer, but the awareness happening between her and Josiah scared the heck out of her.

He'd kissed her. Without reason, he up and kissed her. It hadn't been deep and hot like the one they shared at Hammered, yet her stomach was now a field of butterflies. Her lips tingled remembering his touch.

Jessie trotted to a wooded gully looking for clues. Around a bend, she found a telltale sign on the side of the road: a fresh cow chip.

Sliding off Lucy, Jessie walked along the side of the road. The thick vegetation made it hard to traverse until she found a critter trail. She pressed past a tree. The trail led downward to a spring, nothing more than a muddy puddle. In the small oasis, a cow and calf hid in the cool shade. She crinkled her brow and studied the pair. The little one was knee deep in mud and struggling. Jessie ran to Lucy, hopped on, clucked her tongue, and they set off in a trot.

She needed Josiah. He had a genuine gift with animals. He could sooth both the frightened and the angry beasts. A man who loved animals was special. She grinned and envisioned the way he'd held a newborn calf.

What was happening to her?

The memory of his cocky grin and bare chest from this morning tugged at her heart. Josiah hadn't said a word to B.J. but let her handle the angry man. He'd been wise in that regard, and she felt grateful to him not overstepping any boundaries.

Josiah had never left her side either. The argument was between two adults, but he'd witnessed a man abusing her before and wasn't about to leave her alone. *Always the protector.*

She scanned ahead for him. Her father held open a novel and pointed to a page. Josiah slapped him on the back, and her father's laughing face turned bright red.

Josiah was a good man, a handsome, kind-hearted soul, but he was younger. Soon he'd be twenty-five, a quarter of a century. Even though there were less than three years between them, his age had been an issue, one that had bothered her since they met. Time and friendship had spanned the difference. Could love?

Both men glanced up, merriment dancing in their eyes.

Jessie searched Josiah's face, for what she wasn't sure, but he must have sensed it. The smile changed from humor to a crooked smirk. His blue eyes sparkled as if she'd lit a fuse. It was a familiar expression. The one he'd worn before pressing her against the counter. Words stuck in her throat and she swallowed.

She trusted Josiah with her life and property, but could she trust him with her heart? She blocked out the answer her thundering heart gave and shifted her gaze to her father. "I found two of them, Daddy. Cow and calf but the baby is knee deep in mud." Jessie's cheeks blazed red with excitement.

"Mud. How in tarnation is it stuck in mud?" Brad scratched his chin.

"There's a spring," she answered.

"Ah, around the corner. Smart. There's protection there," Brad said.

"Let Josiah use Duke, please."

Josiah dusted off his legs then pulled off the gloves. His gazed volleyed from daughter to father.

"What's wrong with your old man?" Brad asked. His mustache twitched as his hands found his hips.

Nothing, but Josiah's butt looks better in a saddle. "You can come if you don't mind fishing in mud for the baby." She shrugged, pulled the reins and turned Lucy, but winked at Josiah.

"I suppose I could let him help you," Brad dabbed his forehead with a handkerchief, "but you might need both of us."

Josiah mounted Duke and prodded him onto the road.

"No, Daddy, I need my man."

Brad tilted his head with a lopsided grin and crossed his arms over his chest. "Your man?"

"My hand," Jessie corrected as her face heated. She pointed past her father toward Curly and Cole. "You've got two of your own."

"Able to rescue a calf single handed," Josiah quipped.

CHAPTER 19

Josiah

AS THE HORSES' HOOVES RHYTHMICALLY beat the pavement, Josiah studied Jessie's profile focusing on her sweet full lips.

"I don't know if I've gotten you out of work or made more for you," she said. Without turning her head, Jessie gave him a quick glance then her cheeks turned pink.

Josiah leaned forward in the saddle and patted Duke.

They tethered the horses to a bush and followed the path to the muddy spring. The small calf cried at their approach. Josiah made low soothing sounds to put both mother and baby at ease. He moved slow, walking out into the mud without a second thought.

The baby tried to bolt but couldn't lift a leg.

Josiah ran a hand over the calf, assessing injuries. "The little critter isn't hurt, Jess, but the poor guy's heart is beating fast." He frowned and rubbed the calf's back like a cat. The little guy panicked, fighting the hold the earth had on him.

Jessie clutched her hands together. "You're scaring him."

"Yeah, I'm one big scary dude."

She giggled. "Look at the prints in the muck. They're around the puddle. The mama wants to help her baby."

The cow bellowed and the calf replied.

Josiah pushed up his sleeves and knelt next to the calf. The little guy had dark eyes and long lashes, a velvety muzzle, and a long pink tongue. His coat was golden tan with lighter color around his eyes. Josiah slid one hand under the belly and put one on the back then lifted, keeping the animal steady. The deep mud was reluctant to release his legs.

She rubbed and comforted the calf while Josiah diligently dug out his little legs until they freed him. Together they moved him to solid ground and released him. Josiah took Jessie's hand and pulled her away from the mother and baby. The cow nudged the calf and he kicked up his heels as he frolicked around her.

"Josiah?" Jessie cooed. When Josiah glanced up a ball of mud struck him in the chest. He rocked back shocked and swiped it away to have it replaced by another. Filth covered his hands, half his arms and most of his legs, and thanks to Jessie, his t-shirt too.

Her gaze held an evil glint as she scooped another mud ball. He slowly stood and walked toward her but she threw two shots before ducking away from his hand. Josiah took his muddy fingers and drew double stripes on his cheeks. War paint. "It's on."

"Aw, hell, I didn't want a war." Jessie danced out of his reach.

Josiah laughed low and kept after her nearly catching her but missing because of the mud. When he caught her, Jessie tried to trip him but that backfired and she teetered off balance. He tried to hold on to her, but her weight threw him forward. She landed on her backside in the thick sludge, and he landed on top of her.

Josiah froze. Jessie's palms rested on his chest, her eyes wide. She took shallow gulps of air. Then her gaze left his face and traveled their bodies. He'd fallen right between her legs and damn if it didn't feel right. He fought the urge to grind against her.

The calf made a noise, and Jessie's knees squeezed his hips. He groaned, and her expression matched the frightened calf. Dammit, he'd scared her again.

The calf stumbled forward and sniffed Jessie's head then tasted her messy mop.

"There, there little bit, my hair isn't hay." She touched the baby. "He's cute."

"He's a muddy mess." Josiah laughed and rolled to the side of Jessie, enabling her to sit.

Jessie followed them, but Josiah grabbed her belt and with a yank, he tossed her back in the mud. Arms flailing, she yelped and landed with a face-plant. Her hands twitched then she stilled. He knew there'd be hell to pay, but he couldn't resist.

A moment passed then another. He took a step closer. It had been too long. "Jess?"

Envisioning his twin, Moriah, laying on the playground blacktop, motionless, he froze. All the kids thought Moriah was fooling, but she wasn't. She'd hit her head and cracked her skull and died hours later. He gulped and took several staggering steps forward.

"Jessie." He touched her shoulder and shook her. Nothing.

The slippery earth smelled dank and old. He fell to his knees beside her and, with trembling hands, tried to flip her.

Attacking with an Amazon yell, she flung herself at him. He jerked back. She maneuvered him onto his back. A brown banshee, she waved her mud-encrusted hands at his face.

Josiah caught her hands as relief rolled over him. He blew out a long breath then chuckled. Only the whites of Jessie's eyes remained clean. She squirmed over him, inadvertently priming his gun.

A groan escaped as he spun her onto her back. "I've always wanted to mud wrestle a woman," he teased, his lips against her ear. He straddled her as she wiggled deeper into the mud.

Jessie tried to buck him off. "Yeah, well, I never thought I'd take a mud bath with a guy."

"Let's make sure you wash behind your ears." He reached for her head, and she pushed him back. He caught her elbow and got one ear.

They tussled with each other, laughing and growling becoming mud monsters. Eventually Josiah pulled Jessie to her feet, and they stomped uphill following the cow and calf.

Jessie

Raucous laughter reached Jessie, then she spied Curly and Cole doubled over and pointing at her and Josiah.

Her father's red face told another story. She glanced away. When Jessie bit her lip, she received a mouthful of grit.

Jessie and Josiah herded the Longhorns on foot. As they led the horses, every movement made clods fall off. She must resemble Pigpen from Peanuts with dirt dropping off with every step.

Jessie handed Lucy's reins over to her father's cowboys. Cole and Curly would lead the animals to the nearest gate and back toward the herd.

The new wire was cinched tight across the replacement pole. With Jessie and Josiah on one side and her father on the other, the barbed wire remained a prickly divider between them. She tilted her head inspecting her father, trying to ascertain why his blood pressure had skyrocketed.

"Little girl, you have a business to run, a responsibility to the animals, and to our employees," Brad ground out in a rumble.

"Yes, sir," Jessie replied. *Where is he going with his lecture?*

"It's not appropriate to go gallivanting over the countryside while others do your work." His dark brows dipped into a V.

Jessie's temperature rose, and she took several deep breaths to stymie her annoyance. She'd been working. She gave Josiah a sidelong glance. Okay, they'd played a little, but they'd worked more.

"Dad, would you heckle Randy Fellows if he showed up here with lost cattle and covered in mud?" Jessie asked her father, mentioning a long-time neighbor.

Her father didn't answer but continued to stare. Jessie climbed the wire on either side of the new post, using it like ladder rungs, then jumped to the other side.

"You wouldn't read Josiah the riot act if it was him so please save the speech." Jessie waited for Josiah to follow her then she stepped toward the ATV. Her legs trembled as she climbed on Cowboy behind Josiah.

"Little girl." Her dad used his pet name, she stopped. "I don't want you hurt. I want you safe and happy. You need to be responsible."

A light clicked on, and Jessie chuckled. Her father thought she and Josiah did more than rescue a calf and roll around in the mud. Her blood raced and she clenched her fists. "Daddy, we kept our clothes on while retrieving the strays. You're welcome. And one more thing: Josiah is moving in with me."

Jessie poked Josiah in the side, and he gunned Cowboy.

"Can you believe him? What the heck." Jessie mumbled. "Did you see his face when I dropped the bomb? Priceless."

Josiah nodded and chuckled. She'd shouted twice that Josiah was moving in with her. Of course, she hadn't said it was temporary. Poor Josiah, the rumors would run amok with his reputation.

Jessie

Quiet permeated the ranch house. Jessie glanced at the wall clock; the afternoon was shot. Josiah had held the door open for her. Their caked boots stayed outside, but that hadn't kept the mud out.

"You need help?" he asked when she froze. It was wiser to shower in the spare bath than track dirt through the entire first floor.

"Loads," she replied.

Josiah chuckled. He took her hand and pulled her through the hall but didn't enter the bathroom. He continued to the laundry room. A slop sink in the corner next to the washing machine shined like a beacon of hope. He left but soon returned with shampoo from the shower. He turned on the water, adjusting it until the temperature warmed.

"All right, let's get rid of the mud," Josiah said as he rubbed his hands under the water.

Jessie bent and pointed to a pile of clean towels in a laundry basket. "Grab one of those, please." She pulled off her shirt then wrapped her torso with the towel, trying to ignore the fact he watched. "No sense pulling a dirty shirt over a clean head," she murmured, leaning in to wet the clumped mass on her head.

"Here, let me." Josiah adjusted the faucet and got the back wet. His long fingers worked to get the big chunks out then he squeezed shampoo into his hands. He massaged her sensitive scalp then rubbed behind her ears. The gentle strokes racked her body with sensations setting off alarm bells in her head. The water swirling the drain started the color of coffee but gradually cleared.

"Sorry, I got you pretty good. It's out now." Josiah's voice sounded husky and deeper than normal.

She wrung out the hair and wrapped it in another towel, refusing to meet his gaze. "Thank you."

She dumped soap in the washer and threw her shirt in, then unzipped her jeans and added them too. Next went the socks. He tossed in his shirt and socks. As she changed the setting on the machine to accommodate the filth, she listened for his zipper, but none came. She turned to investigate. He blushed, grinning sheepishly.

"You've got to be kidding," she teased. "Commando?"

Josiah shook his head, the red on his face intensifying. "No. These are my church boxers."

Jessie's gaze dropped to tight front of his jeans. His long fingers unbuckled his belt then unbuttoned the jeans. She swallowed and blinked dry eyes. He fingered the zipper pull. She raised her gaze to his sparkling blue eyes.

His lips turned up with a cocky grin. "They're holey."

Jessie ran, her heart in her throat. Darn, if she didn't want to get on her knees and play.

CHAPTER 20

Josiah

THE INSTANT JOSIAH STEPPED INTO the foyer of his parent's house, both brothers raced past hurling insults and pushing him against the wall. "Watch it," Josiah yelled after them.

"Whatever, jerk," Matt shouted as he disappeared around the corner chasing Gabe.

High pitch squeals hurt his ears, and an awful stench met his nose as he continued through the hallway.

"Mom!" His sister's patented whine tattled, "Gabe and Matt are bothering us."

From the kitchen, his mother responded, "Boys, leave Tori alone."

Josiah paused at the dining room, finding the source of the smell. Nail polish bottles littered the table while Tori and two friends painted their nails. The longer he watched, the louder the girls' chatting seemed to get.

In the kitchen, his mother hummed as she pulled out a cutting board. She nearly dropped it when she caught him hovering in the shadows. She placed a hand over her heart. "Don't scare me like that."

"Sorry, Mom." Josiah kissed her cheek then took the sweet tea she offered him. "I've got some news for you."

Her brows lifted. "Oh, what's that?"

"Jessie and I saved a calf today."

"I knew it. My son, the hero." She grinned. "Tell me about it." While he spun the tale, she continued with the dinner prep, peeling and chopping onions. After the story ended, silence descended. He fingered his empty glass.

"There's more news, isn't there." Prairie put the knife in the sink, glancing at him.

Josiah nodded then blurted, "I'm moving in with Jessie." Heat spread across his face as he stared at his hands.

"Don't get your hopes up," she cautioned, adding the onions to the pot. With a frown, his mother turned to face him.

"I'm on the sofa not in her bed." Josiah crossed his arms, ready for whatever lecture she planned. "I came home to get my things."

His mother hit him playfully on the arm. "That's not what I meant. You already like her. I don't want your heart broken."

"Don't worry." He kissed her again, earning a smile. His mom and dad liked Jessie; she'd always been welcome in the Barnes' home.

"I'm turning Don's old barn office into a bunkhouse." Josiah couldn't keep the excitement out of his voice. The space wasn't bigger than a studio apartment. He'd love to be out on his own, but Josiah couldn't protect Jessie from Kuntz if he wasn't on the property. The upside to sleeping at the ranch was being nearer to Jessie. He'd keep her safe from the things that go bump in the night. Of course, he wouldn't mind bumping her in the night.

Taking the steps two at a time, he hurried to his old bedroom to pack. Closing his eyes, he took a deep breath before returning to the family room. He left the duffle full of clothes and a few other items at the entry. Guy Manning sat on the sofa reading on his phone. Josiah thought he owed it to his sister to make sure Guy had Maggie's best interests in mind. He shelved his desire to run out the door to meet Jessie and plopped on the sofa next to Guy.

After an awkward silence, Josiah said, "So you and my sister…"

"Yeah, me and your sister." Guy's lopsided smile appeared genuine, and he scratched the back of his head.

"How'd you meet?" Josiah knew Maggie's version. Guy approached her at the library while she studied.

Guy glanced at his hands where he picked a nail. "She'd bought lunch for a homeless woman who'd come into a fast food restaurant. The bag lady had enough money for a coffee. She sipped it in a corner away from most people."

Josiah frowned; this didn't fit Maggie's story. He shifted and bumped his knee up and down.

Guy glanced up at Josiah. "Most everyone ignored the woman. She was dirty and smelled horrible. But not Maggie."

Guy's face turned red. "This next part is embarrassing." He cleared his throat. "Most people ignored the woman, but I didn't even see her." He swallowed and glanced at the door where women's laughter sounded. He explained, "When I get into study mode I totally zone. I don't see or hear anything."

"So what happened?" Josiah leaned toward Guy.

"Maggie happened." Guy's face softened, and he smiled. "She bumped my chair as she walked by. It was an accident, but it knocked me out of the zone." He chuckled and rubbed his chin. "At first, I was irked, but as I watched the simple act of kindness, I became curious. I asked around about her."

Josiah crossed his arms, not happy about this revelation.

"I didn't stalk her. Well, maybe a little." Guy rolled his eyes and chuckled. "She made me curious. I wanted to know if it was a dare, or if she lived like that all the time. After a few weeks of observations, I knew she was the real deal."

Guy sighed and relaxed against the sofa. When Maggie entered the room, the man's gaze followed her with such love it amazed Josiah. She winked at Guy then picked up her purse and exited the room.

Josiah cocked his head to the side and smirked at Guy. "There's a reason for this visit, isn't there?"

Guy nodded, and his face bloomed into a goofy grin. "I love her," Guy whispered.

Josiah wished his future brother-in-law, "Good luck with Dad."

Maggie returned and handed Guy an iced tea. Guy no longer could see or hear Josiah because he now resided in the Maggie zone. Josiah exited without interrupting them.

Whistling, he threw his bag in the car and headed to Hammered. Nothing could dampen his mood. By the end of the night he'd be moving onto Double D property with the love of his life.

Josiah

There were several vehicles in Hammered's lot. Mona's compact, Sawyer's shiny pickup and the Greene's minivan. Jessie's truck made Josiah smile.

Oh, there's Johnson's un-dented truck. Huh, doesn't that beat all.

Josiah rubbed his chin. Now he worried Jessie might have a knock-down

116

drag out with Johnson in Hammered with Sawyer taking bets. He needed to inform Jessie of Johnson's innocence.

As he pulled open the door, the smell of fried food and stale beer assaulted him. He searched the bar, finding Jessie in the corner, behind the pool tables, giggling at something Mona whispered in her ear. Jessie wore snug jeans and a pale yellow t-shirt. She hadn't fought anyone. He let out the breath he'd been holding. Glancing around the bar, Johnson wasn't anywhere in sight which meant he was next door in the hardware store Nailed.

Sawyer and Ben played a game of pool with the girls watching. Sawyer bent over the table sticking his butt in the girls' direction. He swung it back and forth. Mona watched as if hypnotized, but Jessie smiled at Josiah, ignoring the other man's bid for attention. She winked. That was his cue.

As he walked through the restaurant, several couples sat together, hunched over a book either reading or talking. They cuddled close together. Singles read too, most of them men. He grinned at all the romance and hoped one of these days he could cuddle up with Jessie as he read to her. Maybe he could perform a role for her. His face hurt from smiling.

He could tell Jessie was in a good mood by her mannerisms and sassy grin. Her father hadn't upset her. Hopefully, Josiah wasn't banished from the ranch. At the Double D that afternoon, Brad came barreling up the drive as Josiah left. He jerked the wheel to stay on the road. Her father glared at him as he passed. Josiah had felt like a coward as he kept driving but Jessie could handle Brad. Evidently, the talk with her father hadn't been bad because Jessie smiled and greeted him with a big hug.

Jessie pulled back and scanned his face. Ruby red lips parted to tell him something, but Sawyer elbowed in and shook Josiah's hand.

"Man, you're a jerk. I can't believe you asked the girl I wanted to ask to the dance. How could you? Bros before hos, dude." Sawyer slugged Josiah playfully. Behind Sawyer, Jessie put her hands together, begging him to play along.

"You should have acted faster. How many girls have you asked?" Josiah winked at Jessie, and she blew out a breath.

"Well, Jessie was the third, but the others don't count." Sawyer studied Ben as he took another shot and sunk the ball.

"Jessie is a first choice kind of woman," Josiah stated then frowned, crossing his arms. *Since when did Sawyer want Jessie?*

"What is it with this dance? It's not yet autumn and everyone's scrambling for a date for the Cattlemen's Ball." Sawyer smiled because Ben missed. "Anyway, I'm glad you finally got the balls to ask her. Bravo." He gave a mock bow.

Josiah bit his tongue and glanced at the girls. Neither seemed pleased by Sawyer's musings.

Ben held his cue next to Josiah. He leaned close. "I swear, Sawyer believes he's God's gift to whoever he can impress. He asked Jessie when she had her mouth full. She tried to find a nice way to tell him off. She politely told him she'd already been asked. He pestered her until she said she was going with you."

Josiah took Jessie by the hand and pulled her to their usual spot. His heart thundered like a hundred horses.

Jessie stared at the ground and blurted, "I'm sorry. I couldn't help it." Her cheeks turned a pretty pink. She gulped in air, sucking in her bottom lip then gazed at him, her green eyes begging for understanding.

Reaching out to touch her arm, Josiah's fingers skimmed her warm skin, her hand covering his gave a tiny squeeze. Heat hit him, simmering in his heart. She didn't need to worry about him rejecting her. Josiah ached to pull her into an embrace. He glanced around Hammered searching for curious eyes. Finding none, he retrained his thoughts on Jessie. He hooked a finger under her chin, tilted her face upward and leaned close. Her eyes widened, but she didn't move.

"Would you like to go to the dance with me, Jess, because I'm asking you now?"

Her gaze traveled around his face, his eyes, a full day's beard growth, and lips. He licked them making her gasp.

"Jessie?" Josiah drawled in a throaty voice. She trembled at her name. He pulled her into his arms and whispered her name next to her ear. Again, she shivered. Somehow he'd gotten to her. "Jess?"

Like a dream come true, Jessie's arms wrapped around his back and she replied, "Yes." His heart leapt.

With a quick glance over her shoulder, Jessie returned to her friends, but he stayed trying to digest everything. He sat on his stool and drank a beer. He didn't want to frighten Jessie away, but he wanted her in a bad way. His body ached as much as his heart.

Jessie was healing. She was opening up, exposing her soft spots. As much as Josiah hated it, letting Johnson in then having the confidence to kick him out, was proof she was returning. She'd come to him, and he'd be waiting. What he needed was patience and maybe a cold shower.

CHAPTER 21

Josiah

SATURDAY NIGHT SAWYER CHALLENGED JOSIAH to a game of pool, but Josiah stayed ahead of the game this time. He tucked his fingers into his front jeans pocket and grinned. Sawyer didn't get rattled often, and Josiah planned to take full advantage of it while it lasted.

Mona leaned close to Ben and smiled. "So have there been more visitation arrests?" Ben's face blazed red at Mona's attention.

Or maybe he's planning a visitation of his own. Josiah grinned and sunk a ball.

Ben cleared his throat. An amber bottle lifted to his lips, and he sucked a long swallow. Josiah chuckled, understanding Ben's flustered state. *Welcome to my world, bro.*

Mona touched Ben's arm with wide eyes. He coughed, having inhaled a sip of beer. Mona's brow dipped with concern, and she patted his back. Once he found his voice Ben tried to answer, but Sawyer cut him off. "Haven't you read the paper, Mona? There's been three arrests."

Her hands flew to her hips, Mona growled, "I didn't ask you, Sawyer Hickey, so just butt out."

Sawyer shrugged and circled the pool table, spying the perfect shot.

Josiah could tell Sawyer listened and watched Mona and Ben. Not long ago they'd been playing for kisses with Mona eager for Sawyer to win. Now she flirted with another man. It had to eat at Sawyer's pride if not his heart.

Ben's gaze traveled those closest to him but landed on the pretty girl holding onto his arm. "We've collected a few fines from those who run around without clothes." His face turned a deep shade of red. "Only one true arrest. I can't tell you much other than you shouldn't be naked in the park after hours." He cleared his throat again and a lopsided grin formed. Mona giggled and sighed closer to Ben.

Sawyer muttered, "But it's okay to be naked in the park when it's open." Josiah chuckled at the childish quip.

"Well, that's where the fines come in. I wonder how much it costs to get ticketed for indecent exposure?" Josiah leaned glancing at the balls on the table.

"Pretty damn high. Have you seen these people?" Sawyer threw his hand out gesturing to the people of the bar. "Seeing them naked could do immutable damage to my innocent eyes."

The men laughed then Sawyer sunk another ball.

Crap.

Jessie scanned the pool table as she scooted closer to him. Ben and Mona were in their own world, ignoring all else.

Sawyer winked Jessie. "Let your girlfriend hold your staff for you while I shoot," Sawyer teased. Jessie crossed her arms and blushed.

"Gee, Mr. Hickey, are you jealous because his staff is getting more tender loving care than yours?" Mona shot back. She'd paid more attention than Josiah thought, and Sawyer's features pinched as he whipped around to confront Mona.

Before Sawyer could speak a word, Jessie ran her hand along his cue moaning, "It's so long and hard." Josiah's jaw dropped. The room overheated. He envisioned a private gun polishing session.

"Barnes, she's quite the vixen. I'm happy for you." Sawyer took a shot and missed. He asked Josiah, "Have you seen Holden's balls?"

"Um, no." Josiah glanced across to Ben, who grinned as if he knew a secret. Even Jessie covered her mouth to hide a giggle.

Sawyer leaned against the table and crossed his arms. "You should. They're shiny." The girls laughed. "And new."

"I don't care to see his shiny, new balls or his old ones either. Thank you," Josiah replied.

Sharon Dix's chunky form put a brown tray on the green felt of the pool table. She handed a draft beer to Ben, a bottle to Sawyer and Josiah then cola to the girls. "Do you know anything about my husband's balls, Sawyer?" Sharon wiped wet hands on the front of her stained apron.

"No, Ma'am. I don't know anything. I'm surprised you're asking me."

Sharon narrowed her eyes and pointed the order book at him. "It'd be the kind of prank you'd pull."

"I'd never touch another man's balls, Sharon. I swear I didn't." The cocky man crossed his heart.

Josiah sucked in a deep breath, he hated to ask, but curiosity was killing him. "What happened to Holden's balls?"

"Somebody broke in and stole them. Can you believe it? Not one but all of them. It's the strangest thing." She sighed. "Good thing he had extra in the storage. You never know when you'll need spares."

Through the bark of laughter, Mona snorted. Jessie doubled over, laughing so hard tears leaked out the corners of her eyes.

Sharon shifted a pencil from the apron pocket to behind her ear. "Did you hear about Nailed? It got hit too. Whoever stole the balls took a wooden dowel rod too. Weird, huh?"

The guys started a new game, this time Ben playing the winner of the last game, Sawyer. Instead of gloating and kicking Sawyer's ass, Josiah now stood next to Jessie making small talk and watching the way her lashes moved when she blinked.

Ben held his cue stick waiting for Sawyer. "There have been several small prank related incidents but the prankster hasn't done any permanent damage."

"How many dowels did he steal from the hardware store, Ben?" Mona asked.

"Only one and it was worth $1.15," the officer replied.

"Whoa, the crime of the century," Sawyer mumbled, rolling his eyes.

"It's still theft," Jessie pointed out. "How did the Nailed employees know someone took the rod?"

"That's the good part," Ben chuckled. The smile softened Ben's features, reminding Josiah that the girls, including Jessie, thought Ben a handsome man. "First off, Nailed had this long, thick piece of wood forever. It's been on clearance for a year. It's been behind register two so long the employees have nicknamed it 'Woody.' When the manager, Wayne Kerr opened that morning, a giant, neon pink poster board read: Nailed, my new owner is taking me pole dancing. I'm free! No more being stuck in this pole vault. Signed: your Long Hard Rod."

Jessie

Jessie recruited Josiah to help carry a load of romance novels into Hammered. Together they hoisted the heavy plastic tub out of her truck bed to the bar counter.

Blushing, Pixie hurried to them. "Oh, Dad will be so happy. He loves these stupid things."

As they unloaded, Pixie stashed them under the bar out of sight. Near the bottom, a book caught Jessie's eye. On the cover, a scantily clad man with a rocking hot body wearing red pointy horns and a devilish grin leaned over a sleeping woman. Jessie couldn't believe her luck finding the second in *The Visitation* series. No one in the town had read it yet.

The Temptation was the story of a male friend of the guy with angel wings. It wasn't set in an apartment this time but a cabin near a lake. Same story, but different characters and setting. The poor woman sleeping spread eagle on the bed was clueless a man with a magic mouth hovering over her. A not-so-rude awakening was in store for the heroine. Jessie put it aside until they were walking out to the truck.

"Look what I found," she said handing the novel to Josiah.

Glancing at the cover, Josiah gasped. He grinned then flipped the book to read the back cover. "No freaking way." Josiah offered it to her, but she pushed it into his hands.

"No, you read it first. Tell me if it's as cheesy as the others." Jessie smirked as she closed the gate of the truck.

"Thanks, Jess." Josiah reached for her and pulled her against him. She thought he intended to give her a hug but held onto her longer. "Happily ever after isn't cheesy," he breathed next to her ear.

A shiver traveled down her body and she pushed him away. "Whatever you say, Romeo."

Josiah crossed the parking lot to his pickup and opened the cab. She couldn't peel her gaze away from his tight jeans. His muscular form leaned into his truck and stuck the book somewhere.

When she heard a noise behind her, she jumped. B.J. stood a few feet away. His five o'clock shadow and reserved cockeyed smile gave him a mysterious aura. A swift mental kick resulted in a poker face. A puff of his cologne preceded him but not as strong as before. Jessie wouldn't need to hold her breath.

Out of the corner of her eye, she checked for Josiah but he stayed silhouetted in the dark, hidden and ready if she called for him.

B.J. approached cautiously, as if he'd frighten a small animal. Dark hair peeked out of his polo shirt, the material stretched taut across his muscular chest.

No, B.J. might have damaged the fence.

"Hello, Jessie, I saw you bringing in new books."

Jessie started, "Listen B.J., I-"

"You were right," B.J. interrupted. His liquid velvet voice continued, "It wasn't my place to say anything to you and I'm sorry. It's just, ah hell." He pulled her into his arms and crushed hot lips against hers.

This wasn't the confrontation she expected. Her treacherous body liked the attention, switching on places she'd turned off. As her body revved its engine warming up, warning bells clanged in her mind. It told her to call out, kick and run away.

Jessie's noodle arms pushed against his chest, but when his tongue wrestled hers she forgot the day. Her brain turned to mush. He pulled back and searched her eyes.

"Why?" It was all the cognitive thought Jessie could muster. Her heart thundered in her ears.

He smirked like the guy on the cover of the romance she'd handed to Josiah. Just add a pair of devil horns and tear open his shirt.

"I've been wanting to do that for weeks." B.J.'s words, murmured with pent up longing, whispered against her ear. He took her earlobe between his teeth then suckled it. Jessie pushed against his chest again. "Don't count me out, Jessie. I will try my hardest to win you."

She froze, surprised by the declaration. Jessie hoped Josiah hadn't dared him. B.J. took dares seriously. She gasped, clenched her eyes shut and squirmed in B.J.'s arms. *Josiah is watching.*

Wednesday morning she was a liar and Satan's spawn and by Saturday night he wanted to date her. She leaned back and narrowed her eyes, giving him a once-over. He needed therapy.

"I'm going to the Cattlemen's Ball with Josiah." Jessie shifted her gaze trying to find him. Her own cowboy guardian angel. Would he rush in or let her handle B.J. again?

"Is he your boyfriend?" B.J. asked before working his way, nipping, licking and kissing, down her neck.

"No," Jessie moaned. Her arms had turned into Jell-O, refusing to push against the hard-muscled wall of his chest.

He chuckled low against her neck wracking her treacherous body with bolts of pleasure. "Then I have a chance. Barnes is going to have competition." B.J. tugged her blouse to the side as his tongue traced her collarbone.

That is some serious competition. She sighed and closed her eyes. *Too bad he's psycho.* The warning bells kept clanging.

Jessie found her head and shoved him, detaching his mouth from her neck. "Enough," she muttered. She stood beside her truck and watched him walk away. Dazed, she pulled open the pickup's door to make an escape.

Josiah appeared concerned. "You okay?" She shrugged. "He didn't take out the fence. I checked his truck. It's fine. He didn't do it." He stared at her swollen lips, his own dipped in a frown.

A few toe-curling kisses and Jessie forgot the fence. She rubbed her forehead. "I don't know what to think about B.J. He's angry and accusing then turns apologetic and seductive. He says you have competition." She glanced at Josiah, mortified she'd repeated the words. She gasped reading his cocky grin as the challenge's acceptance.

"Bring it," Josiah muttered low. He leaned closer. "Maybe I should kiss you senseless too." His jocular tone gave her pause, but the thought thrilled and scared her. Jessie's heart went into overdrive. He'd been watching. Watching and not stepping in.

Did he want her to push B.J. away or maybe Josiah wasn't attracted to her? After all, he'd rejected her once before.

The truck's ignition turned over. She tugged on the seatbelt.

Josiah leaned in the open window, the intent obvious in his eyes. Another sexy man wanting to kiss her and this one was coming home with her. Sure, technically they weren't sleeping together but…What was wrong with her? She was half tempted to seduce Josiah, and that frightened her more than B.J. She ground the truck into gear and whispered, "I'll see you at home."

CHAPTER 22

Jessie

"MY FEET HURT," DESIRE COMPLAINED. She kicked off her shoes and wiggled her toes.

"After all the walking we did around Nockerville, I'm surprised they haven't fallen off," Jessie teased. After fixing them each a sweet tea, Jessie joined Desire at the kitchenette. She removed her shoes too. They'd spent way too much time shopping, and now they paid the price.

"You did well. The lovely woman who owned the fabric store seemed very accommodating."

"She should be." Jessie chuckled.

"Oh, I smell a secret." Desire slapped her hands together and rubbed them.

Jessie shook her head. "It's not a secret."

"Pray tell, dear."

Jessie glanced at the floor and giggled before meeting Desire's eyes. "She has one of my bra and panty sets. I've made her a beta tester."

"That's smart. I'll beta test your thongs. I'd be happy to model them too." Desire grinned. She sipped her tea while rubbing the ball of a foot.

"I've sent two gowns to a friend in Austin. Both Kelly and Mona are testing panties." Jessie laughed at the excitement in her own voice. "My college roommate's family owns a business, and she's mentioned The Double D to them."

"Austin, huh? You might need to plan a sales trip." Desire took a drink then closed her eyes and relaxed. "I could model something for Tim."

"The teen sales associate at the fabric store?"

Desire had flirted with the young man. By the time they'd left, Desire and the teen seemed chummy. "What happened?"

Desire waved her hand in the air. "I was working my magic. Lookee here." She unbuttoned the top button of her blouse, and her hand disappeared inside. A moment later, she removed a small wad. She smoothed it on the table and handed it to Jessie.

Jessie pulled the scrap of paper toward her. She gasped at the number written in red ink. "This isn't what I think it is."

"Honey, it's his phone number." Desire raised her glass of tea in a salute.

"No way. He's a minor, and you'd go to prison."

"He's legal, I asked." She grinned and leaned back against the chair. She stretched her short legs out and crossed her ankles.

"So will Josiah massage my feet? I could offer to massage something of his in return." Desire waggled her eyebrows.

"You can try to use your magic." Jessie laughed. She believed Josiah would help Desire out even if it included rubbing her feet but he wouldn't want any reciprocal deeds. She squeezed her eyes shut at the thought.

"Those Harlequin Inspire books you donated were a big hit at the church bazaar, dear. They're too tame for my taste but romance is romance. The volunteers cleaned out most of the tote before the doors opened. All the books sold in record time." Desire chuckled.

"I'm glad I could donate something of interest. I kept one with a gown on the cover I'll try to make."

"Speaking of which, I want to see that little number you're working on. The one the shop owner told me about." Desire stood. "Come on, dear. I'm not growing any younger."

Jessie nodded and reached for a bag containing the yards of fabric she'd purchased. She motioned for Desire to follow. The two women trekked upstairs toward Jessie's work room. Still surrounded by stacks of paperback sex, the sewing machine rested in the center of the room. Jessie hadn't gotten around to moving it to the downstairs office. Mainly because she'd bump elbows with Josiah and she wasn't ready to divulge what she'd been creating.

"There it is." Jessie pointed to a dress form wearing a cream colored gown with a beaded and lace bodice. Pinned to the wall behind it was an aged pencil drawing.

Desire gasped and covered her mouth with her hands. Her eyes sparkled with unspent tears. Her weathered fingers reached for the satin cloth and caressed the material. "Oh Jessie dear, it's heavenly. Your grandma would be so proud. There were three things your grandma loved more than anything: her family, sewing some kind of do-dah, and reading a good book."

Desire shuffled to the center of the sewing room. "I miss her," she whispered, staring at the books. "Your grandma could read a book in mere hours. The same book would take me days."

"How'd she move them here?" Jessie asked in a soft voice.

Desire turned in a complete circle, taking in the contents and acting as if she hadn't heard the question. She answered "Does it matter?"

No, not really. But why they were there was another question Jessie wouldn't mind having answered.

The book conversation had been shelved because Desire exited, leaving Jessie alone. She flipped the switch and closed the door.

Back in the kitchen, Jessie refilled their glasses. She glanced out the window. Josiah closed the barn door with Tippy weaving between his feet. He reached down and plucked the cat up, holding and petting her. Tippy's chin tipped back allowing for better access and Josiah obliged. His lips moved as he rubbed the little cat. She'd love to have heard what sweet things he'd said and wouldn't mind letting his fingers work on her too. Josiah gave the best massages. Warmth spread through her body. A grin tugged at her lips as she returned to the table.

"What about this trickster pranking the town?" Desire glanced at her with raised penciled brows.

"It's funny but wrong."

Desire puckered her lips in a wet pout. "Nothing evil has happened, and it's the most excitement Fortuna has seen in a long time."

Jessie sighed and rubbed her forehead. "It's still vandalism and stealing."

"But who'd want a dented and crooked rod?" Desire cackled and slapped her knee.

Josiah pulled open the back door. Covered from head to toe in dirt, he wiped his boots before entering. "Afternoon, ladies." He took the iced tea offered to him.

"Care to rub my feet, handsome?" Desire's lashes fluttered. Josiah was a piece of meat Desire would love to devour.

More like, she'd love to swallow his meat. Jessie slapped a hand over her mouth to keep from laughing.

Josiah smirked and held out his dirty hands. "Another time. I need to get cleaned up. Excuse me, ladies." He winked at them then exited the room, heading toward the shower.

Desire waved her hand in front of her face, fanning herself. "Honey, you let that gorgeous man shower alone? Shame on you."

Envisioning water streaming over Josiah's muscled chest had Jessie's body hot. She took a long drink of cold tea, but it didn't help. She didn't want Desire to gossip about her and Josiah so she countered. "Have you smelled him?"

Jessie

With a wave, Jessie dropped Desire off at the Tease Me Salon & More's back door apartment. She loved that ornery old woman. Desire's mouth shouldn't surprise her anymore, but it happened every time they were together. Usually, after the shock wore off came a fit of giggles.

Jessie drove through the town square glancing in the shop windows with the Independence Day displays. In the center of Fortuna, the Greek Revival courthouse, a red brick building with fluted columns held Mayor Jasen DeLay's office. B.J.'s novel reaching talons extended into the heart of town. It was rumored the mayor's shelf held romance books containing bondage. Even though her curiosity was strong, Jessie never had the nerve to visit the office or ask her father. The mayor was in B.J. and her father's book club.

The streetlights cast a homey glow as she drove around the central park. A small group of people gathered around the larger than life bronze statue of the town's founder, William T. Stoker. According to myth, William had been a gambling man and won the parcel of land in a card game.

The group around the statue seemed older than high school students. They weren't tourists but normal town's folk. Every single one of them had a smile on their face and most laughed.

What the heck?

Jessie slowed and lowered her window to question someone. The prankster had made an addendum to the statue. She snapped a picture with her phone and drove off, giggling.

By the time she arrived home, tears streaked her face. She couldn't breathe, and her sides hurt from laughing. Between breaths, she called for Josiah. He ran out of the barn and grabbed her arms. His gaze scanned her face and roamed the rest of her body. "What's wrong? Who did this to you?"

His concern touched her, but for some reason, Jessie giggled even harder. She couldn't talk, shaking her head she pulled him toward the house.

"Are you okay?" Josiah scrutinized her expression.

She nodded. "I need to make a phone call." Jessie held his arm as he tried to leave the kitchen to give her privacy. "You'll want to hear this." She dialed and waited.

"Sharon? Hi, it's Jessie. I found Holden's balls. You know? Of course, you do. Half the town is there." She glanced at Josiah, who leaned closer.

Holding the handset so they both could listen, Sharon ranted. "God, it's embarrassing. The whole town has seen my husband's balls except me. What sick bastard steals another man's balls? I'm going to kill the pervert who touched them." Sharon took a deep audible breath. "Maybe I'll castrate him so he can have his turn as the ball-less wonder." Sharon harrumphed, and Jessie could envision the plump woman with one hand on her hip and the other raised with finger wagging. A hand flew over Jessie's mouth to stanch the giggles.

"Uh oh. Someone else is calling me. Got to run, Jessie. Thanks for the call." The line went dead, and Jessie replaced the handset.

Josiah shook his head, his eyes crinkled with merriment and he laughed without making a sound. Jessie pulled him into the living room and they sat.

"You're not going to believe what I saw tonight."

"Holden's pool balls?" Josiah surmised.

"There's so much more." Where did she start? She told him about the crowd at the square. "You know, Willie Stoker's statue in the square. He grew a pair."

"The balls? No way." He chuckled.

"That's not all. The stolen rod stuck out of the proper place too. The town's customized phallic symbol." Jessie wiped tears again. "That's on the bottom half. On top, Willie had on a pair of those feathery angel wings from *The Visitation*. I swear this town is obsessed with that book."

"It had a happy ending." Josiah shrugged.

"This visitor dressed Willie Stoker in more than angel wings. There was also a lacy, white full-figured bra thanks to more pool balls. Look Josiah, here's a picture."

Turning the small screen in his direction, he held it and stared. "Well, I'll be damned." He rubbed his chin. "Willie will be on the front page of the Fortuna Forum tomorrow."

CHAPTER 23

Josiah

"WAKE UP, JESS," JOSIAH SAID in a grim voice, shaking her. "We've got an intruder."

Her green eyes fluttered open briefly.

"Jessie," he said, this time caressing her face.

Her eyes flickered open again. Yawning, she reached out and touched his leg. Jessie's warm fingers ventured up, under his boxers to his backside. Goosebumps broke out on his skin, and he stymied the urge to crawl into bed with her. Heat flooded his body pooling between his legs.

"I told you not to stop," Jessie murmured.

Josiah wouldn't have minded her probing hands but not when there might be thieves. Plus, he wanted her awake when she touched him. He didn't want to compete with a dream man. His lips pressed together as he pushed her hand away then he shook her again.

"Josiah?" Jessie blinked as recognition dawned in her sleepy eyes.

"Wake up, Jess. Somebody's here."

"You should be more careful, I might have gone for my gun," Jessie said with a groggy voice.

"You went for mine." Turning his body to hide his tent pole, he asked, "What were you dreaming?"

Jessie yanked her hand away, sat up and yawned again. Flinging the covers back, she jumped out of bed. "Somebody's breaking in?" A lacy pair of panties peeked out from under her white t-shirt.

Josiah ached to touch her, and he reached for her then dropped his arms clenching his fists.

Jessie caught him staring. "What? I need to do the wash. Dang, where are my jeans?" She pulled them out of the hamper and tugged them on.

"The intruders-" Words stalled in his throat. He squared his shoulders and pointed toward the door.

"My gun." Jessie groped under her pillow and pulled out a pistol. Grabbing his hand, she crept to the bedroom door and canted her head, listening.

She trembled and Josiah pulled her into his embrace then nosed her hair. His lips brushed her ear. "Jess, they're not inside the house. They're out by the new barn. Noise woke me and I saw lights. I used binoculars but they're staying to the shadows." The sweet smell of strawberries coupled with her soft sigh had him longing to nibble her neck. Jessie splayed her fingers, grazing his abdomen and making it twitch.

Jessie lifted her chin. "Let's go."

Josiah released her then led the way. He didn't want to expose her to danger but there was no way in hell he'd leave her behind. Not with possible criminals on the property.

The lights had ceased moving, but they crept forward to catch the culprit. Jessie held her pistol while Josiah carried a shotgun.

Tippy mewed welcome. They hushed her.

While Josiah kept a lookout, Jessie tried the front barn door. Locked. They followed the building's length until they emerged behind the barn. The outside light at the back of the building illuminated a wide swath of yard. The doors remained locked and there weren't any vehicles. They faced the road but heard nothing but night noises.

"I don't get it," Josiah said, lowering the shotgun. "I saw flashlights, but whoever it was didn't go in the barn."

"They're gone," Jessie stated. She lowered the handgun and knelt to inspect a wadded paper towel.

"I hope so. I'll check out the road." Josiah walked hunched, primed and ready. He strained his eyes peering into the dark brush, but nothing moved. He sighed and returned. Gasping, Josiah froze, his gaze cemented to the barn wall.

Hearing him, Jessie pivoted. "Josiah," she whispered. "Why are you standing like a statue?"

Josiah pointed to the building. High on the gable, under the light, someone had painted a girl.

"Holy crap," Jessie squeaked, a hand flew to her throat. "What is that thing?" She backed away until she stood next to him with her hands on her hips.

"I believe it's you." Josiah couldn't help the grin tugging at his lips. If someone waved a wand turning Jessie into a hot Japanese cartoon, it would be the spitting image.

Emotions scrolled across Jessie's face—shock, anger, amusement and disbelief. "The painter thought himself funny," she said in a flat tone.

Josiah put a hand on her shoulder. "Jess, just think. You have a free new logo for the Double D."

She glared at him. The night breeze blew her hair like the girl pictured on the barn.

"Oh come on, it's not that bad."

"Josiah, it's practically cartoon porn." She sucked in her bottom lip.

The head and bust of a manga cartoon, with long auburn hair flying, graced the barn. The girl winked extra-large eyes and smiled a toothy grin. Her clothes, what little she wore, barely covered her nipples. The Double D logo, a pair of capital Ds back to back so the first one faced backward, were the cups of her bikini. The Ds, and everything painted around them, were unusually big. Like an afterthought, the word 'ranch' appeared stenciled under the Japanese caricature.

Jessie stomped her foot. "I'm nothing like that... that... monstrosity. My boobs are not that big!"

Josiah glanced to the t-shirt where her breasts strained against the thin material but suppressed a comment. Instead, he mumbled, "Come on, let's go call the sheriff."

Jessie

Before Sunday service, a group of people hounded Jessie and her father like paparazzi. They hovered wanting information about the risqué graffiti. The vandal's art made her a local celebrity. A weird phenomenon at church.

"Who painted it?" Sawyer asked.

"I don't know," Jessie grunted for the umpteenth time. She took a deep calming breath. All morning long, she'd denied having anything to do with the art. Her head hurt from shaking no and her shoulders ached from shrugging, and denying the artist.

"I don't know who painted it. I didn't commission the painting or know who did," Jessie said through gritted teeth.

A Japanese cartoon caricature on a Texas barn was a strange sight. And everyone seemed interested in the story.

For ten minutes, Jessie hid in the ladies' room, behind a stall door. She hoped the mob would check their watches then find a seat in the sanctuary. She pushed the bathroom door open a crack and peeked out. The Barnes family arrived late, as usual.

At the last minute, she hurried down the aisle and sat next to her father.

The organ played, and the robed choir entered. Sometimes Jessie's mind wandered as they sang and she imagined what they wore under the robes. Were they naked or wearing pink tights? She giggled but thank heavens the loud music masked it. Her gaze roamed the room. B.J. caught her eyes. His tongue traced his upper lip before his lips curled into a seductive smile. Heat rose up her neck to her cheeks. She swung her gaze away and Desire winked.

A sidelong glance uncovered Josiah's furrowed brows and clenched jaw. She swallowed and squirmed in the pew.

As the service progressed, Jessie's mind pondered the prankster. She hadn't been the only victim. Who was he? Why the Double D?

The pastor introduced a guest pianist for the offering's special music. The woman appeared to be in her fifties, thin and short with a military flattop. Prim and proper, wearing a navy skirt suit with shiny brass buttons; she could have been a matron of a military school.

Next to the choir a shiny, black baby grand piano awaited. The piano bench's cushion matched the red carpet. As the woman took her seat, she farted, and the congregation jumped. She leaped up examining the seat. Snickers broke out, then an all-out laugh riot.

"Special music indeed," Pastor Peacock quipped before succumbing to a fit of laughter.

The pianist lifted the seat cover and gasped. She plucked a round pink item off the bench. A deflated whoopee cushion swung pinched between her thumb and finger.

CHAPTER 24

Jessie

FROM THE BARN, JESSIE HEARD a car door shut. She glanced out the door and grinned. "Kelly, over here," she said waving.

Halfway to the house, Kelly stopped and reversed course. The women hugged. "Wow, that is quite a side show you've got going on. I swear I almost got rear-ended."

The Double D Ranch was now the current Fortuna hot spot as the locals came to see the halfway naked woman advertising the ranch. Like art critics, the gawkers drove past surveying the graffiti.

Jessie thumbed over her shoulder to the weathered wood building behind her. "This barn doesn't get attention like the other one."

"I don't know," Kelly said as they strolled into the barn aisle. Her gaze swept the crowded space. "Looks pretty busy to me."

"Howdy, Kelly." Matt stepped out of a framed doorway. He tipped his black felt hat and grinned. Even with a broom in hand, he struck a handsome pose wearing a formfitting Fortuna Seniors t-shirt and faded jeans. Strange how his confident poise reminded Jessie of Josiah.

"Congratulations on graduating," Kelly said to Matt. "Where are you going to college?"

Propped against the wall, Matt crossed his ankles. "Well," Matt drawled with a cocky grin. "I'm taking a year off to weigh my options and work."

"Stop lollygagging with the girls, Matt, or we're never gonna get done." Gabe frowned at his older brother.

Before Kelly could ask, Jessie explained. "We're turning Grandpa's old barn office into a bunkhouse. Josiah's insulated and repaired the walls. He's done a great job." Jessie stood tall and grinned. "Matt and Gabe are the construction crew and movers. They helped move all the old furniture out."

Josiah exited the tack room turned junk closet with a gallon of paint in one hand and supplies in the other. The women followed him into the bunkroom. The smell of drywall mud and cleaners assaulted them. Josiah handed the can to Gabe, who placed it on the ground. The teen pried open the lid then stirred the liquid.

"Make sure you cut in before you roll," Josiah instructed. His gaze shifted around the ceiling line.

Gabe glanced at Josiah and narrowed his eyes. "I know how to paint," he grumbled. "Make sure Mr. God's-gift-to-women over there tapes off the ceiling."

"I'm glad you know me so well, bro." Matt wiggled his brows at Kelly and Jessie. Jessie rolled her eyes, and Kelly covered her mouth to hide a giggle.

"You wish." Gabe snorted.

"No. You do." Matt took the painters tape and opened the roll.

"Whatever." Gabe continued to stir the paint undaunted. Jessie couldn't yet decide if Gabe had the makings of a cowboy. He always had a sketch book at hand doodling cartoon characters.

Matt let the plastic wrapping fall to the floor. "Hey, looks like you gave Pikachu a big zit."

"What?" Gabe bounced to his feet. He pulled the Pokémon shirt away from his body and examined it. His brows dipped into a frown when he found it paint free. "Jerk."

"Geek." Matt laughed holding his sides.

"Hick," Gabe growled.

"Do you need any help?" Kelly glanced at Jessie, but Matt smiled and leaned close.

"You can help me anytime." Matt touched Kelly's arm.

Josiah frowned and pointed to the ladder. Matt swaggered over and climbed it without a word. "You see, Kelly, my brothers made a deal with me." His eyes held an evil glint.

Jessie laughed and tugged her friend back out into the main hallway. As the women stepped further into the dark hall, Jessie slid a desk drawer shut on her grandfather's old steel desk. The desk was empty but heavy. Nothing but dust and a few dead bugs inside but Josiah opted to keep it. He was sentimental about her grandparents too.

"Matt and Gabe are jealous Josiah is moving out and want to stay with him sometimes. He's smart to bargain for the privilege and now has free manual labor." Jessie smiled at Josiah as he leaned on the doorjamb with his arms crossed. The eighteen- and sixteen-year-olds helped Josiah claim the space. Jessie pulled Kelly close and said, "Who knows, maybe more Barnes will live in the barn."

"Hey, can I talk to you alone?" Kelly pointed to the loft. Jessie nodded and climbed the ladder.

"I wanted to tell you B.J. has a date to the dance. He wouldn't say who." Kelly glanced around the rafters. She tugged on the end of her long dark braid. At five foot four inches Kelly was petite and had a smattering of freckles.

"You're not going with him?" Jessie tried not to sound too curious.

"God, no. But a man with those looks, hm, I wouldn't mind him asking." Kelly's lips widened in a sheepish grin as she stuck her hands in her front pockets.

"Did you finally choose a date?"

Kelly nodded and blushed. "Sawyer."

"And you said yes?" Jessie hoped she hid the shock from her face and voice. *Who'd have thought Kelly would accept Sawyer, the man who flirts with anything with a vagina?*

They moved to the loft door, and Jessie pushed it open. Overlooking the drive, they could see the sightseers as they slowed for the barn-side spectacle.

Jessie tried to ignore the strange sensation rolling through her as she gazed down to where Josiah had moaned her name. Thank God for the breeze through the loft door.

"Sawyer worked for it. I reminded him I wasn't his first choice, hinted I had another offer, and I liked the guy." Kelly giggled then she sobered. "He seemed so unhappy."

Josiah's words, "Jessie is a first choice kind of woman," sounded in her mind. She'd been Josiah's first choice. The warmth radiating from her face made her glad she faced away from her friend.

"Sawyer admitted asking you to make Josiah jealous," Kelly said.

Jessie swung around to Kelly. "Why would Sawyer want to do that?"

Kelly tilted her head scrutinizing Jessie's face. "Because."

Jessie crossed her arms and rolled her eyes. "Because why?" Her pulse tap danced in her ears.

Kelly's small hands rested on her hips and her eyes narrowed. "Because everyone can see he's sweet on you. Sawyer figured Josiah needed a nudge to act."

Sucking in her bottom lip. Could the cowboy love her? Her lungs stopped working. Besides the Cattlemen's Ball, he'd never asked her on a date. Winning the pool game could explain the spectacular kiss at Hammered. But how did she reconcile the tender kiss in the kitchen the day of the fence mishap? A comforting kiss? She touched her lips and sighed.

"Hey, Jessie?" Josiah called from below.

Jessie jumped and spun around again. She'd been caught staring at the driveway. Shifting her weight, she tried to ignore the ache between her legs. "We're up here," Jessie answered.

Josiah popped his head over the top but didn't climb the rest of the way. "I didn't interrupt anything, did I?"

"I was informing Kelly of our elopement plans," Jessie teased. Kelly's jaw dropped.

Josiah climbed up and sat on a bale. "You found a babysitter?"

Kelly's wide eyed gaze volleyed from Jessie to Josiah. "I got a date for the dance but that's nothing compared to a wedding."

"Well, we've been planning it for years, since we first tried to kill each other," Josiah admitted. Jessie kicked his boot. It moved a bunch of straw from the bottom of the support post.

"I forgot about that," Jessie said pointing to the bottom. Scratched into the wood were several sets of initials. "It's a list of boys that visited the loft with me."

"Boys as in dates?" Kelly got on her knees and touched the carved letters. "Your grandparents never knew?"

"They knew, but my father didn't." Her dad would've skinned alive any boy caught in the hayloft with her. Most were innocent make out sessions with dinner guests of her grandparents. Back when the Double D had horses, it'd been a good excuse to get out of the house and boring adult conversations.

"I can hardly read these. R.F.? Who's that? He's on the bottom, was he your first?" Kelly asked inclining her head.

"Rodney Fillmore, a brat from Nockerville. His father and my grandfather were both members in the International Texas Longhorn Association. The group met regionally. The Fillmores came to dinner one evening, and they had a son. He was cute, but he knew it. He had braces." Jessie stuck out her tongue and grimaced remembering him. They'd come up to spy on the dinner party in the backyard. Rodney charmed her with compliments. Flattery led to the hayloft make out session. "He was a horrible kisser, way too wet and his braces cut my lip."

"It's a rating system," Josiah guessed rubbing his chin.

Jessie nodded. "The lower the name the less I liked the kiss. Rodney was the absolute worst kisser. He had an ego as big as Texas."

The bulk of the initials were carved low, but a few reached knee height.

"Who's your favorite?" Kelly asked. Hands clasped on her lap, she sat on the bale next to Josiah.

Josiah's forehead crinkled as he examined the post, no doubt trying to see who he knew or how he ranked.

Jessie ambled to the wood support. Josiah and Kelly gazed near the base but the favorite had a special place. She'd carved the initials at lip height, his lips not hers. She'd been twenty-two and leaving the next day for college, her final year. It was always sad to say goodbye to her family. She'd escaped a moment to compose herself.

"Here." Jessie pointed to the small lines. Admitting her secret caused her face to heat, and she fiddled with a hangnail.

"It looks like J.B. Is that Jim Beam? I knew you had a thing for Jim once." Kelly squinted at the letters, trying to guess.

"I had a crush on Jim in first grade. Ugh," Jessie laughed uneasily.

The favorite had worked for her grandfather and the whole incident had been an accident. She hadn't set out wanting to kiss him. Lost in thought, he'd startled her. Seeing the tears, he held her then... She didn't remember who'd started kissing who, but it'd been fast and furious. When they landed in the hay, he'd slowed it down. They'd lain next to each other taking slow, deep heart yearning kisses. Jessie closed her eyes and sighed.

"J.B. stands for jail bait." Josiah teased.

Jessie's eyes snapped open and narrowed. "You were nineteen, Josiah." She placed her hands on her hips and tapped her foot.

"Oh. Josiah's your top kisser? Way to go." Kelly high-fived the grinning man. "So what made him so special, if you don't mind me asking?" Kelly's gaze slid from Josiah to Jessie.

Jessie smiled. She'd been carefree and happy, her grandparents were both healthy and living, she didn't own a ranch and her future was free. She'd thrown caution to the wind, willing to give herself to Josiah. He'd been sexy as sin. Josiah the sweet, gentle and level-headed cowboy.

"Maturity," Jessie answered peering into his brilliant blue eyes.

Josiah stood and took a step forward. His gaze locked on hers. Her heart raced, and she swallowed.

Even as a young man, Josiah had considered the future. They'd have to live with what they did forever. Being rejected hurt, but they weren't ready for that deep of relationship or the consequences yet. He'd known it.

Transfixed, Jessie stared at his lips the same height as his initials. They'd always been friends but there was attraction too. She sighed. There had always been attraction. Ever since their traumatic meeting, she'd thought he was cute. "It wasn't the first time I kissed him," she admitted throwing a sideways glance to Kelly.

"What do you mean?" Josiah asked with brows dipped in suspicion.

Jessie felt her face heat and knew she'd turned bright red. She glanced at the tips of her boots. "After the accident, when you were in the coma."

"You kissed a guy in a coma?" Kelly chuckled.

Jessie put one hand on a hip and grinned at her friend. "Hey, he was cute, even with a bump on his head." Jessie shrugged.

"What did you do to me?" Josiah put his hands on his hips and leaned into her space. His brow hung heavy over narrowed eyes. He struck an opposing pose, but Jessie knew better. A slight smirk gave him away.

Jessie closed the space between them, then took his face in her hands. "I wanted to meet you. The guy who'd risked his life to save a dog had to be special. I thought it might be like sleeping beauty: one kiss to wake you." She rubbed her thumb over his cheek. It was a miracle he'd lived. The warmth of his skin was magic. "Your face was angelic, and I talked to you when your family wasn't there."

Prairie Barnes had been frantic having already lost one child, his twin. Jessie should have offered to babysit his siblings but she didn't want to leave Josiah. She hadn't wanted him to die. Jessie pressed her eyes shut trying to keep the tears at bay but one slipped out. She'd wanted to meet him and attempt a happily ever after.

Josiah cupped her face, wiping the moisture away with a soft caress of his thumb.

Jessie opened her eyes and her lips tipped up on one side. "I had a visitation with you." His eyebrows rose. "That's right, Josiah. I whispered sweet nothings into your ear. It was romantic stuff, not dirty, though."

"Well, that's a shame." His husky voice made her shiver.

"You have nice lips." Her thumb skimmed the soft skin.

"Did you ravish them?" Josiah asked, leaning into her touch.

"Completely."

"I don't remember." He pulled her into his arms. "Maybe you can show me."

Jessie baulked, pushing against his chest. "Josiah, we have an audience."

"Who?" he asked. Her gaze scanned the loft but Kelly was no longer there. She'd left them alone.

CHAPTER 25

Jessie

JESSIE PLANNED THE TRIP TO Austin alone, but Desire had hinted she wanted to come along because she wanted to reunite with the girls. *The girls? With Desire, it was all about uniting with the men.*

Now the old woman sat beside her with a satisfied smile. She'd suggested several marketing ideas. "You should use the funny cartoon lady from your barn. Nobody came forward and claimed to be the artist, did they?" She twisted in her seat to face Jessie.

Jessie pressed her lips together. She could use it, but that was a matter of principle. Someone had trespassed and vandalized her property. She'd talked about it with Josiah. They waffled between using it and painting over the abomination. Locally, the painting was on its way to becoming legendary. It identified the ranch with a sexy new image. And God help her, she could use the cartoon likeness of herself to jump-start branding of the Double D intimate apparel line.

"Nobody's claimed anything," Jessie lamented.

"You can't buy that type of publicity, dear. It's an odd but pretty work of art and it's got a great story you couldn't invent." Desire smiled and tapped her finger on her chin. "Why don't you see if one of those Barnes boys could build you a web page?"

Jessie had spent years living in the capital while attending the University of Texas. *Hook 'em horns!* Not much had changed, especially the traffic. It still sucked. Now the rancher, turned intimate apparel entrepreneur, was taking a bold step, the next step for Double D Intimates.

The five hours in the car had been productive. While brainstorming with Desire, they'd cataloged several crazy and a few realistic ideas. She followed the GPS's directions until she parked in a small lot next to the first store, Flirt.

Jessie got out, then reached for the bag of merchandise. According to Desire's friend, Emma, the woman they planned to meet was no nonsense and hardcore. The boutique catered to the sexy side of a woman and showcased unique high-end items. It sounded like a perfect fit for Double D Intimates.

Jessie swallowed and inhaled a deep breath as Desire held the door open. The sales clerk led the women to a large office with plush carpet and two club chairs for guests. Rhoda Mahn stood stiffly in a dark gray business suit with black rimmed glasses. She gestured for them to have a seat while she gave orders to whoever was on the other side of the phone pressed against her ear. Her tone was firm, but she wasn't rude.

Jessie watched the fish in the large tank against the wall.

"Soothing, aren't they?" Rhoda remarked as she set the phone aside and took a seat in the plush leather desk chair. "I find the sound of water and watching the fish can help bring calm to my life." She closed her eyes and took several deep, cleansing breaths. She folded her hands on the desktop then opened her eyes, glancing at the visitors with a welcoming smile. "That's better."

"Rhoda, thank you for sharing your valuable time today," Desire said.

Flirt's owner leaned forward with raised brows. "Emma told me a few stories about you, Desire." Rhoda's green eyes flicked to Jessie. "She swore whatever you said regarding this young woman's talents were true. I'm curious after this high praise."

"My Jessie won't disappoint. Show her your artwork, dear."

Jessie nodded, her mouth dry. Her hands shook and excitement filled her. This was it. The beginning to the new division of the Double D. She opened the case and presented the items one at a time.

Rhoda touched and explored the intimate apparel before her. She ordered twenty pieces—spaghetti strap nightgowns and matching panty sets. Each piece had a small tag with care instructions. On the small cotton fabric was the Double D Ranch logo, a pair of Ds back to back.

After the meeting, Jessie started the truck but sat there and stared out the windshield. A dreamy smile clung to her lips. The first appointment had been a success. Her first order completed, she felt energized and encouraged. Desire patted her hand. "One down."

Josiah

Josiah turned Cowboy off and was unloading tools when his phone rang. Pulling it out of his pocket, he checked the caller. His heart kicked up a notch when Jessie's face appeared on the screen. "Hello, thanks for calling the Double D Ranch where we grow them big. How can I help you today?" he answered.

"Josiah, what on earth?" Jessie giggled.

"Trying a new slogan. Matt's been coming up with them left and right." Josiah filled her in on a well needing repaired. After the ranch business, he lightened the mood. "Jessie, you aren't going to believe it, but Nockerville got hit by the prankster."

"Oh no. What happened?"

He snickered, and she begged, "Come on, Josiah. Don't leave me hanging."

"The prankster hit Nockerville's bronze statue this time."

"Isn't he on a horse?"

"The statue is Barnabas 'Buster' Highman and, yes, he is riding a horse. Both Buster and his horse sported a pair of Holden's balls." Josiah laughed hard now.

"I'm afraid to ask, but what about the rod?"

"Yeah, Woody was there too. Both males were en'*dowel*'ed."

Jessie giggled and he pulled the phone from his ear smiling. Her laughter was music to the soul. He closed the barn door and stepped over Tippy.

Jessie asked, "Angel wings?"

"Not this time. Buster wore devil horns and so did the horse. They had pointy red tails too." Josiah wandered to the house and washed his hands, careful not to drop his phone.

"Whoever is pulling pranks is familiar with *The Visitation* series. We need to check Grandma's stash for more of those books. It might be a trilogy or a whole series." Jessie's voice rose with excitement.

"Matt and Gabe are coming by later. Since we haven't found the culprit who took out the fence Matt and I will run a perimeter check. He's keen to see the property. I want to check on Muddy Buddy too. I think he'll be a good breeding bull someday."

"What about Gabe? What's he going to do while you're out?"

Josiah could picture her biting her lower lip. "I'll ask him to pull weeds. Your garden is full of them."

"Thanks. Listen Josiah, where are you?" Jessie's voice quieted. His gut rumbled. Something about her tone worried him but he couldn't put a finger on it.

"In the kitchen," Josiah replied. He glanced around the pale yellow room. "What are you wearing?"

Josiah's heart stopped and his brain stalled. The whole world silenced so it could hear his heart start again. *What the hell?* "Why?" Smirking, he should have answered "nothing but my birthday suit."

A soft gasp then Jessie's words rushed together, "Well, if you're clean, you can go to town and get dinner. My treat. There's a boot shaped cookie jar in the corner. See it? It's got a stash of money. Use it to buy dinner for you and the boys tonight as thanks for their help." Jessie took a loud breath and continued slower. "There's a list of carryout menus in there too. My favorite is the Fu King Chinese restaurant."

As if he didn't know her favorite. He chuckled but covered his mouth. "How's the trip?"

"It's going well, so far. We've got another meeting around dinner time."

The excitement in her tone made him picture a beautiful smile on her face. "That's great. You'll have to tell me about it, especially if Desire misbehaves. I'm glad you got there safe." Josiah shook his head, hearing the longing in his own voice and prayed she hadn't picked up on it.

"I'll keep you posted. Talk to you later."

Josiah rubbed his jaw. He stared at the phone in his hand. The confounded thing vibrated the second he'd hung up with Jessie. The timing of the text was a shock, but the message began "Howdy, sexy cowboy, this is your heart's Desire." He closed his eyes and gulped. What could the ornery woman want? He glanced around, making sure his brothers weren't close. He sat before reading the rest of the text.

"Find Paige Turner's contact information. A.S.A.P."

Jessie

After driving south on I-35 for forty-five minutes, they found the hotel. Jessie checked into the room and dropped off the luggage. Desire took a minute to freshen up.

The large stucco restaurant, Twig & Barry's, had a black and white awning over a wide patio filled with couples who sipped glasses of wine and snacked on appetizers. Jessie's stomach rumbled. Desire held open the door. Jessie pulled her tote full of special garments.

"This place smells so good I could eat it," Desire said with a smile.

"The meeting room is this way, ma'am." A tall server with dark hair and pressed white shirt led the way. Desire pointed to the young man's butt and elbowed Jessie.

"He's a little young, isn't he?" Jessie asked arching a brow.

"You're no fun. You're grumpy because you miss your man," Desire teased.

It was true. He'd been living on her property for a few weeks, and she'd gotten used to having him around in the evenings. They'd each read a book while sitting on the porch swing. She missed his presence and the way he'd blush when he read the naughty parts. She'd only been gone a few hours, but it already felt like an eternity.

A thin man with graying hair stood when they entered the room. He towered over them but had gentle, brown eyes and a thick mustache. "You must be Neil Lowe." Jessie offered a hand.

Jessie had called him because he had multiple boutiques in Austin, San Antonio, New Braunfels and Dallas. After checking out the company website, instinct told her the Sheer Delights chain would be a great fit to represent Double D Intimates.

Neil had ordered an appetizer, and the ladies nibbled while they perused the menu. After the meal, Jessie gave her spiel while she displayed the varying pieces. With a big grin on her face, she answered Neil's questions. She hoped she didn't seem too eager.

"What's next for your business?" Neil sipped his coffee and leaned back.

"Besides growing it?" Jessie answered tilting her head. "We had a meeting about this particular thing, Neil." It had taken place hours before on the truck ride to the big city. Desire shot a toothy grin at Jessie. "We discussed several items but one of the hot topics was the next line of lingerie. We will model the line after romance book covers. There are sexy models on the books and people want to emulate them. We have an appointment to coordinate a book cover with a gown."

Jessie bit her lip throwing Desire a glance. The older woman promised to put in a call to a local author from outside of Nockerville but had received no response yet. Jessie swallowed and reached for her drink.

"It's a grassroots venture." Desire swirled her wine.

"That's exciting. Which publisher?" Neil asked leaning forward.

"I'm sorry we're not at liberty to say. I hope you understand," Desire said in a diplomatic tone.

"Of course, I understand. I'm interested. Please, keep me informed."

Neil paused then asked, "Have you considered a fashion show?"

Again Desire glanced at Jessie offering a conspiring smile. The ideas churned in Jessie's head. A lingerie fashion show. Her grandmother would have turned it into a production. "A test market for the new line. Who should we invite?" Other boutique owners? Jessie tapped her chin with a finger

"Men." Desire smirked.

Jessie entered Neil's order information then folded the samples. Another successful meeting.

Desire's gaze followed the handsome server around their table. When he left, Desire shadowed him, her gaze affixed to his rear. A few minutes later, Desire returned with a satisfied smile. The waiter blushed when he refilled their glasses. There was a story somewhere. Jessie bit her tongue trying to stymie her curiosity.

The conversation turned to Austin events for the upcoming Independence Day celebration. Concerts, parades, and dinners. Neil had his hat in everything.

Walking to the truck, Jessie felt more exhilarated with each step. She sent Josiah a text. "So far, so good." He wasn't yet aware she peddled lingerie. Communicating with him spanned the distance.

"Call me," came Josiah's brief reply. She sucked in her bottom lip, dismayed and excited the tingles those two words caused. The air conditioning couldn't cool the truck cab fast enough as Jessie returned to the motel.

Desire still wore a smile, even though she leaned back against the seat with her eyes closed. Jessie couldn't stand waiting any longer. "Okay, out with it. What happened with the server?"

Desire's petal pink lips split exposing teeth. "Nothing twenty bucks couldn't solve," she said and popped one eye open then closed. She sighed like a contented cat. "That young number was a hottie. I paid him to drop his pants for a full minute." She crowed like a Halloween witch.

Jessie giggled. "Twenty dollars?"

"It was worth it. He was hung like an ox."

Jessie

The phone vibrated in Jessie's hand. It was the ranch, the original part of the Double D. More importantly, it was Josiah. She excused herself and answered as she walked outside the motel room to the relative quiet of the street.

"You want to tell me how Matt got a black eye?" Josiah demanded in a low tone.

"What does he say about it?" she countered, knowing good and well the eighteen-year-old had earned his shiner by being fresh.

"He's being stubborn. When he arrived at the ranch, he had a swollen and bruised eye. Matt wouldn't disclose any information other than it hadn't happened in town. I'm about ready to give him a matching one." The quiet, intense tone spelled trouble. When Josiah had rescued her from Rusty Kuntz, she'd seen his angry side and it was no joy ride. Matt might have to dodge Josiah's angry fists if Josiah thought he needed to protect her. But Matt was a hothead too, and they'd go at it. She didn't want to cause a rift in the brothers' relationship. Also, Matt was becoming a good hand. He had natural talent with the animals and loved the outdoors. If Josiah was grooming Matt to take over for him, she didn't want to push the kid away.

"There's no need for that. I've already taken care of it," she said in a business-like tone.

"What happened, Jess? I can't have Matt here if he's going to get into trouble. I don't want him hassling you."

Jessie sighed, she had to tell him the truth even if it was embarrassing. "It was my fault. I started it. You can't blame Matt."

"He's responsible for his actions. I'm not holding you accountable for those. Did he hit you?"

"God, no." Hit on her was more accurate. "I said I started it. I'll tell you, but I don't want you to take any further action against Matt. Promise me."

"Fine," he grumbled.

"Not good enough, Josiah. Say the words."

"I promise I won't touch Matt. Satisfied? Now Jessie, my dear, ante up."

"Matt worked in the barn and I went out to find you. He had dressed in a plaid shirt and jeans. You have a shirt like it. He must have snatched it. He wasn't wearing a hat. That should have been my clue; but as it was, I thought he was you." She bit her lip.

"You wanted to punch me in the face?" he asked.

She laughed then sighed again. "No, of course not. He leaned into one stall. I thought he was you so I pinched his backside." Matt and Josiah were the similar height and coloring. Matt's right cheek had a dimple when he grinned. Josiah had a fuller beard, and he wore a brown hat most of the time around the ranch. As Matt leaned into the stall, the denim pulled tight over his perfect rear. She'd wanted to touch it, so she did.

"He wasn't me so you punched him?" Josiah's tone turned jovial. He must've liked the fact she tried to grab him. "Or did you hurt him, and he said something?"

"He liked it a little too much so I punched him. I took care of it. You don't have to worry. He won't say anything like it again." She clenched her eyes shut and rubbed her chin. Poor Matt, he was going to get it.

That morning, Matt had turned around as startled as she but he'd been quick to recover. He grinned and stepped towards her. She should have stepped away and apologized but her brain stalled, not comprehending how alike the brothers were.

Dressed in a short dress with pumps and a light-weight jacket, she'd been ready for her first business meeting. Matt had made her feel cheap.

"Jessie," Josiah said his tone soft but firm.

"He said 'Honey, that's a nice set of legs. What time do they open?'" There was silence on the other end. Jessie imagined him turning bright red with fury. Then she thought he might bite his knuckles trying not to laugh. It infuriated her, and she'd decked Matt. It must have hurt like hell, because he'd stayed down on his butt where she knocked him, one hand covering his eye, his mouth wide open.

"Don't you ever talk like that to me again unless you want to sing soprano." She'd turned and walked out, got in her truck and left to pick up Desire.

CHAPTER 26

Jessie

DESIRE'S OLD STRIPPING GAL-PAL, Emma Royds, wished to meet in a dive they used to frequent. Even at one o'clock in the afternoon, the sketchy location gave Jessie the heebie-jeebies. The rundown building sat across from a pay-by-the-hour motel. The neon in the windows gave more light than the grimy bulbs overhead, and square tables had chipped butcher-block Formica with wobbly legs. Metal chair pads sported duct tape attempting repairs, but some still leaked yellow stuffing. Jessie's feet stuck to the floor as she walked and she tried not to guess when the last time it'd seen a mop.

The bar might have been remodeled in the sixties but she'd made that assumption based on the dark wood paneling caging them in. The jukebox in the corner crooned twangy country music. One old TV hung above the bar. Three scruffy men sat watching a game and drinking. The bartender was a woman that, at first glance, appeared twenty-five with a blond ponytail and big perky chest under the low, tight pink shirt. Staring longer, crow's feet appeared under the heavy makeup.

"I might know that woman," Desire said. She pushed up and moseyed to the bar. The women exchanged words and smiles then Desire came back with two tumblers filled with amber liquor. It smelled horrible. Who knew colored rubbing alcohol was the house special? Jessie tasted it with the tip of her tongue. It burned. She was wrong, it was gasoline.

An older woman opened the door, wearing a red dress, hat and shiny stiletto heels. Jessie sighed as the door closed cutting off the fresh air and sunlight. The woman pushed her dark rimmed glasses up her nose and righted her hat. Caked foundation, penciled eyebrows and fire engine red lips were distracting but the smile was genuine. This was one of the famed Cork and Screw dancing girls. Desire and this businesswoman used to strip together.

Maybe she'd known Grandma too.

"Ah, Desire, my friend. It's been too long." Emma embraced Desire. The woman's strong floral perfume could have given B.J. a run for his money.

"This is my Jessie," prided Desire. "This is Emma Royds. She owns the Goose & Gander."

As the women shook hands, Emma shrugged. "You know what they say—what's good for the goose is good for the gander." Emma winked and tilted her head studying Jessie's face. "My dear child, you are the spittin' image of Undine." Her gaze dropped lower. "Yes siree, you're your grandma's kin. Ever thought of dancing?" She arched penciled brows.

Jessie's eyes widened, and she felt her face heat. She fingered the tumbler of gasoline.

"Emma, she designs intimate apparel. Some of them from Undine's drawings," Desire stated coming to Jessie's rescue.

The bartender gave Emma a glass of matching amber liquid. The women raised their glasses. "To friends," Desire toasted.

"Both old and new," Emma said, her tone wistful. She turned to Desire, "Do you remember the excursion on the party barge?"

"Ah, yes." Desire smiled, glancing into the whiskey. "There was dinner and dancing. We were entertained, not the other way around." She chuckled.

"Oh, we had fun," Emma reminisced. "The night ended too soon."

"And in tragedy for one woman. None of us knew what happened to the girl until later." Desire lifted the glass to her lips. Her pink lipstick stained the tumbler.

Emma frowned. "We thought the poor girl did a swan dive into the lake to end her life of ill repute. But that wasn't the case." She paused, and the women shared a look.

Jessie's gaze bounced from one woman to the other. Gripping the table's edge she leaned forward. "What happened to her?"

Desire moved her hand as if she shooed away a fly. "She had a lover that wanted her exclusively. They eloped."

"The real tragedy was Jim Dimwitty's decline in business and the extra

150

hours we had to put in to fill her place. I hated her after that." Emma took a long swallow then sighed again. "All those wasted tears."

"How about we look at some fancy drawers?" Desire asked. She rubbed her hands together and tilted her head. The older woman took the lead with the business and the Double D's history while Jessie opened the case and Emma touched everything.

Emma took a gown, turned it inside out and examined the seam stitching. Every touch and critique made Jessie feel violated. Emma was picky and knew her stuff.

"Unfortunately, my clientele will not pay premium prices. They're cheap. I'm sorry, my girl. You make beautiful things. May I order for my personal wardrobe?"

Emma ordered over three hundred dollars' worth of items. Jessie measured the woman and made notes. It was hard to sit still while the Cork and Screw dancing girls reunited. She sent another joyful update to Josiah. When she couldn't stand it any longer, Jessie slipped out to call Josiah but frowned when he didn't answer. She returned to the table, sulking while she emptied a second glass.

Josiah

Josiah took Cowboy to the back-country. The engine could spook the cattle so he opted to make repairs. The morning heat made a sweat breakout. A windmill water pump wasn't functioning as it should and it was a necessary watering hole for the Longhorn. The herd would move his way soon and it was his job to get it running. He parked the ATV and took off his shirt.

After examining the rusty mechanism, he tinkered with parts trying to unfreeze the metal. There weren't any bees in the gearbox. His upbringing and college education hadn't helped him fix the pump. Hopefully, they'd help him figure out how to save the Double D.

The sound of hooves on dirt brought his attention to the distance. Brad Davidson rode toward him, like a cowboy out of the Wild West. His Stetson shadowed his sharp eyes. He wore a red plaid shirt and jeans and rode with authority. He dismounted, walked over and bent to inspect the work. Brad said nothing as he scanned the metal.

Josiah hadn't expected to see him. "What's up, Brad?"

"Have you heard from Jessie?" Brad took off his hat and finger combed his hair.

"She's texted me a time or two." Josiah raised his hand to shield his eyes from the sun.

"How's it going?"

"Good." Josiah opened a cooler, twisted the lid off a water bottle and downed it. He offered one to Brad who waved it off. There was a reason for this visit. Jessie's father and Johnson were in the same book club; Johnson might have let something slip. Or Kuntz got out of jail. Josiah coughed and wiped his chin.

"Do you know what she's doing in Austin?" Brad asked fingering the brim of his hat.

"She and Desire are peddling clothing." He didn't know the details but the amount of time she spent locked away had him curious. She'd never shown him any of the completed work and when he asked to see them she shook her head and blushed.

"Son, we've got to talk."

That didn't sound good. Josiah swallowed, heaviness clung to his gut. "You know more about the trip." Josiah put his hands on his hips waiting.

"Yes and you need to hear what she's up to." Brad sat his hat back on his head. He launched into a story describing the sewing room, neglecting to mention the books. Jessie found patterns from her grandmother's time as an exotic dancer. Classy, yet sexy, lingerie pieces had stoked Jessie's curiosity. "She has talent for sewing, like Mom did," he said.

"Wait, you're telling me Jessie is making…"

"Negligees, bras, panties, you name it, she's made it." Brad's face blushed speaking of his little girl's handy-work.

"Huh. I didn't know." A slow smile found a way to Josiah's lips. The knowledge affected him in other ways but it was best to not let Brad see. He cleared his throat. Sawyer had been right. Jessie was a little vixen. "Why are you telling me?"

Brad sighed and stared at his boots. "She's good. Desire called to let me know they have orders from two boutiques. The owners love the quality of her work. This is just the beginning, they'll be more orders but Jessie's already worried about finding the funds. Desire suggested asking around to get a silent partner to help a startup business." Brad straightened and caught his gaze. "I'm asking you for help. I know you were a business major. Any ideas?"

"How much money are we talking?" inquired Josiah.

"I don't rightly know." Brad shrugged.

"I'll try to help. Someone will invest in her dream." Josiah thought he knew everything about Jessie Davidson but that wasn't true. This new knowledge excited him.

Jessie

Dee Flowers owned a Boutique in Round Rock, a suburb of Austin, called Britches and Hose. The high-end clothing and intimate apparel store was the kind of store Jessie had dreamed of having her merchandise sell in.

"Why did Dee want to meet us here instead of her store?" asked Jessie.

Desire glanced around the room of the old stagecoach inn turned microbrewery then leaned forward. "I believe she has a crush on the owner. She kept sighing when mentioning his name or this place."

The S'Wheat Spot brewed its own collection of ales while boasting to be the home of paranormal activity. The main room had a large stone fireplace with a rough-hewn mantel. Antique lanterns littered the mantle. The furniture was quaint but comfortable.

"Welcome to the S'Wheat Spot. We hope you enjoy your visit." A short-haired young woman with glasses led them to a small table near the stone fireplace where they could watch the door. The girl had round owl eyes and a short beak-like nose. She handed Desire a list of their house brews. "My favorite is the Zombie Six Shooter, but the bestseller is the Headless Woman."

"I don't want to end up headless," Desire whispered wiggling her eyebrows. Jessie tried to stymie a giggle because the older woman wasn't referring to the loss of her noggin, she alluded to certain men's body parts.

A middle-aged woman entered the pub and inquired with the hostess. Dee Flowers, the last client for the night, had short, wavy hair and wore stylish yet casual clothes. She reached for Jessie's hand and held it in greeting. "It's a pleasure to meet you both. I've got to tell you I'm excited to see your selection." She took Jessie's hand and squeezed. "I hope you don't mind, but I'm starving. Have you ever been here?" Dee asked glancing around.

"No," Desire said, her eyelids heavy. A blossom wilting, she hid a yawn behind her hand.

Dee raised her hand and a skinny teenage girl with a blinding white smile approached with coffee. She sipped from the mug, glancing across the room. "Oh, I'll be right back. You gals are in for a treat," she breathed out in a rush. She stood, smoothing her wrinkle-free shirt and hurried away.

The next moment, the owner sat beside them. "Dee says you've never heard about us. I'm Gooden Small. I bought this building fifteen years ago." The short muscular man spoke with a spooky campfire voice. "I'd heard rumors it was haunted, but I didn't believe it. I thought I could use the lore to capitalize on business and pay homage to the ghosts by naming a few ales after them." He shrugged and winked at Desire.

The Fortuna women ordered then listened to Gooden recall stories of various employees. Incidents had involved the basement where a temporary jail used to be. Several people reported being touched. "They said it felt like icy fingers. There are cool spots and the lights sometimes turn on and off on their own."

"We have twelve ghosts. There is a pair of young children. They're pranksters. Then the headless lady. A woman died giving birth to a baby. The child died too." He lowered his voice and leaned forward. "When there's a full moon people hear a baby crying and a woman sobbing. There's a cowboy ghost. No one knows his story but sometimes he appears in this room." Gooden's gaze shifted from their table to the mantle.

Jessie giggled, pleased the owner took the time to entertain his patrons. Desire straightened in her seat and peered around the room.

"What brings you ladies to town?" Gooden asked.

"We have business to discuss," Dee replied. Her cheeks turned a pretty shade of pink.

Gooden's brows rose, and he blushed. "Well, I'll leave you to it." Gooden went to schmooze with other patrons but didn't stray too far.

Dee inquired about the Double D intimate apparel line. Jessie opened the tote and Dee took her time pulling out and examining items. She held a red one high enough it caught Gooden's eye, acting like a red flag catching a bull's attention.

"You made this by hand?" Dee sounded hopeful.

"Yes, Ma'am. The lace is handmade, but I didn't make it."

Dee nodded and turned the garment inside out inspecting the seams. "It's beautiful work. I'd like to try Double D in the store. Can you send me samples?"

"I can do better than that. You may select a few of these if you'd like."

Dee grinned and placed an order. Jessie had another check before the evening ended.

Jessie

As soon as they returned to the hotel, Desire kicked off her shoes, collapsed onto the bed and pulled out a romance novel. Jessie closed the bathroom door to have privacy and called Josiah. It rang and rang. She bit her lip, at the last second he picked up. She blew out a relieved breath.

"Hey, Jess."

"Josiah," she paused tears stinging her eyes. The sound of his voice made her heart ache. What was happening between them? After a few weeks of living in the same home, she'd become used to his presence. She wasn't lonely anymore. Not until she'd left him.

"Are you okay, Darlin'?"

Her breath hitched at the endearment. "Desire had a bunch of ideas for the new business. She's got a great mind for it," tumbled out as one long word.

Somehow he'd understood her. "She's had the salon for thirty plus years," he reminded.

Jessie took a deep breath and tried to focus on business. "She might have found a silent investor for the Double D. I don't want to get my hopes up but that's what the clothing line needs to start with a firm foundation." She tried to tone down the excitement in her voice, because after all, it wasn't a done deal yet.

"I," Josiah paused and cleared his throat, "I've got good news too. I spoke with Miles Long, the farmer? He's interested in renting your property to grow feed grain."

"How would he pay us? Product or money?" Jessie asked.

"Maybe both. I'm investigating it. Your father won't mind. I've already asked him. Also, Matt and Gabe will work on Saturdays for the next month. Matt will alternate weekdays with the Double D and the Big Deal. I hope you don't mind."

"We can't afford them now," Jessie said with a sigh.

"I'll pay them out of my check. I'm the one who hired them," Josiah stated.

Jessie squabbled with him about paying his brothers. She brushed her teeth listening to his tale about how he fixed the water pump.

She exited the bathroom and claimed her spot on the starched white sheets. Jessie would rather cuddle with Josiah on the sofa. It had happened twice since he moved to the property, but she remembered the warmth of his body and his touch. They didn't kiss, he only held her, but it'd been enough to make her eager for more.

"I miss you," Jessie admitted to him. Silence. "Hello? Josiah?" Still silent.

"You just made that cowboy speechless," Desire murmured.

"Are you all right?" Jessie asked.

"Yeah, Jess. I'm fine." His voice cracked, "I miss you too. Dream of me."

He didn't have to worry. Josiah had been starring in her dreams since he'd sneaked into her room acting out *The Visitation*. She needed to stop reading Grandma's romance novels because she and Josiah became the hero and heroine almost every night. She smiled as she pulled the covers over her body while envisioning Josiah wearing angel wings.

CHAPTER 27

Jessie

JESSIE'S FINGERS CLUTCHED THE STEERING wheel on the drive to the restaurant, Making Waves. She'd already packed and checked out of the motel, now she had to meet with big-wig potential clients. Her stomach ached with worry about meeting this powerful couple.

Cheri Robbins, a college roommate of Jessie's, had married into one of the founding families of the company. She'd sent her friend two gowns with matching panties and heard nothing but praise from her friend. When Cheri mentioned the owner of the Double D custom-made intimate apparel company would be coming to Austin, Cheri's relative had insisted on an appointment with Jessie.

According to Jessie's clients, the restaurant had fabulous food with a panoramic water view, located on the northern shore of Lake Austin, a lake created by the Tom Miller Dam.

"Tom Miller. Wasn't that a band?" Desire asked Jessie as they entered the building.

"You're thinking of Steve Miller."

"No, that's not right either." Desire paused, her forehead crinkled in thought. "It's Glenn Miller. He had a big band."

A hostess led them to the large back deck. The overcast sky and the air smelling like rain did little to dampen the peacefulness of the view. The breeze fluttered their hair and skirts. Jessie checked to make sure her hair stayed in the clip. She bit her lip and glanced around.

Desire perused the menu boasting an extensive seafood selection. "I wonder how the crab cakes are. I hear they're catching," she said with an evil grin.

Jessie glanced up, recognizing Randy and Fonda Peters as they walked towards the table. She silently thanked Cheri for sending a link to the Peters, Beaver, and Associates website. The couple's faces matched their likenesses from the company page. They were a cute pair in their forties, in business suits showing off style as well as their trim figures. Petite and busty, Fonda Peters clung to her husband's hand. Randy Peters stood six foot but didn't have much hair.

They wanted to see the goods before they presented the Double D to their partners. It seemed handmade underwear was something treasured by the board.

"Thank you for taking the time to meet with us today," Desire greeted the owners when words failed to spring forth from Jessie's mouth.

Jessie's lips tugged into a lopsided smile. She stared at her simple white blouse, khaki skirt, and dressy brown boots. An overdressed cowgirl next to such classy people, she wiped sweaty palms on her skirt.

They ordered, and the waiter delivered the drinks.

Finding her courage, Jessie opened the tote. She explained the materials and stitching. Fonda gasped and reached for the beautiful skimpy pieces of clothing. She fondled them with excitement. "Randy," she said in a husky whisper. "I'll wear these for you."

Randy shifted in his seat and smiled seductively. "You don't need to wear anything to please me."

Fonda tittered and blushed. She fished in her black Hermès purse, pulled out a phone and took a few pictures. "I've got to show these to Lillian. She'll love them." The reply was instant. Fonda appeared pleased and leaned back. "See. She wants to see the panties and sample them if possible."

Desire's brows raised and the Fortuna women shared a look and a smile. It appeared the Peters and Beaver ladies wanted to buy the handmade garments for themselves. Jessie nodded and put her hand on her chest. Her thumping heart tried to hammer its way out. It would be great to acquire clients who wanted quality merchandise and wouldn't balk at the price.

The food arrived, and they ate. Fonda asked Jessie how she'd thought of Double D Intimates. With a smile, she and Desire reminisced about her grandmother. Fonda seemed enamored with the Davidson's love story and Undine's love of romance novels. After dinner, Fonda whispered in her husband's ear. He gave a nod.

"Peters, Beaver & Associates is having a board meeting here in the conference room at the top of the hour," Randy informed with a tap to his watch. Fonda nodded as she typed a text on her phone. "We'll get you a few orders. Would you mind sticking around until then?"

Again Jessie and Desire shared a smile. "That would be great, Mr. Peters. We'll be happy to wait."

The Peters excused themselves to prepare for the meeting. Jessie sent a thank you text to Cheri. Desire and Jessie retired to the truck to sit in the air conditioning and contemplate their good fortune. The women arranged the gowns, panties and teddies by size. They didn't have price tags, only size and care labels.

"This will deplete the stock, but gaining a base clientele will be worth it." Jessie glanced at the in-dash clock. Fifteen minutes until the meeting. Enough time to call Josiah.

Josiah

Josiah sat in Warren Teed's office, his knee bouncing up and down, as he waited for the man to read a document. The lawyer inspected him over his black-rimmed reading glasses. "Are you sure about this, Mr. Barnes?"

Mr. Barnes. Josiah swallowed a laugh and cleared his throat. "Yes, sir."

"This is a nice chunk of change to throw into a venture of..." Warren paused, removed his glasses and rubbed the bridge of his nose. "Uncertainty. You're rolling the dice here, son."

Josiah frowned, at the man's assumption he'd be throwing money away. Was he calling Jessie a failure? He shifted his weight and felt his face warm.

"I'm not saying it's a bad business," Warren placated, "but there are other ways you could use the money. A nest egg or a honeymoon for starters."

Honeymoon? He hadn't thought of funding it, only getting naked with Jessie. The room seemed stifling.

"There's more. This isn't all of it." Josiah glanced at his good boots. They pinched his toes. He'd put on his church duds to make a good impression but he still felt like a kid. "I've got investments."

"Don and Undine would be proud of you," Warren said as he laid the document on the desk. "I'm sure they're looking down and smiling. I know for a fact, Brad appreciates your interest in his daughter." He coughed and cleared his throat. "I mean, the business." Warren grinned and spun the paper so Josiah could read it. He opened the desk drawer and pulled out a fancy ink pen, offering it to Josiah.

Josiah took the pen and scooted forward on his seat. The legal jargon made his head spin; that was why he'd made the appointment with Warren. He studied the blank line asking for his signature. Josiah signed and initialed until his hand cramped then walked out of the lawyer's office with his head raised high. Everything in the manila envelope was legit.

Josiah nodded at people and waved to Officer Ben Moore as he pulled into a parking spot across the street. Ben gave a friendly salute then disappeared inside the Pink Taco. Josiah grabbed his stomach when it grumbled. *Yeah, Ben's got the right idea but lunch will have to wait.* He continued on his mission, attempts to ignore the tantalizing smells wafting out the front door failed.

A blast of cold air hit him as he pulled open the bank door. This time he didn't pause at the counter to fill out a deposit slip, instead striding straight to the loan officer's door and peered inside. Stephanie Malone had a handset pressed to her ear but motioned for him to have a seat outside the door. Excitement or nerves? He didn't know, but it felt as if he sat he'd spring right up. He carved a path on the tan marble floor while holding the envelope with a death grip.

"Hi, Josiah," a feminine voice greeted.

He continued to the teller counter where Mona Little stood grinning. "Hello, Mona. You look pretty."

She blushed and glanced away. "Thanks."

"Seems busy in here." He peered around the building. All the tellers were engaged, except Mona.

"It comes in waves." Mona shrugged. "I've got the drive-thru today." She leaned forward taking in his fancy attire. With a raised brow she asked, "You got a date?"

"Uh, kind of." Noting the frown on her face, Josiah clarified, "A business meeting." He resisted the urge to tug on his collar and loosen his tie. Instead, he scratched the back of his head. The last thing he needed was one of Jessie's friends telling her he'd gone on a date.

"Mr. Barnes?" Stephanie called from behind them.

Josiah smirked. "I'm never going to get used to that."

He followed Stephanie into the small office and handed her the envelope. Stephanie slid the documents out and examined them. She was Gimme Malone's older sister. Sweat broke out. He bumped one leg up and down. If she'd heard of the scuffle he'd had with Gimme, maybe she wouldn't hold it against him. She glanced at him, then smiled. "Everything seems in order." She stuck out her hand and shook his. "It's a pleasure doing business with you. Wait here a minute while I get the account number ready."

Josiah blew out a long breath and relaxed into the stiff chair. That went easier than expected. Of course, the bank wanted money, personal beef aside. And Stephanie had been more than accommodating the first time he'd been in her office to explain what he wanted to do for the Double D clothing line.

Ten minutes later he walked out of the air-conditioned bank into the warm Texas afternoon. His stomach protested louder but this time, he planned to satisfy the hunger. A small brass bell rang as he pulled open the door to the Pink Taco. Brad glanced up from a menu and motioned him over. He slid into the booth as Clint Torres handed a sweet tea to Brad.

"What can I get you, Señor Barnes?" Clint asked. "Or are you getting the regular?"

Josiah chuckled and rubbed his chin. He loved the chimichanga, but he felt exhilarated and wanted to celebrate. "I'll have a steak fajita and sweet tea, please."

Clint smiled and nodded. "A good choice. And for you, Señor Davidson?"

"Make it two."

Clint disappeared from view to return moments later with Josiah's drink. Josiah took a long gulp of tea and leaned back. He tried to wipe the smile off his face as he glanced around the restaurant. The noise seemed minimum as most of the lunch rush had passed.

Brad's mustache twitched, and he shifted the paper placemat around three times before asking, "How'd it go?"

"Well..." Josiah leaned forward pretending to examine the fork. "I had some luck." He ended the older man's torture, setting the envelope on the table, then pushed it towards him.

Brad pulled out the items one by one. Josiah watched the man's gaze roam the official document. Brad's eyebrows lifted in unison as he whistled. "Ten thousand dollars? Wow." He stuffed the envelope again and set it aside. Brad's gaze bored into his. "Who's helping my daughter, son?"

Josiah swallowed and straightened. He suspected Brad knew. He cleared his throat and opened his mouth to speak but his phone rang saving him. "It's Jessie." Josiah smirked at her father's grin and took the call.

"Josiah?" Jessie's happy squeal sounded like music to his ears. He stifled a sigh and kept glancing sideways to see Brad listening to every word. A few moments later, when the sizzling food arrived, Josiah ended the call.

Jessie had a big meeting in minutes. Josiah envisioned her sucking in her bottom lip. Standing in front of a group of successful business owners, peddling a bunch of lingerie was like the only cow in a field of bulls during mating season. He'd admired her gumption. On the way to the ranch he would call her back.

Now it was time to celebrate the successful business transaction. Satisfaction had little to do with the food in his belly. He took another bite of the savory fajita. He was halfway done before he noted Brad had hardly touched his food. The wrinkled brow on Brad's forehead matched his frowning lips. Josiah swallowed the now tasteless food.

"Son, we've got a problem," Brad said in a thick voice. His gaze held Josiah's.

Josiah felt as if he'd been sucker-punched. Dread settled in his gut leaving him cold. He tried to breathe but found oxygen lacking. His heart beat so fast he thought it might explode. He swallowed then sighed. "What now?"

"We knew this day would come." Brad released a long breath and pulled his tea closer, fingering the cool condensation on the side. "They released Rusty Kuntz from jail."

CHAPTER 28

Jessie

JESSIE WRUNG HER HANDS. SHE and Desire stood outside the conference room. Fonda blocked the way in and asked, "Jessie, would you mind if I showcased your items?" With a beguiling smile, she pleaded, "Please. I'll get you orders, I promise."

Jessie couldn't help but giggle at her enthusiasm. "Okay. Let's see what you got."

With a stiff nod Fonda squared her shoulders before she turned and disappeared into the room with the tote full of goodies. Eager eyes gazed fascinated as Fonda Peters unzipped the tote. "Wait 'til y'all see what I have here. You'll want to caress the material and order one in every color."

Desire clapped her hands together with excitement. "Honey, your friend Cheri came through. I'm optimistic about this meeting."

Jessie nodded as she grinned. The excitement threatened to swallow her. She wiped damp hands on her shirt.

"I'm going to step outside for some fresh air." Jessie headed toward the front entrance. Pushing the door open she took a deep breath to steady her nerves. She wanted to run around squealing her excitement but instead, she closed her eyes trying to relax. She rolled her shoulders and minutes ticked away. Faint tapping made her jump. Desire, standing with Fonda, motioned from behind the closed glass entry door. She inhaled deeply and opened the door.

Fonda jabbered away regarding the various women in the conference room, their tastes, and styles. She talked fast and her words blurred together, making it hard to decipher.

Stepping into the quiet room, ten pairs of eyes stared awed in her direction as if she held the answer to their prayers. She smiled timidly then bit her lip.

"I'm sorry Jessie, but I'm afraid we all want something. I want this jade negligée. Randy, get my cash. Oh, Jessie dear, I'd like to order a set like those over there," Fonda pointed to an exquisite underwire bra and thong set. "But can I get it in red lace?" She leaned in and spoke as if to tell a secret but the whole room heard, "Randy loves lace. It turns him on."

Desire laughed and elbowed Randy. "Good choice." Randy impishly grinned, rubbing the back of his head.

Jessie took the tablet and recorded their wishes and measurements. Each woman chose a handmade piece. Two men ordered something as well. Randy wanted a matching thong and bra in lacy red. With the tailor's tape, Desire measured the men paying particular attention to their nether regions. She wanted to "get it right" but Jessie suspected she wanted to cop a feel.

Jessie

Jessie sipped the latte she'd bought for the ride home. The rain pelted the window at a steady rate keeping the windshield wipers busy. It'd been a harrowing few days. Both she and Desire were road weary and saddle sore. A soft snort came from Desire as she rubbed her face. The older woman had fallen asleep as soon as they hit the highway. A smile teased Jessie's lips when Desire snored.

She'd enjoyed her time spent with Desire and loved the feisty lady. With the insight and help Desire had given Jessie they'd wrangled enough orders to keep her in the sewing room for weeks. Desire had earned her nap.

Lightning flashed, and Jessie jumped when it thundered. The downpour made it hard to see. With hands clamped to the wheel, she slowed the truck. The weatherman had forecast rain all day, but she hadn't expected it to be this hard. She bit her lip worrying about the river and the herd. She didn't want to lose any more cattle because of rising waters.

Jessie called Josiah when she stopped for gas. Visualizing his sparkling blue eyes eased her nerves. Turning on the radio, the soft music helped carve away the miles.

After dinner, Desire insisted they stop at an adult bookstore along the highway. "You stay here, dear. I won't be long," Desire said as she slid out of the truck. She stalked to the store, a tigress entering a lion's den.

Moments later, out came Desire with a smile and a medium-sized plastic bag. Jessie glanced at the bag. "Just something for my girl. You've been working hard. I thought you could use a little time with some manly parts."

"It's chocolate." Jessie giggled.

"Too bad they aren't all like that." The older woman buckled the seatbelt. "Oh, Pat Downe, the owner, is interested in placing some of your items in his store."

While Jessie appreciated Desire's enthusiasm, the adult bookstore and toy shop wasn't the place she wanted to represent her company. She would not make crotchless panties just because of a friend of Desire's.

"His other store, dear. Do you know Gogh-Downe? Patrick is co-owner."

"Gogh-Downe, the boutique in Nockerville?" Jessie couldn't afford to shop there. The jeans were over two hundred dollars a pair. "Desire, you're the best."

"I am." Desire grinned big.

Josiah

Josiah bolted out of the leather sofa, dropping the romance novel onto the table. He glanced out the picture window into the dark stormy night. He could've sworn a light scrolled across the room, signaling Jessie's arrival. Twice he'd already jumped up, losing his page, hoping she'd be home. Both times he'd been disappointed. He hurried to the window and peered at the night sky. The storm had gone from bad to worse.

The book had been an excellent distraction, with great characters, and had kept him engaged most of the evening. Josiah might want to try a few things on Jessie. He yawned and stretched.

A faint sound in the kitchen startled him. Jogging into the room he found a lone piece of luggage. He glanced around then peered out at the dark vehicle. His thumping heart drowned out the pelting rain.

"Josiah," Jessie purred.

Twisting away from the door, Josiah reached for her and pulled her into his arms. The scent of strawberries hung in the air. Moisture seeped through his clothes. "Hey Jess, I'm sorry I didn't help you. I was reading."

Jessie pushed away and glanced at him. Her hair sparkled with droplets of water. Her gaze searched his face and her lips tipped upward. "That good of a book? Or were you at the sexy parts?"

His face heated, and he laughed. "Both."

Jessie's arm stuck out from her body, away from him. In her hand, she held a white stick with a dark lollipop on the end. The thing had lost its shape. "Oh it's a little something, used to be a big something, that Desire bought me." She giggled and stuck it back in her mouth. She closed her eyes and hummed her pleasure. "Mm."

Josiah swallowed, watching her suck on the stick. Her breath smelled like chocolate. The little blue words on the side of the stick caught his eye, "Penis pop?"

Jessie laughed and pulled it out again. There wasn't much left on the stick. On the corner of her mouth a smudge of chocolate remained. God, he wanted to lick the spot. He led her into the living room and they relaxed on the sofa.

"Did you know Desire knows the owner of the adult bookstore?" Jessie asked.

"No, I didn't but, let's say, I'm not surprised." Josiah drank her in, the crinkles at the corners of her eyes as she smiled, the uneven part, and water droplets on her chest. It was nice to hear her exploits and the ornery, old woman's antics but it was even better to have her home. He kept his hands clamped to his thighs so he wouldn't pull her into his arms. Again.

"She ordered me to stop there then disappeared into the building." Jessie gave a one shoulder shrug. "I thought she wanted something naughty, you know how she is, anyway she comes out wearing a big smile."

"And her clothes, right?" Josiah hissed at the thought of a naked Desire.

She reached out and swatted him. "Of course." Jessie laughed. "She handed me the chocolate for working so hard and told me she thought I could use quality time with some manly parts."

Josiah shifted in his seat debating if he should mention his parts were available if she wanted something more to nibble on.

"She spoke to the owner, Pat Downe, about selling my items." His mouth hung open. She blinked wide eyes then squeaked, "Oh!" and put a hand to her hair and pulled a piece straight. "Not at the adult store." She chuckled nervously. "He co-owns a boutique in Nockerville called Gogh Downe. It's high-end. I can't afford to shop there but it's a beautiful store and a great opportunity."

The smile that lit Jessie's face came from her heart. He grinned too, knowing she'd be walking on clouds once Desire and Brad broke the news about the silent investor. She leaned back and closed her eyes. Even though she relaxed, the smile stayed glued to her face. He gazed, mesmerized by her delicate features, the straight slope of her nose, the plumpness of her lips. Her tongue darted out, licking the top lip. Josiah's body became an inferno of desire; he wanted to strip off his clothes and even then he'd spontaneously combust before he could touch her. She caught him staring at her lips—at least it wasn't her boobs. Her gaze held his for a moment, dropping to his smirking lips, then darted back to his eyes. Her cheeks bloomed deep pink, and she gazed at her hands folded in her lap, mumbling something he didn't understand.

"What was that?" he asked.

"I missed you." Jessie kept her gaze focused on her hands while chewing on her lip.

Josiah's heart froze for a micro-second then took off like it'd been turbo charged. This small admittance gave him hope she cared for him. Breathing became hard, and he dared not move or speak. Moisture gathered in his eyes, he closed them to stave off the tears. Damn, he was getting emotional in his old age. When he opened his eyes again, her face had turned upwards wearing a frown, inspecting his while she wrung her hands. He paused to get his emotions in order so his voice wouldn't crack.

Josiah cleared his throat. "I missed you too, Jessie." He reached out and caressed her cheek. Leaning close, his voice lowered. "I worried about you driving in this weather. I'm glad you're home." His fingers touched her thigh, tracing the seam on her jeans.

Jessie pushed his hand away and jumped up, her chest heaving. Her gaze bounced around the room as if she might bolt. Josiah scrubbed his face. He had no intention of scaring her but, dammit, it had happened again. Two steps forward, one step back. He sighed and relaxed onto the sofa.

Jessie honed in on the romance novel on the table. *"The Cowboy's First Love,"* she whispered then picked it up. She walked around the coffee table reading the back blurb. He'd wanted to read it ever since his encounter with Gimme Malone. He swallowed as she opened to the place he'd saved. She glanced at him wide-eyed and smiled.

"Oh, Josiah, no wonder you didn't hear my truck." She read, *"'His fingers skimmed the outside of her breasts, causing her to moan and squirm. His gaze held hers as he leaned in and took a pebbled nipple with his lips. He tortured her with his teeth and tongue watching her eyes fill with longing. Her hands, deep in his thick mane, held his head in place. He bit harder and she cried out, 'Yes!'"* Jessie's voice had turned husky. She closed the book, her face a pretty shade of pink again.

He wished he could see her thoughts. Wearing a funny expression, Jessie stared at his lips again. The tip of her tongue found the chocolate at the corner of her mouth. He held his breath as the chocolate disappeared. He forced himself to stay seated.

Jessie swallowed glancing at the book. She grinned and tossed it to him. He snatched it out of the air. He righted the bookmark but when he glanced up, she'd fled the room.

CHAPTER 29

Jessie

"THAT'S AWESOME!" JESSIE SQUEALED. SHE squeezed her eyes shut and danced a jig of happiness.

On the other end of the phone line, Desire chuckled. "I'm glad you approve. Bunny Hopkins' oldest daughter is getting married, and they wanted to rent the space for a luncheon bridal shower, but I offered Holden fifty dollars more than usual to get the time slot. That guaranteed the banquet hall for us and ruled out the Hopkins."

It hurt to smile. "Thanks for thinking ahead. Maybe I can make something for the Hopkins girl."

"Dear, that's why I'm calling. When Bunny called me trying to negotiate, I suggested that her daughter might earn a skimpy boutique item for her honeymoon. Now you have a model for the fashion show. She's tall and slender and would make a great exotic dancer."

Jessie covered her nose and mouth to muffle a snort of laughter.

Pounding on the front door startled Jessie. "Somebody's here. You didn't send Bunny's girl over did you?"

"No, Dear, I hope it's your hunk of a cowboy looking to get saddle sore."

Jessie pulled the cord tight as she leaned to see the front door. She had a straight shot from the kitchen. She could make out the backside of a man in cowboy hat, tight jeans, and boots. "It's not Josiah."

"Ah, that's a shame." Desire sighed.

"It might be B.J."

"That one's so hot he could fry my bacon." Desire cackled. "I'd better let you go see what the young man wants."

Jessie hung the phone and peered around the corner inspecting the profile of the man in the sidelight. He rang the bell, and she sucked in a deep breath. *What the hell did B.J. want now?*

She sighed and swung the door wide.

"Hi, Jessie, I came for my weekly dose of romance." B.J. waggled his eyebrows, leaning toward her with a cocky grin.

Frowning, she crossed her arms and didn't move. "I told you I'd bring the books to Hammered."

"Listen, Jessie, you're not keeping up with the demand." B.J. spread his hands in a placating manner. "Holden's stock is low, and he threatened to never let me eat there again if I didn't work things out with you. You don't want Fortuna to take up arms, do you? They need their fix of paperback love."

Her father had mentioned grumblings coming from the men in his book club. New books equaled ambrosia and happy townsfolk. She sighed.

"Fine. Come on inside." She didn't want all hell to break out in Fortuna as the men revolted. Many unsatisfied wives and girlfriends would call demanding more books.

B.J. followed her upstairs to the novel hoard. Books still lined three walls floor to ceiling. The skylight cast an eerie glow reflecting the spine colors like a mosaic. She'd cleared a pathway through the center. The room wasn't a stuffed closet anymore. The spaced opened diluting the potency of B.J. cologne.

She threw a quick glance to the wall near the closet where she'd pinned a few of her grandmother's sketches. Luckily, she'd stowed all finished lingerie pieces downstairs in the office closet. A few swatches of cloth and lace remained for curious eyes.

Waiting beside the door were four empty plastic totes. B.J. took one and the stepladder. Climbing a few steps, he reached for, then handed, her books and she filled the bottom. They worked in tandem filling half the tote before he said, "I've got a good view, but it could be better. Do you mind taking a step closer?"

Jessie glanced up with her brows dipped in confusion. He ogled the front of her V-neck shirt. She gasped, and her hand flew to her chest. She cleared her throat. "The first time we did this you said women were the devil's spawn. Now look at you. You're flirting. I'd say that's an improvement." A nervous chuckle escaped.

B.J. handed her more books. "I haven't changed my mind. They still are."

"I try," Jessie mumbled. She placed the novels in the tub. "You've read enough of these books to see those ridiculous points, right?"

"You mean the one where the man satisfies his woman more than once with his magic mouth or hands before joining in the fun? I disagree with you. It can be done." He jumped off the ladder with a handful of books and dumped them into the tote. He licked his lips. "I could prove it to you."

Jessie watched his tongue. Her mouth as dry as the Sahara. *Now?*

"I told you I have a magic mouth."

Jessie tried to swallow. "Yes, you did. You boasted that before but what about making all the preexisting bad stuff go away? And getting married three months later?"

B.J. shrugged, squeezing one last book into the tub. "One thing at a time." He carried the plastic container downstairs and through the door as she held it open.

In the bed of his truck, he already had three containers. "Do you want to go with me? I have to go to Nockerville too. Last time didn't turn out like I'd planned when work called with the emergency. I'll take you home whenever you want to go. No strings and all that." He glanced at his boots and his cheeks turned red, giving her the impression of a shy man.

This was her chance to learn how B.J. got the men hooked on romance books. Jessie chewed her lip. The mystery called to her, but she didn't want to be with B.J. if he suddenly thought of her as demonic.

Across the way, Josiah with crossed arms leaned against the barn door watching them. She smiled, weight lifted from her shoulders. Raising a hand, she beckoned him then met him halfway.

"You okay?" Josiah asked, scanning her from head to toe.

"I'm fine. B.J. wants me to accompany him on his romance book deliveries."

Josiah glanced over her shoulder, his blue eyes narrowed as he studied the competition. His gaze returned to her face, and his features softened as he uncrossed his arms and stuck his thumbs in his front pockets. His lips quirked in a smirk.

Jessie focused on his lips. She found air in short supply as she remembered them pressed against hers and their tongues dueling. Afraid her body might overheat, she closed her eyes and took a deep breath. She needed a distraction. "I get to find out how he started the trend."

Josiah chuckled. "You want to know how it began?"

Jessie placed her hands on her hips. "What's wrong with knowing? It's not a secret, is it?"

Josiah reached for her, pulled her close and traced a finger along her chin. His warm breath tickled her ear as he spoke, "We all have our secrets, Jessie." She closed her eyes and sighed. He added, "And remember—I'm taking you to the dance."

Jessie

Riding in B.J.'s truck, Josiah's parting words "I'm taking you to the dance" remained fresh in her mind. Jessie gazed out the window, recalling Josiah's touch and his mysterious words echoing in her thoughts. He had a secret. She chewed her lip until the vehicle lurched to a stop.

The senior center's sliding doors opened, and the older folks flocked the couple as they came in with new books. B.J. lifted an eyebrow in her direction. No beating with canes allowed. She giggled.

The list of novel stops was extensive: government buildings, police & fire stations in both towns, the nursing homes, assisted living facility, hospital, Hammered, Tease Me, three barber shops and a handful of other places. The last place they stopped in Fortuna, before heading to Nockerville, was the Stitts' truck stop. Jessie couldn't believe they had a full-size bookcase by the entry with a sign reading "Take one, leave one."

B.J. had opened Jessie's door and gave her many cheek kisses. The man chatted with the others addicted to cheesy romance novels. He'd compared and contrasted two books in a series with Bunny Hopkins and saluted Mayor Jasen DeLay before leaving the office. He'd even hand-delivered three books to a blushing Ophelia Cox.

All afternoon, B.J. acted different. The familiar chiseled scowl had morphed into a relaxed smile. He still wasn't floating in blissful love-land but he hadn't been pessimistic. After making a delivery, every time they'd got back in the truck he'd sing "On the Road Again."

"I have to drop books at the Nocker Ranch." B.J. gripped the steering wheel tight.

"Okay." Jessie glanced out the window at the iron gate as they pulled off the main road onto a private lane. "I've always wanted to see their home," Jessie whispered in awe as they approached a hotel-like lodge house.

B.J. turned off the truck and stared out the windshield. She moved to unbuckle her belt, but he stopped her and shook his head. "I need you to stay in the car." He lowered his voice and glanced around. "The Nocker boys aren't the nicest, and I don't want anything to happen to you. If they said something stupid or crass, then I'd end up on Barnes' shit list."

She nodded. "I'll wait here."

B.J. climbed out of the truck, took a pile of books and pressed the doorbell. The shirtless man who fell out the opened door was drunk. His blond hair stuck up, but he was still drop-dead gorgeous. She'd heard rumors about the Nocker boys. Hardcore partiers with plenty of money to do whatever they'd like.

B.J. returned the truck. They bumped down the lane and turned onto the road to Nockerville. His jovial mood had turned introspective. "He won't tell me his real name and always tells me to call him Little Nocker. I've been making book runs out here for weeks. I've never seen him sober, and he's always alone."

Jessie said, "I felt sorry for Little Nocker. Anyone he dates knows him, his family's history and his money."

"Would you date him?" B.J. slid her a sideways glance.

Jessie laughed. "No way. A guy that handsome knows he's a hunk and uses it. He's probably slept with all the single girls in the county." She stared out the window.

"So what do you like in a man?"

Still facing the window, a smile tugged at the corners of Jessie's mouth. *Desire would correct him and remind him the man belongs* in *a woman.*

Jessie listed personality traits. "Sweet, funny, a hard worker, loyal-"

"Sounds like you're describing Barnes." His tone neutral, she turned to see both hands gripped the wheel. B.J.'s jaw ticked as if he was forcing it closed.

"He's a good man and, you're right, he's every one of those things." Jessie watched the side of the road. *I forgot good with animals, eyes as blue as the Caribbean Sea and sexy as sin.* "If you like those qualities in a man, I could fix you up."

B.J. chuckled, turning the truck onto the main thoroughfare. "How did you meet Barnes?"

She faced B.J. again, noting the tension had gone, and his arms had relaxed. Jessie arched an eyebrow. She surmised he wanted information about his competition. "It's a funny story. We almost killed each other."

B.J. parked near the fabric store then relaxed back against the bench with an arm stretched over the back. "Sounds interesting."

"Yes, we had a collision. He swerved to miss a dog, and his little compact car got swallowed by my huge truck." Jessie continued the story about the comatose sixteen-year-old boy, his recovery, and guilt, her grandparents taking a chance on the kid and ended with Josiah's rescuing her.

"Wow, that's some story." B.J. rubbed his chin.

Jessie patted her knees. Remembering all Josiah had done for her warmed her soul, and she longed to see him. She considered sending a text to Josiah, but it wouldn't be proper etiquette. Fisting her jeans, she kept her fingers away from her phone.

Jessie

B.J. pointed to the building right in front of them and broke the prolonged silence. "I have to deliver to the barbershop. The owner loves to read and has been infecting his clientele." He lowered the tailgate and opened a tote while she watched a woman enter the fabric store two doors from the barbershop.

"Would you mind if I don't go in with you?" Jessie asked hugging her arms around herself.

B.J. froze with half a dozen books in his arms. "What's wrong, babe? Do you want to go home?"

"No." Seeing the store reminded her of the fabric she'd ordered for the fashion show. Now, thanks to Desire, she had a model for the show. She grinned. "I'd like to check out another business. I special ordered material and want to check the status." Even to her own ears, she sounded excited.

He nodded and smiled. "I'm glad you aren't sick of me." B.J. shifted his weight and glanced to the end of the street. "That's fine. I'll drop these then I have to make another delivery to the firehouse at the end of the strip. I'll meet you back here in a few."

"Sounds great."

Half an hour later the shimmery red bolt of fabric she'd bought was starring in her daydreams. She visualized several ideas, including a babydoll nightgown. She grinned, eager to start.

"What's that? Are you making a dress for the dance?" He touched the long bag.

A dress? Josiah might like it if it's short and sheer. A wave of heat rolled over her at the thought of pleasing him. Not wanting to go into detail about her creations she shrugged. If she couldn't find the courage to talk to Josiah about it, she wouldn't be disclosing anything to B.J. She itched to sketch her designs and talk to someone, like Desire or Kelly.

All the way to the outskirts of Fortuna, B.J.'s banter regarding men picking novels at his book stops kept him laughing. Jessie listened with half an ear, her mind preoccupied brainstorming negligées, panties and robes.

B.J. turned into Josiah's parents' subdivision, returning Jessie's full attention to the road. "I hope you don't mind, I needed to stop by my house. I have a few books I need to return," he said, shooting her a mischievous grin. They rounded a corner, and he slammed the brakes. "Shit."

CHAPTER 30

Jessie

JESSIE TRIED TO SWALLOW BUT couldn't because her heart was in her throat. She inhaled and inspected the two-story house where B.J. stared. A sedan waited in the driveway. He gaped and gripped the wheel with white knuckles. After a few deep breaths, he pulled beside the tan vehicle and turned off the truck. He froze, continuing to stare at the house.

"It's Carlotta," B.J. mumbled, then groaned. "Why?"

Jessie's mind echoed the same question. What more did Carlotta want from B.J.? She'd been having an affair for years then got pregnant by her lover. Carlotta had changed his attitude toward women and not for the better.

B.J. had been divorced less than a year, but he was making progress. Jessie had witnessed the scowl being replaced by a smile. Hell, the whole town loved him and his book deliveries. The men in the book club B.J. and her father belonged to, developed friendships.

Glancing at B.J., the pale-faced man appeared as if he might be sick. Gone was the usual boisterous, if not cantankerous, yet confident flirt. Carlotta had emotionally castrated him.

His ex-wife wasn't sitting in her car waiting. *She must have a key. He doesn't deserve this.* Jessie's anger flared.

Paralyzed and helpless, Jessie chewed her bottom lip. This wasn't her business. Closing her eyes, she tried to stay calm. Carlotta was B.J.'s equivalent of her Rusty Kuntz. But B.J. wasn't lucky enough to have Josiah here to save him.

He has me.

Jessie pushed open the truck door, straightened her shoulders and took a deep breath then stomped in through the front door. She stopped inside the entry to get her bearings. She'd never been in his home before, and something smelled good. Surprised, she took a deep whiff. *Cookies?* Letting her eyes adjust to the dark room, she glanced around then blinked. Every picture frame held Carlotta's likeness. Jessie was in the woman's shrine. Perhaps B.J. wasn't making as much progress as she'd figured.

A noise came from the hall. She tiptoed to the kitchen. A beautiful -no, exotic-woman bent and slid a cookie sheet into the oven. She wore frayed denim shorts and a tight half-shirt tank top. She hummed moving around the room. On the counter, two cookie sheets with baked chocolate cookies sat cooling. Carlotta turned; that's when Jessie spied the bellybutton piercing, lack of bra, and tattoo. The blue ink swirled from her back down her arm.

Not a strand of her curled, ebony hair was out of place and her heavy makeup was flawless. Her mascara made her lashes long and luxurious. Jessie might have dressed similar to go clubbing in college. Although she was never brave enough to go braless.

B.J.'s booted footsteps announced his presence and Carlotta spun around with a stunning smile. Seeing Jessie, Carlotta demanded, "Who are you?" Her penciled brows formed a V.

"Not anybody's ex-wife." Jessie gave her a sweet sappy smile.

"What the hell are you doing here?" B.J. stood behind Jessie but had a hand on her shoulder as if he needed the support. His voice sounded like a wounded little boy.

Carlotta's gaze softened. Her deep raspy voice purred "I've come to see you, baby." Opening her arms for him, shoulders back, breasts jiggling, she stepped forward.

"Where's the baby daddy?" Jessie asked. B.J.'s fingers dug into her flesh as he released a soft gasp. She hated to cause him any pain. Jessie put her hands on her hips but she scanned the room searching for the man. Maybe Carlotta wanted to rob B.J. of some family heirloom. God only knew why the ex had returned.

Carlotta crossed her arms, and her glossy lips glowered. "Who is this woman and why is she in my house?" Her lime green lacquer-tipped toes peeked out from the sandal she tapped.

Jessie smiled a genuine grin and relaxed her arms. She took a step into the room and studied the dark granite countertops and maple cabinets. The dream kitchen had an island and all stainless appliances. A cat calendar hung on the wall next to the fridge. Upon further inspection, it was the previous year's and had doctors' appointments written in a feminine script. Huh? He hadn't even thrown away his ex-wife's calendar.

"This is Jessie Davidson. She owns the Double D Ranch." B.J.'s voice sounded stronger. Not quite himself but getting there. Jessie gifted Carlotta with a nod and a princess wave.

Carlotta's gaze dropped to Jessie's chest. "I can see that." Her lips pursed in a pout. "B.J., I need to talk to you."

"Like I asked before, what the hell do you want?" B.J. snarled. Jessie covered her mouth to hide a smile. B.J.'s gonads had grown back.

"I wanted to make sure you're healthy and doing well. I—I missed you." Carlotta stared at her hands and picked a perfect nail.

"You've got to be kidding me," B.J. retorted, the familiar chiseled scowl at home once more. "If you got something to say, you should talk to your lawyer."

Carlotta harrumphed and threw Jessie a glare that could have singed off her eyebrows. Jessie leaned against the counter and crossed her ankles. "I don't understand you, Carlotta." Jessie shook her head and continued, "B.J. is drop-dead gorgeous, charming and sexy. He's an excellent provider. He's sweet and funny." When he's not brooding. "And both Fortuna and Nockerville consider him a hero. I don't understand why you left."

Carlotta wore a sour expression as if she smelled rotten eggs. On the other hand, B.J.'s predatory smile had returned. Jessie sucked in her lip. She was butting in where she shouldn't. B.J. was a friend, sorta. Jessie witnessed, along with the town of Fortuna, how bitter and angry he'd become because of Carlotta. He'd been making strides forward with his life. Women weren't the devil any longer. Hell, he pimped love and romance in the form of books to every man around. She didn't want him to get knocked back down.

A baby whimpered then full on wailed. B.J. and Jessie gazed at each other. Carlotta had brought the other man's child with her. She retreated into the dining room, and Jessie followed and stood at the entry. A chubby foot stuck out of a sky blue blanket and kicked when his mother cooed at him.

Heat radiated off B.J. as he stood behind Jessie. They watched Carlotta change the little guy on the table. She played with his toes and a gurgling laugh erupted from the baby. Jessie couldn't help but smile at the sound.

She leaned her shoulder against the doorjamb and glanced at B.J. His face bore an anguished expression and tears pricked his eyes. He exhaled a stuttering breath and blinked back the tears. It had to hurt like hell. What should have been his wife and son belonged to another man.

"That's better, isn't it, my little man?" Carlotta cooed and picked him up. She cuddled the baby against her rocking to an internal rhythm.

The baby gazed at Jessie and blinked big, blue eyes then smiled a toothless grin. "Gah!"

"Well, hello to you too," Jessie said. With the light colored eyes and downy yellow hair, he must favor his father and not his dark eyed, dark haired mother. "He's cute."

"Say thank you, Erick," Carlotta said in a sing-song mommy voice then moved the baby to her hip and waved one of his arms.

"You named the baby Erick Junior?" B.J. grunted.

"Carlotta, it's time for you to go home," Jessie spoke in a soft voice.

"I am home." Carlotta shifted the baby to the other hip, and she stomped a petite foot.

"Not anymore. Go home." B.J. pointed towards the door.

Carlotta pointed at Jessie. "Why would you let this bimbo dictate your life?" She pouted her lips again. It wasn't as effective while holding another man's child.

B.J. laughed, howling until tears streamed down his face and he bent holding his stomach. When he could manage he said, "Jessie is as much a bimbo as I am a saint."

Carlotta's lips turned down as if she'd swallowed a lemon. "B.J. please."

"Get the hell out of my house and don't ever come back!" B.J. bellowed. He stormed into the kitchen.

Jessie jumped when he'd yelled, but that was nothing next to the pale, fearful face of Carlotta. She'd frozen with eyes opened wide and quivering lips. Probably not the reception she'd expected. Picking up the diaper wipes, her hands trembled. Erick hiccupped, and a steel facade replaced any emotion. Her gaze narrowed on Jessie.

"I don't know why you're here. Honestly, I don't care but what I do care about is B.J." Jessie put her hands up in surrender. "He's already had his heart broken once. Don't do it again. He deserves to find happiness and love." She paused, and her voice softened, "And so do you."

Carlotta gave her a stiff nod and put the baby in the carrier.

"You should leave the house key here. You won't need it again." Jessie held out her hand.

With the diaper bag over one shoulder and the infant carrier hooked on the other elbow, Carlotta passed Jessie and dropped the key into her open palm. B.J. watched his ex make a hasty retreat through the kitchen to the front door. He stood at the window scowling with his arms crossed long after she'd left.

Jessie

The smell of burning food alarmed Jessie. A wave of acrid smoke met her face as she pulled out the forgotten cookies. The black discs resembled hockey pucks. She pulled open drawers searching for a spatula.

B.J. remained in the other room facing the window and Jessie left him to his thoughts. He had a lot to reconcile.

Jessie frowned and chipped at the hard cookies. If she hadn't gone with B.J., he would have faced his demon, or as he called it "Satan's spawn," alone. She was glad for the opportunity to help him. She couldn't fathom how he felt.

I don't understand cheaters.

Her parents and grandparents had been faithful. Josiah would get on his knees begging if he ever had an inkling of a wayward thought. *No, Josiah is loyal.*

Something nagged at her. She'd spent the afternoon with someone other than Josiah.

"I'm taking you to the dance," he'd reminded her.

Jessie swallowed. Her time spent with B.J. might be considered venial, but her heart disagreed. *Am I a cheater?* An overwhelming desire to run home to Josiah hit her. Her lips quirked into a lopsided grin: Josiah equaled home. Wiping her palms on her jeans, she'd give B.J. a few more minutes then she'd ask to return to the Double D.

"Thanks for all you did today. That adulteress will no longer barge in and make my life hell." B.J. rubbed his face. He tossed the extra key into a drawer.

"You're welcome. I hope she hasn't made another copy of the key." Jessie put the cookie pan in the sink.

B.J.'s bloodshot eyes and red nose contrasted his bright smile. "You're awesome, Jess."

Jess. That was what Josiah called her. Jessie closed her eyes and pictured Josiah with a hat ring in his wavy hair and the simmering look he gave her when he'd catch her staring at his lips. A blanket of warmth covered her body.

"Carlotta didn't like being replaced." B.J. touched the side of her face and stepped close. His cologne overpowered the burnt cookie smell.

"I didn't replace her. She replaced you." Jessie stared at her feet. She'd tried to help him. It was what Josiah would have done.

B.J. leaned, his warm breath caressed her neck. "Thanks." His lips pressed against her pulse point. Taken by surprise, she froze. Her heart raced as he nibbled and his tongue teased.

"What are you doing?" Jessie asked, her voice quavered a higher pitch than normal.

"Magic mouth," B.J. murmured against her skin.

A nagging in her head warned it would end badly if she let it continue. Jessie didn't want to be a rebound. She wanted to be wanted because he loved her, not for physical comfort.

"Stop," she whispered. "Don't you want to talk about what happened?"

"With my hands." He unsnapped her jeans and unzipped them. She grabbed his wrists and pushed them away.

"B.J., I can't do this." Fixing her pants, Jessie stepped away from him.

One step and his body pressed hers, trapping her against the counter. One hand cradled the back of her head, and the other rested on her hip at the top of her jeans. His thumb skimmed her flesh. "I've got protection if that's what you're worrying about."

Her breath came in gasps. Jessie hated being pinned, and she pushed against his chest. She needed to get out. Now. "No. I mean yes. That's not all. You're not over your wife leaving."

A throaty chuckle met her ears, and his body vibrated against her. "I've kept busy. You know I've changed."

Not enough. The first time she'd seen B.J., love had radiated from him. He was capable of giving it, but he wasn't there yet.

His hands promised more, but all she wanted was her freedom. Jessie felt tears sting her eyes. She pushed against him again. "Please," she begged.

"All right, babe." B.J. crushed her against his hard body, his arousal evident. One hand dipped and squeezed. His wet, hungry lips threatened to devour her face.

Unable to breathe, panic welled. Josiah's face flashed before her, making her guilt-ridden heart race. Josiah had been right about B.J. She half-expected Josiah to burst the door in and save her from B.J.'s embrace. She took a deep breath trying to dislodge the heaviness settling in her stomach. This time, she'd remained sober, and B.J. wasn't Rusty Kuntz.

Jessie jerked her head to the side and broke their connection. "I can't breathe," she huffed.

"I feel the same way, baby." B.J. resumed his assault on her neck with a moan.

"No. Not ready," Jessie hiccupped. "No!"

B.J. pulled back and must've seen the fear because he let her go. Running his fingers through his thick dark hair, he growled and turned away from her to pace the room. Bending over, she gulped air. When she'd caught her breath, she inched toward the front door.

"But all those things you said? Sexy, drop-dead gorgeous, charming and sweet." B.J. grabbed her arms and squeezed, shaking her.

"That's the truth. I protected you from her. I didn't want to see you hurt again." Jessie's wide gaze stared toward the exit.

His fingernails had dug into her skin before B.J. pushed away with disgust. "You didn't want to see me hurt? Then you reject me?" He sneered, red faced.

Her fear evaporated, replaced by anger. Jessie rubbed her arms where he'd hurt her. How did it come to this? Josiah wouldn't harm her. He's been plenty angry at her before, but he'd stomp off then come back and talk. B.J. wanted to screw to resolve his problems, and she would not be manipulated.

With her hands planted on her hips, Jessie declared. "It's all about you. I didn't want this."

B.J.'s tone turned acid, "You lied to me. You're just like Carlotta."

Jessie snorted masking the pain that hit her heart. Shocked, hurt and angry, she matched his glare but said nothing. After three deep shuddering breaths, she pushed past him before the tears could fall and stormed out.

"I'm not into infidelity," Jessie muttered as she retrieved the bolts of fabric from the truck. She bit her lip hoping Josiah stayed calm when he learned about B.J.'s dreadful behavior. She hoofed it down the street aiming for the Barnes' home. One thing was certain: *Josiah would never do this to me.*

CHAPTER 31

Josiah

JOSIAH HAD HIS BROTHERS WEEDING and mulching the Double D landscape when his father's Mercedes pulled into the drive. One of his brothers must want out of work. But Jessie sat in the passenger seat. *What the...?*

He leaned on the shovel handle and waited until the vehicle came to a stop. Jessie averted her eyes. Something twisted in his gut. It had gone wrong with Johnson or else the man would have brought her back gloating. Wiping the sweat off his brow, he fought the desire to rush over and pull her into his arms. *If Johnson hurt her—there'll be hell to pay.*

Jessie and Bridger exited the car and walked toward the porch. His father, stepping over piles of weeds and dead branches, carried bolts of fabric. Jessie surveyed their work. The two younger Barnes raked while Josiah shoveled the debris into a wheelbarrow.

Gabe paused, smiled and waved at his father. The shirtless teen worked on his tan, but at least he wore gloves.

Following Jessie, Bridger carried a large package inside. After a while, Jessie and his father brought them lemonade. His father offered to buy food for the younger two but only Gabe took the offer.

Josiah walked his father to the car. "Thanks for bringing her home, Dad."

"She's been crying." Bridger glanced at Jessie and waved. He turned to his son and frowned. "She didn't say much."

"I know who upset her," Josiah growled. He had the urge to hunt

Johnson and… *what?* Gut him like a fish? Normally, he wouldn't fight but for Jessie, he'd go to great lengths to protect her.

Josiah watched as Jessie moseyed out to the barn and opened the loft door overlooking the property. She sat on the floor cross-legged. Despite the emotional turmoil she'd been through, her closed eyes and relaxed features radiated calm. The sun washed her face and wisps of hair blew free giving her a fiery halo. He remained transfixed and gawking until Matt slugged him in the shoulder as he passed. Josiah rubbed the sore spot ready to wipe the cocky grin off Matt's face.

"Jessie frowns and you turn into a lazy caveman wanting to hit something with a club." Matt grunted then thumped his chest like an ape. "Me Joe-joe. Save sexy babe."

Josiah pursed his lips, placing his hands on his hips. Matt hunched and swung his arms like an ape, making squawks and grunts. Josiah glanced at Jessie. She watched them from her perch with a hand over her mouth and her eyes crinkled with mirth. He relaxed and laughed at his brother's ridiculousness.

"All right, let's get back to work."

"No more monkeying around?" Matt asked and lifted the handle of the cart. Matt wheeled the yard waste to the refuse pile and dumped it. Josiah used the shovel to scrape it. Stretching, Matt groaned as he rubbed his lower back. His younger brother looked beat. A few more hard days labor and his body would be ready for real ranch work.

Matt pulled out his phone and whistled. "I can't believe how late it is."

Glancing at the screen Josiah pivoted, almost ramming Matt. "Oh crap, I gotta go. Can you do me a favor? Tell Jessie I've got a meeting and I'll see her later." Josiah walked to the house to shower.

"Sure, Bro." Matt cocked his head sideways. "I'll tell her."

Josiah hurried. After a full day of working in the yard, he stunk. The warm water would relax his aching muscles and he'd smell a whole heck of a lot better too.

This meeting was important to Jessie's Double D Intimates and the secret financial partner. Josiah couldn't skip it nor could he tell her about it. He sighed as he started the truck.

Josiah wanted to scrap the meeting and figure out what happened with Johnson. He was half tempted to call the man, but he wouldn't be able to keep it civil. Besides, getting this meeting lined up had taken conniving by Desire and Brad.

He hoped Jessie would be okay.

Jessie

It felt good to be alone. The peace of the breeze rolling along the plains soothed her. Jessie sat on the patio enjoying a glass of Josiah's homemade lemonade. The cool glass and tangy flavor were quintessential to summer, but it felt wrong to drink it without him.

Jessie worked cutting the new red fabric and matching lace. A cardboard box full of U-shaped wires sat at her feet. After inspecting one she slid it into a narrow tunnel of fabric. She finished the set for Fonda and Randy Peters and hung the negligée on the dressing form and took a photo of it. She wrapped each item in tissue paper then put it in a small box for mailing.

Satisfaction rolled over her. Jessie smiled, envisioning her next creation as she cut small pieces of pliable fabric. After a while, her back ached, she massaged her lower back. She stood and paced the room twisting her torso trying to get the kinks out. The spines of romance novels attracted her. The pile nearest the wall was sci-fi romance, including a few space operas.

How would the men of Fortuna act out alien penises? She giggled and shook her head at the musings.

Turning, she spied the box with her grandmother's diaries. She'd ignored them for a while because it'd been hard to envision her grandmother as a stripper. Undine Love had been a dancer, entertainer or whatever working title, but when it came down to it she'd been a call girl.

On one worn journal cover, the side tabs were still bright, but the outside had faded to a dull pink. She opened the book to the first page. Before focusing on what the string of words meant, she examined the scrolling letters. Jessie tried to envision her grandma young as she sneaked a few minutes to write about her day. Jessie's heart quickened, and she took a deep breath.

She let the letters coalesce into words and the words formed a sentence. She lowered the book and wiped the tears away. It was their story—Undine and Don's.

The first page was how they met. He'd been walking in a park when a child missed a ball. Don retrieved it and tussled the child's hair. Undine had pined for children but thought how she'd never have them unless she could break away. The way the gentleman treated the child, his smile and mannerisms attracted Undine's gaze and she watched him.

Don noticed Undine watching him and he started a conversation, bumbling over compliments and turning red. Undine's observations had made it clear she'd been smitten with Donald Davidson after the first day.

This book was a love story. Jessie hugged the journal to her chest and sighed.

It was the essence of Undine Love. Their love's sweetness lasted their entire married life modeled for Jessie and all to see. Tears streamed down Jessie's face. She wanted that kind of love. It wouldn't come from B.J. It'd take a man like Josiah. He was steadfast and loyal. She wondered if it was too late to have a relationship with him.

Josiah's appointment probably had been a date. He had so-called meetings before.

Josiah cleared his throat.

"Oh," Jessie squeaked glancing at the silhouette in the hallway. Her cheeks heated. He'd caught her crying. She wiped the tears from her face.

Josiah stepped into the room with a pinched expression. His gray t-shirt clung tight across his broad shoulders. "Jess, are you okay?"

She pointed to the diary. "It's Grandma and Grandpa's story, Josiah, and it's beautiful." Jessie wiped her face again.

Josiah placed a hand on her shoulder and squeezed. A hint of a floral fragrance clung to him as he leaned close scanning the piles of red fabric. "I'll be right back."

Jessie watched him go with a heavy heart. Glad he'd found a girl, but at the same time it plagued her. The contradictions rubbed her raw emotions. Jessie squeezed her eyes shut, wishing her grandma was there to talk too.

She'd tidied the sewing room before he returned. He knocked, startling her.

"Come with me," Josiah requested offering his hand. She took it and her heart hammered as he led her toward the master bedroom. The humid air held a fruity scent. He tugged her into the bathroom where the garden tub was filled. "Take a nice long relaxing bath. I'll get you something to eat."

Jessie

The scent of strawberries hung in the air and bubbles towered over the hot water. She closed her eyes and relaxed. He cleared his throat again but stayed in the other room out of sight.

"It's okay." Jessie waved a bubbly arm.

Josiah blushed, handing her a plate with a sandwich and chips. She dried her hand on a towel next to the tub then took a big bite of the sandwich. She moaned a happy sigh making him smile.

"Dad told me you showed up on his doorstep today. Things didn't go as planned with Johnson?" He sat on the floor.

"He was fine at first. Did you know all the places he takes books on Saturdays? We had fun. He was a perfect gentleman and in a good mood. Until Carlotta." Jessie described the house and the conversation. "Was I wrong to help him? Maybe I should've let him face his demons alone?"

"You are a good friend, Jess. I'm sure he'll appreciate your concern later."

"I wish he wouldn't have kissed me," she grumbled.

"You were a hero to him. You didn't slay the dragon, but you made it turn around and leave the villager alone. So it was hero worship."

"I didn't do that to you when you rescued me from Rusty. What would you have done if I tried to seduce you afterward?" Jessie moved sloshing water over the edge.

"After making sure you were safe, I would have turned you around and marched you inside. You weren't ready for a relationship, no matter how temporary," Josiah said.

"Thank you." It proved Jessie's point. She was sane and B.J. was an ass. The quiet hung in the air. The bubbles had disappeared, but Josiah sat on the ground and couldn't see into the water. "How was your appointment?"

"Good. Kinda boring but necessary." Josiah glanced at his watch.

Heaviness settled in her heart again. She didn't like it.

"Do you know the ex-Mrs. Johnson's new man's name?" Josiah asked.

The change of subject shouldn't have surprised her. She sat forward to see his face. Yep, it sounded like he was smiling. "No, I never heard."

"The guy's name was Erick Shen." The lines around his eyes and mouth famed his laughing face.

Josiah's tanned face, turned upwards in mirth, floored her. She could have studied his features all night except his laughter became contagious. Did he say "erection?"

"Yeah." A new wave of laughter hit him.

After they quieted again. She explained why she'd been crying. "You found me reading Grandma's story about how she met Grandpa. I thought I knew their story. The fast courtship. But I didn't know Grandma and Grandpa eloped. It's an interesting read, but it's hard not sharing it with someone. Would you like to read it together? I know they were special to you." Jessie bit her lip while holding her breath.

"They were special people. They taught me about ranching. Age didn't matter to them. Don always treated me as a man." He wrapped his arms around his legs in a childlike manner and tilted his head. "They were special," he repeated.

"Want to see how my Grandma fell for Grandpa?"

Josiah grinned. "I'd love too."

Jessie grinned too. "Go get your pajamas on, and I'll get out of here then we'll read it."

Jessie

Jessie emptied the tub as she got ready for bed. After she'd brushed her hair and teeth, she found Josiah sitting on the edge of the bed holding the book. His excited grin coupled with the tight t-shirt and plaid boxers made her mouth go dry. *Maybe this isn't the best idea.*

He cocked his head and turned the book over in his hands. "I'm curious to find out how they met."

"It's a good story. Grandma watched Grandpa interacting with children and thought he was sweet." Similar to Jessie and Josiah. He didn't want to hurt an animal. She shook the similarity out of her head.

Jessie propped the pillows and sat back on the bed. She signaled for him and he crawled as if he was afraid he'd frighten her. Josiah settled next to her and smiled. She felt the heat cover her face. They sat side by side and opened the book. While he skimmed the pages she already read, she covered their legs with a quilt. He reached the place she pointed out where she stopped then read out loud. She watched the words as he read. "Don sat across from me at the restaurant. He was handsome in his suit. He's clever and quick witted. His smile is beautiful. I could get lost in the depths of his eyes. I want to be with him forever. We are a perfect fit but I don't deserve him. I'm not good enough. Besides my job, he's years younger."

"What?" Jessie leaned over the page. "I didn't know that."

"Yeah, Don married an older woman. He said he never pointed out that fact to her or else he got in trouble." Josiah smirked. "Aren't you older?" He poked Jessie's side.

"Older than what?" Jessie raised a brow.

"Dirt?"

Jessie mumbled, "I wonder how long Grandpa would have lived if he said that?"

"Desire?" Josiah continued to tease.

"When I'm an old lady, if I have an ounce of Desire's spunk then-"

"Your husband will be thrilled." Jessie elbowed him this time. "Ouch.

Mona called you a cougar." She gasped then Josiah chuckled.

"Mona and Kelly tease me but they know the truth about us. Anyway that's not as bad as what Sawyer calls you."

Josiah's body stiffened next to her. "Oh yeah, what's that?"

"Whipped."

He laughed. "Darlin', that's better than anything he calls me to my face."

Jessie stared into her lap and whispered, "God, Josiah, I'm sorry. Half the town considers us a couple. It's gotta be hell on your love life."

Their weekly dinners at Hammered helped to make the town's folk believe the rumors. They were always together picking up supplies. Then Josiah moving in with her and the way they behaved in front of Kelly in the loft.

Here they were in bed together, again. So far it was innocent, but who'd believe it? Heck, Desire would be proud of her. Two men in one day. First B.J. tried to bed her and now Josiah was in his boxers under her sheets. "Your reputation is shot."

"Everyone thinking I'm attached to a pretty woman isn't bad. It impresses the guys, and keeps girls like Pixie Dix away." Josiah shrugged as his cheeks pinked. His gaze held hers.

"But it's fake. I mean, we aren't dating." *Josiah thinks I'm pretty.* Her face burned but she couldn't tear her eyes away.

"Aren't we going to the dance together?" One of his brows rose. Josiah shifted and his leg brushed hers.

Jessie nodded, her heart in her throat.

"That's a date. Aren't we going to elope?"

Jessie giggled and snuggled next to him with a sigh. Josiah stretched his arm around her shoulder and together they held the book and continued reading.

The Undine Love Davidson Jessie knew had been a woman who'd known her mind. Her grandmother had been strong willed and opinionated but reading the diary she became a young woman with insecurities. Grandma hadn't known how Don would respond to her profession. She worried herself sick thinking he'd reject her. She'd loved him within the first twenty-four hours of meeting him. The day-dreams included running away with him and having his children. Grandma had filled one journal with hope for a new life with Grandpa.

Jessie sighed and laid her head on Josiah's shoulder.

Don had fallen hard for Undine too. They'd fallen in love within six days. They planned a life together, and it was everything she'd ever wanted but still her work had been the albatross in the closet. Jim Dimwitty wouldn't let her leave easily. They were in danger.

Josiah

Jessie's warm breath against Josiah's skin melted his heart. He wanted to pull her into his arms and kiss her slightly parted lips but she'd fallen asleep with her head on his shoulder. He lowered her to the pillow then turned out the light.

Now he faced a dilemma.

Josiah could sleep on the sofa or he could stay there and sleep next to Jessie. His groin and his heart agreed even though he wouldn't sleep much because every soft sigh or slight movement caused him to focus on her.

Half tempted to pull *The Visitation* move and whisper into her ear, instead he folded his arms behind his head and relaxed. The king bed was big enough for both of them. Taking a deep breath his eyes drifted shut.

CHAPTER 32

Jessie

JESSIE WORE A SPECIAL GREEN *negligée to match her eyes. A man slid his hand over her backside and nuzzled his nose in her hair murmuring she smelled good enough to eat. "Don't stop. Please, don't stop." She turned and pulled him closer. This was her husband and the love of her life.*

The beat of his strong heart lulled her into a peaceful, contented place. Until he murmured her name and his lips suckled the sensitive part of her neck. She arched against him pressing their bodies closer. Instead of the calm flow of blood, it raced causing rapid, short breaths. Just like oxygen she couldn't get enough of him.

Jessie was loathe to get up even though there were chores to do. Cuddled and warm, she heard a long sigh. Her eyes shot open and she stiffened. Glancing over her shoulder Josiah's slumbering face tipped toward her.

Relaxing, she rolled over. Her gaze raked his serene face with lips tipped in a smile. The hair above his forehead stuck up and growth sprinkled his chin. She itched to touch him. Another soft sigh escaped his parted lips. She swallowed the desire rising from her heart. Balling her fists, she refused to touch him.

With heaviness, she forced herself to twist away. It had been folly to allow him into her bed. She'd grown accustomed to the companionship. A warm body, *his* warm body. She rolled out of bed then tiptoed to the kitchen to start breakfast.

The smell of bacon and coffee must have woke the man. Josiah entered with a lazy grin and scratched his bare chest. His arms encircled her as he placed a sweet kiss on her cheek. "How'd you sleep?"

Jessie shrugged and flashed hotter than the frying pan she held. She longed to lay her head against his chest and close her eyes but the bacon couldn't wait. Josiah stepped away from her and sat at the table. Flipping off the burner, she set the pan aside then removed the crispy strips.

Facing the table she stared at Josiah with confusion. He'd had a shirt on when they'd read together. Ah. He must have taken it off before climbing into bed.

Another version flashed in her mind. He'd starred in her dream. Longing stole her breath. She grabbed the cool counter to help keep her upright.

"So how'd you sleep?" He asked again. An ornery smirk resided on his lips and his blue gaze held hers.

Jessie swallowed then answered in a shaky voice, "Very well, thank you. How 'bout you?"

"Not so much. You kept making funny noises?"

"Noises?" Jessie handed him a cup of coffee.

"Yeah. What were you dreaming? It must have been good." Josiah shoveled the food into his mouth but his gaze never left her face.

Jessie covered her cheeks with her hands. Her face was hot enough to be a solar flare. A squeak escaped from her mouth. She cleared her throat and laughed nervously. "Pretty good." *Desire would have liked it. Well, maybe not. Too tame for her usual finesse.*

"Ah, about a man. Who, Johnson?" Josiah focused on his plate.

"No way." Jessie frowned and shivered. Josiah grinned, nodded and his cheeks turned pink. "My husband," she admitted in a wistful tone.

"Didn't know you had one. I mean, we haven't eloped yet. It's good to know you're practicing." Josiah smirked a cockeyed grin and his face flamed red.

Jessie hit him on the arm. "How do you know it wasn't about his job or building a house?"

"Mostly because you said 'don't stop' more than once and now you're turning bright red. It must have been realistic to have you talking in your sleep."

She dropped her gaze to the plate not wanting to discuss the nature of the dream with him. "It was realistic. Have you ever had dreams so detailed you swear they were real?" she whispered. She boldly raised her eyes to his.

Josiah nodded then his gaze blazed hot and full of longing. Maybe she projected that because she didn't want to discuss the dream but act it out.

Josiah

Ophelia Cox had coaxed Brad to sit next to her leaving Jessie alone in the aisle. Bridger offered Jessie his elbow, and she accepted with a smile and followed him into the pew. Josiah hadn't minded his father's kindness; however, he wished his little sister, Tori, hadn't squeezed between him and Jessie.

It's a good thing. Keep my mind pure. Josiah sighed and straightened his shirt. If he glanced across Tori's lap he could see Jessie's knees and a good portion of her thighs her short skirt revealed. He prayed for strength because his gaze kept straying.

As a distraction, Josiah let his gaze wander the sanctuary until they settled on Johnson. The man seemed drained and had bags under his eyes as if he'd been sick. According to Jessie, Johnson hadn't tried to contact her. One side of Josiah's lips tipped in a smirk, satisfied Jessie would have slammed the receiver down if B.J. had called.

Johnson must have a sixth sense because the man glanced over. The longer they kept eye contact the redder Johnson's face became. Josiah almost pitied the guy. He could relate to being Jessie-less. *Well, until recently.* Now he'd graduated from the sofa to her bed. So far, it'd been innocent and he wouldn't make a move until she was ready. Remembering her curves spooning against his body brought a smile to his face and blood rushed below the belt. He turned his attention forward while covering his tight pants with the open bulletin.

The church service remained antic free. No whoopee cushions or funny vandalized Jesus pictures.

Afterward Josiah's mother pulled Jessie aside. "Jessie, we're having a picnic at our place on Independence Day. We'd love for you to come."

"Say you'll come," Tori added with a timid grin.

From his vantage point a couple feet away, Josiah could see Jessie struggling for an answer. Her lips formed a polite smile and her cheeks flushed, but nothing like the deep rose his kiss could bring out.

"Dad and I usually spend the Fourth together," Jessie said tilting her head then swinging it to search for her father.

"I already spoke with your father before church. Ophelia invited him for dinner so he declined our invitation but suggested I ask you." His mother took Jessie's shock in stride.

Jessie accepted the invitation and offered to make a side dish. Josiah knew what awaited Jessie at the get-together. It would be more like a family reunion with his dad's side of the family. His uncles would assume he had a girlfriend. His heart thumped faster at the thought.

Josiah

Josiah hadn't seen Jessie all Monday morning. The humming of the sewing machine drowned out the first knock on the door. He knocked harder then silence met his ears.

"Yes?" she said, pulling open the door. Jessie's green eyes twinkled as if she knew a secret. In her hand a swatch of red material edged with lace shimmered.

He stared. Why had he knocked? He cleared his throat. "I'm making a list for Nailed. Do you need anything?"

Jessie glanced to the right above his shoulder and sucked in her bottom lip. "Can you check to see if they have clothes pins?" Her eyes scrunched making her adorable 'I'm thinking' face. "Oh yeah, packing tape. Thanks, Josiah." She pushed the door closed.

Josiah grinned and stuck his boot out to keep it from closing. "It's lunch time. You might want to eat. I'll send Matt to the store after we have lunch."

Jessie took the elbow he offered, and he escorted her to the kitchen. Thankfully she agreed to stop, instead of retreating into the room. All three sat at the table eating sandwiches.

"What are you working on in there?" Matt asked, talking around a mouthful of peanut butter and jelly.

"Trying to get the custom orders finished." Jessie poured sweet tea from the pitcher on the table.

The phone rang and Josiah hopped up to grab it giving Jessie a chance to swallow. "Double D ranch," he paused listening to a happy feminine voice. "Hello, Kelly. I'm not sure but I'll check for you. Hold on a minute." He lowered the handset. "Kelly wants to know if you're still on for tonight?"

Jessie nodded and took a sip of tea then took the handset from him. She squeezed his hand before leaning against the counter and watching out the window. "Hey, girl. Sure, you and Mona come on over. I've got a few things you can help me with. I'm trying to get Gogh-Downe's order finished before the fourth."

Matt leaned close to Josiah and whispered, "Isn't Gogh-Downe that hoity-toity clothes shop in Nockerville? What's she selling there?"

Josiah shrugged and pretended he had no clue. He settled against the chair back and watched her butt, the skin-tight jeans hugging her backside. Jessie swayed to some internal rhythm and both men stared, mesmerized.

Matt crossed his arms. "Hm, lunch and a show. I like this job," Matt said with a grin as he tipped his chair backward,

Josiah frowned and pointed to the door. "Your plate is empty. Time to get back out there." Matt complied with slumped shoulders but not before throwing Josiah a sad puppy face. Matt moved sloth-like to the kitchen sink then disappeared out the door. Josiah relaxed and enjoyed the view while eavesdropping.

"If you want to bring a pizza that will be great." Jessie paused and curled the phone cord around her finger and laughed quietly. "I know, he does have a sexy phone voice."

Josiah sat up straight, a slow smile spread across his lips. *This could be worth taking an extra-long lunch.*

Jessie's voice dropped an octave as she mimicked his greeting, "Double D ranch." Kelly said something sending Jessie into a fit of giggles. "Don't say stuff like that. Why? Because it makes me hot and tingly."

Without making noise, Josiah walked behind her and tapped her shoulder. She spun, brushing her nose against his chest. He tipped her chin and she gaped, red faced. A tiny squeak escaped. "I'd be happy to oblige," he uttered in a low velvety voice. Whatever Kelly had suggested, he wanted to try on Jessie.

Heat radiated off her body. Jessie stared at his lips and swallowed. She licked the corner of hers and he almost came undone. Her chest heaved up and down, the form-fitting V-neck teasing him with every quick breath. He took a step closer aligning his hips to hers. The phone nearly fell from her fingers.

Josiah couldn't stand it. He had to taste her. As he leaned in a loud knock sounded, followed by the unmistakable voice of B.J. Johnson.

"Jessie?" More banging. "I'm here to get the books."

She thunked her forehead on Josiah's chest and sighed. "Ugh, Kelly I've got to go. Somebody is at the door. See ya tonight."

"Let him be." Josiah said wrapping his arms around her. "He doesn't know you're in here. You could be out on the range."

"Hey baby, are you in there?" B.J. called.

The tote with the novels had been placed on the porch so Jessie had an excuse not to answer the door. B.J. made such a racket, Matt came out of the barn and suggested he leave. Josiah could kiss his brother. Instead he opted for the girl in his arms.

Jessie slipped from his arms and fled the kitchen but not before glancing over her shoulder. He could've sworn she zeroed in on his lips again.

It was getting harder to resist her. Every time she sighed, giggled or touched him it strained his reserve. It was only a matter of time until he gave in. Undine's face flashed before his eyes, a reminder of his promise to protect Jessie. He balled his hands into fists. How could he protect her from himself? Love and desire dangled like a yo-yo.

CHAPTER 33

Josiah

INDEPENDENCE DAY MORNING, JOSIAH, WITH the help of his brothers, did the chores around the Double D. They took the truck out to check the well's water pump while Jessie cleaned the house, worked on some lacy project he wasn't supposed to know about, and concocted an asparagus salad.

Jessie met them at the truck wearing a jeans skirt with a pale blue blouse. Even in heels, she still wasn't near his height. He opened the door for her while Matt took the container.

"Mm, that looks good," Gabe said as he leaned forward between Josiah and Jessie. "I don't like veggies but I might try it."

"It'll make your pee smell funny," Matt stated. He laughed at the face Gabe pulled then they argued about whether it would or wouldn't. By the time they arrived at the Barnes home, Gabe had decided to try some to see if it was true instead of taking his brother's word.

Cars lined the Barnes' street and filled the driveway. He pulled into the neighbors drive and parked.

"Wow. This is some party. What's going on?" Jessie inquired.

"The Burks are out of town. It's fine if we park here." Josiah helped her out of the truck.

"Dad's brothers and family are visiting Josiah gets to introduce you to the entire family," Matt informed with a wink. He chuckled at Jessie's shocked expression and took the salad, carrying the container away from his body like it might burn him.

"Guy is getting the third degree from Aunt Laura. Check it out." Gabe pointed to Guy standing with his arm around Maggie. The poor man tugged on his polo collar, nodding like a bobble-head. Gabe trotted to his aunt and cousins. Guy welcomed the reprieve with a visible sigh and a wave.

"You'll get to split the attention with Guy," Matt teased.

Josiah sighed, letting his brother pass. He put a hand on Jessie's arm. "My dad has three brothers and all are married with children. My cousins are married with at least two children, one with four year old twins. My father is the baby of the family so my cousins are older." Add neighbors, friends and other relatives—it made for a colossal gathering.

The family had erected a large white tent in the backyard to accommodate overflow seating. It was a party planning nightmare. Josiah's mother, aunts and sisters had been in charge of coordinating all the food.

Josiah felt Jessie slowing her pace as more and more heads turned toward them. Matt disappeared through the open garage.

Josiah needed to reassure her. "Listen, Jess, all my uncles are great guys. Uncle Bill is an attorney and Uncle John is in realty in the Dallas area." He smiled down at her.

Jessie stopped walking. "You could have warned me about the family reunion."

"You would have worried." Josiah tilted his head when she opened her mouth but she shut it again. He glanced at the few family members watching them and his heart swelled. "They'll love you. We'll elope so don't worry about planning a big wedding." She giggled and they continued walking towards the house.

Jessie stopped him near the side door. "Josiah."

He placed his hands on her shoulders and massaged gently. "Don't worry, Jessie."

"I just wanted to say you look nice." She rolled her eyes as she pushed past.

Josiah caught her wrist and she lifted emerald eyes. "Thanks. You look beautiful." He leaned and kissed her cheek, earning a pretty blush. He opened the door and they stepped into the kitchen.

If she could handle Kuntz and Johnson, she could handle the Barnes family. It would be similar to dealing with a herd of longhorn, only this herd could talk. He chuckled.

Jessie walked straight to his mother, who was cutting watermelon. "Hi, Mama." She placed a kiss on the woman's cheek.

Josiah followed smooching the other cheek. He introduced Jessie to the ladies in the kitchen. Two aunts and two cousins. Jessie offered her tiny hand but was engulfed in his aunts' hugs. His cousin Lindsay gave him a thumbs up while her mother embraced Jessie.

"This salad looks divine," Aunt Laura said pulling the plastic container to her nose and inhaling.

"Smells good too," Aunt Janice added. They both nodded to each other.

Matt hovered near the food, swiping tidbits. Finally his mother ran him out. "Ah, Mom, you're starving me. Look, I'm nothing but skin and bones."

Josiah grabbed Jessie's hand and pulled her into the living area. He found the older Barnes men. Being introduced as "Josiah's friend" translated to girlfriend, so he watched her for signs of annoyance or embarrassment but Jessie smiled and shook his uncles' hands.

They made the rounds and found his brothers and younger cousins. Some played the pinball machine in the basement. There was a pool table and darts down there too.

"Hey, Josiah," his father called from the top of the stairs. "Come help me with something."

Josiah hated leaving Jessie's side but she waved him off. Tori had wrangled her into a deep conversation about nail polish.

Jessie

After a while, Jessie went in search of Josiah. His cousin Lindsay stopped her. She swayed, keeping her newborn asleep. "I've been curious. Has Josiah finally gotten serious with you?"

Jessie sucked a quick breath. Heat radiated off her cheeks as she surveyed the living room for Josiah but didn't find him. Matt gave her a sidelong glance, giving her a nano-second of his attention before returning to the Xbox game. Ears were everywhere. She had to watch what she said. "What's Josiah told you?" Jessie probed.

"Well, he acts like you hung the moon." Lindsay chuckled.

Jessie laughed and put her hands on her hips. "That all?"

The corners of Lindsay's eyes crinkled as she smiled. "He's always talking about you, the ranch and your friendship. I thought it'd turn into more." She shrugged.

"Well, we've talked about eloping-"

"I knew it." Lindsay turned and disappeared into the kitchen.

Jessie's stomach twisted into knots. *What did I unleash onto Josiah? It serves him right for not warning me about the family reunion.* Jessie bit her lip. Spying an empty metal folding chair in the corner, she sat and tried to blend into the wallpaper.

It would seem the Barnes family talked about her often. They talked about them as a couple. A fleeting image of Jessie holding Josiah's baby appeared in her mind. Her breath caught. She tried to banish it before it became a permanent thought. Over the eight years she'd known him, Josiah had become her best friend and now they shared a bed even if they weren't intimate. The thought of her and Josiah naked, tangled and sweaty had her temperature rising.

Jessie liked Josiah, and they might have a chance at happily ever after. It'd been so long since she'd considered having a relationship with a man. Even though it scared her, excitement outweighed the fear. But did he have another girl? He had more appointments in the evenings. When she'd asked his brothers, they'd been reluctant to say much. *Guess they didn't want any black eyes.*

Josiah never acted on anything. He'd teased but hadn't asked her out. At night, in the same bed, he never reached for her or kissed. He wasn't aggressive in anyway.

Ernestine, an elderly aunt sitting closest to Jessie, reminisced about her younger years when Jessie heard a voice she had not expected.

B.J. Johnson. She swallowed and pressed back against the chair.

He'd walked in the front door with a bottle of wine and shook hands with Bridger. She let out a breath as the men went into the kitchen. They were neighbors. She shouldn't be shocked to see him there.

B.J. could pitch a fit if he overheard one of the Barnes' say something about Josiah's girlfriend. Jessie sat on her hands and chewed her lip. She'd tried to play down the girlfriend thing but everyone expected the girl, or Guy, brought to the family reunion-holiday bash to be a done deal. They'd soon get married like Maggie and Guy.

Hidden in the corner with no means of escape, she kept still and listened to Ernestine. Her eyes focused on every person to walk past the room. Matt and one of the Dallas cousins played Xbox. Jessie and Matt exchanged a look.

The minutes ticked by and Jessie relaxed again, forgetting about the intruder.

"She's in here," Daniel Barnes said as he held open the door.

Jessie stared at the entry, hoping Josiah had returned but B.J. followed Daniel into the room. Jessie's heart sunk. She turned her head to hide behind a plant.

Matt watched warily. He lowered his controller and frowned.

"Hey Jessie," B.J. said attempting to get her attention. Jessie wanted to climb in a hole.

"That young man is trying to get your attention," Ernestine said. She waved at Daniel and B.J.

"Thanks, Ernestine," Jessie said sarcastically. The older woman with a white afro patted her knee. Sitting straight, Jessie didn't make a move. "Yes?"

"May I have a word," B.J. glanced around and added, "privately?"

With an exacerbated sigh, she stood, about to leave the room with the one man she wanted nothing further to do with.

Matt jumped to his feet stating he needed something to drink. "Hey, Jessie, can I get you anything?"

Jessie recognized the covert offer. "Sure. Something tall, strong and good."

Matt grinned and headed into the kitchen with a determined stride.

B.J. took Jessie by the elbow and urged her out the front door. They walked into the lawn but she stopped, not wanting to get too far. An awkward silence developed as his mouth dropped open, forming a cave. She half expected bats to fly out, especially after the squeak. He cleared his throat. "Look, Jessie, about the other day. I was-"

"A jerk."

"I know. Carlotta threw me off."

"I'm just like her." Jessie crossed her arms, wishing he'd leave. B.J. had crashed her safe house and it infuriated her. Jessie wouldn't sleep with him and that had pissed him off. She refused to be a rebound relationship.

"I'm an idiot and a fool."

"That sums it up," Jessie snipped.

"Listen, dammit, I'm trying to apologize." B.J. grabbed her elbow.

"Ow!" Jessie yanked away. She rubbed the place he'd hurt. "You have a funny way of showing it," she growled.

"If you weren't being so damned unreasonable-"

"That's right, B.J. Blame it on me. Who came here to apologize? Sounds like you're a little mixed up in the head."

"I don't have to stand here and listen to this." His nostrils flared and face turned red as he leaned into her space.

How had she ever found him attractive? "That's fine. Go home, B.J. I don't want you here." She pointed in the general direction of his home.

Josiah rounded the corner of the house with a murderous expression. His jaw tight and gaze fixed on B.J. Jessie couldn't take her eyes off Josiah, her savior once again. His gaze shifted to Jessie then back to the man who had no clue vengeance was about to give him a beat down.

B.J. turned to catch what she watched then backed away surprised. The immediate threat evaporated.

Josiah locked eyes with Jessie and tilted his head. His expression softened and instead of continuing toward B.J., he walked straight to Jessie. Her stomach flip-flopped. She reached for him with open arms and he folded his arms around her pulling her tight. A moment later he pushed back. "You all right?"

"I am now." Jessie felt safe, at home and complete.

Her heart hammered, realizing how much Josiah meant to her. The depth she read in his blue eyes was more than friendship and boss-employee relationship. He cared for her. Her mouth went dry. She hugged him tight, buried her nose in his chest and inhaled deeply. This felt right. Breathing his spicy scent made her long to kiss him. Josiah stroked her long hair, making her shiver.

Over his shoulder, she noted every window was full of faces. Matt's was in the window next to the door. He appeared ready to storm out as backup. Behind Josiah's back, she gave his brother thumbs up.

A lump formed in her throat; this family could be hers if she reached out and grabbed it. The thought made her weak in the knees. She held tight, closed her eyes and sighed.

"This is what I meant," B.J. grumbled. "I never had a chance, but every time I felt I did, something like this happens."

"This happened a long time ago," she muttered quietly. Josiah let out a sigh, and he squeezed tighter. She'd fallen for Josiah when he was a sixteen-year-old boy and again as a young man. He'd grown into a man—a loyal, sweet, gorgeous, kind man. She loved him. Jessie sucked in a deep breath.

"Jessie, would you mind going into the house? Mr. Johnson and I need to have a conversation." Josiah glanced into her eyes.

Jessie nodded but refused to let him go yet. "Don't kill him. You don't have your gun do you?" She bit her lip.

A wicked grin formed. "Darlin', you know I always carry that with me."

Jessie's cheeks burned but a sly smile graced her lips. "I know. I can't easily forget. Anyway, you should keep from shooting it unless you're on Double D property."

Josiah arched a brow. His gaze turned intense, her lungs failed her. She took a few steps toward the front door and pointed at the house. "Too many witnesses."

"Private showing later?"

Hell, yeah. Jessie's brain failed to find words and her heart stalled then kicked-started into overdrive. Her gaze raked his body, starting at his boots and ending with his sun-kissed, wind-tussled hair. Heat filled her body and she longed to touch him. She swallowed, enjoying the slow simmer of desire.

B.J. cleared his throat.

"Don't count on it." Jessie's gaze darted around. She tried not to appear too eager, the tension released and everyone dispersed.

Josiah and B.J. remained in the front yard talking for half an hour. Matt pulled her away from the window.

"It's like putting two bulls in the same fenced area," Jessie said, glancing back. She'd karate chop B.J. then kick him in the gonads or maybe replace them with some of Holden's missing balls.

"Well, I suppose they might butt heads," Matt said as he handed her a beer, "or they might toss cow patties."

Jessie went to help Mrs. Barnes in the kitchen. It was a safer place than the front yard where all she would be able to do is stare at Josiah. The longer she gazed, the more she yearned for him. She'd been tempted to run out and snatch him by the hand and return to the Double D.

"Time to eat." Bridger sounded the alert.

Jessie went to get Josiah and found Matt standing at the entry window watching his brother. She touched his shoulder causing him to jump. "Sorry. Are they still at it?"

Matt shook his head. "I don't get it. Josiah shook hands with Johnson and now they're laughing and smiling like old chums. I don't like it."

Jessie didn't either. A strange sensation filled her stomach.

Matt pulled open the door and yelled, "Time to eat. Better yet, stay out there yapping. There'll be more for me and I'll sit next to your date."

Jessie

The smell of grilled hot dogs and hamburgers hung in the air of the kitchen and dining room as Jessie walked through to the outside patio. The hot food had been lined on the island like a buffet. Chips, salads and other items were in the dining room. She'd eyed watermelon slices. Once the family and friends assembled on the back patio spilling out into the yard, they held hands as the eldest Barnes family member said grace.

Jessie stared at her hand, fingers laced with Josiah's. The simple touch fascinated her. They didn't let go immediately after the prayer ended. She peeked at him. Josiah grinned like a fool.

Throughout the meal, they touched hands or knees and stole glances. Before the meal she'd felt hungry but now she couldn't eat a bite. The butterflies in her stomach launched every time Josiah smiled at her. It was horrible and wonderful.

Josiah sat on one side of her and Guy and Maggie filled the other seats. Matt and Gabe ate at the card table next to them.

"Hey," Gabe said catching everyone within earshot's attention. "Did you hear the prankster struck again? He took Rain-X and marked all the police car's windshields with words or drawings. They could have been put on weeks ago but only showed when it rained recently."

"What'd they draw?" a male cousin asked.

Gabe squinted as he chuckled. "One said 'Help Me' in giant letters. One had a picture of male parts. The back of Ben Moore's said 'Stolen'."

"The vandal has been changing the signs of businesses in town like Harry's Meat Market. Their sign has the changeable letters and boasted a Black Angus meat special. Well, the G went missing."

"Black Anus?" Someone said then laughed. The others at Jessie's table joined in.

"That's not all—the Meat Market sign had been hit before. It read: No one can beat our meat prices. They removed the 'prices'." Gabe returned to his cheese burger while his cousin quizzed him and Matt about the vandal. So far, he hadn't damaged anything, just left the missing letters on the ground next to the signs.

"Hey, Jessie, have you picked a dress for the Cattlemen's Ball?" Maggie asked, her gaze shifting from Jessie to Josiah.

"No. The only thing I've picked is the eye candy I'll be toting along on my arm all night." Jessie giggled and felt the heat radiate off her cheeks. She chanced a glance at Josiah; he'd leaned back in his chair with a wide smile.

Maggie shifted forward and described her style of dress and proposed hairstyles. Throughout the conversation about the dance Guy doted on Maggie. He took her empty plate then brought her a refill. He tucked a wisp of hair behind her ear. When Maggie laughed Guy smiled.

After Maggie and Guy left the table and Josiah joined in the conversation with his brothers speculating about the vandal.

Jessie nibbled on a brownie while considering the dance. Because of

Sawyer, Josiah asked her. She hadn't given the dance much thought but a night in Josiah's arms made her body ache with longing.

"Hey, Jess, are you okay?" Josiah asked with a furrowed brow. He leaned close, his warm breath tickled her neck, sending ripples of pleasure coursing through her. "Out with it."

"The Cattlemen's Ball." Jessie glanced at the napkin in her lap and bit her lip.

Josiah cupped her chin and gently turned her so she had nowhere to stare but his fathomless blue eyes. "Jessie, what are you worried about?"

She pressed her lips together, not wanting to voice her fear. Jessie closed her eyes unable to face the intensity of his gaze.

"Look at me." Josiah's tender voice pleaded. His thumb skimmed her cheek and her heart started an uphill climb. "If you don't tell me, I'll kiss you." He uttered the warning his voice low and raspy.

Jessie's breath caught and her eyes popped open. She scanned the crowd and no one but Matt watched them. "Fine. I want to make sure you wanted to go to the ball." Jessie stared at the napkin again. "With me. I don't want you to feel obligated because of Sawyer." She shrugged and offered him a shy smile.

Josiah's brows knit together and his lips tipped into a frown. He placed his hands on her shoulders. "If you hadn't agreed to be my date I wouldn't be going. Does this answer your doubts? You or no one."

Jessie gulped and nodded. Grateful to be surrounded by strangers or else she'd launch herself into his arms and press her lips and body against his. She took several deep breaths willing her heart to slow. "Only me," she whispered in disbelief.

Josiah's hands traveled up her neck until they held her face. His thumbs caressed her skin and she sighed. His serious expression melted into desire, stealing her breath.

Jessie longed to hold him. To have his flesh sliding next to hers. Her body heated as desire pooled in her core. She placed a hand on his thigh, making him gasp. He covered her hand with his and moved it closer to his knee. An impish grin played on his lips and she couldn't help but echo it.

"Josiah," Bridger called. "Let's get out the fireworks."

Matt jumped up, sending his chair to the ground. Laughing at his brother, Josiah pulled Jessie to her feet. He held her hand and she participated in all the planning but after dark she watched with Tori, Maggie and the rest of the family.

After the display, Josiah returned Jessie to the Double D then went to help his parents clean up. The large master bedroom had never felt lonely until Jessie snuggled under the sheets alone.

CHAPTER 34

Josiah

ONE EARLY JULY EVENING JOSIAH found Jessie sitting in the loft. It was dark and her profile showed as she watched the stars. She kneaded her lower back as she turned to him.

Josiah took over massaging. She slumped with a sigh. "You need to take a day off," he said.

"I can't. I've got deadlines and I need to get things ready for the show." She groaned at his gentle touch.

Josiah wasn't overjoyed about people coming to an exposé, fashion or otherwise. Being in the loop with Desire and Brad, as the secret partner had proved insightful. He'd made many suggestions but Desire pooh-poohed most but taking the show off Double D property and having it hosted elsewhere was a suggestion everyone had agreed on.

"You can stay and protect me." Jessie had mentioned this multiple times.

He would receive an invitation to the show along with the other male guinea pigs. It seemed the men's reaction to the various outfits could guarantee the success of the business and, ultimately, the ranch. He didn't want her to catch on he knew more about her intimate apparel line than he should.

Josiah changed the subject. "I don't want you too tired for the dance. I plan to wear you out good." He moved her hair and pressed a kiss against her neck.

"My feet will be fine."

"It's not just your feet I intend to abuse." His chuckle sent a shiver down her spine which he felt as he rubbed her muscles.

"Do tell," she purred.

"If I told you my secret I'd have to kill you."

"You've tried to kill me. It didn't work."

Josiah snapped his fingers. "I know, then you retaliated by trying to kill me."

"I feel horrible about it too." Her voice turned soft.

"So horrible you corrupted a minor with your mouth." He scratched his chin with a long finger. "I wonder if my mother knows. She might have a different opinion of you."

"Your mother loves me. If she would have caught me, my explanation would have sufficed. I was only trying to wake you." Jessie leaned back onto him.

"You were besotted with me. Admit it, Jess. What else did you want to do with my studly body while I was asleep? I was a kid and you were a woman of the world." Josiah's voice turned husky as he thought of things he wanted her to do to him now.

Quick as a wink, she spun and pushed him onto his back. Surprised, he chuckled.

"It's not what I wanted to do, Josiah, it's what I did." Jessie straddled his body and wiggled her fingers in front of his face. "I took advantage of your body, your beautiful, sleeping body. I touched every inch. Your mind might have slept but other parts of you weren't so sleepy." She shifted slightly. Her gaze devoured his body starting at his zipper until locking on his lips. One delicate eyebrow lifted. A corner of her mouth teased upward into a smirk.

Josiah put his hands behind his head. This was the woman he'd met in the hayloft. The vixen on top of him curled her fingers into the fabric of his shirt, grazing his chest. The light touch gave him goosebumps.

All too soon, the tease left her face as Jessie studied him. Her finger traced his face. "I'm glad you woke up. I would have died if you did." She leaned close.

"I'm glad I did too or I wouldn't have my name carved in the post, at the top of the list too." He wiggled his brows at her.

"Hey, Josiah, you up there?" Matt called as he climbed the ladder and found the owner of the Double D straddling the help. He flashed a mischievous grin. "Job perk?"

Jessie threw an arm wide. In an announcers voice she said, "This too can be yours, if you make it to the top of the hayloft post."

Josiah squirmed beneath her with a frown. She glanced at him and winked. "However, the position in the current loft has been filled. You'll have to find a vacancy in someone else's barn."

The young man examined the wood support and the lower names of the rejects. "This might take some time." Matt rubbed his chin.

"It'll be worth it," Josiah said as he sat up keeping Jessie on his lap.

Jessie put her arms around his neck and touched his hair. "Trust your DNA. You've got it in you."

Both Matt and Josiah grinned.

"Thanks, Jessie. I guess I'll, uh, go do a load of laundry or something." Matt climbed down the ladder then popped his head up. "Oh yeah, Mom said no grand-babies until the time is right."

"Get out of here." Josiah threw a boot at his laughing brother.

"If that's the case, my dad and your mom are going to have a knockdown drag-out. My dad wants grand-babies yesterday."

"We could work on that now." Josiah leaned forward and nuzzled her neck. His hands dipped low on her backside and he pulled her closer.

"Not with your brother listening to everything going on up here."

"I am not," Matt shouted from below.

Jessie

Jessie hadn't talked much with Josiah after the conversation about making babies. Two full days had passed of teasing and smiles but no real expressions of commitment. Ever since the night of July fourth he'd slept in the Double D bunkhouse. She missed him in bed, but this way her hands wouldn't stray. They still read the journals but sat on the porch swing enjoying lemonade and the evening air.

Jessie paced the kitchen, pausing to stare out the window at the driveway. She thought she'd heard his truck again. She sighed. *I should go find a book. A good romance will take me away.*

She kicked at the chair. A hot romance would make her want to jump Josiah's bones the minute he walked through the door. She was half tempted to give him a sneak peek of the items to be debuted at the fashion show.

The night was going to be a long one. Jessie stomped upstairs to the hoard and read the spines. She pointed her finger at them, "Eeny, meeny, miny moe." Picking up the lucky shape-shifter book, she headed to her bedroom.

She sat on the bed and crossed her legs. Her heart felt heavy. If Josiah had a girl, she needed to let him go. It would be hard now that she acknowledged she loved him. Tears threatened to spill as she recalled earlier in the evening.

Jessie made dinner for the Barnes brothers then Josiah ducked out for a meeting. Gabe left with him, begging a ride to a friend's house. Matt helped clean the kitchen. As the sun set, they watched from the back patio. She couldn't help but speculate where Josiah had gone.

"It's not what it seems." Matt gazed at her with pale, blue eyes so much like Josiah's, it made her heart catch. One cheek sported a dimple. "I know what I'd think if the person I loved disappeared at night going to mysterious meetings. My brother isn't seeing anyone. He has an appointment, that's all."

"Is he in a book club?"

After all, her father, the mayor and B.J. belonged to one. Men reading naughty romance novels brought a smile to her face.

"Might be, but I'm not sure." Matt grinned and patted her arm. "Trust him."

In her bathroom mirror, she stared at the sad eyed woman in a silky black nightgown. She'd been prolonging getting ready for bed, waiting for Josiah's return. She pulled the brush through her long hair again.

Trust Josiah? She did, didn't she? Tension between them had been intensifying. Sometimes the all-consuming way he gazed at her made her feel as if her skin would sizzle right off. The sexy cowboy made it hard to think.

It was all the romance swirling around Fortuna. Jessie shook her head. This was Grandma Undine's fault. Her and those blasted novels. The arousal avalanche started with the discovery of the provocative hoard, for the town and her, a sexual awakening. Could she embrace the sexy, sensual side of life?

She sighed. Not yet.

Was she tempted to face it with Josiah? *Heck yeah.* Life with Josiah Barnes would be like riding a mechanical bull, every second would count and it'd be one hell of a ride.

Josiah

Josiah leaned back in the stiff chair and shook his head. "She hasn't shown me a single thing. I mean, she doesn't scurry around and cover things when I enter a room. I've seen bits of material and lace but nothing completed."

Desire and Brad exchanged a look of surprise. "Jessie must be waiting for the show. She invited you." Desire gave him a patronizing smile.

"Yeah, I'm invited and so are other guys," Josiah muttered, frustration apparent in his voice.

The three met secretly at the Big Deal ranch in Brad's dining room. The details of the show remained a mystery to the men but Desire wasn't about to spoil it for either of them. Josiah's involvement included more than moral support; financially he was in for the long haul. From what he has seen, the numbers were good. Double D Intimates was holding its own and, beyond that, it was earning money. It had promise.

"Have you told her how you feel?" Brad asked.

The switch in topic earned a startled expression from Josiah. He chose to ignore it. "How am I supposed to act with other men ogling her?"

Desire tilted the wineglass she held, staring at the burgundy liquid. "Who says she's the model?" She lifted a Vulcan eyebrow and took a sip then placed the glass on the table. "It's the clothing we're showing off, boy."

Josiah's mouth dropped open. He'd assumed Jessie would strut around in tiny swatches of fabric barely covering her... double Ds. He'd prefer one man in the audience—him. According to Desire, if Jessie had a small percentage of Undine's dancer talent and spunk, she'd be a diva. He swallowed and blew out a long breath.

"This is a fashion show, first and foremost," Brad said sounding as if he was trying to convince himself. Hard enough to believe at one point his mother had been a stripper, but now his little girl pimped intimate apparel.

"Brad asked you a question, Josiah," Desire prompted.

"Hm?" Josiah stared at the woman. Question. About the show? His brows dipped in confusion. The older woman tapped her foot.

"Have you told Jessie how you feel?" she repeated.

"Oh." *That question.* Of course he hadn't told her. He wasn't stupid. "I don't want to scare her. She's healing and the last thing she needs is an overload of my emotions." What if the attraction wasn't mutual? He would ruin any chance at winning her. He'd lose her trust and it would be awkward to work alongside her knowing he'd made a fool of himself.

"Josiah," Desire warned. "You don't want some other man to swoop in and steal her away."

"Like Johnson," Brad reminded with a sigh.

Josiah frowned. He'd talked with Johnson and hoped the man was moving on. Johnson didn't have much of a choice with Jessie blasting him on the fourth. But Johnson wasn't one to roll over and play dead though. He had Jessie in his sights and would play nice until he sneaked back into her good graces. Jessie had a soft spot for the man because of Carlotta's actions. Josiah wouldn't let his guard down; Johnson already proved dangerous.

"Oh, that one's a looker. Tall, dark and sexy." Desire hummed. Both men stared in awe. "What? A girl can dream."

"Son, something has changed. Jessie's acting different." Brad glanced to Desire.

"Yes. She's happy, like she made a hard choice and pressure is gone."

"You mean, like picking out silk versus satin?" Josiah scratched his chin.

Brad threw up his hands. "She's happy because she's in love."

"I wouldn't go that far, Brad." Desire wiggled a finger. "Let's say she's crushing on someone in a major way."

"Crushing?" Hope crept in. After all this time, could it be? A smile tugged at Josiah's lips.

"She's walking on cloud nine. As far as I can tell, she keeps busy so y'all don't get busy." Desire grinned then cackled at Brad's pale face.

Brad cleared his throat. "Actually, Desire has a point-"

"She does?" Josiah leaned forward. He had to be kidding.

"She's keeping busy because she doesn't want an idle mind." Brad took a deep breath. "Son, she thinks you have a girl on the side."

Josiah laughed, he couldn't help it. He sobered up when Brad crossed his arms. Josiah stood and paced the room. "She thinks I'm dating someone?"

"It's these business meetings," Desire said with a wink. "She isn't wrong. Come here and give me a big hug. I'll rub my perfume on you."

Josiah returned to his seat and smiled. If he hugged that ornery old woman she'd get more out of it than him, a couple of handfuls more.

CHAPTER 35

Jessie

"COME ON, JESSIE. FESS UP." Kelly wagged a finger in Jessie's direction.

Jessie stared at the brown liquid in her paper cup and chewed the cinnamon donut hole. Kelly had something on her mind when she appeared that morning offering to whisk Jessie away for some girl time. Jessie shook her head. "About what?"

Kelly squinted and leaned forward. "The truth."

Jessie sighed and watched a couple sitting in the ridged faux wood seats of A Hole In One Donut Shop. Their fingers were laced on the tabletop while they talked in hushed tones.

"What truth? That my grandmother was a stripper or a book hoarder?" Jessie popped another donut hole in her mouth savoring the doughy goodness. *God bless Kelly and her meddling.*

"No, silly." Kelley giggled pulling the box of confections toward her. She scrutinized the contents before picking a jelly filled. "What's the deal with B.J.? Do you like him?" The donut hole disappeared into her mouth. "He is tall, dark and sexy."

"Desire would call him eye candy." Jessie giggled. She took a sip of coffee then sat the cup down relaxing back and crossing her legs. "I feel sorry for him. He's been through a tough time. He lost the love of his life, and his heart is broken."

"That's sad, but nothing is going on with you two?"

"No, but I'm glad he started spreading the love of romance novels." Kelly grinned. "Now you can tell me all about you and Josiah."

Jessie fingered her coffee cup. "There's nothing to tell." Jessie shrugged then took a long drink of the mocha-flavored java.

"Like hell, there's not."

"There's not." *Hopefully he will make a move soon.*

"Don't give me that bullshit, Jessie." Kelly slammed her hand on the table.

"Oh!" Jessie squeaked then laughed. "Honest Kelly, Josiah and I aren't an item."

"Come on, Jessie." Kelly rolled her eyes. "That's complete bullshit." She crossed her arms and stared at her friend.

Jessie bit her lip and fiddled with her fingers in her lap. She wasn't dating Josiah, but she wouldn't mind if he asked her out sometime. Her heart raced at the thought.

"This is a ranching town, so I know bullshit when I see it." Kelly's voiced quieted, "There's the kiss you shared with him at Hammered. It wasn't a quickie either. You had your tongue trying to touch his tonsils."

Jessie groaned and covered her hot face with her hands.

"You carved his name at the top of a barn post, for crying out loud."

"Stop," Jessie said as she put her head down on the table, her hands trying to hide her head.

"You guys are always looking at each other and turning red, smiling and sighing." She picked up her coffee and held it. "It's sweet. I wish I had a guy to flirt with."

"Can I refill y'all's coffee?" a skinny teen with buzzed hair asked. His name badge read: Ted, A-Hole of the Month.

Jessie sat up and pushed her cup to the edge of the table. "Hit me."

"Mocha, right?" He winked then filled it to the top. "How about you, gorgeous?"

Kelly blushed and accepted the refill. After the kid returned behind the counter, she said, "I used to babysit him and his little brother."

"How's your classroom coming along? Hear anything from your favorite student's dad?" Jessie sipped her coffee and relaxed.

Kelly laughed nervously. "My room is almost ready for the school year. I saw Andy and Dakota at the open house. Andy waved at me."

"Did he ask you out again?"

Kelly sighed and smiled. "He did, but I can't date him. That would be weird."

"Why?"

"Because he's the parent of one of my students."

"Kinda like me dating my employee?" Jessie grinned when Kelly's eyes narrowed.

"If I was interested in Andy Felterbush as long as you have been mooning over Josiah Barnes then I'd be married with a couple kids by now."

Jessie rolled her eyes and ate two more donuts. "He might have a body carved by the gods but Josiah is too young for me, Kelly."

"That's not what he said to Pixie Dix."

Jessie froze with her coffee cup halfway to her mouth. Her heart had gone cold, and the donuts danced hip-hop in her stomach. "What did he say?"

"Nothing you'd be interested in." Kelly Jo grinned and ate the last two chocolate donut holes.

Kelly had her. *Dammit.* Curiosity was going to give her an ulcer. "Kelly, please."

She grinned and leaned over the table. "Pixie hit on Josiah. Called him Joey-baby and told him she came free with his meal."

"Oh really?" Jessie tried to keep any emotion out of her voice, but it sounded angry. She clamped her hands together so they wouldn't shake.

"That's the bad part. Pixie offered everything for takeout, but Josiah politely smiled and told her he preferred older women." Kelly laughed and leaned back. "You should have seen Pixie's face. Her smile seemed glued on, and she nodded. Sharon waited on Josiah after that."

Jessie sighed and rubbed her face. His words delighted her, and her body tingled as if she was lightheaded. She tried to take deep breaths to calm her racing pulse. B.J.'d told her Josiah loved her, and Josiah chanced a visitation with her. He'd moaned her name with such raw emotion the memory of it shot a shiver down her spine.

"Everyone in Fortuna can see you and Josiah are a perfect fit. Why can't you?" Kelly asked in a soft voice.

Jessie gazed into Kelly's eyes. "I'm afraid. After Rusty-" Her eyes filled with tears, and she tried to blink them away.

Kelly reached across the table and squeezed her hand. "Honey, Josiah is nothing like Rusty. If fact, he's the opposite. Josiah would never put you in a position of compromise. He wants to protect you. Haven't you ever asked why he showed up at Rusty's place?"

Jessie bit her lip. She tried not to visit the past. But when the nightmare resurrected in her memory, she dwelt on her stupidity leading to her vulnerability. She'd made the mistake of trusting Rusty. Josiah arrived at the perfect moment, but she hadn't questioned why.

It hadn't made sense for Josiah to travel to Rusty's mother's place. Far from Fortuna, the trailer was in another county. Jessie rubbed her forehead. "I don't know why he was there," Jessie admitted.

Kelly smiled with a dreamy expression. "My guess is: he wanted to ask you out. He had to ask around to find out where you were."

"Oh. That was me." She'd bumped into him twice before heading out to Rusty's. "I told him my plans."

Kelly's voice lowered to a whisper. "Jessie, what if he's been in love with you since then?"

"I guess I'll have to ask him," Jessie mused.

"What? You want to ask if he loves you?" Kelly's eyelids disappeared.

Jessie rolled her eyes and tossed her head. "No way. I'm going to ask him about that night." She reached into the donut box and swiped the last one. She closed her eyes savoring the flavor. She needed to find the right time to talk to Josiah.

Jessie

Jessie half expected Josiah to appear that night. She dreamed a man visited her.

He wore angel wings, and they kissed and teased one another. He liked her silky gown, but it didn't stay on long; soon they were naked. His body pressed against hers. His lips trailed from hers to her neck down her torso to her core. There he paused, making her squirm. His fingers helped his tongue. She bucked with pleasure. He had a magic mouth. He worked its way up her body again.

They were about to unify when he murmured against her neck, "I've been waiting for this for so long."

Her heart stopped. It was a voice she recognized. She reached for the bedside light as he thrust into her. She turned on the light and B.J.'s sexy body was naked on hers.

Jessie gasped and bolted upright. In the darkness, she fumbled for the light and fell off the bed. *It was just a dream. No, not a dream but a nightmare.* She went to the kitchen and brewed a cup of tea. She wasn't going back to sleep anytime soon.

Josiah

Jessie shuffled into the kitchen and grunted. Her hair stuck out a haphazard ponytail and she'd forgotten to put on makeup. Not that she needed any but the fact she'd forgot all of it said oodles. Josiah tilted his head and examined her from head to toe. Worry balled in his stomach. The plaid blue and yellow shirt was mis-buttoned, one of the tails was tucked in and the other hung out of her unzipped jeans. Her tiny size six feet were sporting different socks, one blue and the other with a striped pattern. The unkempt appearance made him frown.

He handed her a mug of fresh coffee and she sat at the table. He filled a cup for himself then sat across from her. Half the liquid had been drained from her cup and she slumped over with elbows on the table, rubbing her temples.

Josiah waited, observing and hoping the caffeine would hurry and kick in. As he sipped, the rich flavor jolted his taste buds. He closed his eyes and leaned back with a satisfied sigh. When he opened them again, he found Jessie studying him. Her gaze lingered on his lips, making him smile.

Her puffy half-closed lids had bags under them. Even with a slight frown, she still tempted him. Josiah wanted to take her back to the bedroom but putting her to bed alone wasn't on the agenda.

Matt entered the kitchen after wiping his boots on the mat. He glanced from his brother to Jessie then back to his brother. Puzzled, he advanced to the coffee pot and helped himself. He glanced again at the table and announced, "You both look like crap."

"Good morning to you too," Jessie snipped then huffed out a sigh. "I'm sorry, Matt. I didn't sleep well and I need more coffee." She lifted her cup toward Matt, and luckily his brother caught the hint and refilled it.

Behind Jessie's back, Matt gave him a thumbs up. Josiah gave a shake of the head and frowned. Matt must have gotten the nonverbal cues because he shrugged and leaned back against the counter.

"Dreams?" Josiah asked because he hadn't been there to keep her up.

She stared into space and swallowed. "Nightmare. It was horrible." He reached across the table and patted her hand. Her cheeks pinked up and her gaze refocused on him. She clasped her mug with both hands and sucked in her lip. She pulled her cup to her lips and took a large gulp. "It was along the lines of Rusty Kuntz."

"I'll, uh, go do something in the barn." Matt left the house but not without shooting a worried glance over his shoulder.

"I'm sorry, Jessie. I wish I was there with you last night." He'd let the longing seep out and hoped it wouldn't further upset her.

"I do too." Jessie stared into the depths of her coffee but it did nothing to hide the pink blush spreading across her cheeks. "Ever had a dream within a dream? That's what happened. It was all good until the light came on. Then it was all wrong. Seeing someone in my room who shouldn't be there, to wake up and turn on the light for real." She huffed a loud sigh. "It was horrible. Why is my mind playing tricks on me?"

"You haven't had a relationship since before Rusty. He didn't have his way. You know that, right?" Josiah asked.

"That's not what I remember." Jessie glanced at him with watery eyes and sucked in her lip.

"You had underwear on. He didn't violate you. He'd be dead if he had." Josiah took a deep calming breath. "He wasn't excited, if you know what I mean."

"How is that possible when he was all over me?" Jessie hugged herself then shivered.

"Seeing you in any state of undress is exciting. Kuntz was a crazy, drunk fool. I don't know if it was the alcohol. Whatever the reason, I'm grateful he couldn't get it up." Josiah scooted the chair closer then pulled her into his lap. "I wish I could have got there sooner."

"Why were you there at all?" she asked. "I never expected help with his mother's trailer being out in the backwoods." Jessie twisted so she could see his face.

"I found the nerve to ask you to the Cattlemen's Ball. I chickened out three times," Josiah admitted. "You mentioned where you were going but your father gave me the address."

"Really?" She relaxed against him.

"I wish I hadn't been such a coward." He clenched his jaw. "If I would have had the nerve, then maybe you wouldn't have been there at all."

"Oh yeah, where would I have been?"

"In the hayloft—with me."

Jessie's fingers curled on his shirt, pulling him closer. "You're pretty sure of yourself." Josiah opened his mouth to reply, but she beat him to it. "I would have preferred it, that's for dang sure."

Their faces hovered close together, eyes locked on the other, neither seemed to breathe.

Matt barged in the door with a mischievous grin. "Sorry guys, but you gotta hear this."

Gabe followed him in, stopped short then blushed and rubbed his head. "Maybe now isn't-"

"For Pete's sake, just tell them," Matt demanded.

"Fine. There's been another prankster strike. Willie Stoker is now pink. The vandal painted the statue pink. Bubble gum, Pepto Bismol, whatever, but he's pink!"

Jessie

After Jessie got her act together she met Desire for lunch. They relaxed at The Pink Taco's bar and sipped margaritas while eating burritos, the lunch special.

"Ladies, did you see the pink man in town today?" Clint Torres, the owner, strummed his fingers on the counter. In his fifties, with a salt and pepper goatee, he was a handsome man Desire fancied.

"Yeah, Clint, what's up with him? Who's the vandal?" Jessie studied Clint for signs of guilt.

"I don't know, man, but I'd love to thank him. My sales have doubled today. This place is packed. Everyone who thinks pink thinks of the Pink Taco. It's been great for business. I could give the guy a hug."

"Would you settle for giving an old lady one?" Desire asked with a shy smile and flung her arms open.

Clint grinned but pointed. "Ah, Ms. Desire, anything for you, but hands off the cojones." He came out from behind the counter and spread his arms.

"Clint, you're no fun." Desire accepted his hug nonetheless but goosed him on his way to the kitchen.

CHAPTER 36

Josiah

JOSIAH PULLED OPEN THE DOOR to Hammered and glanced around the empty restaurant. He'd never seen the place so dead or the romance bookshelf so plundered.

From behind the bar, Pixie waved a hand holding a white cloth but turned away. "Everyone is upstairs." She returned to drying a tray of glass mugs.

"Looks like you'll have an easy afternoon." Josiah inhaled a deep breath reminiscent of stale beer before turning into the hallway leading to the stairwell. He trekked the narrow passageway two steps at a time. His stomach churned. The other men's presence tempered his excitement to see Jessie's creations.

Gabe stooped over a laptop placed on a card table. The soft light washed his face with an eerie glow making him seem angelic. His blue eyes flicked in Josiah's direction and he nodded welcome. "'Bout time you showed," he said pushing away from the table.

Josiah continued into the small space before studying the attached party room. The room didn't smell like a greasy spoon but fresh paint. Rows of folding chairs surrounded a runway built for the occasion. He whistled. "Holy hell, this place is different."

"Check this out." Gabe pushed a button and the main lights dimmed and a colored spotlight shined on the stage then another faded in on the other side. The murmurings of the guests quieted as they glanced to the stage.

"Wow. Have you orchestrated the entire event?" Josiah asked. His

220

brother had always been the family IT guy. It was nice to see him tap his creative side.

Gabe's chest swelled and his lips spread in a wide smile. "Yep. Wait until you see the show. It's going to be nothing like you imagined."

Josiah had imagined Jessie showing off her lacy skivvies and dancing around for him but not for others. He frowned and counted the chairs. It promised to be one hell of a shindig.

"You've done a great job, Gabe."

"The show hasn't even started." Gabe laughed and reached into a backpack and pulled out a sketchbook and pencils.

"No. I mean it. You've been helping Jessie in ways I couldn't have fathomed. Thank you for that."

His little brother's cheeks flamed red, and he returned his attention to the sketchbook, flipping open to a blank page. "You're welcome."

Across the room, Brad leaned against the long wooden bar. He raised a hand in greeting. Josiah meandered through the room, across a designated aisle. He noted several folks had already arrived and a majority of them stood sipping cocktails in the back. Josiah recognized the boutique/adult bookstore owner, Pat Downe. A few business women chatted with men in suits.

Holden pushed a cold long neck toward Josiah. "Looks as if you need it."

"You have no idea." Josiah chuckled and clinked Brad's bottle. "Here's to Jessie and the Double D."

"Hear hear." Brad took a long drink, and the three men remained quiet, observing the guests.

Mayor Jasen Delay hustled across the room and shook their hands. He thumbed over his shoulder and asked. "Who're the suits?"

Josiah grinned at him. In dress pants, white button up shirt and red tie, the mayor could blend in with the newbies.

"A few of my daughter's business associates," Brad acknowledged.

The mayor rubbed his hands together and his brows lifted as his eyes lit. "Guess I'll go introduce myself."

A few locals moseyed to the bar. Holden filled orders. Josiah leaned against the bar, drinking and inspecting the room. He'd been in the party room several times. The receptions, graduations and birthday parties had balloon and flower decorations, tablecloths with centerpieces. He'd never seen it with a raised stage. A skirted runway split the center of the front of the room. Chairs lined both sides. The polished wood floor gleamed.

Josiah scrubbed his face, hoping Mona or Kelly planned to model the skimpy wares and not Jessie.

The curtain over the door fluttered and Desire stuck her head out. "Hey boy," she called to someone on a ladder hanging a sign of the Japanese caricature logo. Matt finished hanging it then shifted one side so it hung straight. Josiah frowned; even Matt had been a part of the show's set up.

"Hey, tight pants," Desire tried again.

"What do you need now?" Matt's exasperated tone made Josiah chuckle. Matt tipped his head back and pinched the bridge of his nose.

She crooked her finger and her smile turned sappy sweet. But Josiah couldn't read their lips.

Others from Brad's reading group mingled with the men and a few women gathered near the bar. Sharon joined Holden, both working up a sweat.

Josiah kept his eyes on the entrance. He'd invited Paige Turner but wouldn't recognize the local author's face. Well, Desire wrote the note, and he mailed it.

During one of his meetings with Brad and Desire, she'd informed them Paige had replied with the cover of an upcoming release. Jessie had set about the task trying to emulate the nightgown.

Josiah swallowed and rubbed his damp hands on his jeans. He felt under dressed. At least he'd put on a clean polo shirt and his good boots.

A short skinny man with a broom-bristle mustache hesitated near the entry. His owlish eyes peered through thick, round glasses. Gabe greeted the man and handed him a piece of paper.

Before Josiah knew he'd moved, he stood between the stranger and his brother with his hand out. Gabe offered a program. Josiah skimmed the paper with the Double D Intimates logo. It thanked him for being a part of the show and promised an exciting night.

"Oh boy." The man glanced up from the brochure. A wide grin broke out on his face. "I'm glad I didn't bring any women with me tonight."

Josiah chuckled, inspecting the man. He appeared the bookish sort, especially when he pushed up his glasses.

The stranger leaned closer to Josiah and said, "I hear one of the show pieces is based on Paige Turner's novel's cover."

Josiah's brows skyrocketed and a small gasp escaped his mouth. *How did he know? It must have been Desire dropping juicy bits of information. In Fortuna, it'd only take a small spark to start a gossip inferno.*

"That's what I've heard too," Josiah offered with a nod.

"Interesting." The man's shoulders rolled back, and he stood straighter.

He strutted into the main room.

Gabe handed programs to the next group of men as they arrived. After they'd passed, Josiah turned to Gabe. "Who is that odd man?"

"It was Paul Ennis."

"Who?"

"He writes under the pseudonym you might know."

"Oh?"

"Yeah. Paige Turner."

"The romance writer is a guy?"

"Yep."

"No shit."

Gabe pointed to Brad. "Mr. Davidson needs you. You better not keep your future father-in-law waiting."

Josiah tried to smack his brother's arm but the laughing teen dodged it. He swallowed and crossed the now bustling room. Damn, the place had filled. All these men would know Jessie's business.

"Son, you look as if you're going to a funeral." Brad placed a hand on Josiah's shoulder.

Josiah tried to smile but probably appeared constipated.

"You're doing fine."

Fine? He wanted to pull the fire alarm and make everyone leave so he could view the show alone. "I don't know how I feel, Brad."

The older man's brow crinkled and a pained expression crossed his features. "Yeah." Brad took a deep breath. "Well. We better get to our places. Yours is in the front row."

Brad pointed but walked the other direction. Josiah found a card printed with his name on a front row chair. Other names along the front included Pat Downe, Randy Peters, Neil Lowe and, oh shit, B.J. Johnson. Josiah stifled a growl.

Jessie had made it clear to Johnson she didn't want him in the romantic way. So why the hell is he invited?

Johnson entered the room making a beeline for the bar and his book club members. The man was welcomed by other men in the community, including Jessie's father. Josiah crossed his arms certain Brad was unaware of Johnson's advances toward his daughter.

Jessie had handled it encouraging Josiah, Maybe the Kuntz incident was behind them too and he had the old Jessie back. He enjoyed the way she'd told Johnson to buzz off. Josiah couldn't help the sly smirk that found a home on his lips. He didn't want to sit next to Johnson but this way he could keep an eye on him. He sat back, closed his eyes and took several deep breaths.

"Is this seat taken?" Johnson asked.

Josiah's eyes popped open, and he swept his arm. "All yours."

"How'd I get this primo spot?"

"Hell if I know," Josiah muttered as he crossed his arms again.

CHAPTER 37

Jessie

JESSIE BIT HER LIP AND glanced in the full length mirror. She loved the gown but couldn't believe she'd be the one showing it off.

"Hey, quit chewing your lip. You'll ruin your makeup." Gloria Sass spun Jessie around so fast she tipped into the girl's arms. "You should put your boots back on."

"My boots? So I can kick your ass?" Jessie grumbled.

Gloria threw her head back and laughed until tears streamed down her face. She squeaked, "As if."

Desire stepped into the room wearing a soft gray wool skirt suit with an ivory-colored blouse. "Time to get this show on the road." Desire glanced at her diamond encrusted gold watch. With a clipboard in hand, she resembled a cruise director. She winked and held the door open for Jessie.

Jessie closed her eyes and took several deep breaths. Her knees shook. She needed to pull her act together, or she'd fall off the runway.

Desire led the way to the curtain. She stuck her hand through and the lights dimmed. The music started. A hush fell over the audience as they anticipated the show. Desire closed the black material then faced Jessie. A wistful expression softened her features. "Jessie, you're stunning. Undine would be proud of you, my girl." Desire wiped a stray tear then squared her shoulders. "Don't forget the walk."

Jessie nodded and blew out a long breath.

Desire grinned and stepped through the curtains. The audience clapped. "Shucks, y'all know how to make an old woman feel young again. Anyone looking for a date to the Cattlemen's Ball come and see me afterward."

After the laughter died, Desire explained the romance hoard leading to the creation of the Double D intimate apparel line. "Welcome to the premiere unveiling of the Double D Intimates. Modeling the first item tonight is the owner and creator, Jessie Davidson."

The audience again applauded and Gloria nudged Jessie forward. She blinked into the bright spotlight aimed at her. Having practiced using the stairs from the runway, she'd felt comfortable in heels, but now with the crowd watching she froze.

Desire began the spiel about the floor length gown and Jessie moved again. "Inspired by the 1940s, this masterpiece in black is elegant and mysterious."

Jessie gathered courage as she stepped to the rhythm of the music. The lightweight material of the robe was shimmery and sheer and delicate black lace lined the bottom hem. The sleeves ballooned at the shoulder then gathered at the elbow. Satin ribbons accented the elbows and matched the tie around the waist.

Butterflies fluttered in her stomach but she pasted a smile onto her lips. *I can do this. I just need to channel my inner call girl.*

Glancing over the audience, she spotted her father. He wore a pained expression as if his appendix had busted. She blew a kiss to him making him swallow and blink.

Beforehand, both she and Desire had tried to reassure him she wouldn't be naked. Under the lingerie, she wore a nude colored bodysuit, like an old fashioned one piece bathing suit with tight mid-thigh shorts and sleeves to the wrist. Bracelets hid the edge. This trick she learned from Desire.

Jessie turned around and met Desire half-way. "They're speechless. That's a good sign." Desire said, earning more laughs.

Jessie strutted to the end, and the robe slid off the shoulder she rolled. It was a polyester blend but the men in the front row probably wouldn't care. It wasn't the polyester of yesteryear. Pulling the hem out she held it for the men to touch.

Jessie stepped down the two front steps and stopped in front of Josiah's chair. He leaned back scanning her face and swallowed. She refused to bite her lip.

Josiah raised his hand as if to touch her but stopped himself. He blew out a soft whistle. She giggled and had to glance away.

Like a fishing line, she dangled one end of the slippery, satin tie in front of Josiah. "Hold on to this and don't let go." She winked, and he nodded.

"Yes, ma'am." He pinched the thin strip of material between his thumb and fingers.

Jessie stepped backward, and the bow slid apart, untying the front of the robe. She turned in a circle panning the room. Many familiar faces gawked as the robe slid off one shoulder and arm then the other. It fell to the floor and stayed there, a soft black puddle.

Josiah still held his end of the satin ribbon, his face resembling a fish as he stared at the bodice. The neckline, edged with scalloped lace, plunged into a deep V exposing maximum cleavage. The spaghetti straps had a cuff of matching lace on the shoulder. A diamond of lace started on the underside of the bosom and ended at the belly button. The back also had a lace diamond. Both sides of the skirt had slits.

Her body heated, and she graced Josiah with a seductive smile.

"This material is a Poly-Acrylic Lycra blend. The Lycra adds to the flexibility of the fabric." Desire had entered teacher mode.

Inhaling deeply, Jessie placed the pad of her shoe between Josiah's legs on the edge of the chair. The material slid away exposing her leg.

Desire continued, "A long skirt in any material is confining but with two slits the legs are free and mobility gained."

"So is easier access," B.J. pointed out with a grin.

Josiah slid his hand up the backside of her thigh where it disappeared in the soft black material. He winked at Jessie. "I agree." Offering her guests a smile, Jessie pushed off the chair and returned to the runway, leaving the robe on the floor.

"This line comes with several styles of matching underwear French cut, bikini and thong," Desire stated as she shook her behind, "none of which I'm wearing."

Jessie tried not to walk faster as she neared the end of the runway. She gave one last wave and disappeared from sight behind the curtain. She took a large gulp of air but grinned so hard her face hurt.

"You were awesome," Daisy Hopkins said. She drew in a deep breath and gave her arms a loosening shake. "Now it's my turn."

"Thank you for helping me." Jessie took the tall girl's hand and squeezed. "Good luck."

Daisy giggled and stepped through the curtains. Desire's voice introduced the ensemble as "a classic bridal set." The white bustier, a fancy push-up bra, covered most of Daisy's athletic waist. She wore matching bikinis and stockings. A white feather boa rested in the crooks of her arms and she twirled the ends as she strutted down the runway in high heel vinyl boots.

Through a sliver between the curtains, Jessie watched Josiah. Her stomach ached as his gaze scanned Daisy's body. Next to him, B.J.'s eyeballs bulged and tongue wagged reminding her of a cartoon character. Josiah opened the program and read a page when Daisy stopped and turned at the end. He reached for the black robe at his feet. Jessie smiled as a wave of relief rolled over her. Josiah brought it to his nose and closed his eyes as he took a deep breath. His lips curled in a small smile and warmth spread through Jessie.

"Stop watching the men. Come on. We don't have much time." Gloria grabbed her elbow with a yank. Jessie nodded and followed her into the room. Gloria helped lift the gown over her head then hung it on a hanger. Jessie slipped off the shoes while Gloria held the next item.

Jessie passed Daisy again. She hated heels higher than two inches and focused on walking. She didn't leave the runway as she did on her first trip but headed to trade places with Daisy again.

In the room, Gloria once again helped remove the gown. "This is my favorite," she said as she helped Jessie into the next garment. Gloria touched the pale blue material.

The compliment shocked Jessie, but she agreed. "Mine too."

Jessie snapped the crotch. This piece fit Jessie tighter than the others. The light blue silk reminded her of Josiah's eyes. The ecru lace plunged, exposing half a rack and edged her hips.

When Daisy pushed through the curtain Jessie hit the runway again. A favorite, the teddy was one of the first pieces she'd embellished. Jessie held Josiah's rapt attention again. She winked at him and his sultry, hooded eyes did more to raise her temperature than the spotlights.

Once in the changing room, Jessie tugged on the snaps. They wouldn't release. The plastic snapping system she'd used at the crotch had stuck. Neither she, Gloria or Desire could unsnap the dang thing.

"You need a man," Gloria said pointing to the pinnacle of Jessie's legs.

"What do you need?" Matt asked sticking his head in the doorway.

"Go get Josiah," Gloria ordered before Jessie could respond. "I don't have time to mess with it. I need to get my red sexy thing on." She disappeared behind a screen at the back of the room.

Jessie hadn't expected her to bail but Gloria was right. The encore was fast approaching. She put hands on her hips and blinked away tears. She'd wanted to be in the audience to watch it.

Josiah entered breathless. He took Jessie by the shoulders as his gaze roamed her body. "What's wrong?"

"My snaps are stuck." Jessie's face felt as hot as the sun. Her hands flew to her cheeks.

His gaze dropped, and Josiah chuckled. "Matt made it seem like an emergency."

"My help's gone." She pointed to the screen where Gloria muttered. Jessie grinned and teased, "If you want to go back out there to watch the show I suppose Matt could give it a tug."

Josiah's smile fell off his lips, and he leaned closer. "That won't be necessary."

He knelt before her and she showed how she pulled the garment. Josiah reached out his hand but hesitated to touch. He frowned as he glanced up with pinched brows. "Jess?"

"Don't worry, I'm wearing a leotard. Please, be gentle. I don't want it ripped."

He moved his fingers under the delicate fabric brushing against the most intimate place. A leotard did little to protect the area, and she gasped. His eyes sought hers and she nodded. He tugged; of course, nothing happened.

Longing threatened to overwhelm her as her body heated to a molten level. She yearned to run her fingers through his wavy hair but kept her arms at her side. Her fingernails dug into her palms.

Josiah yanked harder, then blew out a long sigh with frustration. "I guess you'll have to leave it on," he said with a smirk.

"That would be a shame, because you'd miss the grand finale."

"Such a shame," he teased moving his fingers against her. She gave in and plunged her fingers into his thick brown hair.

"Josiah," she purred, "fix it. Or I will let B.J. take a look-see."

Josiah knit his brow in consternation and leaned to inspect the little bugger. His warm moist breath fanned her. He ran his hand along her backside and grabbed the material. "What is this some sort of chastity belt?" he said as he pulled again.

"Not if you can get it off." Jessie's body responded to his touch with a shiver.

It pulled free. Josiah grinned at her triumphantly.

"Now isn't the time to get on your knees and play, Josiah dear." Desire stood in the doorway holding the clipboard and tapping a pen. She smiled and winked at them. "Thank the man proper, Jessie, so we can continue the program."

Josiah got to his feet and Jessie put a hand on his chest. His heart raced like hers. Jessie tilted her head and tiptoed. She intended the kiss to be a sweet peck but her body had other ideas. The kiss deepened, his soft moan making her pull him against her. Both their hands dropped to the backside. His hands massaged her back under the unfastened material and she pulled out his shirt, caressing hot, damp skin.

"Children," Desire snapped.

"Wow." Gloria clapped.

They pulled apart and smiled at one another. Jessie's lips tingled. *Good God, that man can kiss.* He hugged her to him, burying his nose in her hair. "Thanks," Jessie whispered.

"Any time," he offered with a husky laugh.

"Come on, Gloria, the show must go on."

Gloria stood with her arms folded across her chest. Her foot tapped and her head tilted as if she listened for a musical cue. Jessie worried Josiah's eyes would stray to the red lace and satin Gloria wore but he remained focused on her.

"I need a knife," Jessie stated, shocking the others.

"Why do you need that?" Desire asked.

"I have to carve a pole," Jessie said.

Josiah grinned. "You liked it, did you?" Jessie hummed her pleasure, and he chuckled. Holden wouldn't appreciate if she carved initials on anything.

Desire's penciled brows rose as she pointed to Josiah's crotch. "There's one." Jessie stifled a giggle.

"On that note, I'm out of here." Josiah fled the room.

Dressed in a sundress with a white short-sleeve shrug, Jessie slipped into the room next to her father. Gabe had the spotlights swirling around the room and moving to a funky beat as they changed colors.

Brad placed a hand on her shoulder and squeezed. He pointed to the corner where Matt helped Paul arrange books on a table. "This has been quite a show, little girl. You've done well."

"Thanks, Daddy."

Desire took the stage again as the music faded. "Thank you for attending The Double D Intimates inaugural show. We hope you've enjoyed viewing the sampling of Jessie Davidson's work. There are items for sale at the other side of the room including Paige Turner's latest novel. The author is here and will be signing books."

The excited murmurs of the audience made Desire pause. People twisted around in their seats. Jessie hoped she'd had time to make enough of the Turner novel's gown. If she ran out, they could always place an order. She rubbed her hands together and bit her lip. Her gaze panned the crowd again but stopped when she found Josiah staring at her. Her mouth went dry, and the room faded around them.

"Now ladies and gentlemen, our finale." Desire moved offstage after a few more words, then the lights dimmed. A hush fell then the music played. The spotlight blazed to life on Gloria as she stood facing away from the crowd. The red strapless, topless corset was the raciest thing Jessie had ever created. She hoped to gage its popularity by sales and orders from the show. Gloria wore a sheer, red robe with lace edges and a G-string. The leotards made the show PG-13.

In strappy heels, Gloria strutted to the end of the runway and grinned. She bent her legs and moved her arms as if she lassoed something off stage. The imaginary rope flew behind the screen and caught something. She giggled and tugged and tugged.

"Hold still, you varmint." Gloria gave a heavy pull, and a man came into view.

"Ya caught me, now what are you going to do?" Sawyer grinned wearing black cowboy boots and red thong.

"Brand you. Do you like it hot?" Gloria asked in a silky voice.

"Hell, yeah." He licked his index finger and poked his tush making a hissing sound. He swayed his visible cheeks at the crowd, earning laughter mixed with a few groans.

Desire stepped onto the stage again and swept her arms. "Double D intimates can cater to both men and women. Custom orders are available."

"You too can have your own marble sack," Sawyer declared gyrating his hips. Desire had picked a perfect man. Jessie held her hand over her lips to stifle a laugh.

The spotlight focused on Desire who stood alone and reminded everyone about the books and lingerie being sold. "Now let's give a big hand to the woman with the creative genius who brought us these captivating items."

Jessie stepped onto the runway. The audience clapped and yelled her name. The noise drowned out the sound of her racing heart. Her tongue was pasted to the roof of her mouth yet her cheeks hurt from smiling.

She tried to swallow and cleared her throat. "Thank y'all for coming and making Double D Intimates introduction a success."

Jessie thanked her models, stage and sound crew then mentioned her supporting father. Her gaze landed on Josiah who stood clapping, others joined him. Someone in the back whistled.

Josiah

Josiah carried a tall glass to the far end of the room. Behind the book signing table, Jessie faced the corner and drew in a few deep breaths. The murmuring of the crowd had dissipated but a few people still held drinks and compared purchases.

The empty rack once holding the book cover gowns was behind the table. Jessie had sold out of the gowns.

Paul ran out of books too. He had foresight to put an extra case of an older book in his trunk. When he ran low, he sent Gabe out to fetch the box.

Double D Intimates gained a large following, according to the extensive number of names on the email sign-up sheet. He suspected she'd have a large deposit on Monday.

He'd caught Jessie yawning and rubbing her eyes while sitting at the table next to Paul while schmoozing with her clientele.

"Jess, here's a drink for you." Josiah held out the sweet tea.

She gulped the liquid then smiled at him. "Thanks for looking out for me."

"Always." He aimed to keep that promise. His hooded eyes held her gaze as pink spread across her cheeks. Her lips parted, tempting him.

He needed to step away and break the mesmerizing spell she'd cast on him or he might lose control. His restraint was wearing thin. Josiah turned to go but Jessie grabbed his wrist.

He halted at the warm touch. Breathing through his mouth, he scanned the room for an escape. He clenched his lids shut. Leaving wasn't an option if she needed him.

"Josiah," Jessie's soft voice beckoned him like a siren's song.

"I'm listening, darlin'."

She made a quiet mew-like noise, but didn't reply. He twisted toward her but she stared at her toes. His heart lurched. Something troubled her. He caressed her cheek, and she leaned into his touch with a sigh.

Lifting her head, Jessie's green eyes studied him. What did she see? How much he loved her or how much he wanted her? He tucked a wayward strand of hair behind her ear. Her thumb skimmed his skin where she still held his wrist. Tingles of pleasure caused goosebumps.

"I need to ask you a question." Jessie broke eye contact. Her gaze strayed to his belt buckle.

"Shoot."

She giggled, and an impish grinned played on her lips. "It's nothing to do with guns."

Josiah rolled back on his heels. "That's a damn shame." He chuckled, enjoying the shade of red her deepening blush produced. Her eyes narrowed a second then swept his body.

"Remember the day we found Muddy Buddy?"

"Yes."

"You kissed me in the kitchen. Why?" Jessie's intense stare had his blood boiling.

Johnson had visited and together they'd gotten rid of him. Josiah had caught her staring at various parts of his body. He'd been turned on and feeling high after she called him perfect.

"We've kissed more than once, Jess, why that kiss?" He cocked his head.

Jessie sucked in a deep breath. "Well, I can understand the others. We were young when we rolled in the hayloft. One kiss was a prize for winning the pool game. Tonight's," her voice stammered, and she cleared her throat. "Tonight's was a thank you."

"You can thank me again, if you want," he teased.

Her lips twisted into a grin then she bit her bottom lip. Josiah leaned closer, and she put her hand on his chest. Her eyes widened. His heart raced. Would she bolt like a frightened rabbit or did she want to learn the truth?

"It was different. It wasn't prompted. There wasn't a reason." She stared at his belt buckle again.

He swallowed, hoping her gaze stayed above the belt. "Don't you enjoy kissing?"

Jessie rolled her eyes. "Hello? I needed a knife, remember?" She chuckled and crossed her arms.

He raised his arms in surrender. "Yes, I remember." Josiah couldn't forget the hayloft, or the morning in question. He could still feel Jessie's hungry thank you kiss. "That morning, we were alone…" He shoved his fingers in his front pockets. He couldn't tell how he felt. Not yet.

"Yes?" Jessie said. She placed both her palms on his chest and gazed into his eyes.

Josiah sighed and rested his hands on her shoulders. "That morning, I had a moment of weakness and lost control." He pressed his eyes shut. Shame washed over him. Losing control could end their friendship. Or worse, hurt Jessie. He'd never be able to live with himself if he hurt her.

"You mean, you didn't want to kiss me?" He recognized the doubt in her voice.

Josiah's eyes popped open. He'd upset her trying not to hurt her. He sighed again. Better to have a broken heart than to break hers. "Jessie, I want to kiss you every waking moment." He rammed his fingers through his hair. "I'm afraid I'll lose control and won't be able to stop."

"I liked that kiss." She admitted glancing away. "It was sweet, gentle and hot too. Just like you."

Josiah sucked in a breath.

"I thought you've been ignoring me because you had a girlfriend." Jessie shrugged wearing a sheepish smile.

His fingers squeezed her shoulders as his gaze bored into hers. "There's no one else for me but you, Jessie."

With tears in her eyes, she slid her arms around his waist and hugged him. "I guess Desire was right. You were trying to be good by staying away from my bed."

"You've talked to Desire about us?" Josiah asked as Jessie turned cherry red.

"Jessie," Brad called.

"Over here," she said, letting Josiah go. She bustled to her father, and they talked pointing to different parts of the room.

In a happy fog, Josiah floated down the stairs. Sitting in his truck he yelled, "Jessie didn't reject me."

CHAPTER 38

Josiah

JOSIAH PUSHED THE BLANKET ASIDE. The morning light filtered into the old office-turned-bunkhouse through the slats of the mini-blinds. He rubbed his eyes then scratched his head. After a yawn, he glanced at the bunk bed where he'd heard whispers.

His brothers sat on the lower bunk with their heads together in quiet conversation. Both wore rumpled clothes as if they'd only woke.

"What's going on?" Josiah asked, making the teens jump.

Gabe hopped up and spread his arms. "Happy Birthday!"

Josiah's mouth went dry. He groaned and threw his body back onto the mattress covering his eyes with his arm. God. He hated his birthday.

"Aw man, don't be like that," Gabe said sounding hurt.

The kid had been five when Moriah died. *He hadn't been her twin.* Being alive was a constant reminder of her death. Josiah pushed himself up again and forced a smile. *No need to ruin anyone else's day.*

"Did we wake you when we came in last night?" Matt asked.

"I didn't hear a thing." Josiah noted Matt's somber face. Either he wasn't quite awake yet, or he was tired from the night before. "Thank you for helping Jessie. The show's presentation was professional."

"Thanks. It was challenging yet satisfying." Gabe beamed and elbowed Matt who grimaced.

With a tonsil-exposing yawn, Matt scratched his chest. "I'm so glad to be away from Ms. Hardmann. That woman is a tyrant." He frowned and stared at the wall.

"She liked you." Gabe laughed.

"She liked my ass. She kept pinching it. I'll have a bruise for a month." Matt shivered.

A smile teased Josiah's lips. Ms. Hardmann, what an ornery woman. "Did she pull any stunts after I left?"

Matt and Gabe glanced at each other, then burst out laughing. "You won't believe it," Matt said.

"After you left, the locals went downstairs to get books and dinner. A few of those business owners stayed and talked. Desire stood gabbing with Jessie, Gloria and Daisy." Gabe glanced at Matt who prompted him to continue. "B.J. Johnson approached the group and asked 'Ms. Hardmann, can I offer you a ride?'"

Matt jumped in and continued, "That old lady smiled and turned to the girls. She switched on the teacher voice she used for the show and lifted a finger, pointing to the ceiling." Matt's voice rose as he mimicked Desire. "Always accept free rides from handsome men, especially ones you'd like to ride all night long."

Gabe laughed, holding his sides while Matt snorted with disgust.

"Yep, that's Desire." Josiah rubbed his chin still grinning. "What did Johnson do?"

"He laughed really loud." Gabe smiled. "And he turned as red as a chili pepper."

"That's not what Josiah means. Johnson didn't take her home. She sent him on his way telling him he didn't have the stamina she required." Matt shook his head.

While Josiah made his bed, Gabe rambled on about the breakdown of the show's electronics and stage. Both his brothers had stayed late to clean and help Jessie and Brad.

When Josiah pushed open the back door, the smell of fresh-brewed coffee assaulted him. On the kitchen table a blue envelope with a Mylar balloon attached to it awaited him. It moved one way flashing Happy Birthday then twisted back repeating the message as the ribbon rotated the balloon.

Jessie walked into the kitchen. A smile lit her face as she changed course from the oven to him. Wrapping her arms around him, she tiptoed and kissed his cheek. "Happy Birthday, Josiah."

As he stared into her green eyes, time stood still and the longer he held her the hotter the room grew. The desire to fling everything off the table and ravage her struck him like a solar flare.

The oven timer sounded, and she jumped away from him, hurrying to the oven. She opened the door and peered in. A new delicious smell hit him and his mouth watered. "It's almost ready." Jessie took a deep breath and smiled.

"Do I have time to shower?" he asked. She straightened and her gaze swept him from head to toe. His mouth went dry. A lopsided grin formed on her lips. God, he wished he could read minds.

Matt and Gabe entered behind him. "Oh my God. That smells great." Gabe moseyed to the oven and took a deep breath. His eyes rolled back in his head. "Breakfast casserole. Mm."

"Wash up," Jessie ordered.

"Yes, ma'am," Matt replied and soaped his hands at the kitchen sink.

Josiah struggled to get an adequate quantity of food from his plate into his mouth so not to disappoint Jessie. He didn't have much of an appetite, unlike his teenage brothers who wolfed down a majority of the casserole before he'd sat at the table.

"Thanks Jessie, that was phenomenal." Josiah put his empty plate in the sink. The smile on her face was worth his effort.

"Josiah," Jessie called as he opened the door. She met him there, tiptoed and kissed him on the cheek again. "Try to have a good day."

The urge to pull her into his arms and weep hit him. He sucked in a deep breath. With a stiff nod, he forced a smile.

Jessie

Jessie sat at the sewing machine and tried to create but she found it a chore. Her mind kept slipping to a melancholy cowboy. She'd ruined two pairs of panties.

She wanted to pull Josiah into her arms and hold him. Jessie hated seeing him sad and itched to fix the situation. But she couldn't fix death.

She left the Double D. She hoped getting away from his essence would help ease the obsessive thoughts.

While in the fabric store in Nockerville, Tori called and invited Jessie to the Barnes' home to celebrate Josiah's birthday with cake. Jessie had time to kill before arriving. She ended up at Hammered.

Holden handed her a long neck. Sitting in her usual spot, she sipped while she tried to read the last pages of a novel. A contemporary western romance. New girl in a small town fighting for acceptance. She found a friend in the local vet and eventually they became lovers. Then the man she ran away from comes after her to find her in a Podunk town and he wanted to rescue her. Great sex must equal great love because she stayed.

Unrealistic hogwash.

Jessie smelled B.J.'s cologne before he sat next to her. She ignored him and kept reading. She reached the happily ever after, sighed and set the book aside.

B.J. placed his order then turned to Jessie. "I've read that."

"Yes, I saw. You're not the only one. There are seven sets of initials. Did you like it?"

He thought for a while. "Yes. I guess you didn't."

She shrugged. "It's not realistic."

"They lived happily ever after." B.J. grinned. "It's got some good points. The lonely girl needed friends. The vet guy was nice to her."

"He saw a needy, pretty woman and lured her in."

"They were attracted to each other. Raw animal attraction. It happens," he said.

"I guess." Jessie remembered the way Josiah had moaned her name, and a shiver ran down her spine. "But what about her original boyfriend who traveled after her? He cared for her. He wanted to make a life together."

Now she turned to him, reminded of the first day they opened the room full of books. "See point number two: all problems disappeared after the vet and heroine had magic sex. The town loved her-the outsider, the girl's family loved the vet and the ex-boyfriend, who wasted money to save her, went away without a fight."

"Listen, honey, all sex is magic." B.J. took a long pull of the amber liquid. His voice lowered. "Problems will always be there but it's easier to face them when you're not alone. It's nice having a partner to share things with. Did you like anything about the book?"

Jessie accessed the pros and cons of the story. The vet had been a softie for animals; it wasn't a job but a lifestyle, and it chiseled the hardness around the heroine's heart. It made a hole big enough for the man to wiggle his way into. "He liked animals, and she liked men who liked animals."

"Hm." He took another drink and stared at the flat screen on the wall. "Sounds familiar, doesn't it? Wasn't there a girl smitten with a local boy who swerved to miss hitting a dog?"

Jessie pushed away from the counter, threw money on it and patted B.J. on the hand. "Thank you."

CHAPTER 39

Josiah

MORIAH'S GRAY GRANITE HEADSTONE GLEAMED in the evening sun. Josiah stuck his hands in his pockets, glancing over his shoulder at his truck. He walked closer to his twin's resting place. A large bouquet of pink, red and yellow roses reminded him his parents had visited. With a twinge of guilt, he mentally kicked himself for not going home sooner.

"I still can't believe you're gone." Josiah squeezed his eyes shut, hoping to stem the tears. He sat on the grass cross-legged, listening to the birds. Moriah would've known which birds made the tweets and chirps.

"You'd laugh. I've become a cowboy, not an old time sheriff like we used to play, but I help run a ranch." Josiah sighed. "I've met someone. I don't know if you ever met her. She was older than us in school but I love her. Jessie is special and the two of you would have gotten along at my expense." He chuckled envisioning his sister's mischievous face, the way her eyebrow rose before saying something witty.

"Today I had to work the longhorns into a chute. With their wide horns, you wouldn't think they'd fit but the chutes have horizontal bars to accommodate the width." He rubbed his chin recalling the vaccination process.

The wind fanned him and he relaxed. Stretching out his long legs, he continued to tell Moriah about his day. Time passed, and the heaviness weighing on him began to dissipate.

Several cars came and went, circling the small cemetery but one truck parked behind him. At first glance, he thought it was Jessie, but she wouldn't come to the graveyard today. She hadn't any reason. He stared at the trees and watched the leaves dance with the breeze.

A car door shut, then another followed by footsteps, made him swivel his head. Jessie approached with a handful of flowers. Her knees kicked the edge of her teal skirt making it flutter with each step. He couldn't help but admire her toned legs as she approached him with a shy smile. Words stalled in his throat. He took a deep breath and rose to meet her, noticing a devilish glint sparkled in her eyes.

Jessie

Daylight had started to wan when Jessie pulled into the lane of the Fortuna cemetery. She hadn't visited it a while and made a florist stop first. She hoped Josiah wouldn't mind the intrusion.

When she spotted his truck, she smiled. She pulled behind him and turned off her vehicle. She'd brought his birthday present. It sat wrapped and waiting on her front seat. She'd bought it as a gag gift and knew he wouldn't be in the mood for a laugh now. That's why she quietly opened the door to his truck and hid the package under the passenger seat. She giggled and shut the door. She picked up the bunches of flowers. Using her rump, she closed her door then headed toward him.

Their eyes locked, and he stood. She swallowed. Rays of sunlight, touched his hair giving him an ethereal glow. *If he only knew I shoved a pair of angel wings under his seat.* She giggled again, feeling her face heat.

"Howdy," he drawled.

"Hi." She bit her lip. "I hope you don't mind. I brought flowers for Moriah. For my grandparents and mom too." She handed him a plastic sheath full of white daisies.

He glanced at the flowers. She knew his loss of words had to do with the emotion clogging his windpipe. She rubbed his arm. "I'll be right back. I'm going to drop these off." He nodded and watched her turn.

Her grandparents' headstone was near Moriah's. Jessie knelt and placed the yellow mums in the container. She dusted off her knees. She pressed her lids together as tears welled. "Thank you for always loving me, and Josiah too."

Jessie didn't like to visit her mother's grave for a few reasons. For the longest time she'd been mad at her mother for leaving her. She'd worked on the grief, thanks to her grandmother. Her father's name and birth date had been engraved on the stone with a dash as if waiting for him to die. She didn't want to be reminded of her father's mortality.

The red granite had small bits of crystal shimmering in the sunlight. Her father mentioned her mother would've liked the bling. A smile tugged at Jessie's lips. She knelt, placing the flowers. Tracing her mother's name, she sucked in a breath. Her mother had never met Josiah. She'd never know he had saved her little girl from Rusty. A tear escaped. Trish had died too young, just like Moriah.

Jessie stood but covertly watched Josiah. He had resumed his seat on the grass with long legs stretched out and crossed while leaning back on his hands. She envisioned him wearing only those white wings. Her breath hitched, and she yanked her gaze back to her mother's stone.

Returning to Josiah's side, she lowered herself next to him before he could stand. Not wanting to interrupt his thoughts, she smoothed out the gauzy material of her skirt. Her gaze strayed to his face. The slope of his nose and the curve of his lashes, then his lips.

He met her gaze and held it. Tilting his head, he said, "Thank you for bringing the flowers."

"I wanted to do something." She reached out her hand and he took it. Warmth filled her when his thumb traced a line across her skin. "I know how it is to feel alone."

His brow dipped, and he leaned towards her. "You're never alone, Jess."

"You're always there when I need you. I wanted to return the favor." She threaded her fingers with his and squeezed gently. "I'm here for you."

He glanced at his sister's name. "Daisies were her favorite."

"Oh?"

"Yes. Moriah liked to pick them and put the stems in water with food coloring. They would change colors." A whimsical smile touched his lips. "Of course, Daisy was her best friend."

"Daisy Hopkins?"

Josiah nodded. "They'd been friends since third grade."

"I never knew." They remained quiet for a few moments and Jessie folded her legs under her skirt. "I remember Moriah," she whispered.

"You do?"

She faced him again. "Yeah, she impressed me back in the day." Jessie bit her lip and shivered at the memory. "One summer day, we went to the park to swim at the spring. I loved watching the teenagers jump off the cliff. Then I saw a little girl disappear up the trail to the top. I waited to see if she'd jump. And she did." Jessie chuckled. "Like a screeching banshee, she yelled as she flew off the cliff. She flailed her arms as if trying to fly. When she hit the water I thought the worst, but she popped her head out, flung her hair out of her face and laughed. An elementary kid who could jump off a cliff is brave."

"I don't know if it was bravery or stupidity. I dared her to jump. And Moriah never backed down from a dare." Josiah's faint smile hinted of the mischievous manner of the sibling's relationship.

"Bravery," Jessie said with a nod. She glanced at their entwined fingers.

Josiah squeezed her hand, sending a wave of warmth up her arm. She tipped her face to gaze into sorrowful, red-rimmed eyes. "What's wrong, Josiah?"

He squeezed his eyes shut and took a shuttering breath. "I should have been there."

"For Moriah?" Jessie scooted closer and touched his arm.

He nodded, and she reached for him pulling him against her. His arms encircled her waist as he sighed. With one arm on his back, Jessie hugged him closer. It felt right to hold him, to feel his heart beating against her.

The sorrow seeped from an old wound and grief born in the past. A fierce desire to protect Josiah from the pain arose within her. The sensation burned so strong, she ached to comfort him. She kissed the top of his head.

"That morning," he drew a quick breath and continued on, "the morning Moriah died, she'd asked me to go with her." Josiah closed his eyes and in a raspy voice continued, "She'd gone early to meet a bully she'd been dared to fight."

Jessie rubbed his back. "She didn't back down."

"No. The bully had picked on Daisy for weeks. Poor Daisy was a twig with a head. Bucked teeth and glasses, too."

"If he could see her now," Jessie murmured. The beautiful woman could vie for a cover model.

Josiah pushed back to meet her eyes. "It was Bobbi McCormick. That's Bobbi with an I."

"Oh," Jessie squeaked.

"Bobbi was tall and thick. She was the biggest kid in our class. She should have been a football lineman. No guy wanted to piss her off. Yet my sister got into a verbal sparring match defending Daisy. Bobbi dared Moriah to a fight. When she hesitated Bobbi called her a chicken and insinuated she was a crappy friend. They met before school on the basketball court next to the playground. Moriah kept out of reach of her for a while and even bloodied Bobbi's lip before..." he shuddered and swallowed. "Before Bobbi lashed out with a wild punch that broke Moriah's jaw, lifted her up and tossed her like a rag doll. The fall cracked her skull."

"I'm sorry, Josiah," Jessie whispered.

"I know what happened because Sawyer told me. But I wasn't there." His voice shook. "I'd stopped by a friend's on the way to school. He'd gotten a new video game, and we played. I should have been there for her. I could have saved her." Josiah's fists balled at her back and his jaw tightened.

She understood his protectiveness. He couldn't stand the thought of loss. Jessie glanced at him with a consuming hunger to protect. Josiah's eyelashes curled onto his cheek and his chin rested on the swell of her breast. The image seared into her heart. She could envision him resting on her bare chest. Her knuckles brushed his smooth cheek then rubbed stubble creating a tingling sensation running up her arm. His lips opened and his blue eyes, rimmed with red, stared into hers.

Mine. This man was hers. Jessie's heart raced at the revelation. Excitement, not fear. She smiled, her grandmother was right. Josiah was her happily ever after.

Jessie cupped his face. She wanted to express what words couldn't fully explain. Her gaze dipped to his tempting lips as the pad of her thumb skimmed them. Jessie leaned closer, close enough to count his freckles and feel his warm breath coming in quick bursts.

"Defending a friend was the right thing, Josiah. Moriah was brave amid adversity. She's a hero with a legacy that will be hard to live up to."

Josiah's eyes sparkled with unspent tears and he turned his head and kissed her palm.

"You and your sister are a lot alike. You both protect people you love." She pressed her forehead to his and whispered a truth she'd given up trying to deny. "Thank you for loving me."

Josiah pushed her onto the ground so fast, Jessie's stomach became lodged in her throat. Even with his speed, he'd cradled her head. His hard body pressed against hers in all the right places. Fire ignited. Heat threatened to consume her.

His hooded eyes studied her face then watched her chest rise and fall. An impish grin formed on his lips. They'd been in this position before. *The hayloft.* He would not reject her this time. Not if she could convince him they were ready. Grateful for the loose skirt, she hitched her leg around his thigh and tugged him against her.

Josiah closed his eyes and moaned. "Jess, you don't know what you do to me."

"Yes, I do," she said wiggling her hips. "I like it." He groaned again, making her body quiver.

He dropped his lips to hers and she opened for him. Her hands slid under his shirt and explored the contours of his back.

Both their phones chimed. He sighed when she pushed him back. "That's probably your mother. You haven't been to your parents. They seemed worried."

Josiah groaned, sitting up he checked his phone. "I know. I wasn't ready to face them yet." He rubbed his face and stood, offering her a hand. He pulled her to her feet, and she smoothed her skirt.

His eyes narrowed. "How do you know I haven't been to my parents'?"

Jessie blushed, and they walked toward the trucks. "Tori invited me for cake so I stopped by. I thought you'd be there. I wanted to give you something."

His lips tweaked into a smile as his simmering gaze raked her body. "Something you made?"

She chuckled nervously. *If he only knew the truth.* "I left it there. So you won't know until you go."

He tried to hide the disappointment with a small smile. Jessie strode to his truck and pulled open the door. "Come on, cowboy. Don't keep your mama waiting."

She glanced at the passenger floor, relieved the package remained hidden.

Obediently, Josiah climbed into the driver's seat and fastened his belt. He tilted his head. "Jessie, why are you smiling?"

She glanced in the side mirror and felt her hot cheeks. "You'll find out," she purred. Jessie bit her lip, not wanting to spill his surprise.

He reached to unbuckle his belt, but she slid a hand across his waist. "No sir. You are going to your parents. I won't let you shirk your responsibilities." She kept her hand over his, leaned forward and sucked his bottom lip in and traced it with her tongue. A moan met her ears but she couldn't be sure who'd made it.

Jessie pushed back and gazed into the startled blue eyes of the man she loved. She needed him to know how she felt. She stroked his cheek. It wasn't enough. She needed more. Quick as a lightning strike, she consumed his lips as if they offered life support. He responded with a happy sigh then moaned. The sound sent a shiver straight to her core.

She enjoyed affecting him and smiled against his lips. "Happy Birthday, Josiah."

Jessie hopped out of the truck and closed the door. He stared out the windshield with both hands clamped on the wheel.

"Follow the instructions on the card," she said into the open window. He whipped his head toward her. Before jogging to her truck, Jessie winked and said, "Make sure you open the second one alone."

CHAPTER 40

Josiah

JOSIAH TOOK DEEP GULPS OF air and wrung his hands on the steering wheel. He'd turned off his truck when he'd arrived at the ranch minutes ago. He could have driven back to the ranch blind using his dick as a divining rod. His knee bounced up and down and he clenched his eyes shut. He was a fool not to run inside to Jessie's waiting arms. Hell, he was as skittish as a mailman at a dog show.

He opened his birthday card and read it again. On the front a herd of cattle with party hats stood in a grassy field. On the inside it read "Happy Birthday! You're old and that's no Bull."

Back at his parents' home, his family had laughed at it. There he'd opened gifts from his parents. After the gifts, he'd forced down cake and ice cream. He stayed long enough for his brothers to start wrestling then he excused himself. He'd kissed his mother and sister and hugged his father before leaving.

Jessie had penned a funny message about him being a quarter of a century but nothing mushy. A line suggested a second clue. "I cleaned out your glove box." He'd been dying to open the glove box and find the second gift but had returned to the ranch for complete privacy.

He reached and opened the compartment. A small wrapped package with another card waited. Plucking the rectangular present, it was a paperback book. Hastily unwrapping the romance novel, he laughed. Signed by the author, Paige Turner's latest story with the red gown from the show had Josiah fantasizing about Jessie. He took another deep breath and picked up the card.

This one featured a picture of a cartoon Popsicle reading "lick me." The stuffy cab of the truck overheated. He opened the card, and it was blank except for two short sentences. "Look under the seat" and "in your laundry basket."

Josiah searched under his seat but found nothing. He bent, peering under the passenger seat. Wrapped in the same birthday paper something peeked out. He tugged on the wide package. The gift was flat and square like a pizza box. Tearing the paper, his jaw dropped. Angel wings. She'd bought him a pair of feathery, white wings.

He rubbed his face. Could this mean what he hoped? Jessie wanted him to visit her. *Lick me.* His mouth went dry.

Darkness met him as he pushed open the house's back door. He listened but heard nothing. Josiah strode for the laundry room and flicked on the light but only found empty baskets. He spun and entered the bathroom. Turning on the light, he found a wrapped shoe box in a basket.

Grinning as he lifted the gift, he gave it a shake. He stuck his head out in the hallway, hoping Jessie was near. He peeled off the paper and lifted the lid. Inside something shimmery and ruby red lay folded. "Holy crap," he murmured. *The book cover gown.*

He reached in and pinched the garment. As it unfolded, a card fell to the floor. He held a pair of boxers. Lifting the material to his face, he smelled a hint of Jessie's lotion.

He opened the card with a picture of an angel. The front read, "Touched by an Angel." Inside she'd written: I hope you like them. They match my gown. Stop by for a visit.

Josiah gripped the sink and took deep breaths. Jessie had invited him to bed. He'd been waiting years for this moment, holding onto the hope one day Jessie would love him. He'd seen love in her eyes when she thanked him for loving her.

He wanted her. Once they took this step, they couldn't go back. He undressed in record time and slid the satin boxers over his junk. Jessie had made these for him. The boxers felt light and soft, the opposite of the itchy and awkward wings. To be Cupid, he needed a quiver full of arrows and a bow to shoot them. He had no bow, but had a primed gun. Glancing in the mirror, he didn't recognize the man with a smug smile.

Josiah nudged the master bedroom door. Moisture and a fruity scent clung to the air of the dark room. She'd recently bathed. A lone candle flickered on the night table on Jessie's side of the bed. She'd lain on her side facing away from him. She'd pulled the sheet up but he could see the dark straps of her gown against her creamy skin.

The floor creaked as he stepped over the threshold. Sitting upright, her gaze inspected the wings, his bare chest then dipped lower. Her cheeks blushed as she met his gaze. "What took you so long?"

"Somebody ordered an angel. I was trying to find my halo." He smiled and padded to her bedside. "I've enjoyed my birthday scavenger hunt. Do I have anything else I have to unwrap?"

"Just me." Her raspy voice went straight to his groin. The pretty blush remained as she pushed the sheet away from her body. Her painted toes slid over the edge to the floor when she stood. The satiny red gown hit her above the knee and clung to her curves. Edged with lace, the neckline plunged, revealing the creamy swells of her breasts which rose and fell with each quick breath.

Jessie reached for him and his arms encircled her, kneading her back. Her hand tentatively touched the wings. He pressed his arousal against her belly and she squeaked.

"Jess, are you okay with this? We can stop." He kissed the top of her head. When she didn't answer, he glanced at her face, tilted upward. Her eyes brimmed with tears but a sweet smile grew on her lips. Her hands rested on his chest.

"There you go protecting me again," she whispered. Her fingers explored, sending waves of heat through him. Her eyes locked on his as her hands dipped lower but stopped at the waistline of the boxers. His heart hammered in his chest. He craved her touch. Covering one of her hands with his, he placed her hand on his erection. Her fingers curled around him, making him moan.

"Oh yeah, we're good." Jessie's lips formed a devilish grin.

"Awesome." Josiah met her lips with a ferocity equaling hers. She continued to stroke him until, panting, he pushed her hand away. "Wait. I've got points to prove first."

"What?" Jessie breathed through dewy lips.

"Point number one-"

"Oh, magic mouth." Jessie giggled.

Josiah picked her up and spun, sitting on the edge of the bed with her on his lap. Her legs crossed behind his back, pulling her warm, soft body against his hardness. His mouth consumed hers as her fingers snaked their way into his hair. As their tongues dueled for supremacy, his fingers skimmed along the skin of her thighs to her backside. He moaned into her mouth and squeezed her round cheeks. He broke the kiss. "No underwear?"

With one finger, she skimmed from his lips to his bellybutton. She shrugged and the impish grin appeared on her lips again. "I didn't see the point. They'd just end up hanging from the ceiling fan." Jessie raised her hands over her head as if she surrendered. "Unwrap me, Josiah."

He swallowed and nodded. His hands gripped the hem and pulled it upward. Inch by tantalizing inch, he exposed her toned thighs until they met at her apex. He stared at her core, pausing to explore. She squirmed at his touch and sucked in a breath.

He resumed sliding the gown, longing to touch the smooth skin of her belly and swirl his tongue around her navel.

"Too slow," Jessie rasped. Hopefully, his leisurely perusal of her body excited her as much as it turned him on. Her chest rose and fell, tempting him.

"I'm taking my time unwrapping my last birthday gift," he said as he unveiled her breasts. He pressed his nose between them and inhaled her feminine strawberry scent then nuzzled her.

Her heart thumped wildly and her chest heaved with short puffs. "Josiah, there's more to unwrap," Jessie purred seductively. Her gaze shifted and both index fingers now pointed to the night table.

He glanced at the box of condoms with a bow. "Thirty-six?"

She giggled. "I have plans."

He licked a line between her breasts and hummed. "Sounds good." The gown went flying, landing on the floor. She arched into him, her hands once again in his hair. His mouth claimed one breast while his hand caressed the other. The perfectly shaped double Ds fit into his palms. His hands worked her body, gliding over smooth skin and making her mew.

One of his hands slid down and her breath hitched. She hummed when he brushed the warm spot between her legs. Her lips parted for him and his tongue plundered as his fingers explored. He pulled away studying her hooded eyes, flushed cheeks and damp lips.

When he couldn't stand it any longer, he stood, taking her with him and turned. He gently laid her back on the bed. Her luminous, emerald eyes raked his body. He smirked as he pushed the boxers down and his erection sprang free. Her gaze focused on his groin and her tongue licked the corner of her lips.

Josiah climbed on the bed and settled between her legs. The pure contented arousal on her face compelled him to make love to her, but first his mouth needed to preform magic.

He rubbed his hands together, kneeling with a wicked smile. "And now to prove point number one." He traced his lips with his tongue and mesmerized, her gaze followed. "Somebody has asked to be licked and touched by an angel. I'm going to combine those two requests by, as Desire would say, getting on my knees and playing." He shrugged when her eyes widened.

Josiah leaned to play. He started on her inner thigh, nipping and licking. Going from one thigh to the other, he continued closer to her core. Every soft moan she uttered, sent a lightning bolt of pleasure between his legs. He gazed at her sweet spot and sharply inhaled. "God, Jess, you're beautiful."

Jessie giggled and touched his face. "You sound like a romance novel hero."

With a smug grin, Josiah lifted his gaze to hers. "I'll pleasure you like one of them too."

CHAPTER 41

Jessie

JESSIE SWALLOWED AS SHE RAISED her fist to knock on her father's back door. Inside, the light was on and moments before a shadow passed by the window. The sun hadn't risen over the horizon yet the sky had lightened since she'd left the Double D. She rapped on the wood and glass door.

Across the yard, Curly exited the bunkhouse and strode into the barn where the horses nickered in greeting. He hadn't seen Jessie hidden in the morning shadows under the stoop.

Her father pulled open the door with wide eyes. "Good morning, little girl, what brings you here?"

Jessie walked in, not minding the obvious spring in her step. Her face held a smile that had been tattooed on her lips for three days. She grabbed her father in a tight hug and he squeezed her back. "I love you, Daddy."

Brad chuckled and gave her another bear hug. "I love you too but I won't believe you left your home at this hour to come tell me you loved me." He released her.

She stood with hands on her hips and her head tilted but smiling. "I don't tell you enough." She giggled. "But you're right, I came here to talk with you."

Jessie glanced around the large kitchen. The aroma of bacon and coffee clung to the air. Except for a dirty bowl and spoon in the sink, the kitchen appeared little lived in.

"Come on and sit down. Let's get coffee. I'll need more caffeine to deal with whatever you have to tell me." He poured her a mug then refilled his, emptying the pot. He started another pot brewing then lowered himself into a wooden chair at the round table.

Her mother had scolded her for kneeling in the chair at the table. But the scold came accompanied by her mother's dazzling smile as she sat a plate in front of Jessie. Her mother could make a masterpiece out of boxed mac and cheese. She sighed and glanced at her dad. Did her mother haunt his thoughts as often as she haunted Jessie's?

Jessie picked up her mug and inhaled the bold scent. Her father's mustache twitched, signaling he was nearing the end of his patience. "It's about Josiah." The smile beamed until she took a sip of the bitter liquid. Grimacing, she stood, "I need a spoon of sugar." *More like a cup.*

"Corner cabinet." Her father rubbed his chin. "Josiah?"

Jessie opened the door of the top cabinet in the corner "We've come to an understanding." On her tiptoes, she glanced into the dark space and pulled out a few spices, searching for a ceramic sugar bowl.

"So he finally told you?"

"Yes, he did." The smile found residence on her lips again. Her cheeks hurt.

"How do you feel?"

She turned to inspect her father. His face remained neutral. "I'm happy. I don't believe I could be any happier."

Her father relaxed back and smiled then. "I'm glad he told you about it. I mean, you didn't tell him about the nature of your business so I suppose it's fair." He picked up his cup and toasted her.

"My business. What does Josiah confessing his love have to do with the Double D?" She stood with hands on her hips.

"Uh." Brad's mouth closed. He stood so fast his chair crashed to the ground. "He did what?"

"Josiah loves me, Daddy." Jessie giggled and felt her face heat as she reached for the middle shelf. Behind the cinnamon, she found the ceramic sugar bowl. One of the handles had broken off, and it had a chipped lid. The dainty sugar spoon reminded Jessie again of her mother.

A knock sounded on the kitchen door. The door opened, but the visitor remained hidden behind it.

"Mr. Davidson?" Jessie recognized the voice.

"What do you need, Malone?" Brad moved to the doorway.

Gimme laughed as if something tickled his funny bone. "Your son-in-law is here." He guffawed.

Her father's grip on the door handle tightened then relaxed. Her father must be a saint to deal with Gimme daily. She had no such luck.

"Who would that be," Jessie demanded, jerking the door open. Startled, Gimme stared like a fish.

"Er," Gimme swallowed. "I... uh. Miss Jessie, I'm sorry." He swiped his hat off his head and shuffled his booted feet while staring at the ground.

Should she laugh or yell? She forced a frown. "Don't you mean Mrs.?" she snipped. "Who am I supposed to marry, anyway?"

Gimme pointed toward the barn where Matt led Gabe and Josiah inside. Jessie's blood rushed as her heart raced at the sight of Josiah. She couldn't stop staring at the cowboy until he disappeared into the barn. Gimme's face held a smirk. Even her father grinned at her. She raised a hand to her mouth to check to see if she'd been drooling.

"The Barnes brothers are working with Curly. They're moving the three-year-old cows and their calves." Brad glanced from the barn to his daughter but ended on Gimme. "Tell Curly to send Josiah back once they reach the windmill. I need to talk to him about the vet bill."

Gimme nodded and replaced his tan hat. He was tall and muscled, Jessie noted. He was a decent looking guy; too bad he had a big mouth. She shook her head.

Jessie resisted the urge to question her father in front of Gimme but she remained curious regarding his comment about the Double D. Her heart beat faster at the thought of Josiah being so close. She stayed while her father dealt with the intruder.

Gimme tipped his hat, still red faced and took a step back. "Guess I'll go tell the Barnes posse."

Brad closed the door behind him and scratched his head. When he turned around, he wore a frown. Lost in thought, he retraced his steps to the table and sat with a huff.

"Daddy?" she hesitantly asked.

The lines of his furrowed brow softened when he glanced at her. "Little girl," he sighed. "I need to talk to you."

Jessie returned to her seat. She tapped her foot and chewed her lip, the coffee forgotten. Her father grimaced as if the bean soup had gone bad.

"Little girl," he cleared his throat. "We need to talk."

"Yes, Daddy, you've already said that." She stared at her father watching his eyes shift to the window then to his mug.

"It's about Rusty Kuntz."

Jessie sucked in a deep breath. "Oh, crap."

A wistful smile flickered on his lips but she blinked and it disappeared.

Her stomach twisted into knots and her heart fluttered so fast she clutched her chest. "What about him?"

"He's out."

"Out… of jail?"

He nodded. His lips pulled into a firm line.

"Oh crap," she repeated then slumped against the chair and squeezed her eyes shut. After a few moments and many deep breaths, she opened her eyes and inspected her father. "Has he been to see you?"

"No."

"Has he tried to contact you?"

"No."

"Good." She took another deep breath but relaxed her shoulders. "Does Josiah know?"

"I've been keeping him informed." He scratched his chin again.

Jessie frowned. She didn't like them keeping secrets from her, even if it regarded Rusty. "From now on you tell me everything."

"He's been out a while now. If he comes anywhere near you…." He gripped the mug so tight she thought the ceramic would crack.

"He won't come back, Daddy. There's nothing left for him here." She heaved a sigh and fingered her mug. "He's severed his relationship with you. He wouldn't come near me either. That leaves Curly, and I don't believe Curly would stop and listen to anything he has to say."

Her father rubbed his eyes and nodded. "I know. You'd think he'd stay away but then again, Rusty has always been a fool."

"Well, he did pick you as a friend," she said trying to lighten the mood. She shrugged when his eyes narrowed.

"You got me there." He chuckled. "I guess we should go out and see your fiancé."

Jessie's face heated, and she glanced at the table. "Daddy, I need to talk with you." She lifted her gaze to his. "It's about Josiah."

Josiah

Josiah helped Gabe saddle Sundance. The kid hadn't ridden as much as Matt but he'd shown no fear. In fact, he was positively giddy. The smile lighting his face only rivaled the smile a coveted video game or graphic novel brought. Josiah adjusted the stirrups for Gabe's legs. The horse stepped back.

Gabe took the reins with confidence and Sundance moved where Gabe wanted. "I'm a cowboy," Gabe hollered with glee.

"Yeah, yeah, keep it down, you hick," Matt teased as he rode past Gabe on a black mount.

"Takes one to know one," Gabe yelled, and he nudged Sundance in the side and took off after his older brother.

Josiah grinned after the two of them. Both brothers had surprised him, learning the nuances of ranching quickly. The summer had flown by, and soon Gabe would go back to high school. Matt hadn't made his plans clear. The kid needed an education. Besides, it worked for Josiah. His business schooling hadn't been in vain.

Josiah walked his mount out of the stable and into the yard. He shielded his eyes from the sunlight, studying his brothers. Both had reported to Curly who waited patiently next to the corral.

"Josiah!"

The excited feminine voice had him weak in the knees. He turned and Jessie flew into his arms. She'd hit him hard but he couldn't care less. She wrapped her arms around him. Her hair flared, smelling like a field of strawberries. His hands rubbed her back. She tipped her head and his lips touched hers. At first, he'd been vaguely aware of her father and Malone's presence. He'd heard Matt mutter "here we go again" but it all faded. The kiss deepened, her fingers plowed through his hair, knocking off his hat. It didn't stop her. She tasted of coffee and passion. His body trembled with need. Addicted to Jessie, only her love could grant his fix.

Brad cleared his throat. Josiah pulled her hands away from his neck and broke the kiss.

"I love you," she whispered as their foreheads touched.

He clenched his eyes shut and breathed. His heart soared. Those words touched him and tears welled. He still couldn't get used to her love. "I love you too." Opening his eyes he found both Brad and Malone wore smirks and Josiah couldn't help the grin that spread across his lips. They no longer had to pretend to be friends. "We've got an audience."

"Oh, kind of kinky." She giggled and fisted his shirt.

"Later."

"Promise?" she pouted.

"Yes, darlin'. I've got plans for you." He wiggled his eyebrows.

"I will hold you to it then." She released him and let him leave.

Curly planned to have his brothers moving cows and calves. It would prove a good experience for them. Especially Gabe. The kid was green. He still wore the goofy grin.

Matt morphed from teasing his big brother into a cowboy. He'd be better than Josiah one day. And that'd be okay because one day Josiah and Jessie would have kids. He could trust the ranch details to Matt while he did the books. The accounting, not the romance novels.

He shifted on the saddle. Romance books, he chuckled. He'd promised Jessie they'd read a romance together.

At Hammered the other night, three couples read together and they wanted to try it. Two days in and they'd become hooked. Of course, they'd dared each other to act out certain sexy parts.

When the men reached the windmill Josiah hopped off his horse. He climbed to the top and inspected the gear box. Everything remained in working order.

Josiah dusted off his hands and climbed into the saddle. His brothers had continued down the trail around a bend and out of sight. He should hold their horses' reins to keep them safe. As older brother, that was his duty. He pinched the bridge of his nose and blew out a long breath. He needed to let them go.

Josiah's gaze shifted to Curly who waited, inspecting him with a tilted head. His black hat tipped back so Josiah would see his face.

"Brad wants to see me," Josiah started.

"Yeah, I saw." Curly laughed. "Malone told me, of course, but now I know the why."

"Malone," Josiah growled.

"He didn't say a lick about you and Jessie, only that Brad wanted you for a conference. You and Jessie told me the rest. And quite a telling it was. About time you two got together."

"Malone didn't say anything about us? Wow. That's a first."

"He didn't know or he would've." Squawking birds shot into the air. Curly glanced after Matt and Gabe. "You better not keep your father-in-law waiting." He laughed again and spurred his horse away before Josiah could recover from Curly's teasing.

With a shake of his head, Josiah turned his horse toward the Big Deal homestead.

Brad awaited Josiah in the office. He glanced around for Jessie.

"Jessie has gone home, son." Brad peered up from the ledger on his desk. "Have a seat. We need to talk."

"This doesn't concern the Double D, does it, sir?"

"Sir?" One of Brad's eyebrows lifted. "Not directly. This has to do with Jessie."

Josiah pulled the chair back and sat. He swallowed and rubbed his palms on his jeans. The small office seemed stuffy and dusty. He longed to be out riding again. "What's up?"

"She visited me this morning. We had a nice conversation." Brad focused on Josiah. He didn't seem mad, but he didn't seem happy either. "I told her about Kuntz. She deserved to know the truth."

Josiah gripped the edge of the big wood desk and leaned forward. "How'd she take it?" His heart felt like lead.

"Better than I thought." Brad rubbed his chin and a hint of a smile touched his lips. "Actually, she reacted calmly and rational. No crying or paranoia."

"Did you expect her to freak out?" Josiah wished he could have been there for her.

"I expected some reaction but..." he sighed. "She asked reasonable questions and acted almost as if it never happened to her."

Hm. That was strange, but it'd been years since the incident. And he'd never let the man near her if he could help it.

"She's better because you two are finally a thing."

"A thing." Josiah chuckled.

"Her smile is back, son. And you're the reason. You make her happy." He stood and offered Josiah his hand. "I'll be eternally grateful."

Josiah rose and took Brad's hand. "One more thing. I intend to marry your daughter. Sooner than later."

Brad smiled and nodded. "She didn't mention any grand-babies."

The phone on Brad's desk chimed. He glanced at his desk and a soft tender expression crossed his features. Brad tapped the screen of his smartphone and chuckled, which became a deep laughter. Closing his eyes, he leaned back in the chair. Josiah waited, he knew it had to be something good to have Brad laughing hard.

"What is it?" Josiah asked once his curiosity reached an end.

"Ophelia Cox sent a picture of a sign the prankster vandalized. Here take a look." Brad pushed the device toward Josiah. He glanced at it and chuckled. The sign itself was funny. But Desire had used her hands to show it off like Vanna on The Wheel of Fortune. "What's that cantankerous woman doing there? Desire is always in the middle of everything. I wouldn't be surprised if she's the vandal," Brad surmised.

"Or writes the stuff for him," Josiah suggested. "It's not like she could crawl between the bushes at the church to change the letters or climb above the grocery store to get the Marquee or have the key to get into the school."

"You're right," Brad agreed, rubbing his chin. "She probably is writing the one liners. You'd need a dirty mind to concoct all those sayings."

Josiah leaned forward, raising his eyebrows. "So Ophelia keeps you abreast of the shenanigans in town, huh?"

"That she does." Brad grinned but said no more. Changing the subject, Brad asked, "When are you going to propose to my daughter?"

"Soon." Josiah wanted to elope but needed to make arrangements. Buying a ring was top priority. His stomach churned as he studied Brad's calm exterior. "At the dance," he blurted. His face heated, and he swallowed.

Brad's brows rose and one corner of his lips tipped. "It's less than two weeks away." Brad whistled, leaned back and threaded his hands across his chest. "You have nothing to worry about, son. Curly Moe, your brothers and I will care for the ranch. Y'all plan on taking a couple weeks. We'll call if we need anything."

"You're forgetting Jessie needs to say yes first."

"She'll say yes." Brad winked and held his gaze. Josiah narrowed his eyes, suspecting Brad knew something more but his gaze fell to the paperwork on the desktop. "About the vet bill. I talked to Claude Oliver, and it seems he duplicated the bill. He hired a new assistant, and she charged both the Big Deal and the Double D for the same service." He glanced at Josiah. "Can you imagine? Billed twice for the cattle treatment. He's credited us now. Here's the new invoice." Brad slid the paper across the desktop to Josiah.

He glanced at it and appreciated the figures. "This will make Jessie happy. She was stewing about it."

Brad nodded. "One more thing. Are you planning on disclosing the secret investor to Jessie?"

Josiah scratched his chin. "I hadn't thought about it. I mean, I want to tell her-"

"You need to come clean. She didn't appreciate us withholding information about Rusty from her. She doesn't want secrets. Consider telling her about the business partner soon." His phone chirped again. He glanced at the screen then tapped it. "What the...?"

Josiah crossed his arms and waited. Brad's eyes widened then lifted to meet his. The older man studied Josiah before saying, "That silent investor has been whispering ideas into Desire's head. Good Lord, son, Jessie will want to parade her nighties in another show. I don't think my heart can take it." With elbows on the desk, Brad rested his face in his palms and groaned.

A wry grin twisted Josiah's lips. He knew exactly what Desire schemed. It had been his idea. "It's more of a personal show. Mine."

Brad's face blazed red, and he shook his head. Josiah laughed as he straightened his shoulders.

CHAPTER 42

Jessie

JESSIE PULLED OPEN THE DOOR of the Pink Taco. Mexican food smells swirled in the air, making Jessie's stomach rumble. Desire lifted her bony hand and waved. Jessie smiled and slid in the booth.

"Jessie dear." Desire grinned. "Love looks good on you."

Jessie felt her face heat but she couldn't help the smile. "It's been a roller coaster of fun."

Desire appeared ready to go on a date with her Vulcan-like hairdo neatly trimmed and crisp shirt and pants. Jessie glanced around the restaurant, searching for a gentleman in waiting.

Desire fingered her iced tea glass. "The silent partner had an idea. Since the show-"

"He was at the show?" Jessie leaned forward.

"Of course, I sent the silent partner an invitation. *They* wanted to see your items. You didn't disappoint." Desire flashed Clint Torres a smile as he walked past.

"*They* liked my creations?" Jessie had an inkling who the silent investor could be. Desire didn't like when she used the word "he" and preferred to use the pronoun they. *Maybe it's Desire.*

"Do you want to hear the idea?" Desire asked raising one eyebrow.

Jessie nodded. "Why not? It's the least I can do." She picked up her sweet tea and sipped.

"Well, here's the scoop. You're to use the activity of the dance to test the endurance of your products." Desire glanced around the restaurant then leaned closer as if telling a secret. "Beta test your own products."

"But Kelly and Mona are testing the bras and panties for me. I've received great feedback from them."

"This is the same but different. You're busty like your grandma Undine. Those other girls aren't so gifted in that department." Desire winked.

Jessie glanced at her chest. She'd given little thought regarding fuller bust sizes and the business.

"Ladies with big hooters want to wear pretty things too." Desire smirked.

"Yes, we do," Jessie agreed. She leaned back, recalling the items she'd created for herself. Gowns and the teddy but no bras. "I don't have much time. Did they mention anything specific? Like a certain piece from the show, or give you a number of items to test?"

"No, nothing specific. Use your discretion."

The brass bell clanged as the door yanked open. All eyes turned to the entrance where Gloria Sass stumbled in with tears streaming. She swiped them away. Gloria doubled over laughing, something Jessie had never seen.

"A Hole In One's sign has been vandalized again. Whoever keeps switching the letters is hilarious." Gloria took a breath. "It says 'Nuts: 2 for $1.00'."

The 'do' from donut had gone missing. The prankster had struck again.

Desire flicked her hand in dismissal. "The sign has been like that all morning. Gloria should keep up with the rest of the town."

After lunch, when Desire suggested they go dress shopping at Gogh-Downe, the boutique in Nockerville. Jessie agreed.

"I want to see how they display the Double D items, dear." Desire said as she shut the truck's door.

Jessie stepped onto the curb, smiled and pointed to the window display. One mannequin wore a Double D Intimates gown.

"Desire, the boutique has placed a second order after the official debut and the show." Jessie pulled open the boutique's door and held it for the older woman. "Thank you for talking to Pat and introducing us."

"You make quality pieces that are darn sexy, too." Desire winked and stopped at the first rack of shirts. "I hope this comes in pink." She tilted her head and grinned. "I do."

Jessie giggled. She shifted hangers glancing at the beautiful clothes near the cash register while Desire moved deeper into the store.

After a few minutes, Desire waved over the racks then headed to Jessie's side. "You've got to try this dress on. It's stunning and will make your eyes pop. That cowboy won't be able to keep his hands off of you."

"I hope so," Jessie breathed, taking the hanger and touching the material. The surplice neckline, with the fabric criss-crossing over the bosom, dipped in a daring V neck. She liked the style as it complimented her Double D bra size. She grinned at Desire. "It's pretty." Red wasn't a good mix for Jessie's auburn hair but emerald green worked. "You know, I'm going to suggest the name Emerald to Forrest Greene as another baby girl's name. Em for short."

"Are they expecting?" Desire asked as she moved to the right observing the street.

Jessie turned around. "Not that I'm aware. Jade's only two." She watched as Lisa Ford and Linda Hand paused and admired the display. They pointed then pulled the door open. Small bells announced the newcomers.

Lisa wore a genuine smile. The tide had turned in the Ford's relationship. Rumors about their abhorrent relationship turning into something passionate swirled around town. No longer did Parker yell at her in public, now he read to her. Jessie had spotted them more than once in Hammered's corner booth red faced and reading.

The Fords had become something of a legend in Fortuna and the envy of many women when police arrested Parker for streaking while acting out a favorite hero.

Desire glanced at Linda and rolled her eyes. Once out of ear shot Desire whispered, "That gal is such a snob. She doesn't care for most people but especially me." Desire smiled, "I'm not afraid to show her what I think of her."

As Lisa walked past, she tipped her head in greeting and smiled sweetly but Linda passed with her nose in the air, ignoring them altogether.

Desire twisted her head to make sure the sales associate wasn't listening. "Your poop does stink, Linda," the old woman muttered under her breath.

Linda and Lisa ventured toward the rear of the store, near the intimates. Lisa selected a Double D gown and touched the blue shimmery material. She held it against her and twisted side to side making the fabric sway. Seeing the price, she returned the garment to the rack.

"Oh my gawd. Who would pay seventy dollars for a nightgown?" Linda whined.

"I can't," said Lisa, not that she wouldn't.

"It's exquisite," Desire egged as she walked nearer. "A handmade quality piece. Thought you could tell those kind of items, Linda?"

"Yes, of course, I can. This was probably made in China." Linda shifted the indigo Michael Kors handbag on her shoulder.

Monitoring the conversation, the sales associate tipped the fabric on the neck exposing a small cloth tag with the Double D logo and Lone Star flag. "Quality over quantity. A quality piece is worth the price because it lasts longer. Handmade in Texas by a class act, that's the expense."

Recognition flashed in Lisa's eyes.

"I have three," Desire lied, and she walked away giving Jessie a wink.

Linda snapped up hangers with two gown styles and stomped to the fitting room.

Josiah

A blast of cool air hit Josiah as he pulled open the door to The Family Jewels. His father, of all people, had recommended the store. His mother's jewelry gifts came from the small family owned business. Josiah's gaze swept the rows of cases as he entered. He paused in the entry to take off his hat.

"How may I assist you today?" asked a slender blond woman with Jean Poole on her name badge.

"I need an engagement ring," Josiah answered. He couldn't help but smile as he fingered the rim of his hat.

Jean returned a warm smile. "Congratulations."

"Thanks," Josiah nodded adding a nervous chuckle.

"Follow me," Jean said, curling her finger and walking further back. She unlocked a case filled with treasure.

Josiah threw one last glance out the large storefront window. "Well, I'll be damned," he muttered under his breath. Jessie's truck wasn't parked too far from his. Josiah inspected the sidewalks around the square but didn't see her. He'd have to watch the door. He didn't want Jessie to ruin her surprise.

"Can I show you something?" Jean asked.

Josiah studied the rings. Besides price, how did a man choose? Yellow or white gold, platinum or titanium. A single diamond solitaire or something with a nest of diamonds. Eeny, meeny, miny, moe wouldn't cut it.

Josiah took a deep breath and envisioned Jessie's hands. She had petite slender fingers. "How about that one?" He pointed to a shiny ring with three princess cut stones. The large center diamond had smaller ones on either side. His heart hammered, and he closed his eyes. He couldn't wait to claim Jessie as his wife.

"Do you know her size?"

"Yes, ma'am." With a wry grin, he reached into his pocket and fished out a ring. "This is her grandmother's ring. Jessie tried it on the other day and it fit. I don't know the size but I was hoping you'd be able to figure it out."

"I can." She held out her hand and Josiah placed the small opal ring onto her palm. As Jean worked with the sizers, Josiah walked to the window searching for Jessie again.

"All right, I've got it. We'll need to resize it."

Josiah turned away from the window. "Oh. How long will it take?"

"A week at the longest, but usually it takes two to three business days." She handed the opal ring back.

Josiah stowed it in his pocket. Jessie hadn't known he borrowed it. He got lucky a few nights ago when nostalgia struck Jessie. She'd pulled out her grandparents' journals and read about the opal ring. She'd searched until she found it. For a few days she'd worn it on her ring finger but for whatever reason she'd forgotten to put it on that morning. With limited time, he passed his work duties to Matt and drove to get the ring. "As long as it's finished before the Cattlemen's Ball."

"Yes, sir. It will be completed by then." A smile erupted on her face. "Are you going to ask her at the dance?"

Josiah felt his face heat. "I'm not sure I can wait, but that's the plan."

Jean laughed and gestured for him to sit. She pushed a paper toward him. He read the bill of receipt for the ring and signed off to get it resized. He handed her cash then ventured to the window while she rang him up.

The world stood still as Jessie, accompanied by Desire, exited Gogh-Downe. Each held a large bag which they dropped into Jessie's truck cab. Both women's faces held smiles as they chatted and walked away from him. He felt relieved yet disappointed.

Movement caught his eye and his gaze abandoned Jessie to find a scrawny old man staring after them. He hadn't shaved in a while but his beard was splotchy. In the torn dirty clothes, the old man had a defeated, homeless air. Something gnawed at Josiah's conscience. As the man took a shuffling step in Jessie's direction, recognition dawned.

Rusty Kuntz.

"Son of a bitch." Josiah launched for the door.

"Mr. Barnes!" Jean called, making him halt with the door open. "Your change and paperwork."

Josiah narrowed his gaze on Rusty. The old man glanced toward Jessie then at the ground. Rusty turned and ambled in the opposite direction. Josiah watched until Rusty disappeared from sight. Keeping his eyes fixed outside, he took the papers and tried to listen to Jean's parting words.

Josiah tossed the papers into his truck before trying to retrace Rusty's steps. The old man had vanished. Josiah didn't stray too far from the vicinity of Jessie's truck. He wanted to intercept Rusty if he spoke with Jessie. Josiah watched and waited in his truck. When Jessie and Desire drove toward Fortuna, he knew she'd returned toward the safety of the ranch and he could go home.

CHAPTER 43

Jessie

JESSIE GLANCED IN THE MIRROR, tilting her head. Her hair fell in soft waves around her shoulders. She grinned at the image reflected. Grandma Undine had inspired her style from her hair to the green dress.

The muscles in her lower back still ached even though she'd taken a long hot shower. She tried to knead the ache out as she stepped into her heels. She didn't have time for pain.

Clicking off the light she hoisted a small suitcase and hurried down the hall. She paused in the kitchen listening for Josiah. She blew out a long breath; he was still in the shower. The baggage had basics she'd need for a short trip. The truck door creaked when she opened it. She glanced around, hoping no one would see her. Tippy hopped on the hood with a mew and startled Jessie.

"Sorry, girl. I've got to get inside and get my trousseau." Jessie chuckled and rubbed the small feline between the ears. "I get to try out my goodies. Josiah will like the surprise."

The gravel crunched under her shoes as she tentatively opened the door a crack. She listened for Josiah. On the counter three brown paper bags awaited her. She'd slaved the past week to get two bra and panties sets completed. One night, she'd almost spilled the beans about the silent investor's suggestion when Josiah had caught her topless. Besides the sets, she'd fixed the snaps on the teddy. She hadn't worn it since the show but it was a favorite.

The water turned off and Josiah whistled a tune. Jessie's heart kicked up a notch. She grabbed the bags and rushed to the truck. It would be tricky packing the remainder of his belongings with him in the house. She remained hidden until he passed the window moving from the back shower toward the master bedroom.

In stealth mode, Jessie tiptoed to the laundry where she had an overnight bag packed for him. She retrieved his personal items, like the razor, from the bathroom. Luckily, the bag rolled and was easy to manage.

Matt pulled open the back door and Jessie squeaked. "You're going to give me a heart attack," she uttered under her breath.

"Sorry, Jessie. Let me get that for you," Matt said hefting the suitcase as if it weighed nothing. When Matt returned, he smiled like he knew a secret. "Everything ready?"

Jessie wrung her hands. "I hope so." She peered into the hallway. Finding it empty, she continued, "We might not be leaving. It'll depend on Josiah." In another room, Josiah whistled a new song.

Matt laughed, squeezing his eyes shut, he slapped his knee. "You have nothing to worry about. My brother will follow you anywhere. Even to Las Vegas. Seriously, don't worry. Gabe, your dad and I have got the ranch. Take your time and domesticate my brother."

Jessie rolled her shoulders but nodded. She'd never whisked a man away on vacation. "Emergency numbers are in the drawer by the phone."

Matt crossed his arms and furrowed his brow. "Like I don't know you or your dad's number."

Jessie kept from rolling her eyes. "It's just…" Tears welled. "Thank you," she croaked.

"Ah, don't mess up your makeup. It's fine, Jess. You're welcome." Matt's long arms encircled her and pulled her into a hug. She let him hold her as she struggled with getting her emotions under control.

"What's going on here?" Josiah said, stepping into the kitchen.

Jessie swallowed. He'd caught her in his brother's embrace. Matt released her and nudged her in Josiah's direction. Her gaze raked his handsome, tailored body. His eyes glistened with excitement and lips tipped in a full smile. The tie he wore matched her dress, and she bit her knuckles. She took a tentative step toward him.

"Hello, handsome," she whispered.

"Hello, gorgeous," Josiah replied, closing the distance between them. His fingers caressed her cheek.

Jessie's heart jolted when his lips claimed hers with ferocity. The room became too hot, making her want to strip. He ended the kiss and she reluctantly let go. He chuckled when she fanned her face.

"Ready for dinner?" Josiah asked, taking her elbow and leading her to the door.

Her eyelashes fluttered as she grinned. "I'm ready for dessert."

Josiah

Josiah considered getting Fu King Wok carryout and having a picnic but he feared they'd never make it to the dance. In the green dress that hugged her curves, Jessie was stunning. He kept his fingers clamped to the steering wheel to keep from ripping the dress off her tempting body and nibbling her sweet spot.

At Arlon Topp's suggestion, Josiah made reservations at a little-known restaurant tucked away in a Nockerville hotel, the Schagg Inn. The steak dinner surprised him, being one of the best he'd ever had. Although it could have been the company. He worried Jessie's belly hadn't agreed when she'd disappeared for an extended bathroom break. He dismissed it when she returned all smiles.

As he turned the wheel into the fairgrounds a marquee welcomed guests to the dance.

"Look," Jessie squealed, pointing to the sign.

Someone had added a red letter S turning Cattlemen's Ball into Cattlemen's Balls.

He laughed as he selected a spot. The luggage shifted when he pulled in. Jessie glanced over her shoulder into the backseat with a frown.

"Everything okay?" he asked.

"Yes." She glanced once more and nodded.

He exited and rounded the vehicle. Parallel to the truck was a large slick of mud. He hesitated before opening the door for her. "Watch your step. Maybe I should move the truck."

Jessie glanced at the puddle. "There's no need." She dangled her shapely legs over the edge then took his hand and hopped down landing next to the muck. "See. I'm good. Thanks for the help." She fluffed the dress skirt then grinned at him, threading her arm with his.

Proud as a peacock, he guided her under the lights of the cheerful entry.

Other couples entered the large convention hall converted once a year into a ballroom. On the left near the bathroom hallway was a long table filled with snacks and a large punch bowl. A bustling bar with several attendants served patrons on the opposite side. Front and center was a stage with a live country western band. Josiah didn't waste any time and led Jessie onto the parquet dance floor. They smiled and laughed with the others as they two-stepped. Four dances later a slow song played.

"You look pretty tonight," Josiah said. Jessie beamed and her features softened as she blushed. He liked the dress. "That's a great color. Your eyes…" He stopped moving, and his gaze caressed her features. "Jess," his voice turned husky, "you're so beautiful." He touched her face then pulled her against him as if he couldn't get enough. Time lost its meaning.

Laughter met his ears. "Sawyer," Jessie murmured, putting a space between them.

"Hello, Jessie and Josiah," Kelly said as Sawyer twirled her around them. Kelly wore a denim skirt and vest with a red blouse. She appeared to step out of a wild west show. Sawyer's crisp white shirt contrasted with his dark jeans.

"I can't believe Kelly got him to wear a bolo tie," Jessie whispered as the other couple disappeared into the crowd again. After another few songs they took a break and visited the bar.

They'd worked up a sweat but Josiah didn't mind. He'd take Jessie in his arms any way he could get her.

"I need to grab something from the truck." Jessie pulled him toward the door. She finished her beer, handing him the empty bottle.

Josiah's heart thundered in his chest and a lopsided grin formed. "Is this for the secret partner?"

A flush blossomed on Jessie's face and she gazed at the floor. "Maybe." Her gaze rose to meet his. "Or maybe it's for you."

"Is that so?" He swallowed and his gaze dropped to her cleavage.

Jessie fingered his tie working her way upwards as she pulled him closer. Every graze of her touch burned his skin.

His mouth went dry when she tugged on the shoulder of her dress. It shifted, revealing lace matching the green of her dress. There was something about her creamy skin contrasting against the dark lace that lit him on fire. His heart stopped, or its rhythm was so fast it was one long continuous beat. He had to taste her. He leaned to lick her collarbone's divot, but she took a step back.

With an impish grin she swung the truck key on her finger. She'd fished them out of his suit jacket's pocket while he lusted.

"Need any help?" he asked.

Jessie giggled and shook her head as she walked away. Josiah stared, watching the purposeful sway of her hips.

Damn. He needed a drink to cool his internal temperature.

Jessie

Jessie had a hard time deciding between the blue teddy and the other bra set. Closing her eyes, Josiah's hooded gaze flashed before her when he saw the exposed bra strap. A shiver ran down her spine. She picked a bag. He'd like whichever item it turned out to be.

Stepping into the throng of people she spotted Josiah and Sawyer beside the punch table. Jessie greeted a few Fortuna residents along her way to Josiah's side. Pixie Dix tapped his shoulder and ducked behind his other as he turned. He smiled in surprise then Pixie blushed. They exchanged a few words.

Jessie hastened her pace. Josiah winked at her approach. The building anxiety dissipated. He opened his arms, and Jessie stepped in, keeping the paper bag full of goodies behind his back. She was home. He smelled like soap and his warmth calmed her soul.

Her thoughts ran wild but when she refocused Pixie had left.

Sawyer smirked at them. "Get a room."

"Later," Josiah said.

He'd read her mind. While at the Schagg Inn, she'd sneaked to the front desk during a bathroom break. The hotel had vacancy, so she booked a room for the night. Josiah kissed the top of Jessie's head. A shiver shot through her and she pressed against him.

"I hope Kelly is okay," Sawyer said. He stared toward the bathroom with a frown. He shifted his weight then grabbed a glass of punch. "Somebody spiked the punch. Hoo-whee, it's strong." He gulped the rest then refilled his cup. "I'm drinking as much as I can before the volunteer ladies discover it's tainted."

"Where's Kelly?" Jessie asked.

"She's powdering her nose." He glanced at his watch. "She's been gone a while. Jessie, would you mind checking on her?"

"No problem," Jessie said. She needed to visit the restroom, anyway. Phase two of the silent partner's idea. She found Kelly, leaning against the sink trying to fix the hem of her skirt.

"What's going on? Your date's worried about you." Jessie said inspecting her friend in the mirror.

"He is?" Kelly rested her hands on her hips. "I can't spend the evening with him. He's horrible. He flirts with anyone with a vagina."

"Oh no." Jessie opened the door to a stall and unzipped her dress. She hung it on the little hook then opened the bag. The blue teddy awaited.

"You'd think he'd give it a rest while on a date," Kelly huffed.

While changing her undergarments Jessie listened to Kelly give instances of Sawyer's infractions. "Wow. You like him. You need to show him how wonderful you are. Make him jealous. Dance with other guys, especially the flirtatious ones," Jessie suggested.

"Would he care?"

"He'll come around," Jessie said with a shrug. "Why don't you go? I'll be a few more minutes. See you on the dance floor."

Alone in the bathroom, Jessie fastened the new snaps then opened them again, testing the replacements. Satisfied they worked, she stepped into the dress, sliding it over the silky material.

Josiah

Josiah witnessed Kelly stride out onto the dance floor with another man. The couple laughed as they passed.

"How do you like that?" Sawyer muttered, sticking his hands in his front pockets. He grimaced as his gaze followed his date around the room.

"She's your date, go get her," Josiah said.

With a curt nod, Sawyer marched after Kelly. Sawyer cut in. Kelly blushed and smiled.

Out of the corner of his eye, he caught sight of Ms. Hardmann talking to Johnson. They both wore wicked grins. Johnson's gaze darted around until Desire pointed to a woman adding more punch to the bowl. Josiah moved to get a better view. Desire might be up to something.

Josiah knew the woman's league volunteered to keep the punch bowl, lemonade and water pitchers full. A team of women worked to keep the table clean and refreshments filled.

Johnson approached the fifty-something league woman who'd finished refilling the bowl. The older woman became flustered by the attention and kept inspecting her feet.

Desire approached the table with a large older cowboy. Josiah knew the man as Big Nocker from Nockerville's founding family. Rumors said Big Nocker loved to drink. While Johnson distracted the woman, Desire reached for the ladle. Inside her long sleeve dress was a plastic tube. The older woman reached into her other pocket where a small hand pump hid. She pumped clear liquor into the fresh punch.

Big Nocker ladled a cup and took a sip. He frowned and pointed. "More."

Desire smiled and acquiesced. The old man filled his cup then gave Desire thumbs up. Johnson, Desire and Big Nocker faded into the sea of people once more. It wasn't college kids tainting the punch, it was an old lady. Desire didn't disappoint. Josiah rubbed his chin trying to hold in a belly laugh.

"Josiah," a voice called. A slender hand waved over the crowd.

He meandered through the bodies until he found his parents, Maggie, and Guy. An engagement ring sparkled on Maggie's finger. They talked several minutes before Ben and Mona greeted the Barnes party with smiling faces.

"Did you see the truck parked outside?" Ben asked.

"The one acting like a mobile library? Yes, we saw it coming in," Guy said.

"I guess Nockerville likes romance too," Josiah said. He frowned, realizing they'd finished reading a book the previous evening. Perhaps he needed to visit the mobile library.

"That's an understatement. You should see the line." Ben pointed out the door.

Josiah's curiosity piqued. "If y'all see Jessie, tell her I'll be back in a moment."

At the door, he took a deep breath of the cooling twilight air. The breeze fanned him. Men clogged the parking lane two rows over. He headed toward the crowd. It could be a fight. Josiah hurried to see the spectacle but Johnson stood on the gate of his truck and selected novels from the bed. He handed them to the hands of waiting men. The lady from the woman's league had a book open, thumbing through the pages with a pink face.

"Hey, smut peddler," Josiah called.

Johnson tipped his hat. "I'm open for business. What can I do for you?"

"Remind your clients to initial the books."

"Will do. Read this. Good luck." Johnson winked and tossed a book.

Josiah caught it. *Romancing the Rancher's Daughter.* Josiah chuckled and lifted the book in salute, accepting Johnson's defeat. As he walked away, Johnson reminded the others to record their initials and where to return the books.

Josiah opened the truck with the key Jessie had slipped back into his pocket. He stowed the book on the backseat. "What the hell?" he mumbled, spying the two overnight bags. He'd expected to see small bags for the test run but not suitcases. *What did she have in mind? And when can we leave?*

CHAPTER 44

Jessie

WITH THE PAPER BAG CLUTCHED in her hand, Jessie entered the ballroom. Josiah no longer waited near the punch. She scanned the dancers seeing Kelly pass in Sawyer's arms. Jessie tip-toed, craning her neck. She didn't spy Josiah but found Desire talking to the D.J. Jessie headed to her side and waited for a moment to speak. Desire wore a dress with a frilly pink neckline and pearl buttons. Her lipstick was a shade of fuchsia.

The older woman leaned toward Jessie and uttered, "I'm trying to get Phil McCavity to play a song for me. He's not listening." She flashed a fake smile at the man. Phil held up a hand, signaling Desire to wait. She pursed her lips and put her hands on her hips.

"I see you have a bag. Are you wearing something new? Is it causing the frown?" Desire asked.

Distracted, Jessie opened the bag and showed Desire the green lace bra strap. "This is the first set. They fit well and gave accurate support. Honestly, I never realized I was wearing them."

"That's perfect!" Desire hugged Jessie.

A teenage girl ran to the MC table holding a pool ball. "This just rolled across the floor. Somebody kicked it by the entry." She left the ball in the hands of Phil who fingered it, inspecting the writing. The message written in black marker read: "I belong to Holden Dix."

Phil grabbed the microphone and announced, "Holden Dix, if you are in the building and are missing any balls, please come see me at the sound booth." Phil set it out on the table like a display.

After the hubbub and laughter subsided Desire asked Jessie, "What's wrong?"

"I've misplaced my date. Have you seen him?" Jessie bit her lip. She wanted to torture him by showing him the ecru lace.

"Oh dear." Desire frowned then pointed toward the back door. "He went out there with Holden Dix's daughter. I'm sorry, Jessie."

Jessie clenched her eyes shut. Her heart sunk to her ankles. She'd trusted Josiah yet she'd made no claim on him. Did she wait too long? "I need to find him."

Stepping into the cool twilight, Jessie spied couples cuddling, talking or making out. She shook her head and hugged herself. Memories flashed. The way he'd moan her name. His tender touch when they made love. The dreams they'd shared while in each other's arms. She shouldn't doubt Josiah's love so easily.

In the dim glow of an outside light, a man resembling Josiah faced away from her. A woman's hands slithered around his back.

Jessie swallowed a wave of nausea. The reason for Josiah's mysterious nightly meetings became crystal clear. The woman giggled. *Pixie Dix.* Her short dress showed off her slender, toned legs which Josiah touched as he nuzzled her neck.

Jessie's fairytale night had morphed into a nightmare. She crept forward to confront her date. She grabbed his shoulder and spun him to face her. "Josiah!" she growled.

Pixie screamed but Matt jumped. "Holy crap, Jessie."

Air rushed into Jessie's lungs. The emotional roller coaster had her feeling giddy. "Oh God, I'm sorry." She shifted her gaze to the building. "I was looking for your brother. Carry on."

Leaving Matt to deal with a huffy Pixie, Jessie retreated to the dance overwhelmed with desire to claim Josiah for her own.

Josiah

"Ladies and Gentlemen, I' m Phil McCavity. Can I have your attention, please. Welcome to the Cattlemen's Ball. I hope you're having a delightful evening," the D.J. with slicked back hair smiled.

Josiah stopped scanning the room of dancers. Jessie hadn't been waiting for him near the punch table or the hall leading to the bathrooms.

The dancing ceased, and the people swiveled to listen, pressing forward forming a wall around the stage.

Next to the D.J., Jessie stood clutching a paper bag. Her gaze scoured the faces of the crowd. With wide owl-like eyes her petite form appeared childlike and lost. Almost frightened. His instinct was to billow through the mass not resting until he held Jessie in his arms. He wiped his palms on his pants.

"Josiah Barnes. Is there a Josiah Barnes present? Please come up to the sound booth, your date is missing you something fierce. Josiah Barnes," the D.J. said.

His hand shot up. "Here," Josiah shouted. The crowd parted around him.

Jessie's face transformed into a bright smile. Josiah surged forward as she jumped off the podium, lifting her skirt and running towards him. The crowd hooted and hollered.

When they met, he took her into his embrace and spun her in a circle. Warmth radiated through his body as her curves pressed against him. Her giggle sent his heart soaring.

"Where have you been?" Jessie asked in a whisper.

"Looking for you."

"You've found me," she said. Fisting his shirt, she pulled his face to hers.

"No, you found me." Josiah kissed her nose.

Jessie tipped her head with a mysterious glint in her green eyes. She lifted on her tiptoes and kissed him. He moaned and the sweet kiss turned hot.

The crowd went wild with cat calls.

"This song is dedicated to the young lovers," the D.J. said as music began.

Josiah

Later Josiah led Jessie into the relative peace and quiet of the hall. As she walked, the sway of her skirts brought his attention to her shapely calves. "Do you think that was the prankster?" Josiah asked.

"Who else would hire firemen strippers to dance for the folks of Fortuna," Jessie replied.

The thumping bass of the music still rang in his ears. "The nod to *The Visitation* was cool."

Jessie turned to face him. "That winged guy was brave to bungee off of the top of the ladder." She shook her head.

People trickled into the ballroom but most remained outside, looking at the trucks and taking photos with the dancers in their uniforms.

Josiah swallowed and rubbed the back of his head. Time was escaping, and he had something important to ask before night's end.

"How much longer is the dance?" he muttered to himself.

"Another couple of hours," Jessie answered. She grinned at him. "You got someplace to be?"

Her dress shifted, exposing more of her creamy neck but also tan lace. His mouth went dry, and he traced the scalloped edge. Yeah, he had plans, but they were momentarily forgotten. "Is that...?"

"Your favorite, yes." Jessie's face turned pink, and she blinked.

"Holy hell, Jessie. How am I supposed to dance another song?" His voice dropped to a husky whisper. "I can help with the snap again."

"I replaced the defective snap. It should work perfectly now." She gasped when he licked his lips.

"I should hope so. It would be a damn shame to ruin the teddy but if I have to rip it off you, I will."

Jessie pushed back on his shoulders. "You won't tear it. I spent too long making the teddy to throw it away."

A slow smile bowed Josiah's lips as his finger traced the lace across her bosom. "Darlin', I'm going to shoot my gun tonight and if the teddy gets in the way, I will remove it. One way or another. I can't promise I'll be gentle because I want you something fierce."

"It's fixed. I ordered new snaps from another company. I want to make more. Teddies are feminine and sexy." Jessie's face blossomed deep pink, and she toyed with the tip of his tie.

"As long as I get to try out the prototypes, I'm all for it," he whispered against her neck.

"Josiah, I promise, you'll be my beta tester." Her hooded eyes swept his body. "Do you want to leave?"

He sucked in a quick breath. "That's an idea."

People filtered into the main hall as the fire trucks left. Musicians took the stage.

"I shouldn't leave yet." Jessie sighed then bit her lip glancing around as if searching for someone. "The silent partner wants me to try more items. I've only tried two." She held the paper bag and shook it.

Josiah checked his watch. It was about time to meet his folks and Brad. Glancing around the room he spotted Desire dancing with one-eyed Willie. Catching the old woman's eye, he nodded.

"Why don't we put the bag in the truck and get the next one." He winked. "Honestly, if you're comfortable, I don't see why you need to change."

She tapped his stomach. "You just want to play with the snaps again."

"Yes, ma'am." He chuckled and crossed his arms. "You want me to take the bag to the truck for you?"

"No." Shaking her head, Jessie stepped away from him. "I'll go."

"Meet me over there." Josiah pointed to the corner near the sound board and D.J. With a quick nod, she walked toward the parking lot. He paused watching her gait for a moment before he turned to find his family.

"Here goes nothing," he mumbled before wiping his hands on his pants. With a deep breath, Josiah stepped into the throng.

Jessie

Jessie paused on the curb outside the building. Her gaze shifted left then right. The sun had set yet twilight hung on as the shadows grew long. A sensation of being watched had her scanning the area. Glancing over her shoulder she saw Parker and Lisa Ford, fingers intertwined and giggling, inspecting books on B.J.'s tailgate.

I shouldn't be so paranoid. But with Rusty Kuntz out of jail she couldn't help it. B.J. gave her a two fingered salute before turning to converse with the Fords. Jessie blew out a relieved breath, shook off the angst and continued forward.

She had to watch where she stepped in the gravel parking lot. Pot holes made walking precarious. With each step she drew closer to part three of the beta test. She sighed, waiting for a car to pass. The silent partner had eccentric ideas, not necessarily bad but in this case, poor timed. She wanted to keep wearing the teddy and not change. Josiah's reaction to the lacy edge had been hot enough to melt the fabric to her skin. Every feminine part hummed in remembrance.

Circumventing the muddy puddle on the passenger side of the truck, she opened the door and climbed in. She slumped back against the seat and exhaled a loud sigh.

Shifting her dress, the slide of the poly-blend material over the teddy reminded her of the fashion show. The memory of Josiah's fingers along the seam of her legs sent a shiver to her core. Her body warmed, and she needed something cool to drink. Shedding her clothes might alleviate some of the heat, but she doubted it.

Jessie glanced into the backseat then reached for a bag. She dumped its contents onto her lap. The underwire bra offered more support for the girls. Josiah would appreciate the white satin and lace set too, but it didn't have the history the teddy did.

She hit the seat with her fist. "To hell with the silent partner. Josiah comes first," she growled. She stuffed the set into the bag and dropped it on the floor. She checked her makeup in the visor mirror then straightened her dress.

If the secret partner scrutinized her movements at the dance, hopefully they'd assume she'd changed again. Josiah exited the building wearing a frown and scanning the parking lot. Jessie had stalled long enough.

The truck door creaked when she pushed it open. Keeping an eye on Josiah's kissable body, she lowered her feet to the ground. The running board caught one heel, and she pitched forward. She hopped trying to right herself but to no avail. She gasped, heading right for the large mud puddle.

Calloused hands clasped her arms, steadying her. She caught her breath. "Careful, miss."

"Thank you," she said, turning to face her rescuer. She gasped again.

"You're welcome. Couldn't have your fancy duds getting dirty." Rusty Kuntz smiled at her, a few of his teeth missing.

She jerked her arm away, jumping backward. "Y-you," Jessie hissed and pointed an accusing finger.

"Watch the mud." Rusty glanced down while kneading his hands and took a few steps back, expanding the distance between them.

He appeared twenty years older than her dad, not the same age. A white cap of thinning hair topped his head. His splotchy beard was long. The clothes hung off his lanky frame, now painfully thin. Jessie sucked in a deep breath and scanned him. His pathetic existence and sad eyes surprised her. A wave of compassion hit her and she shook her head, speechless. Seeing B.J.'s wounded heart and loving Josiah had made her more sensitive to others' situations.

"I'm sorry, I never meant to hurt you, Jessie. I'll never touch a drop of alcohol again. This I promise you." He glanced up, his yellowed eyes now full of tears. "I don't deserve your forgiveness."

Rusty brushed a tear off his cheek then moseyed in the opposite direction leaving her standing alone, stunned and speechless. The old man vanished into the darkness. There'd been times when she fantasized yelling and ripping Rusty a new one or making him eat one of Holden's balls but the anger had faded, replaced by pity.

Out of breath Josiah reached her side. He scanned her face. "You all right?"

Joy bubbled out from within. "Yes, I'm fine now." *I can turn the page of my past and start a new chapter.* Jessie stepped into Josiah's embrace. His arms closed around her cocooning her in warmth. With a final glance toward the broken old man, Jessie said, "Let's go dance."

CHAPTER 45

Jessie

JESSIE LOVED THE WARMTH OF Josiah's muscled bicep under her fingertips. It comforted and excited her. She needed to make a move soon or the night would be over and they'd return to the Double D.

Glancing ahead, she spotted her father speaking with Dr. Barnes. Long necks dotted the high top table before them. They laughed and her father patted the other man's back. *Probably talking about the novel they're reading.*

Next to her husband, Mrs. Barnes flailed her hands conversing with Maggie and Tori. Next to Maggie, Guy and Matt talked. Guy spotted her and Josiah then elbowed Matt. A big dopey grin broke out on Guy's face and Matt's face changed crimson. Jessie narrowed her eyes studying the younger Barnes. He'd better not have told anyone her plans.

On the fringe of the family, Gabe flipped a page on a book. Even from a distance, she could ascertain the graphic novel by the colorful animated sketches. He picked up a pencil and added something to a notebook. He didn't glance up when Matt poked him in the side. Engrossed, he kept drawing.

"You know," Jessie said slowing, "Gabe's good at drawing those Japanese cartoon characters. I thought he could design something based on the barn graffiti. What do you think?"

"That should be easy since he painted the dang thing in the first place." Josiah admitted with a shrug.

Jessie opened her mouth then closed it. She opened it again. "Seriously?" She'd been a fool. Gabe was a vandal. Could he be *the* town prankster? The shock faded into frustration. She poked Josiah in the ribs. "How did you find out? And when were you going to tell me?"

Josiah didn't slow. His lips pressed into a thin line before he answered. "The other day, I found one of his art books opened to something like the girl on the barn. I wouldn't have thought much of it if I didn't see the date. It predated the barn graffiti."

"But all those other pranks...?"

Josiah stopped and faced her. "Jessie, my brother isn't the Fortuna prankster. He was commissioned to design and paint the barn. Gabe never met the person who hired him. He figured he'd paint over the art later but then you liked it." Josiah shrugged again.

"He got paid to do it?" Jessie asked, incredulous.

He nodded stiffly, giving her the impression there was more to the story. "You can ask him the details." He took her hand, and they started toward their families again.

Her father extended a hand to Josiah, and they greeted each other.

Tori grabbed Jessie around the waist and giggled. "I love your dress," Jessie said.

The French twist hairdo made her look older. Tori twirled the purple dress making the skirt flare. "Do you really like it? I bought it with my babysitting money."

"It's pretty. The same purple as Fortuna high school," Jessie mused.

"Yeah, royal purple because I'm a princess." Tori giggled and leaned near Jessie's ear and said, "I know because my mom is the queen."

"Hey Jessie," Matt greeted.

She took his arm and spun him so she could watch Josiah. With the music loud, Josiah leaned in and had joined their father's conversation. She relaxed some. Focusing on Matt's pensive face she asked, "Have you told anyone about my plans?"

Matt's eyes widened. "No way. I don't want to end up with another black eye or worse yet—dead."

"If that's so why does Guy have that funny smile on his face and why do you look guilty?"

Matt glanced at Guy then he huffed out a sigh. "I didn't tell him. You gotta believe me. But he kinda figured it out. I swear, I didn't tell him."

Jessie's gaze narrowed but then she relaxed. "Fine." She exhaled. "I haven't asked Josiah yet but I'm going to soon."

"Okay," Matt nodded and a toothy lopsided grin formed. "Good luck."

Desire bumped Jessie as she strutted past, One Eye Willie on her arm.

The older woman paused near Phil McCavity's table.

Jessie approached Josiah. At his side, he lifted his arm and she slid against him. He draped his arm over her shoulders. She sighed and wrapped her arms around his middle, marveling how well they fit together.

The moment reminded her of Grandma Undine's fervent declaration Jessie would have her own happily ever after. Grandma had been right. She giggled and hugged Josiah tighter.

"What's going on?" Josiah asked glancing into her eyes.

"Nothing." She giggled again.

"It doesn't sound like nothin'," he said, pulling her into his embrace. He kissed her forehead.

"Actually, I need to ask you something," Jessie said. She quirked a brow as she studied his hooded eyes and tempting lips.

A flash of light made them blink. Jessie frowned and searched for the source. A photographer, whose face remained hidden behind a large camera lens, snapped pictures of the dance. Desire gestured toward the Barnes clan and the photographer nodded, accommodating the old woman's request. He pointed the camera, capturing Jessie's stunned face.

Josiah moved, creating a cool place where he'd been. He patted his front pockets then his back. His sheepish grin and pink cheeks made him appear like an impish schoolboy.

"Your book is in the truck. *Romancing the Rancher's Daughter*?" She smiled, shifting her feet. "That's not fiction, it's reality."

"I wasn't trying to find the book. I was looking for this..." Josiah dropped to one knee, extended a hand and offered a ring.

Jessie gasped. Her hands flew to her face. Tears formed, but she tried to blink them away, refusing to have them blur her vision.

"Jessie Davidson, will you do me the honor of becoming Mrs. Josiah Barnes?"

Not able to speak, she nodded. It felt as if her heart stopped and she floated in a sea of hopes and dreams. The smile on her face stretched making her cheeks hurt. Tears streamed. She offered her hand, and he slid the ring onto her finger. Taking her by the hands, he stood. Jessie fisted Josiah's shirt and pulled him into a hard, needy kiss.

Their families cheered and congratulated as the photographer continued to snap pictures. Desire wiped a stray tear.

Josiah

The music stopped and the D.J. announced, "Ladies and Gentlemen, congratulations are in order. There's been an engagement. Would the happy couple please come to the stage?" The building erupted in cheers.

Josiah didn't want to be in the spotlight. All he wanted was a moment to savor Jessie's decision to be his wife. He kissed her head then let her go. They shared a look then hand in hand they walked toward the stage.

A rogue pool ball rolled across the floor stopping near their feet. Jessie picked it up. As they stepped onto the stage McCavity extended his hand to Josiah. "Congratulations. What are your names and where are you from?" He shoved the mic into Josiah's face.

"I'm Josiah Barnes." He shook McCavity's hand then glanced at Jessie. Her red face held a bright smile. "This is my fiancée, Jessie Davidson. We're from Fortuna." Josiah swallowed. The crowd hooted and hollered, especially Sawyer in the front row.

McCavity pointed to the ball in Jessie's small hand. "What do you have there? May I see it?" He held out a hand. With a giggle, Jessie handed it to him. He read the message and rolled his eyes. "Now Jessie dear, you shouldn't touch another man's balls on the evening of your engagement." This earned a chuckle from the crowd.

"Jessie can handle my balls anytime," Holden Dix shouted. Sharon elbowed him but was laughing with the rest of the building.

The D.J. waited until the crowd quieted before asking, "So when's the big day?"

They glanced at each other. Josiah didn't want to appear overeager, but he wanted to leave pronto.

"Tonight," Jessie blurted. Her cheeks bloomed scarlet. With a firm grip, Jessie clung to his arm.

"Whoa." McCavity's eyes widened as round as Holden's balls. "How's that possible, little lady?"

"We're eloping." Jessie grinned at Josiah. Her emerald gem-like eyes sparkled with adventure. "Technically, it will be tomorrow." She turned to Josiah. "How fast can you drive to Las Vegas?"

Josiah's heart hammered and his mouth felt dry. A fog of happiness settled and he remembered to breathe.

"Wow. Congratulations, man." Phil shook Josiah's hand again. "The lady is gung-ho to hit the bed, er, I mean, the road."

"That might be true," Josiah drawled wiggling his eyebrows.

Jessie shifted her weight to her toes and put her hands on her hips. "It took eight years to see Josiah's love. A long wait isn't an option."

"How'd y'all meet?" Phil smiled and raised the mic to Jessie.

"A car accident. He tried to kill me," Jessie said, quoting their old argument.

"No. You tried to kill me." Josiah poked her in the ribs.

Jessie smirked but relented. "We almost killed each other."

"But we didn't kill each other. It's how I met her grandfather and got my job." Josiah winked at her. "She was smitten with me from the get go."

Maggie cupped her hands around her mouth and yelled, "Look who's talking!"

"No comments from the peanut gallery," Josiah said, laughing as his older sister crossed her arms.

Josiah spied Parker and Lisa Ford to the side of his sister. Parker stood behind Lisa with his arms wrapped around her middle. He nuzzled her hair while his lips moved against her ear. She blushed and one of her hands slipped behind but between them. Parker's eyes widened. Josiah suspected Lisa played Parker's organ Desire-style.

Josiah chuckled. He couldn't believe this couple, who'd once fought in public destined for divorce, now acted like horny teens in love. The Fords showed up in places, like Hammered, reading romance novels together. After the park arrest rumors swirled about Parker's uncanny ability to take on the personae of novel heroes. Josiah rubbed his jaw; he'd preform a few novel characters of his own soon.

"There's an unusual phenomenon happening in Fortuna, isn't there? I've heard tales of a prankster of epic proportion." McCavity tipped his head as his gaze scanned the crowd.

"I'd say you're fondling the evidence in your hand," Jessie said.

Josiah bit back a laugh but the crowd wasn't as refined. Desire's witch-like cackle and Holden's loud guffaw echoed over the riotous laughter.

"What about the hoopla with the books?" McCavity asked.

"Not just any books. *Romance* novels," Josiah clarified.

"The Fortuna folks will understand when I say Josiah Barnes is well read." Jessie smiled as the townsfolk cheered.

"You go girl!" Norma Stitts cried. She elbowed her husband, Hugh.

Josiah swallowed and his face heated but he couldn't deny the smile Jessie's proud words caused. Sweeping the crowd with his gaze he found several regulars staring at him: stylists from Tease Me, patrons and employees of the Pink Taco, Hammered and Nailed. The men from the Big Deal ranch and Brad's book club threw cheers and wolf whistles. Even Johnson gave him a stiff nod.

Jessie's fingers brushed his arm, sending tingles up it. Overwhelmed by her decision to marry him, he focused on her upturned face. She was a sweet, sensitive and passionate woman and he'd do his best, even if it killed him, to keep the promise he made to Undine Davidson. He'd keep Jessie safe, and he'd guard her heart. He closed his eyes, hoping the vision of beauty remained at his side when he opened them. His eyes popped open and Jessie bit her lip. Worry creased her brow. He swallowed. It was too early to fail Undine.

"What's wrong, Jess?" Josiah asked.

"I reserved a room at the Bellagio. I planned on stealing you away for a week of togetherness." Her eyes sparkled with joyful tears. "I hoped to talk you into marrying me." She giggled then shrugged one shoulder exposing a tiny sliver of creamy lace.

Josiah cupped her face, his thumb skimmed the delicate skin of her lips. "Why wait until tomorrow? We can do it tonight."

Jessie inhaled sharply and blushed.

"Well, that too but I was talking about getting married." Josiah grinned and winked.

McCavity turned to a rapt audience. "They want to get married right now."

The place erupted and Jessie hid her face against Josiah's chest.

"There's no reason to wait. We can begin our honeymoon tonight instead of tomorrow." Josiah kissed Jessie's forehead while hugging her soft curves tighter against him. The thought of a proper wedding night got his blood pumping. "Hey, Drew Peacock, are you out there?"

Pastor Peacock's hand shot into the air like a third grader with an answer. The crowd parted, and the pastor made his way to the stage.

"Any groomsmen or bridesmaids we can call up here?" McCavity asked once more, shoving the mic in Jessie's face.

"Kelly Greene, Mona Little and Maggie and Tori Barnes," Jessie said. The girls clattered onto the platform.

McCavity shifted the mic to Josiah. "My brothers Matt and Gabe, Sawyer Hickey and Ben Moore."

The photographer continued to click shots while Desire helped arrange the party. When they were in place the D.J. relinquished his mic to the pastor.

Hands clasped, Josiah faced Jessie. Even though her eyes filled and lips quivered, he'd never seen such tenderness in her expression. His heart hitched. To love this deeply hurt, but it was a good pain.

"Jessie, repeat after me," Pastor Peacock said.

Jessie repeated the words, making it with a warbling voice. She drew in a deep breath before continuing, "Josiah, you were made for me. You're my happily ever after and I can't wait until you see what I've got planned."

Josiah rolled back on his heels and whistled, earning a chuckle from their audience.

"Your turn, Josiah," Pastor said.

"Let's go!" Josiah whooped. He repeated the vows, pausing a few times to keep his composure. Like Jessie, Josiah added an addendum. "Jessie, your grandma and grandpa knew how much I loved you when we were younger. They cautioned me to be patient. Your grandma once asked me to protect you and love you. I aim to never break that promise."

A collective "aw" rose from the gathering.

"She also gave me some advice. She said, 'Josiah dear,'" his voice rose higher as he quoted Undine, "'Jessie is stubborn like me but deep inside is a call girl. It'll take work to coax her out and when you do, you'll both be happy you did.' God bless Grandma Undine."

"Amen!" Desire hooted causing more laughter.

"You may kiss the bride," Pastor said over the din.

Jessie fisted his shirt. "Come here, cowboy."

"Yes, ma'am, Mrs. Barnes." Josiah placed a chaste kiss and smiled a wry grin when she stuck her lip out in a pout. He leaned in and claimed his wife's lips with a ferocity of longing. The roar of the crowd dimmed as the kiss deepened.

They broke apart, Josiah's racing heartbeat ringing in his ears, the scent of strawberries lingering in the air.

Jessie wiped a stray tear. Her lips moved. Not one word was audible but he knew she'd said, "I love you."

The next few minutes simultaneously crept as if time had slowed and leapt forward five minutes for every beat of his heart. Josiah and Jessie hugged their family and friends and shook countless hands of strangers. Drew Peacock had them sign papers Josiah had given him earlier that day, making the marriage legal.

McCavity announced, "This song is for the newlyweds. Feel free to tuck a little something in Josiah's jacket pockets as they dance by."

Josiah breathed a breath of relief when the music started. He took Jessie into his arms and stared into her shining green eyes.

"My face hurts from smiling," she said with a giggle.

"Mine too," Josiah spun her. Unable to keep Jessie close because people kept stuffing money into his pockets, he became eager to be alone with her. Glancing toward the door he sighed when another song played and people kept giving. He shouldn't feel upset at their generosity but, dang it all, he wanted to hold his wife.

"I've booked a hotel room at the Schagg Inn," Jessie said blushing.

"I'm glad." Josiah touched her collarbone where the lace taunted him. "That's why you disappeared at dinner."

She bit her lip and nodded.

"I'm glad," he repeated. "There's no way in hell I'm waiting until Las Vegas to rip the teddy off of you."

Jessie hit his arm. "You will not destroy it."

With his lips against her ear he said, "I'll open it one snap at a time. With my tongue." She trembled in his arms. He sucked her lobe and Jessie hummed her pleasure. The sound shot straight to his groin.

She shoved against his chest and gazed at him. "Let's go. Now."

Josiah found most their family waiting near the stage. Several of Brad's book club members stood around him. Their animated gestures suggested a lively discussion. The mayor handed Brad a book. He glanced at it and his brows rose. The group dispersed with pats to Brad's back when they saw Josiah and Jessie approaching.

Jessie walked into her father's arms. "Have fun making me grand-babies." Brad said, squeezing Jessie in a bear hug.

"Daddy!" Jessie giggled and tried to wiggle out of his embrace.

Josiah shook both fathers' hands while Jessie hugged his sisters and mother.

Desire dabbed the corner of her eye. Her gaze raked Josiah's body from head to toe. "Remember to do everything I'd do. Twice." The old woman threw her head back and cackled.

"Ladies and gentlemen, it looks like our newlyweds are getting ready to start their honeymoon. Please make an aisle for them." McCavity asked the assembly to line either side of a path through the dance floor to the door. The music to Kenny Chesney's Me and You played.

Josiah and Jessie glanced at each other. Smiles crept to their lips. He trailed a finger across the smooth skin of her cheek. She sighed and took his hand. Their fingers threaded then they turned and walked the gauntlet of well-wishers.

Feathers floated from the ceiling. Josiah glanced upward. Bags of white feathers had been attached to the fan's paddles. The fans slowed and the raining feathers stopped. Someone switched them on again and the feathers once more took flight. The small feathers floated like milkweed. He chuckled and shook his head.

"Another prank," Jessie murmured stretching her free hand out to catch the downy snow in her palm.

Josiah searched the periphery trying to find the culprit. His steps stuttered when he spied Desire handing his brothers money. *What the hell?*

At the exit, they paused and waved then stepped into the dark.

"We're married." Jessie said. Her gaze drifted from the gravel beneath her shoes to the star spangled sky.

Joy threatened to consume him. He breathed deeply. "That's a fact, Mrs. Barnes." He couldn't stop smiling.

Jessie threw her head back cackling like Desire while rubbing her hands together. "That's right, Mr. Barnes. Your name belongs to me."

"My body too."

Jessie gasped then tripped, bumping into him. Chuckling, he caught her elbow.

"Let's go, Josiah. I've got our bags in the car." Jessie fiddled with the buttons on his shirt, unbuttoning one. The tips of her fingers grazed his skin, sending a wave of heat through his body. "Like I said, I've got plans for you tonight."

"Yes, ma'am." Josiah took big steps hurrying across the lot. Arriving at the truck he stopped and Jessie ran into him.

"What the devil?" Jessie asked stepping closer to inspect the truck. She covered her mouth with her hands and giggled.

Josiah joined her laughing. Someone had written the message "Just Hooked!" on the rear window. Under it, in smaller letters, "We did it now we're going to do it!"

He helped her in then closed the door. Walking around the rear, he made another discovery. Several ropes tied to the hitch each had a few tin cans. They'd make a racket. Josiah stooped to see what else was tethered to the rope. He flipped a small cardboard box. "Condoms." His laughter began anew.

Climbing into the truck, he wiped a tear, prepared to tell Jessie. He gasped when he saw her dress skirt pulled up, revealing lace. Jessie's hooded eyes held mischief and the impish grin dared him to touch her. He swallowed, all rational thought forgotten. He didn't trust himself to stop caressing her once he started. Pressing his lips into a thin line of determination, he jammed the key into the ignition then jerked the gear shift into reverse.

To leave they had to pass the entrance to the building. His family and a few friends had gathered waving and yelling. He honked but there was no way in hell he'd stop. He planned on setting a land speed record to the hotel. Taking a sharp turn out of the parking lot, Jessie shifted in his direction. She placed a hand on his thigh and he hissed. Stabbing heat radiated from her hand, traveling the short distance to his groin. He gripped the steering wheel with both hands.

"I love you," Jessie said laying her head on his shoulder engulfing him in the sweet smell of strawberries. "I can't wait to unholster your gun. Maybe I should check and see if it's loaded." Her warm breath near his ear made his heart race.

"It's primed and loaded." *Ready to fire.* He gulped when her fingers skimmed his zipper. He pressed the accelerator harder. The sign to Schagg Inn came into view and he blew out a long breath. "Only one mile."

Jessie giggled and his heart swelled. He'd have the privilege of making her laugh for the rest of his life. He smiled and relaxed his grip. "Now let's get on with our happily ever after."

EPILOGUE

JESSIE LEANED WITH HER BACK against the side of the truck while Josiah tightened the lug nuts on the wheel. It figured they'd blow a tire on the way to the hotel. She crossed her arms, watching the way the cotton shirt pulled taut over his straining biceps. "I still haven't figured out what B.J. said to get the men of Fortuna to read Grandma's novels."

"Guess," Josiah said. His mischievous blue eyed gaze found hers before returning to the jack. He lowered the truck.

"Read these and you'll learn the art of magic mouths."

"No," he laughed. A breeze fluttered the skirt of her dress. Josiah's gaze scanned her legs. He put the jack away and wiped his hands. "Try again."

Jessie tapped her chin with a finger. "For a good time, read these books."

"Closer," he teased. "Try again."

"What did he say?" With hands on her hips she tapped her foot.

"Well," Josiah paused as he opened the door for her. "He was wearing an excited smile when he approached me. He said 'Hey man, you've got to read a few of these books. I know why the ladies like them. They're better than porn.'"

Jessie shook her head. He started the truck and pulled onto the road. Clicking on the radio to fill the sudden quiet, her knee bumped up and down as she chewed on her lip. Marriage was what she'd planned, but it happened quick. She rubbed her damp palms and stole a glance at her husband's profile.

"You're awfully quiet over there," Josiah stated keeping his eyes on the road.

She leaned against him and sighed. "We both planned the same thing."

"Yes, we did." He nodded and a charming grin spread on his lips, tempting her to taste him.

"I informed my dad about Vegas. He told you, didn't he?" she asked.

"No. He knew I wanted to marry you but never let on about your plans. He encouraged me to make mine." He chuckled. "The sneaky devil."

"What did Desire say to you when we left?" Jessie plucked a feather out of his hair.

"Words of advice," he said.

"Such as?" She couldn't help her crinkled nose, listing the possible dirty ditties Desire could have spouted.

"She said all women have a little call girl in them and it was my duty to nurture yours and bring her out." His brows rose. "It's a challenge I accept."

It was probably Desire's idea to test and switch intimate apparel items throughout the night. Jessie had a week's worth of lingerie for Josiah to enjoy. *Thank you very much, Ms. Hardmann.* Being reminded of a "hard man," she slid a hand across Josiah's thigh to his crotch.

A small groan escaped his lips, and he stomped on the gas. "I'm not a silent silent-partner."

It took a full minute for this statement to register. "What do you mean by 'silent-partner'?" Jessie pushed back scrutinizing his face.

His gaze darted toward her as his face turned red. He muttered something under his breath.

Jessie sat back, leaning against the door. What did this twist mean for her, for them and for the Double D? Thoughts stalled. She clenched her eyes shut and drew in a deep breath. Her stomach churned.

"I thought you'd figured it out." Josiah's voice turned soft

Jessie exhaled and crossed her arms. Glancing out the window, the hotel came into view and she frowned.

Turning the wheel, the truck entered the parking lot. Josiah found a space near the lobby, parked and turned off the engine. He twisted in the seat facing Jessie.

"I thought your father spilled the beans, or Desire."

Tears filled her eyes. This wasn't how she envisioned starting her marriage. Her fingers played with the hem of her dress and she bit her lip. What else was he not telling her?

"You're the silent partner." Jessie laughed, but it sounded hollow. Could he be after the business? Did he love her or was it a guise?

"Why, Josiah? Or maybe *how* did you become the silent partner is a better question?"

"Desire." Josiah blew out a breath and squared his shoulders. "She asked me to brainstorm with your father to come up with names of people who might invest in your company. I knew how passionate you were about making it work, and even though I'd never seen a stitch of work, Desire insisted you made quality pieces. I believed her." His lids closed and a half smirk rested on his lips. He became quiet as he reminisced and her heart fluttered, hoping it was something to do with lingerie.

"I had no idea you made teddies or anything sexy until you were in Austin. Your dad dropped that bomb." Josiah's gaze dropped to the V of her dress where ecru lace peeked out. He stretched his arm on the seat bench brushing her shoulder with his fingertips.

The touch gave Jessie goosebumps. She honed in on his lips then swallowed. She felt the anger dissipate and her stomach relaxed. He'd invested before he had seen samples. Tears pricked her eyes again, and she blinked. Her heart swelled at his confidence in her and her ability. She wiped a stray teardrop.

"Thank you for believing in me." Her voice a throaty whisper. "How did you find the money?"

"Your grandparents," Josiah said.

Jessie gasped and shifted toward him.

"Do you remember when Warren Teed read your Grandmother's will? I waited until you and your dad left. You were grieving and didn't need to be there for my paperwork. Your grandparents didn't have to give me anything, but they did. I'm sure they'd figured out I was sweet on you." Josiah gazed out the front at the side of the building but his thoughts remained lost in the past.

Jessie drudged up the memory of the lawyer's monochromatic office. Garren and Warren Teed had been present. A box of tissues sat on the desk. Warren read the will to Brad and Jessie. The house, land and herd became Jessie's. It was a surreal moment. First her grandfather's death then her grandmother died of a broken heart. One moment Jessie was a college kid ready to jump into the world and spread her wings, the next she became shackled to a business and property, including a hoard of books.

From that acquisition she received Josiah.

"Jessie, your grandparents left me money. It was a gift they thought could help with my tuition. But I didn't need it; between scholarships and my parents, my schooling was covered." Josiah faced her again. "I took my father's advice and invested the money. For five years I added to it, saving.

I didn't have rent or any major expenses so I collected a nice chunk of change." The confident smirk returned.

"I shouldn't be surprised," Jessie said. "They both loved you." She sighed and placed her hand on top of his. "No more secrets. Like the silent partner or Rusty's whereabouts, okay? We're partners, Josiah."

Josiah glanced at the book on the seat and cleared his throat. "I, uh."

"Out with it," Jessie said restraining an eye roll.

"Forgive me, Jess, but Desire set up regular business meetings. She showed me what you were working on before the show. She pretended to take a bathroom break and came to talk with me. The items in the closet were beautiful. She knew about sewing and stuff and thought they were works of art. I don't know seams or materials but I knew you had talent. Thinking of you wearing those lacy things…" Josiah closed his eyes and hummed. "Well, let's say it made me hotter than a billy goat in a pepper patch." With a red face he added, "I wanted to help, and I had the means."

"Thank you," she repeated. She scooted closer to him and fiddled with a button on his shirt. "I'm sure I can figure out a way to pay you back other than dividends." Her fingers grazed his skin making him quiver.

"Oh, hell yes." He groaned as her lips found his neck. "So worth the investment." He plunged his hands into her hair.

Jessie pulled back. "Should we check in and finish this naked?"

"Oh, hell yes," he said again. Josiah sprang from the truck so fast Jessie almost toppled out.

Entering the lobby with their overnight bags, the couple greeted the smiling desk attendant with a name badge: Sue Kerr.

"We have a reservation," Josiah said.

"Oh, the original reservation has been canceled." The smile never faltered from Sue's face. "It's upgraded to the honeymoon suite. Brad Davidson asked for us to give you this message. 'Grand babies STAT'."

Jessie glanced at her husband as heat blossomed on her cheeks. She took the keycards Sue offered.

"One more thing," Sue said, and she bent out of sight. She reappeared holding a basket wrapped in clear cellophane and tied with a hot pink ribbon. Sue's face matched the ribbon. "Congratulations and have fun."

As Josiah and Jessie followed the instructions to their room, they inspected the basket from Desire Hardmann. Condoms, lube, handcuffs, chocolate sauce, candy, and more. "Chocolate penis pops for sustenance." Jessie giggled.

"You don't need to suck on that," Josiah said, "I've got one built on."

Jessie's brows raised, and she laughed harder, barely getting the keycard in the lock. They entered the large dark room. Josiah clicked on the light and sat the basket next to the flat screen TV.

When the door shut, the lock clicked filling the silence. Neither moved from the entry as they inspected the room. A large king sized bed, full sofa, coffee table, end tables, and a desk filled the large room. The neutral fabrics in warm beiges and taupes gave a modern European air.

Josiah clicked on the light to the bathroom and whistled. Jessie peeked in. The large shower surrounded by glass caught her eye. Her heart rate kicked up a notch, wanting to try the raindrop shower head. They locked eyes then blushed and smiled.

Jessie rolled her bag to a table and opened it. Champagne chilled in ice. "Look." She pointed. Josiah sauntered over and raised the bottle. As he read the label, she pulled out her mobile phone. She had one last piece of business to finish before her mind could rest.

Josiah lifted the bottle, and she nodded as the phone picked up. "Matt?" Jessie said. Josiah's brow frowned. She disappeared into the bathroom and the cork popped.

Standing in front of a wall to wall mirror, sultry expectant eyes stared back at her. The young wife and lover had rosy cheeks and red lips. The long auburn hairstyle was a hot mess but sexy. A sensual smile tipped her lips, and the blush deepened. *Holy hell! Maybe I do have call girl in me after all.*

"What the hell do you want? It's your wedding night! Are you trying to get me killed? That's what he's going to do. Kill me," Matt Barnes' exasperated voice squeaked. He rambled on, but she tuned him out. She fixated on Josiah's long and lanky form leaning against the doorjamb. The room's temperature rose as he scanned her body. He offered her a flute of champagne. She took it.

Jessie couldn't pull her gaze off of Josiah as he slowly raised his glass. Alcohol glistened on his lips and his tongue licked them clean. Her lungs burned. Jessie gulped for air because his presence had sucked it all out.

Muscles flexed as his fingers unbuttoned his shirt starting with the second to the top and moving lower. Transfixed, she froze. Her gaze swept his body from his hair to his toes. His chest hair had returned, and she longed to run her fingers through it.

"Shut up, Matt. Do you want a full time foreman job?" Jessie asked. There was complete silence on the line. "Matt?"

Josiah's brows rose, but he continued shrugging out of his shirt. Next his long fingers worked his belt.

"What about Josiah?" Matt asked with a suspicious tone.

"What about him?" Jessie countered.

"He's the foreman at the Double D." Matt huffed.

Josiah pulled the belt through the loops then dropped it. Jessie fanned herself and turned to watch in the mirror. It did little to calm his effect on her. Especially when the zipper announced his next move. In a blink, his pants fell to his ankles. He wore the boxers she'd crafted. She swallowed at the tent his erection made.

"Not any more. He no longer holds that position," Jesse stated. Josiah stepped toward her with a hooded expression. He pressed his hard on against her backside.

"You fired him? You can't fire your husband!" Matt sounded bewildered. "I'm going to die a slow death and get ran over by Cowboy. I might as well jump out of the loft now."

"Quiet, Matt," Jessie ordered in her boss voice. "Do you want the job or not?"

Josiah lifted her hair to the side, over one shoulder and kissed her neck. Heat radiated from his every touch collecting in her core. Her heart worked overtime to keep from fainting. He unzipped her dress, kissing as he exposed her flesh until the teddy barred him further access. He moved one sleeve off her shoulder. She switched hands, and he tugged the other shoulder until gravity had the dress ballooned at their feet. She kicked it away.

With his chin on her shoulder Josiah appraised the teddy in the mirror. His hands slid around her hips, across her flat stomach to cup her breasts. Jessie gasped, closed her eyes and leaned against his hard body.

She almost dropped the phone when Matt, finished with his internal debate, replied, "Okay. Yeah sure, of course, I do. Thanks, Sis." He laughed sounding giddy. "This is awesome. Do I start now? Am I going to get a raise?"

"We'll bring you a souvenir," Jessie said. "And we'll name a baby after you."

"Uh, thanks," Matt said then paused before saying, "don't call me again. Bye."

"Are we going to try for a baby?" Josiah asked in a soft voice.

"Josiah, I didn't promise Matt the baby would be human. Muddy Buddy could use a playmate named Matthew." Jessie giggled and spun in his arms.

Her mind raced. *A baby? With Josiah?* "I'd like to wait awhile but maybe we could practice." Her fingers traced a circle around his bellybutton.

"Besides, I'm not ready for an expanding waist or swollen breasts. God, I don't want them to get any bigger."

"I wouldn't mind," Josiah teased. His fingers caressed her perky chest. "You know what they say 'everything is bigger in Texas'."

"Is that right, husband?" Jessie's hand slid to his gun. "Mm, that's accurate."

He moaned her name. The erotic sound left her weak in the knees. They wouldn't need the lube from the basket. He lifted her bottom to the counter and kissed her neck. She wrapped her legs around his waist. In between kisses he began an interrogation. A form of sweet torture. "About being fired?"

"I never... said you were... fired. Matt did." She gasped as he traced the lace nearest the apex between her legs. "You've been... Oh, that's nice." All rational thought left when he slipped a finger under the material.

"I've been...?" Josiah prompted.

"Promoted." Her fingers combed his chest hair, leading the way south. She traced his collarbone with her tongue.

"Promoted? To what?"

Jessie murmured the answer against his body then licked his nipple. *Novels don't dwell enough on men's nipples.* Her teeth grazed the tip. His fingers tightened on her buttocks.

"Did you say 'sex slave'? I can deal with that." He chuckled.

The way his hands stroked and caressed made her forget business. His fingers teased under the fabric at the snap. Jessie never wanted a man like she hungered for Josiah. She became tipsy with lust. *Dang, he could make me forget my name.* While his tongue, lips and teeth worked on her neck and lips, his hands fiddled with the teddy's snap. He tugged on the fabric, trying to work it apart.

Grinning like a Cheshire cat, Josiah slipped two fingers under the fabric, making Jessie's breath catch. "You're so wet," Josiah said as he continued exploring.

Jessie whimpered, her fingers plunging into his hair. "Don't stop," she begged as he continued to work her up.

"I need you in me now." Jessie threw her head back and laughed, having reminded herself of Nevaeh and Armando. Perhaps there was something to the romance novels. Her grandmother certainly thought so.

"You want me?" Josiah asked with an alluring smile. His manhood bobbed in rhythm with her heart.

"I've wanted you since you tried to kill me," she answered.

His brow wrinkled with determination as he took hold of both sides of the snap, pinching the fabric. "Ready?" he asked.

"For you? Oh yeah." She was on fire.

Josiah teased as he pulled, purposely rubbing her most intimate place. She writhed with pleasure. The snap didn't give. He pulled harder and gave her an 'I told you so' look. She held one part while he yanked the other. It wouldn't budge.

"This is a problem." Frustration apparent in her tone. "Rip it off."

"But it took hours to make," Josiah sought her gaze.

"I want to make love to you. Now."

"Jess, I'm going to focus on one side of the snaps. If I can get one, then maybe the others will follow." He knelt and examined the stubborn thing. His warm breath made her want him to taste her, and he yanked on one side inspecting the plastic snaps. "There's some sort of hard white goo."

"But we haven't-" she started.

He chuckled, his sparkling eyes met hers with a promise of intent. "Don't worry. We will."

"I don't understand. The snapping mechanism worked perfectly when I reattached it. I tried it several times. And tonight when I put it on I tried it, at least three times," she stated.

Josiah leaned inspecting the fabric then sniffed. "It's some sort of glue."

"Glue! I didn't-"

"I know, Jess. It's probably one of those types of adhesives that hardens when it gets warm or wet. Did you show the teddy to anyone or leave it somewhere?" His fingers stroked her inner leg giving her goosebumps.

Jessie shook her head. "I replaced it weeks ago. So anyone who visited the Double D had possible access to it."

She balled her fists. They'd have to rip the thing off. She wasn't going to give up her wedding night for a stupid teddy.

"The sewing room? Any one visit you there?" He pushed her for an answer although his fingers had slipped under the material again, making it hard to concentrate.

She closed her eyes as he focused attention on her pleasure nub. "Oh, that feels good." Her eyes snapped open. "I showed my ideas about Maggie's peignoir set to Desire."

"Desire!" they both said at once. Jessie laughed then Josiah joined in.

"That dirty old woman created a modern day chastity belt." Josiah frowned and tugged on the fabric again but the snaps remained unyielding. "This will be a night to remember in more ways than one."

"I don't appreciate this prank." Jessie hopped down from the counter. Josiah watched her breasts bounce. Her hands pushed the waist of his boxers. They fell to the floor and his erection sprang free.

"Dammit," Jessie growled, grabbing the material on either side of the teddy's V. She yanked hard and the delicate material gave, ripping down to the lace diamond and exposing her breasts. "I'm not waiting another minute for my happily ever after."

Josiah smirked and pushed the garment until it landed on her feet. He scooped her up like she weighed nothing and, carrying her as a bridegroom carried a bride, deposited her on the bed.

Taking short breaths, Jessie's gaze raked his toned naked body. Her skin tingled with anticipation of his caresses. She lifted her arms to him.

Heat radiated off Josiah as he crawled over her, igniting fire in her veins. His chest hair grazed her breasts and her breath hitched. "Our happily ever after starts now," he whispered. He claimed her lips as he'd won her heart, with passion, determination and love.

SNEAK PEEK

Plumb Twisted
A Fortuna, Texas Novel
Book 2

Cole and Piper arrived at the Stitts' truck stop, where Cole flagged down the owner, Norma Stitts. She waved them in. He took Piper's elbow and led her to a booth.

Piper inspected the bookshelf by the door then gazed around the room, taking it all in. Cole tried not to stare at the girl, but it proved hard not to watch her first encounter with a Texas truck stop.

"There are three men reading romance novels," she said in awe. Packed with men, but also a few women and children, Stitts' was hopping.

"I'm surprised it's not more." Cole said, rubbing his chin.

"Really?" Piper's eyes widened.

"See that bookshelf? It's a major exchange center for the book trade."

"Book trade?"

"You'll have to ask Miss Jessie about how it started," Cole explained.

"Mrs. Barnes, my boss?"

"Yes. Sorry, I've called her Miss Jessie for years."

A man entered the restaurant, placed two books on the shelf then ran his finger down the spines in the line and pulled out another. He paused, reading the back.

"Do you see that man?" Cole asked, and she nodded. "He's a farmer. Owns a couple hundred acres, a modest spread, and he loves romances."

With a smile, the farmer pocketed the book. He picked out two more before leaving.

"Ah, romance books. This is what you meant yesterday?" Her cheeks pinked.

"Yes." He cleared his throat, which had suddenly gone dry. "It started with a personal challenge to one man, a dare. He didn't back down. He liked the books and dared others then it spread like wildfire on dry prairie grass."

They ordered and sipped the rich dark coffee. "This is good." Inhaling deeply, she gripped the ceramic mug like it held ambrosia. He leaned back and relaxed. Warmth spread through his body, happy to have pleased her.

"So who dared you?" she asked.

He nearly spit coffee.

"I mean why do you read them?" She'd gleaned he liked to read.

"I like the stories."

"You mean you like the sex." She tilted her head and grinned.

Sure, he liked the steamy scenes, but that wasn't the whole reason he read them. "I like happy endings," he offered with a shrug. She raised a skeptical eyebrow. "Okay, I like the love scenes but only because of the love." He swallowed.

"Love?"

The waitress placed food on the table, saving him. They ate in silence, except for an occasional comment about the taste of the food. After she pushed an empty plate away, she asked, "Are all cowboys like you?"

Uh oh. "Like, how?"

"You know, crunchy on the outside, gooey on the inside?"

Cole laughed. "Most likely," he answered as another man took more books.

"I don't like romance stories," she admitted in a quiet voice. Before he could ask, she explained, "the heroines are too soft. I don't like to read about weak women. Plus those men always have movie star looks and amazing careers, not to mention they're billionaires. You can't find your soul mate in a romance book."

"But you might find personality traits you like," he offered. She shrugged, not buying it. "I don't see the women as weak—only flawed, with obstacles to overcome."

"I suppose everyone has flaws."

"What's yours?" he asked with a smirk.

"Liking the wrong kind of men," she muttered.

His stomach clenched. "That's a cop out answer." He'd unfairly asked, so

301

he offered his shortcoming. "I'm self-conscious about my looks."

She inspected him critically and sweat broke out across his forehead. "Most people are."

He leaned close and said quietly, "It keeps me from talking and interacting with people. I get nervous and won't go places if there's a crowd." It had been years since the operation and it still affected him.

"You're fine, Cole. You're more than fine. Look, you're out talking to me and I'm a stranger and a woman."

He nodded. "Normally, I'd be a basket case of nerves."

"Looks are all personal taste. Someone might think you're ugly or someone might think you're the sexiest man alive. The thing you have to ask yourself is: does their opinion matter to me?" She smiled sweetly over the edge of her mug.

"What's your opinion?" he blurted, needing to know.

"Does it matter to you what I think?"

"Yes. It matters greatly." It was true, but he didn't want to ask himself why. The smile that lit her face made his heart race. She set her coffee down.

"Well, Cole, I like the crunchy-gooey combo. It's very appealing." She blushed and long eyelashes hid her eyes as she looked at the table. "I find you…" she paused, drumming her fingers against the side of her mug.

"Pretty, right?" A short old woman said as she slid into the booth next to Cole and pinched his cheek. "This one's a hot tamale."

"Hello, my heart's Desire." Cole's face felt like the temperature of the sun. He rubbed his cheek. "This is Piper McCracken. Piper this is Desire Hardmann."

"Hello, young lady." Desire took Piper's hand and squeezed. With a wink, she yelled over her shoulder to a man in a white apron, "Hey, Hugh Stitts! Come over here and meet Cole's Russian mail order bride."

Coming in 2018.

ABOUT THE AUTHOR

Rochelle writes epic dreams. In her mind, they play like a movie with a cast of fun-loving, big-hearted people in a small-town setting.

Born and raised in Cincinnati, Ohio, Rochelle developed a love of nature, art and traveling. Snowbird grandparents first introduced her to Texas when she was a child. Her fondness for the state grew over the years. In college, she flip-flopped between interior decorating and creative writing. Alas, she chose decorating. She worked as a certified professional bra fitter through college and accumulated many interesting stories and a box full of goodies for her soon-to-be Prince.

She made the long migration to Dayton, Ohio after marrying. Taking an early retirement as a decorator, she accepted the full-time position of mother.

In 2008, when her youngest entered Kindergarten, she decided to get the stories out of her head. Midway through her first novel, hurricane Ike (yes, a hurricane in Ohio) rendered the laptop useless with a nine-day power outage. She didn't give up, but continued to pursue her dream.

Rochelle shares her home with one cat, two high schoolers, three lizards, and her Prince.

To learn more about Rochelle's books, please visit RochelleBradley.com.